D1523678

1

FRIENDS

LOVERS

and

LIES

A Casey Quinby Mystery

Friends, Lovers, and Lies
By Judi Ciance
judiciance@ gmail.com
judiciance.com
Published: February, 2016

Other books by this author:

The Casey Quinby Mystery Series:

Empty Rocker (November 2012)
Paint Her Head (October 2013)
Caught With A Quahog (October 2014)
A Tale of Two Lobsters (October 2015)
18 Buzzy Lane (October 2016)

The Detective Mike Mastro Mystery Series:

A Black Rose (June 2017)

Dedication

To My Husband
Paul Ciance

Although Paul passed in September 2019, his words of
encouragement to continue in my writing, his everlasting patience
to listen, and his help from above to keep me in line will have Casey
investigating for years to come.

Casey and I love and miss you, Paul.

Enjoy

To Bob and Judy
Thanks for being a friend
and supporter of all
my endevors
Love ya
Judi
(and Casey)

FRIENDS, LOVERS, and LIES

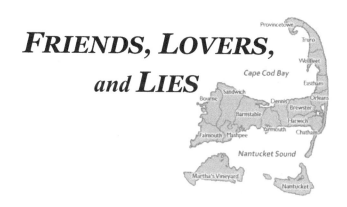

PROLOGUE

June 2006

Buster

Buster Adams came up with an event he thought would excite and arouse those attending the last planned experience of the Barnstable High class of 2006. It wouldn't be for everyone, just those who he guessed may be willing participants—an intimate group of close friends.

He played on his new laptop, pulling up and saving sites that offered ideas for his invitation-only get-together. It was eleven minutes before midnight. *Was it too late to call Betsy?*

Buster and Betsy hooked up all through high school but never had a serious relationship. He was the star quarterback, and she was captain of the cheerleading squad.

Betsy Harper answered on the first ring. "Why the hell are you calling me at this hour?"

"I've got something I want to run by you."

"A boob squeeze and a tongue tickle couldn't wait until morning?" she teased.

"No. And no, I'm not outside your window lookin' to get a quick boink."

"Well then, what do you want?"

"Ever heard of a key party?"

Betsy hesitated. "You mean where people swap room keys, and nobody is aware of who they're going to screw until they open the door?"

"Bingo. You got it."

"Why are you asking about a key party?"

"I think we should have one after graduation."

"You're sick. You know that."

Buster sat forward on the edge of his chair. "Think about it. Nobody will get hurt. It's just a night of fantasy fuckin'. We'll figure out how many people and who we want to invite."

"Sweet dreams, big boy. Half of the 'we' part of this conversation is going to bed. Talk to you in the morning." Betsy didn't allow Buster to respond. She hung up on him.

He didn't care. He wanted new territory to explore—like Betsy's best friend, Tami. She'd be on his party list.

May 2011

Five years later

Betsy

Betsy Harper, always a go-getter, called the class of 2006 reunion committee meeting to order. "Let's sort through the suggestions I received for our event." She handed out copies she'd made earlier.

Annie McGuire, Betsy's classmate, was excited to be on the event planning committee until she read one recommendation.

Mark Mosley, their senior class president, slid his papers across the table in Betsy's direction. "Have you read these? I mean, really read them?"

Betsy smirked. "You have a problem?" She knew she'd get a reaction but didn't care. It was Buster's idea. He died almost five years ago, the morning after he'd talked to Betsy. Buster never made it to graduation, and the key party never happened. His car went off the road two miles from his house and plummeted into Wequaquet Lake. When the police got to the scene, they noted he wasn't strapped in, and his head rested against the steering wheel. The medical examiner ruled his death an accidental drowning. Betsy missed him more than she was willing to admit.

Mark looked around at his former classmates. "I do have a problem with a key-swapping party. What about the rest of you?"

Glances, smiles, and giggles from a few girls sitting beside him caught his attention.

"Who submitted the suggestion of a key-swapping party?" Mark asked.

Nobody fessed up.

Betsy slid her chair back and stood. "Mark, don't get ruffled. I'm sure it was meant as a joke to get our attention." She shrugged and threw her hands up. "Looks like it did."

Annie pounded her fist on the table. "I doubt it came from any one of us." Her outburst had people glancing around the room.

Betsy smiled. *Buster, I did this for you.*

The five-year reunion key party never happened.

September 2016

Ten years later

Casey

Two and a half years ago, I started my dream job. I bought a small vacant building across from the County Court Complex in Barnstable Village and hung my shingle, Casey Quinby, PI. Since last May, when I finished working on a twenty-year-old missing person case, I did some husband/wife spying capers, researched claims to settle family land disputes, and got involved in another missing person case. I did until the missing person came out from under the covers on his mother's best friend's bed.

Life was good. Dunkin' Donuts French vanilla coffee remained my drug of choice, and white zin with ice still quenched my thirst. Sam spent most of his off-time at my rented cottage near Craigville Beach in Hyannisport. We weren't ready for a mortgage commitment—not yet. Sam and I were happy in our life as partners with benefits.

We watched with curious fascination as Marnie and Maloney planned on continuing their relationship through marital bliss. Maloney left the Provincetown Police Department and took a position as a detective with Barnstable PD. Despite my efforts to have Marnie occupy the extra desk in my office, she stayed on as an Assistant District Attorney in the Barnstable DA's office. Since Maloney didn't have to travel back and forth from P-Town anymore, they bought a small fixer-upper off Route 6A in Yarmouthport. Marnie, originally from New York City, and Maloney, from Boston, left city life behind to become permanent Cape Cod wash-a-shores.

Chapter 1

Sunday afternoon

I helped Marnie finish putting away the contents of the boxes she'd marked *kitchen* when we heard Maloney back the U-Haul, loaded with the last of their furniture, into the driveway. Watson, who'd been curled up in the corner watching us, jumped up, tried to get traction, and instead slid across the hardwood floor as he scurried to meet the guys.

Maloney and Sam headed straight to the fridge. "Break time before we unload." Maloney took a beer for himself and handed one to Sam. "Thanks for helping out."

"Helping out, hell. I'll give you my bill as soon as we get the last piece of furniture off the truck."

I put my hands on the back of Sam's damp shirt and pushed him toward the door. "Stop talking and get working. We've got steaks, potatoes, and corn-on-the-cob for the grill, and I'm hungry."

Sam took a swig of beer and laughed. "Casey, you're always hungry. Hey, how come Annie isn't here?"

Marnie spoke up, "It's her ten-year class reunion this weekend. That's all I heard about last week. School and the district attorney's office have been her life. I was trying to finish a brief for the boss, and she wouldn't stop talking, so I sent her to probate to research a bogus address."

I shook my head. "Marnie, you're bad. It looks like happy hour has started. Glass of wine, girl?"

"I could handle a glass or two." Marnie took the glass from me. "You pour, and I'll shuck … as soon as I find the corn."

I poured her some white zin. "It's in the Stop and Shop bags on the deck."

"My steak was perfect." Sam smiled. "This restaurant's a keeper."

"Restaurant, my ass." Maloney shook his head. "If you want dessert, you better help me put the bed up."

Maloney started down the hallway toward the bedroom, stopped halfway then turned.

Sam laughed, "Yeah, yeah. I'm right behind you."

While the boys were setting up the bedroom furniture, Marnie and I cleaned up, then I put a pot of coffee on, and she set a double chocolate layer cake on the kitchen table.

I called down the hallway. "Coffee's done. You guys ready?"

Before I could get back to the kitchen, there was a pounding on the front door.

Marnie ran to answer. "Annie, what's the matter?"

She tried to talk between gasps and tears, but we couldn't understand her.

I put my arm around her and guided her to the closest chair. "Calm down." I slid an ottoman beside her and took both her hands in mine.

Maloney grabbed a box of tissues from the bathroom.

"What's wrong?" I asked.

The tears slowed, but the gasps still broke up her sentences. "My class reunion …" She slid her hands free and covered her face. "My ten-year reunion …."

Marnie handed her more tissues. "Okay. That was last night, wasn't it?"

"Yes, at the Sheraton."

I'd never seen Annie this frazzled. "What happened?"

"Oh, God. After the reunion. Yeah. Right after. I guess after." She looked at Maloney. "You need to help me."

He knelt beside her. "Before I can help you, you have to tell us what happened."

12

"Betsy, my classmate, my friend, Betsy Harper … she's dead."
The tears started again.

I took a deep breath, but before I could say anything, Annie continued, "The maid at the Sheraton found Betsy in her room. She was dead."

I looked from Sam to Maloney, then to Annie. "Did you have a room there?"

Marnie came from the kitchen with a glass of wine for Annie.

"No." She took a two-swallow drink. "I didn't stay at the hotel last night. I went home. I didn't know about any of this until Mark Mosely called me about a half-hour ago."

I kept my eyes fixed on Annie. "How did she, ah, Betsy, die?"

Annie swiped her palm across her cheek and wiped the moisture onto her slacks. "Mark told me he and some of the others were in the bar having drinks and shooting the shit. Somebody saw the police come into the hotel, followed by the EMTs. Somebody, I wasn't told who went into the bar to get Mark. He's our class president, or was back then, and …."

"And what?"

"Mark said the cops told him Betsy was dead. They asked lots of questions, but they wouldn't give him anything more than vague generalities. Due to the nature of their questions, Mark and I assume murder, but we don't know."

Chapter 2

Out of the corner of my eye, I saw Maloney motion Sam to join him in the kitchen.

Maloney looked over his shoulder to make sure they were alone. "Let's take a ride to the station."

Sam gestured toward the door. "Right behind you."

Just before they got to the door, Maloney turned. "We're going to the station. We'll be back soon."

I wanted to go but thought it best to stay with Marnie and Annie until we knew what was happening. Besides, once Annie calmed down, I could ask her exactly what the cops told Mark.

I waved goodbye to the guys and focused my attention on Annie. "You and Mark assumed foul play, but without more information, it could have been a natural death. There was a lot of partying last night. Alcohol and drugs could have been a factor."

Annie sat forward on her chair. "I don't think so."

Marnie appeared puzzled. "I've never heard you talk about Betsy. You said she was your friend and your classmate. You talking before 2006?"

"Yes." Annie looked from Marnie to me. "We've talked since our high school graduation, but not to any great length. And then only because I was on the five-year reunion committee. Betsy was the chairperson. Our 2011 reunion was at the Cape Codder. She called and asked me to be on the ten-year committee. I went to a couple of meetings, then changed my mind."

I figured it wasn't going to be an early night. "Come on, let's move to the kitchen and have a coffee."

Marnie fired up the Keurig and made three fresh French vanillas.

I got the cream from the fridge. "Anyone want sweetener?"

Marnie scanned the counter. "If you do, we'll have to find it. I don't remember unpacking any."

"Annie, why would you think Betsy's death is anything other than natural causes?" I watched her facial expression change from somewhat normal to concern. "What's wrong?"

"Why are you asking?"

"We've been friends for too many years. You wear your emotions on your sleeve. What happened at your reunion?"

Annie stared down at the table. "I think they had a key party."

Marnie's face wrinkled. "A what?"

"Get real. A girl from the Big Apple hasn't heard of a key party?" I twisted around to face Annie. "Did you go?"

Her head stayed stationary, but her eyes focused on mine. "Of course not."

This game of one question and a half answer wasn't cutting it, but right now, she wasn't offering anymore. "Did Betsy go?" I asked.

Annie looked away. "I don't know, but I bet she knew about it."

"Why? Did she discuss it with you?"

"Not recently."

I leaned forward on the table. "There's more to this key party thing. What aren't you telling us?"

"Ten years ago, Betsy said Buster mentioned having one after graduation. Didn't happen. Then there was talk of having one after our fifth-year reunion. Never materialized. When planning the ten-year reunion, somebody again submitted a written suggestion about a key party. Again, never happened."

"Who was involved in the talks?"

Marnie got up from the table, went to another part of the house, and returned carrying a legal pad and a pen. "A lawyer always has writing supplies. I'll write while you two talk."

I nodded enough to let Marnie see it was a good idea, then repeated my question. "Who was involved in the talks?"

"Betsy, for one. She's the one who told me about it."

"I'm sure this wasn't a one-on-one conversation. Who were the others?"

"Buster Adams and Betsy. They were the only ones who originally talked about it."

"Is that what Betsy told you?"

"Yes."

"Then we should talk to Buster."

"He's dead." Annie started to cry. "He died ten years ago last June. His car went off the road into Wequaquet Lake, and he drowned."

Accidental? I leaned forward and ran my fingers through my hair, pushing my bangs off my forehead. Things were getting too complicated for kitchen table talk. *Don't ask. Gracefully close the conversation. Don't get involved.*

My cell rang. It was Sam. "Move away from the girls so you can talk."

I walked into the living room, then down the hallway away from earshot. "Go ahead."

"Maloney and I are at the Sheraton. We'll be here a while longer, then head back to the station. Betsy's death doesn't appear to be from natural causes. I'll fill you in later. We should be back at Maloney's house in an hour. If he's going to be longer, I'll call, and you can pick me up."

I went back to the table where the girls were sitting.

Annie's expression was blank. "Anything?"

"Barnstable PD has opened an investigation. Sam didn't tell me anything else." I hated to lie, but there was nothing to report other than that Betsy's death was questionable. Until there was information as to the cause, I wasn't about to discuss it with Annie. For that matter, I wasn't about to discuss it with her anyway. She'd learn all she needed to, and then some, working in the DA's office.

Marnie got up to make herself another coffee. "Are they going to be long?"

"Sam figured maybe an hour. If they go past an hour, I'll pick him up, and we'll head to Hyannisport."

16

Watson walked over and lay down beside me, resting his head on my foot. I scratched his head, ruffled his fur, then pulled a treat from my jeans pocket. "Good boy."

Annie curled up in a fetal position on the far end of Marnie's couch.

No sooner had I asked Annie if she wanted to stay with Sam and me tonight, I heard a car pull into the driveway.

"Thanks, but I need to go home. I'll be all right." Annie stood and gave Marnie and me a hug. "Marnie, I might take a personal day tomorrow. I'll call you in the morning if I'm not coming in."

I didn't want her to be alone, but it was her choice.

The guys were still outside talking when Annie walked to her car. "It's been a tough night. I'm heading to the homestead."

Sam put his arm around her. "You okay?"

"I am." Annie cleared her throat. "Need a little alone time. I'll call Casey in the morning."

Sam and Maloney waited until she got into her car and pulled out of the driveway before going back inside the house.

I didn't give Sam a chance to sit down. "I'm ready to head home." I hugged Marnie. "We'll talk in the morning."

It's been said that animals can sense when something's wrong. Watson proved that. He slowly walked between Sam and me to the car, then gingerly got into the backseat and laid down. There was no whimpering or looking for a treat.

Once we were on the main road, I reached over and put my hand on Sam's leg. "Anything you can tell me?"

He kept both hands on the wheel and his eyes straight ahead. "At first, they thought Betsy committed suicide. But they changed their finding to homicide. According to Chief Lowe, it was pretty gruesome. Maloney's one of the detectives assigned to the case."

I shook my head. "Annie's a mess. I'm worried about her. I wanted her to come home with us, but she wouldn't."

"Casey, anything you hear either from Maloney or me has to be kept to yourself. Nobody, especially Annie, needs to know what's going on. I'm sure she'll be called to the station for questioning—not for any involvement, but to provide background information on Betsy Harper." Sam glanced in my direction. "You hear me?"

"I do."

The ride home seemed to take longer than usual. Sam took Watson for a short walk. I unlocked the door, shuffled to the living room, and plopped down on my end of the couch. I was exhausted.

Sam brought Watson in, then sat down beside me. He wrapped his arms around me. Neither of us said anything. It felt like forever before we finally got up to go to bed.

"I love you, Sherlock."

My eyes welled up. "I love you too."

Chapter 3

Monday

When I pulled onto the driveway beside my office, I saw Annie sitting at the bistro table outside my front window. I checked my watch—eight-thirty. *She starts work at eight.* I parked, walked up to my back door, unlocked it, and went straight to the front room. Through the window blinds, I could see her silhouette still at the table. I opened the front door, walked out, and sat across from her.

"Mornin' Annie. What's up?"

"I took a personal day." Annie held up a copy of the *Cape Cod Tribune.* "Have you seen this morning's paper?"

"Not yet."

Annie's eyes were red, and the circles around them dark. I imagined it was from the lack of sleep and no make-up.

"I'm assuming you don't want to go to Nancy's Donut Shop for coffee. Go inside. I'll walk down there and get us a couple of sticky buns. We can make our own coffee."

"Thanks."

Annie worked as the district attorney's administrative assistant since she graduated from Cape Cod Community College in 2008, and up until last fall, she lived with her parents. In October, she decided to be more independent and moved out. She found a little place in Cummaquid, not far from Marnie's old home. Living alone, following last night's news, must have been tough.

The coffee was ready when I got back. I tried to lighten the conversation. "We'll sit in the kitchen. I'm not expecting anyone this morning, but if I get bombarded with new clients, then we won't have to move." I noticed a half-smile form on Annie's face, then quickly disappeared.

"I didn't get a chance to talk to the guys. Did Sam tell you anything?"

"Ernie Banks, the medical examiner, is at a convention in Boston, so his assistant was at the Sheraton. Betsy's death could have been a suicide, but the ME's office is running tests."

Staged was the operative word in Sam's on-sight evaluation. Annie didn't need to know that.

"What kind of tests?" Annie asked.

"For alcohol and drugs."

"Alcohol maybe … but drugs." Annie shook her head. "She was totally against them."

I continued, "Annie, you told us last night you haven't been in close contact with her for some time."

"Yeah, but what difference does that make? I know for a fact she doesn't do drugs."

I shrugged. "And what makes you so sure?"

"Her mother died from an overdose when Betsy was in high school. She was devastated. Soon after her mother's death, she started coaching kids who came from families with drug problems."

"Maybe something happened she couldn't handle, and the drugs were her way out."

"Not Betsy."

I opted not to tell Annie that both Betsy's wrists were cut. She bled out. The knife used was on the floor beside the bed. The CSI unit bagged it for prints. Sam said the maid didn't find her earlier because Betsy arranged for a late departure. Her room wasn't scheduled to be cleaned until after five o'clock.

"Did someone plan a key party this time around?"

"If they did, I didn't hear anything. I can ask Mark."

"No. You need to stay out of it. Let the Barnstable PD do their thing. I'm sure they're going to want to talk to you." I muttered as I finished my sticky bun.

"Casey, there's something else."

I reached across the table and squeezed her hands. "I'm not going to get involved in the case unless the PD asks me to, which at this point, I don't think it's going to happen. It's an active case."

Annie lowered her chin to her chest, slid her hands under her thighs, and began to rock. "It's a cold case I want you to look over. No, no—not a cold case, but a closed case."

"Now I'm confused, and confusion doesn't fit well into my routine. You need to give me more than one-or two-word answers to my questions and start telling me what's going on. If you won't, I can't help you." I felt terrible I was so abrupt, but whatever was in her head needed to come out. "Now is as good a time as any, so start talking."

Annie looked around. "Okay, but first, I need to use the bathroom."

I moved to my office and sat down behind my desk to wait for Annie. Five minutes later, she was sitting at my desk across from me.

She talked, and I listened. "I grew up with Buster Adams. We started nursery school together. We lived three houses away from each other. Our mothers would stand by the front doors and watch us walk from house to house. I was five when he gave me my first kiss. I was a nerd in high school, and he was a jock. Opposite sides of the spectrum. Even though my family moved, we remained close friends."

I muted my phone so that I could give her my full attention.

"Betsy Harper's family moved from Truro to Hyannis halfway through the school year. I remember the day she strutted into Mrs. Gordon's sixth-grade class at Hyannis Middle School. She was cute, and she knew it. So did Buster." Annie stood and circled the room. Their on-again, off-again love affair lasted until the day he died. She never got over him."

"Did she ever marry?"

"No."

"Did she have any serious relationships?"

21

"She dated, but I think it was for socializing rather than looking for a mate."

"Did she still live on the Cape?"

"She moved off-Cape — once to Plymouth and once to Quincy. She was gone probably a total of four years."

"Where did she work?"

"Last I heard, Betsy worked at Cape Cod Hospital. After high school, she went to Cape Cod Community College, got a medical science certificate, then worked for a doctor in Yarmouth, but I don't know his name. She left him to move to Plymouth. Then came back over the bridge and went back to work with the original doctor. I bumped into Betsy soon after, and she told me she was leaving again. That's when she went to Quincy. She lived there when we were planning our fifth reunion. She came down for a couple of meetings then emailed us with our instructions. Betsy was in charge. Maybe a year after our reunion, she relocated again to the Cape."

"Quite the timeline squashed into about ten sentences and three breath breaks."

Annie managed a smile. "You told me you wanted more than two-word answers."

"You're right. You said you and Betsy were friends."

"We were. Not best buddies, but friends. She didn't confide in me with her deep, dark secrets."

"Let's get to Buster." I took a notebook from my desk. "Why do you think Buster's death wasn't an accident?"

"He may have had his problems, but he wasn't a bad person. At times he could be mouthy, but I'm sure it came with being a high-profile jock. He was a cut-up. A practical joker. Most people liked him."

"You said most. Who didn't?"

"The tough guys in any class don't like the jocks and visa-versa. Even though he and Betsy weren't an item, only friends with benefits, he was bummed out if anyone tried to get close to her. I think she did things on purpose to get him jealous. She wanted to control him but didn't want him to control her."

"What about drugs or alcohol?"

"Maybe a little too much alcohol at times, but true jocks like Buster trying to advance in the sports world usually don't mess with drugs. He was a true jock. He was up for a football scholarship to UMass." Tears formed in Annie's eyes. "As I said, his death wasn't an accident."

Annie is my friend. Buster was hers. Her emotions were on a roller coaster. I told her I'd look into his death even though I knew when a death was ruled accidental; they were precisely that—accidental.

I checked the time. "It's almost ten o'clock. I need to start making some contacts and getting information on Buster."

Annie stood and hugged me. "Thank you, Casey. I'm going home to rest. That's where I'll be if you need me."

I watched her walk out my front door, cross Main Street and disappear between the cars in the courthouse parking lot.

Chapter 4

I punched the numbers for Chief Lowe's direct line into my cell. He answered on the second ring. "Casey, nice to hear from you."

"Thanks, Chief."

"Monday morning quarterbacking?" He asked.

"You know me too well." I hesitated. "Betsy Harper ... "

Before I could say more, his official chief voice piped in. "Her death is being investigated as a homicide. You're not a reporter any longer. You're not looking for a front-page story, but I still can't share details."

"I'm not calling about Betsy. I'm interested in a ten-year-old closed case. The accidental death of Buster Adams." I emphasized the word accidental.

"Is this at the request of his family?"

"No. If you're free this morning, I'd like to come over and talk to you."

"I'll see you at eleven." The phone went dead.

The abruptness in Chief Lowe's voice spiked my curiosity. The only other case I'd worked on that evoked closeness from the chief was the murder of Mary Kaye Griffin. It was a cold case and not a pretty one. But he was the one who asked me to look into it. Mary Kaye was his friend. I wondered if the chief enjoyed more than a professional relationship with the Adams family, as he did with the Griffins, thus triggering personal memories.

It was just after 10:00. I had one hour before I met with Chief Lowe. I called the *Tribune*.

Jamie recognized my voice at the "hi." "Morning' Casey. You comin' to visit?"

I laughed. "If Chuck's in."

"He is and not on his phone." She passed my call through.

"Well, well, well. We have a murder in town, and I get a call."

"Who said it was murder?"

"Your call said so."

"Gotcha. I'm calling about a closed case. Does my password still work?"

"Barely, but come on over. Coffee's your password, and in case you forgot with cream and one sugar."

I grabbed my briefcase and hustled out the door. "See you in a few."

Chuck Young, my old boss at the *Cape Cod Tribune*, was in the lobby talking to Jamie when I walked in carrying a holder with three Dunkin' Donut coffees. My keys were dangling from my baby finger. My briefcase weighed down my left side.

"Help would be nice. I wouldn't want to drop these."

Chuck laughed and reached over to empty my right hand. "If they were Starbucks, I wouldn't be concerned, but Dunkins' ... you'd go into shock at the loss."

Jamie's phone rang. I set a coffee down in front of her. She mouthed thank-you, winked, and continued with her call. I gave a wave and followed Chuck to his office.

"If it's not murder, what's up?"

I got right to the point. "There was a fatal car accident ten years ago in June 2006. The person who died was Buster Adams."

Chuck put his coffee down and leaned forward on his desk. "Why are you looking into this?"

First Chief Lowe's reaction and now Chuck's.

I mimicked Chuck's position and leaned forward. "Before I go any further, should I know who Buster Adams was?"

"His father, Brian Adams, was the lawyer who defended Dr. Anthony Natale in a murder-for-hire case." Chuck lifted his cup and took a swallow. "It may have happened just before you moved to the Cape."

"Who was Dr. Natale trying to have killed?"

"His partner, Dr. Bernard Goldman. Natale didn't succeed with the murder, but it was a nasty case. If I remember correctly, they cleared the courtroom a few times. Both Natale and Goldman were high-profile, well-respected individuals. But, some of the stuff against Natale wasn't on the up and up. He was found guilty and got a stiff sentence. You'll have to check to be sure, but I think it was twenty years. He appealed it, new evidence was introduced, and the charges against him dropped."

"Was Adams his lawyer on the appeal?"

"I don't know. You'll have to check the files."

"Is Natale still practicing?"

"His license got reinstated, but he moved off Cape. Even though the courts overturned his conviction, his practice took a hit. I believe he moved somewhere close to Boston and opened an office in the city.

"As I said, Natale was well-known … in all living rooms, so to speak. The rumor was, he broke bread with Whitey Bulger on more than one occasion. Need I mention more of his astute associates and his business relations with them? Money has its advantages, but cash often comes with hooks attached."

Things were moving, but I wasn't sure if I wanted to be a part of them. "What kind of doctors were Natale and Goldman?"

"Surgeons."

"A lawyer lost a case. Why would this concern his son, Buster?"

"I gave you a brief, very brief, glimpse into the person of Dr. Natale. This whole fiasco brought out the real Anthony Natale. His exterior façade started to disintegrate, and his true persona showed its ugly face. It was a modern-day *run the bad guy out of town on a rail*."

"So Natale blamed Adams for all this?"

"Basically, yes. Attorney Adams and his family were threatened many times. The pressure, the intimidation, and the state of his legal practice plunged him into debt. After Buster's 'accidental' death and Brian's divorce from Amanda—the father apparently couldn't take it anymore. They found him hanging in his garage."

"Thanks for the overview. I'm meeting with Chief Lowe at eleven. I need to look up as much as I can before our meeting takes place."

Chuck wrote something on a sticky note and handed it to me. "Use my password."

I gathered my stuff and headed across the hall to my old office.

I left the *Tribune* two and a half years ago, and my office is still empty. Every time I talk to Chuck, he reminds me of his offer to return to the newspaper. He always lets me use the *Tribune's* resources, and I write an exclusive if what I'm working on deems one. I tease him by saying we're cohorts in crime.

My search for Attorney Brian Adams proved interesting. I printed all the *Tribune* articles about the Doctor Natale case, then switched to the Boston papers. A case of this magnitude spreads. The *Boston Globe* and the *Herald* both featured stories and extensive follow-ups. I printed everything I could find. I made a note to check Barnstable Courts records, both county, and state, for other cases that could shed light on Attorney Adams. I wanted to understand the father *before* I introduced myself to his son.

It was ten-forty. I had twenty minutes to get packed up and be at the station to meet with Chief Lowe. I stuck my head into Chuck's office. "Thanks. Later."

As I hurried through the lobby, I told Jamie I'd call her for lunch.

Chapter 5

I turned left off Phinneys Lane into the Barnstable PD parking lot five minutes early for my appointment.

The officer in the front lobby buzzed me in and directed me to Chief Lowe's office.

The Chief came around his desk and hugged me. "Casey, nice to see you."

"You too, Chief."

"Did you do your homework before you drove across town?"

"Yes, sir, I did. One of these days, I'll try working on something normal."

"Wouldn't suit you." He laughed. "And, believe me, I wouldn't want you to change. I'd like a few of my detectives to have your skills."

"Don't make me blush."

"What's this about Buster Adams?"

"I'm sure you're aware he was a member of the class of 2006. I understand he was just days short of his graduation when he died in an automobile accident. Otherwise, he would have been at the Sheraton this weekend for their ten-year reunion."

Chief Lowe looked up over his glasses. "Are you familiar with the Adams family?"

"Not personally, but after my research this morning, I'm a little more familiar."

"Who's asking about Buster enough for you to want to see the files?"

"A friend of mine, Annie McGuire, was in the class of 2006. You know her from the DA's office. She attended the festivities at the Sheraton. Many of the participants, even those still living on Cape, stayed at the hotel for the weekend. Annie didn't."

The chief sat back and folded his arms over his chest. "Go on."

"Yesterday morning, she received a call from Mark Mosley, their class president. He told her about Betsy. For some reason, they think it could be murder. I said I'd check it out, but I wouldn't be privy to any information since it is an active investigation. My response seemed to appease her for the moment. Since she works for District Attorney Sullivan, she'll have access to inside information."

"You did right. I know Sam was here with Detective Maloney yesterday, so you're aware we're investigating the Betsy Harper death as a homicide."

I nodded as I bit the corner of my lip.

"You said this was about Buster Adams, not Betsy Harper."

"Annie doesn't think Buster's death was an accident. Given what happened to Betsy, her feelings are stronger now than ever before."

I tried to think of my next set of words.

Chief Lowe spoke up before I could get them out. "Since we're dealing with a ten-year-old closed case, the paperwork is archived in our records room here." He lifted the phone, pushed a couple of buttons, and directed the records room officer to make a copy of the case. "They'll have it here in ten minutes."

I leaned forward in my chair. "When the request comes directly from the chief, people listen."

He smirked. "You're not off the hook yet. There's a lot to this case. In your search, I'm assuming you found information regarding Buster's father, Attorney Brian Adams."

"I did."

"I knew them well. I'm still in contact with his ex-wife, Amanda. They divorced a year before Brian committed suicide. She remarried and is now Amanda Fallon. Include Brian in your research. I'll have his file copied and give you a call. Be careful with that one, though. Choose the people you talk to wisely. Don't pull any of your go-off-on-your-own adventures. I'm here, and, of course, Sam's always available. Make sure you have your ducks in a row."

"Appreciate it." I shrugged. "This is all my doing. It's not because of a paying customer." I was doing this for Annie, but something didn't sit right with me either. "What Annie said and the way she said it just doesn't fit the picture of an accident."

The records officer knocked on the door. "Chief, here's the file you requested. Anything else?"

"Not right now. Thanks." The chief slid the folder across his desk. "Here's the first file. I'll call you when I have his father's ready." He walked me to the lobby, hugged me, and whispered, "Be careful."

Chapter 6

The traffic on Phinneys Lane was light, so it took me only ten minutes to get back to my office. I turned right into my driveway, pulled into my parking space, and sat for a couple of minutes, contemplating my next move. Before getting into Buster's file, I decided to walk over to the Superior Court Clerk's office and pull records on the Dr. Natale case. Since I was doing this pro bono and wasn't under any time constraints, I went inside my office first to drop off the files I'd just picked up from Chief Lowe and check for messages.

The blinking red light on my answering machine indicated I had three calls.

The first was trying to sell me advertising space, the second was Marnie, and the third was a caller unavailable, no message, hang up. I pushed the number two on speed dial.

Marnie answered on the first beep.

"Were you sitting on the phone?"

"Matter of fact, I almost was. What's up?"

"Marnie girl, you called me, so I'll ask you … what's up?"

"Oh, yeah. Annie didn't come to work today. She called in."

"I know."

"Why am I not surprised?"

"She was sitting outside my office when I arrived here this morning. We had an interesting conversation."

"Is she okay?"

"Not really. I've got stuff to look up at Superior Court." I checked the time. "Do you and Maloney want to go to Seafood Harry's tonight? Say, around six-thirty?"

"Sounds good to me. I'll text him." In typical Marnie style, the phone went dead.

I called Sam, left a message about supper plans, then headed to the courthouse.

Fortunately, the courthouse wasn't busy. With Brian Adams as the attorney of record, I looked up and copied docket numbers of the last ten cases he'd worked before his death. There wasn't anyone in front of me at the request desk. I knew the clerk, so within fifteen minutes, the files and I were keeping company in one of the empty offices. From a quick run-through, I determined Brian was primarily a criminal defense lawyer and a good one, at least from his clients' point of view.

The next to last case was Dr. Natale's. I put the other nine folders aside. This case consisted of two folders, labeled A and B, each the size of a Boston phone book and held together with three heavy-duty rubber bands. I scanned the first one for witness names, addresses, and occupations. There were pictures of a 9mm Glock, telephone records, a leather satchel full of hundred-dollar bills, and a meeting between two men shaking hands. There were also single images of each man in the shaking hand's picture, a four-door black Mercedes, a Ford F-250 extended cab, and another view labeled Dr. Bernard Goldman. The testimony would be tedious and certainly, take more than part of an afternoon to read. I jotted down page numbers and identified notes regarding information that might prove valuable.

Before returning the case files to the clerk, I glanced at Attorney Adams' last case. It involved rape. His client's name was Peter Mosley. *Why was the name familiar?*

My phone was ringing when I unlocked the door to my office, and again, I didn't catch it in time. Another unknown caller and no message—the third one in two days. If somebody wants me bad enough, one of these times, they'll leave their number.

It was 3:30. I still had about an hour before I planned on heading home. I took Buster Adams' case file from my briefcase. I'm glad I'm not in the middle of a case so I can help Annie. She's my friend, so a little look wouldn't hurt. If it turns into something more than a 'look-into-favor' for a friend, I'd have to reassess my thinking. At least I wouldn't be taking something on cold turkey.

At the time of his death, Buster's address was 26 Apple Road in Centerville. The address didn't ring a bell, so I fired up the computer and Googled it. It appeared to be a neighborhood of nicely appointed and some customized, cape-style houses four streets in off Phinneys Lane. Just for the heck of it, and because it was on my way home, I decided to ride by. Wequaquet Lake, the scene of the *accidental drowning*, was five miles from his house. I wrote down both locations.

I read through the medical examiner's report. It was cut and dried. There were no signs of drug use, no alcohol in his system, and no marks other than the ones the ME noted not resulting from the accident. The time of death was determined to be 4:30 a.m. They didn't find him until 7:10 a.m. Judging from how far his car was out into the lake, police reports listed speed as a factor. It was also noted there were no skid marks. *It appeared he made no effort to stop or slow down.* In a statement from his parents, there was no explanation of why Buster was down near the lake, especially so early.

The report on Buster's vehicle appeared halfway through the file. Because of the notation of speed and no evidence of him trying to stop, I scanned the pages until I found the entry regarding the brakes. I wasn't surprised the investigators didn't find anything suggesting the brakes or the gas pedal had been tampered with. If so, the case would have, more than likely classified as a homicide.

I closed the file. My head told me to stay clear of Buster and Betsy, but my gut struggled to say, '*go for it.*' Until last night, these two people didn't exist in my world. One at eighteen years old hadn't even started to live, and the other, well, part of her life ended that night ten years ago when Buster died. Now ten years later, she was dead. My sixth sense said to walk away, but my seventh sense wouldn't let me.

Chapter 7

When I turned onto my street, I saw Sam's car already in the driveway. I was glad he came home early. It gave us some personal time before meeting up with Marnie and Maloney.

"You got my message about supper at Harry's?"

"Yeah, about a half-hour before I left the station. I was stuck in meetings all day."

Watson was waiting just inside the door, his tail wagging a mile a minute. I knelt and gave him a tousle. "We're not meeting them until six-thirty. We've got plenty of time for a beach walk with the boy."

Watson heard 'walk' and raced to the door, ready to go.

Sam put a handful of treats in his pocket, took Watson's leash off the counter, and headed out. "Let's go."

"What were your meetings about?"

"Mostly rehashing incidents of the summer, some involving the wash-a-shores." Sam tugged at the leash to slow Watson down. "We can rehash all we want, but the same idiots will be back and pull the same shit next year. How about your day? Anything exciting?"

"Annie was sitting outside my office when I got there at eight-thirty. She took a personal day. I've never seen her so shook up. I mean, she works in the DA's office. She sees lots of gruesome photos, and the reports can be chilling. I wouldn't be able to sleep for days."

"Most of those are Flat Stanleys. They're one-dimensional pictures and cut-n-dry reports of people and events not part of her life. The death of Betsy Harper triggered the memory of Buster Adams' fatal accident." Sam shortened his hold on Watson as a car sped by. "Slow down," he yelled.

I wanted to tell Sam about my research and my meetings with Chuck at the *Tribune* and Chief Lowe but decided this wasn't the time. I'd crammed a lot into one day and needed to sort things out. Nobody hired me. Annie asked me to help her. Now I was in—past my ankles—and needed to decide how deep I wanted to go.

There weren't many people on the beach, so Sam unleashed Watson and let him run to play with his seagull buddies. "Speaking of Betsy Harper, there was some talk of it this morning in Bourne. The guys in the detective bureau were buzzing. They know I'm friendly with a couple of dicks from Barnstable, so they asked me what happened. The word is her death wasn't a suicide."

I shrugged. "I understand the facts about her death, but why did they conclude it wasn't a suicide?"

"News amongst the brotherhood travels faster than a speeding bullet."

"No shit." I sat on the seawall, watching the waves break along the shoreline. "Since we're on the subject, what were they saying?"

"They said it's being investigated as a homicide."

I cocked my head in his direction. "Nothing else? Are you not telling all?"

Sam looked toward Watson to make sure he was within whistling range. "Nothing else to tell."

"I don't believe you, Sam Summers. Let's go home. We'll continue this discussion later."

Watson came on the first whistle. He knew there'd be treats waiting.

Chapter 8

Sam and I pulled into the parking lot at Seafood Harry's ten minutes early. Marnie and Maloney were already there.

Marnie gave Sam, and me hugs. "We just got here ourselves. Five more minutes, and Maloney would have bought the first round."

Sam laughed and started to walk back out the door. "We'll go sit in the car and give him time to complete his mission."

Maloney grabbed Sam's arm. "The only place you're going is with me to the counter to get drinks."

I watched them arm punch each other, then laugh at whatever guy talk they shared.

I ripped some paper towels from the roll on the holder beside the basket of condiments. "We're lucky to have those two."

Marnie's smile said it all.

I smirked. "Now that everything's moved into your fixer-upper, the real work begins. Have you decided which rooms you'll remodel first?"

"One minute it's the kitchen, the next minute it's the master. It's overwhelming, but once we get our heads together and finalize what we're going to do, it'll move fast."

When the guys came with their beers and our wines, we toasted Marnie and Maloney's new house and their upcoming wedding.

Sam folded his hands and leaned in on the table. "So, this wedding … have you guys set the date? I want to make sure it gets on my calendar. And, are we going to New York City or staying on the Cape?"

Maloney looked at me and took a swig of beer. "He sure asks a lot of questions."

I laughed, "Once a cop, always a cop—you should identify."

"Before we can set the date, we have to figure out the location. I'd like to have it on Cape Cod, but my parents want it in New York

City." Marnie shrugged. "I suppose I can't blame them. The City has been their life. My extended family's either in the City or close, and then there are their friends—mine too."

"Marnie's gotten information on several venues. Now she has to run them by her mom."

"Okay, enough answers for now." Sam stood. "Don't know about you, but I'm hungry." He put a paper towel over his arm. "The usual, my dear?"

I nodded. "Of course."

Sam and Maloney placed our food orders.

It wasn't busy, so our food came out quicker than usual.

I was halfway through my fried clams and onion rings. I'd waited long enough. I'm sure Maloney knew I wasn't going to stay quiet about last night. "Have you heard anything from the medical examiner yet?"

"I did. I talked to Ernie earlier today. This one isn't going to be pretty. Betsy's wrists were slit, and she bled out. Probably the cause of death. The thing is, we found marks around her mouth indicating she was gagged. It appeared she didn't put up a fight. Ernie sent some stomach samples to Boston. He suspected she was drugged, just enough to knock her out. Whoever did this didn't want her to die from an overdose."

"Annie stopped by my office today. I mentioned something about drugs to her. She told me Betsy's mother died from an overdose, and Betsy was dead set against drugs in any form. Anything to do with drugs wouldn't have been her choice if she was going to commit suicide."

Sam was quiet until now. "If that's the case, and Annie knew it, then it appears she wasn't the only one. Not hard to figure out this was planned."

Maloney nodded. "True. There's another thing, though. It appears Betsy was raped. The sex doesn't appear to be consensual

38

because of the bruising around her vagina. It may have started as a friendly romp in the sheets but changed to rough sex sometime along the way. There were two empty condom wrappers on the floor under the bed."

I rolled my eyes. "Two wrappers? I suppose there was no semen on her or the bedsheets."

"Nothing."

"What about prints on the wrappers?"

"We're checking." Maloney took a deep breath. "But whoever did this thought he or they were careful not to leave anything that could be traced back to him or them. They missed the condom wrappers. The scene was the perfect definition of rape. So perfect that, in my opinion, it was staged."

"Back up. What's with the him or them?" I asked.

Maloney shrugged, "Because we have nothing definite to go on, we're checking all avenues."

Marnie looked from me to the guys. "Last night, Annie mentioned something about a key party. I had no idea what it was before she explained. It seems the committee discussed having one at their five-year reunion. Annie said it met with disapproval, so it was shit-canned. Do you think had one at their ten-year?"

"Could be." Sam pointed, moving his finger to emphasize his words to Maloney. "There were some key cards on the desk next to the TV. I think there were four, or maybe five. I looked at them quickly before one of your guys bagged them. It appeared the magnetic strips were scratched so badly that a card reader couldn't identify a room number. It was obvious to me that somebody defaced them on purpose."

Maloney took a deep breath. "I'll check first thing in the morning."

"Enough shop talk. Let's move on to the plans for your house," I said. "Are you doing a demo day this weekend?"

Marnie looked at Maloney. "Before we start ripping stuff out, we're going to decide what we're going to replace it with. We'll be checking out flooring, cabinets, and all the good stuff. Gonna be a fun time. Wanna come? We're going to Falmouth, so we can swing by Popponesset Marketplace on the way home and get chowdah and a lobstah roll at the Raw Bar."

Sam piped up. "The cabinets and flooring… ah… don't thrill me, but the mention of the Raw Bar. What time do you want to go?"

Marnie and Maloney took 6A to get home. Sam and I cut across Route 130 to Route 28.

I went right to the bedroom to change into my Joe Boxers.

Sam was playing with the TV when I went back to the living room. "The Sox are playing Baltimore. They started at seven-thirty, so we only missed the first inning. I'll take Watson outside. You make us coffee and plate some Oreos."

He hooked Watson to his leash, then in a soft, sexy voice, he whispered in my ear, "I love you," and sealed it with a kiss.

My body tingled. "Keep it up, and there will be an off-the-field, grand slam home run before the start of the next inning."

Chapter 9

Tuesday

Sam was up, dressed, and had the Keurig ready to go. Two bowls of Frosted Mini-Wheats with sliced peaches marked our spots at the table. Watson was sitting at the kitchen door, patiently waiting to go out.

Sam leaned into the bedroom. "Taking the boy out for a walk around the house."

It was 6:15. Sam didn't have to leave for work until 7:00. As for me, well, I don't have a set schedule. It's a perk for being my own boss. We both like to watch the morning news, so last week we installed an under-the-cabinet TV in the kitchen. When I turned it on, the Welcome to Cape Cod sign at the Bourne Bridge was the lead for the weekend murder of Betsy Harper.

Sam walked in just as the frame changed to a picture of the hotel where they found her body.

"What the ..." He dropped Watson's leash and stood facing the TV. "Unless something happened last night, it hasn't officially been classified a murder. Reporters can't wait to sensationalize."

In some respects, I shared Sam's feelings. When I was a reporter, I didn't put anything into print until I had facts to back it up. The morning newspaper was still in its plastic bag on the counter. Yesterday's edition of the *Tribune* published an article but didn't call it murder or suicide—they referred to a reported death from an undetermined cause. And the Barnstable Police Department was investigating. There was filler for the story, but nothing specific.

I made our coffee and got the milk from the fridge. "Want me to pour?"

Sam pulled his chair out and sat. "Yeah, sure."

The anchor finished his Betsy story and moved on.

"Didn't expect to start the morning with Betsy."

"Me neither." Sam folded his arms across his chest. "Casey, Annie is your friend. And, it was Annie's friend who died. They're treating it as a homicide."

I held my hand up. "Stop right there. Annie knew right from the get-go I couldn't do anything about Betsy's death. It wasn't Betsy's death she wanted me to check into. It was her friend, Buster Adams, who died ten years ago. They ruled it accidental and filed it as a closed case."

"Tonight, we're going to talk. I recall the Buster Adams case. I'm not disputing the fact it's a closed case. What I am concerned about is it's a case that should remain closed. There are skeletons locked in his closet that could reappear and rattle a few cages."

I knew when it was okay to strike up a debate or when to let things mellow out. This was a mellow-out moment. "I'll listen."

Sam checked his watch. "I've gotta hustle, or I'll be late." He kissed me, then patted Watson. "You taking him to the office?"

"Yeah." I walked Sam to his car. "How about we stay in tonight. I'll pick up steaks, and maybe we'll get to watch the whole Sox game—only if someone keeps his hands and tongue to himself."

"But what if they need a little help scoring?"

"Get outta here." I slapped his shoulder, then watched until he disappeared around the corner at the end of our street. *A Marnie and Maloney moment. Are Sam and I ready to commit?*

I filled Watson's bowl and made myself another coffee. Tony Montelli was finishing up his weather report. On Cape Cod, September was the best—like Baby Bear's porridge, not too hot, not too cold, just right. My mother always told me the porridge story when I was a little kid. We spent September weekends in West Dennis. I closed my eyes and cradled my face in my hands. *Memories.*

My reminiscing was cut short when my cell rang. I fished it out of my purse and answered without checking the caller ID. It read *unknown*. "Hello."

No response.

"Hello." I heard a rumble of what may have been papers being shuffled, along with the faint sound of a dog barking, before the call terminated. I held my phone in front of me. "I hate this bullshit. If you're going to call me, then talk. Otherwise, don't waste my time."

I paced the kitchen. Sam was probably right, but I wasn't one to let good research go to waste. I knew Annie's request came because of Betsy's sudden death. I knew it wasn't an accident or a suicide. Annie was sure Betsy's death was somehow associated with Buster's. I would look into Buster's 'accidental' drowning, but Annie would have to understand, I wasn't going to poke my nose into anything having to do with Betsy.

Chapter 10

I hadn't brought Watson by to see Nancy for a couple of weeks, so before I settled in at my desk, I hooked him up to his leash, and we walked to the donut shop to say good morning. I rapped on the window.

Nancy waved me in. "How's my little buddy?" She knelt beside Watson, took a few treats from her pocket, and gave them to him.

"It's no wonder the neighborhood dogs like to stop here." I patted the boy's head. "They get a treat, and the leash holders get a sticky bun."

"Good marketing, don't you think?" Nancy gave Watson an extra yummy. "Casey, do you have time for a coffee? Since it's not busy, I can join you."

I checked my watch. "Works for me."

Nancy smiled. "If you're not in a hurry, sit down, and I'll get our coffee."

Watson curled up on the floor next to me.

"One of the girls from the DA's office stopped in for coffee yesterday. She said Annie didn't show for work. Said it was Annie's friend they found dead at the Sheraton."

Wow, nothing is private. "That's true. Annie and the girl who died grew up together." I didn't want to expand the conversation but knew Nancy would have more questions.

"Poor Annie. Death is hardest when it involves family and friends. Have you talked to her?"

"I have. She's pretty shaken up." *Keep it short.*

"What did her friend die from?"

"No idea," I said.

"Hard for me to believe you haven't heard anything."

I tried to avoid eye contact with Nancy. "When it doesn't involve me, I've learned from past mistakes to mind my own business." It was time to gulp down the rest of my coffee and leave.

When I stood, Watson followed. "I have to get to work. I don't get a paycheck from the *Tribune* anymore."

"Tell Annie if she needs a shoulder. I have two available."

I waved and walked out the door.

Watson was doggy-treated out, so he curled up in a sunny spot by the front window.

I took the notes I'd taken yesterday from Attorney Brian Adams' Superior Court case files out of my attaché and set them unopened in front of me on my desk. From the little I heard, he was an active attorney with no scruples. After he lost the Natale case, Chuck said Adams and his family were threatened many times. Then his son, Buster, died in an accidental drowning, his law practice plummeted, and his wife filed for divorce. They found him hanging, but that doesn't mean he was his own executioner. There was no doubt in my mind the Natale case, and those associated with it may have broken bread with the fine attorney before he called it a night.

Sam's comments before he left for Bourne only sparked my curiosity. He unknowingly baited me to rattle the closet bones. My only hesitation to move forward was that I was doing it out of sheer nosiness—a trait that almost got me killed more than once.

My brain moved in different directions, thoughts bumping into each other and nothing making sense. I needed a robust French vanilla to improve my focus. Watson didn't move when I stood and headed toward my office kitchen. I love this place. Too bad the upstairs wasn't big enough to make it into an apartment. I came back from la-la land when I heard the Keurig spit out the last few drops. With coffee in hand, I moved to my desk. If I lived here, I'd end up married to my job, and the only thing or person I want to be married to is Sam—someday.

Why did Dr. Natale try to have his partner killed?

In a round-about way, Chuck and Chief Lowe shared Sam's feelings about me doing unpaid research on Buster Adams and his father. I found it challenging. I didn't intend to do anything with it, so what the hell.

I'd only skimmed the Superior Court file on the Natale case. My notes were mostly scribbled and unconnected. The file size was considerable, so I needed to organize and create a timeline of events.

My cell rang. This time I checked the caller ID before I picked it up. "Mornin' Miss Marnie." I laughed. "I won't be able to use Miss much longer. I do like the sound of Mrs. Maloney, though."

"Mrs. Maloney—scares me to think of it. It sounds like a name attached to an elementary school teacher."

I laughed. "Is Annie in today?"

"She came in around nine—still's a mess. She's been quiet, so I just let her be. I'm right around the corner if she needs me." Marnie's voice changed to a whisper. "Want to meet me at Finn's around noon for good food and conversation?"

"You going to ask me what I'm working on?"

"Yep. See you there."

"I'm not going to …." The phone went dead—typical Marnie.

Chuck told me Natale was involved in some unsavory things, including his association with the notorious Irish mobster, Whitey Bulger. If this were my case, I could reach out to Dr. Goldman, but since I was researching for myself, this wouldn't happen. I chuckled to myself and wondered if this is how writers Mary Higgins Clark or James Patterson researched for their best-selling murder mysteries. Maybe I should consider writing as a sideline. Wonder what Sam would think. I laughed to myself.

When I checked my watch, it was 10:45. That gave me just enough time to take Watson home, hook him to his lease, set him up with some Kibbles 'n Bits and a bowl of fresh water.

Marnie was sitting on the bench in front of Finn's waiting. "I'm hungry."

"You're always hungry. If I didn't know better, I'd say you were eating for two."

"Bite your tongue, girl."

We settled into our usual table in the corner by the window, and both ordered the Tuesday special—a cup of clam chowder and a lobster salad sandwich on Portuguese sweet bread.

"Have you found something to substantiate Annie's claim about Buster's accident being anything but an accident?"

I shrugged. "Not really."

Marnie leaned forward. "A 'not really' means you've found something of interest. Maybe enough to change history?"

I ignored her and took another bite of my sandwich.

Marnie kept her eyes glued to mine. "If I'm right, are you going to do something about it? Snooping and flipping dirty rocks could right some wrongs."

"Don't get so dramatic. I only agreed to take a look. I'm in between paying cases, and it gives me a chance to sharpen my investigative skills without having to answer to someone. I don't have to take it to the finish line."

"Bullshit. It's me you're talking to. You might not come in first, but you'll always finish."

"Hear me out. I love the challenge, but this case has many appendages and unsavory players. I'm not sure if I want to get hooked to the point where I can't stop. Do you understand?"

Marnie whispered, "Whatever you decide. If you need my help, I'm here for you."

"I offered you the other desk in my office. So, what are you waiting for?" I couldn't resist the dig.

Chapter 11

I'd finished compiling a list of questions. Now, I needed answers. I was on my way to the courthouse to continue my research when my cell rang.

It was Sam.

I could hear traffic noise in the background. "Good afternoon, big guy."

"It's afternoon, but not a good one. There was a fatal on Scenic Highway—at least two dead and several injured. I'm there now. It's a mess. I'll be late—not sure what time. I'll give you a call when I'm on my way. Gotta go."

Sometimes life sucks, and then you die.

When I got to the courthouse, more people were hanging around the lobby and in the clerk's office today than yesterday. I hadn't seen any articles in the *Tribune* noting the start of a new trial. There were four people in front of me at the information desk asking for files. I waited longer to request the trial's transcript than it took to get the actual paperwork. Today I didn't have the luxury of an empty meeting room to re-examine the Natale case. Fortunately, the person I shared the table with took up residency at the far end, leaving ample space between us for privacy.

I flipped through the file until I found Attorney Adams' opening statement. He painted a picture of Dr. Natale as a pillar of the community, renowned heart surgeon, family man, and dad who spent many hours working to advance sports for underprivileged children in the community. They charged his client with trying to enlist the services of a Boston lowlife to carry out a murder-for-hire plot against his partner, Dr. Bernard Goldman—an offense that could get Natale twenty years in prison. Adams acknowledged several meetings between Natale and Willy O'Hara, an ex-con from South Boston, but said he'd prove they didn't have anything to do with a murder-for-hire plot.

Adams went on to say he'd present evidence showing his client was doing a favor for a Boston associate by meeting with Mr. O'Hara to advise him on a heart-related medical condition. The attorney informed the jury there would be pictures showing a satchel of money changing hands, a midnight blue 550 Mercedes belonging to Dr. Natale, a 9mm Glock belonging to O'Hara, photos of Natale, and O'Hara, together and individually. And one of Dr. Goldman, but the pictures were from a meeting that had nothing to do with this case.

Most criminal lawyers, like Adams, should be awarded a doctorate in theatre. They possess the ability to write a script. If performed to the height of perfection, it could manipulate the jury's sense of right from wrong. The poor schmuck who stutters his way through a case with proven facts seems to end up on the losing side. In this case, it appears that Adams met his match. The jury did its job and convicted Natale. Adams' representation ended. Chuck said Natale appealed and won.

I looked at my watch. I had an hour before the clerk's office closed. From yesterday's visit, I remembered the last case Attorney Adams filed in Barnstable Superior Court was for rape. I didn't get a chance to check it out then, so I decided to take a quick look before heading back to my office. I flipped through my notes for the docket number, then turned the Natale file in and requested number 84901. Nobody was in the seat I'd occupied for the last hour. The person I'd shared the room with was gone. My concentration level is better when I'm alone. I set myself up and started to examine the pages. The defendant, Peter Mosley, was charged with rape. I stared at it, closed my eyes, and rummaged the file cabinet in my head. I scanned the miscellaneous section, keeping names for possible future reference.

I lost track of my thoughts and pounded my fist on the table. The noise drew attention from the information desk clerk. A glance let her know nothing was wrong. "Son of a bitch," I whispered.

Chapter 12

Sam was going to be late, so Watson and I took our beach walk. I do my best thinking while sitting on a bench facing the water. September was the start of peaceful beginnings. For the most part, tourists had gone home and, during the week, the natives were still at work.

The tide was starting to come in. The lap of each gentle wave beckoned me to drag my feet in the cool, wet sand.

Watson ran up and down the beach then jumped on me just as another wave broke. I landed butt first in the water. If I didn't know better, I'd say Watson was laughing as he ran circles around me. Good thing I left my phone on the kitchen table.

I reached into my pocket. The only way I would get him close enough to hook him to his leash was to give him a treat. "Come on, boy, let's head home. Daddy should be waiting."

Sam laid back on his lounge chair. "I love sitting on the deck with my favorite girl, the boy, and an empty bottle of Coors."

"Wise ass." I took a frosty Coors Light from the cooler and handed it to him. Then touched the palm of my hand lightly with my lips and blew him an air kiss. "Your reward for a great job with the steaks."

"Thanks."

"So, tell me about the accident in Bourne."

"A drunk in a junky old pick-up cut off a school bus. The bus driver veered to the right to avoid hitting the truck but couldn't escape the concrete power pole."

"Were there kids on the bus?"

"Yep. Fortunately, only four. She had just started her route."

"You said there were fatalities."

"The guy in the pick-up cut in front of the bus then crossed the highway and broadsided another car, killing that driver. As for the kids, one has a broken leg and a possible concussion. The other three were banged up, but except for being traumatized, they appeared to be all right."

"You said two people died?"

"The second one was the bus driver." Sam turned away and stared out over the yard. "She's driven school buses for as long as I've known her. Someone said she was getting ready to retire. I shouldn't say it, but I hope the prison community imposes a sentence over and above the one imposed by the courts." Sam sighed. "Let's change the subject. How about your day?"

"Watson and I enjoyed an early coffee-time with Nancy. Then I brought him home and came back to meet Marnie at Finn's for lunch."

"I haven't heard the word work yet." Sam backed up and smiled.

"Real funny. I spent a few hours at Superior Court today. And, yes, I was working. First, I finished reading the Natale case. Then I pulled another one of Adams' cases.

Sam shook his head. "How far are you going to delve into Buster's case?"

"I'm doing this for Annie. I'll probably continue until I get answers or somebody comes knocking on my door with a retainer check made out to Casey Quinby. Annie's asking about Adams' son Buster. Annie's asking for Annie, not for anyone else."

"You're hopeless."

"Do you want to hear more?"

Sam glanced at his watch. "You've got an hour before the Sox game comes on."

I took my notes and copies of the Natale case, divided them into two piles, and put them in front of Sam. "The case files are on your right ... my notes in the other pile. Read Adams' opening statement. I didn't get much further."

Sam didn't say anything, but he didn't have to. I knew he didn't believe me. It didn't take a whole afternoon to read an opening statement. I purposely left the Peter Mosley file in my briefcase. Until I finished sifting through all the paperwork, there was no sense in sharing it with Sam.

I washed the dishes while Sam read. When he finished, he neatened the piles and paper-clipped the pages together.

"Well, any comments?"

"You're getting too involved in something you weren't hired to do."

"Like how? All I did was make copies of a closed Superior Court case."

Sam rested his elbows on the table. "Casey, you're good at what you do. You could end up opening wounds that may or may not have healed. There were some heavy-duty players involved, and they still might have some influence on the whole situation— if there still is a situation." He inhaled, then let out a deep sigh. "Think about the expression; it's better to let sleeping dogs lie. Need I say more?"

"Your Sox game is coming on." I pointed to the television. "Want some ice cream?"

Chapter 13

Wednesday

I stopped at Dunkins' before heading to Barnstable Village. A silver pickup cut me off as I turned out of the parking lot onto Phinneys Lane. "What the hell." I jerked to the side of the road to avoid a collision but couldn't grab the cardboard tray. My coffee and donut went flying onto the floor. I looked around. The truck was gone and, so was my coffee and donut.

And this is the way to start a new day. The kindergarten song played in my head. My mother wanted me to be a teacher. I should have listened.

It was eight-thirty when I pulled into my parking space and unlocked the rear door to my office. I brewed a cup of French vanilla and sat down at my computer to engage in a challenging game of *Candy Crush*. My cell rang. *Unknown* flashed across the screen. "Casey Quinby, Private Investigator."

"Mornin', it's me."

"Annie?"

"Yeah, who did you think it was?"

"Since the number display read unknown, I wasn't sure."

Annie sounded more like her old self. "I'm on my work phone. You got a minute for me?"

The Buster Adams' stuff was still in my briefcase. And, frankly, I wanted it to stay there. Sam's little talk last night made a lot of sense.

"I can hear breathing, so you're still there." Annie laughed.

"Um, yeah, sure. Come over. I'll have a coffee waiting for you."

"See you in ten."

I'm usually not at a loss for words, but this morning I was. I needed to tell Annie I could not continue checking into her Buster's accidental death theories. She already knew I was staying clear of Betsy's. She didn't accept it but didn't have a choice.

Annie came through the front door at the same time I returned from the kitchen carrying her coffee. I set it down on the desk. "Quiet at the DA's office?"

She swallowed. "Same old, same old."

I was almost afraid to ask. "So, what's up?"

"I received a call yesterday from Amanda Fallon … Buster's mother."

"I've never met her, but know who she is."

"Amanda said she read about Betsy and asked if I was all right. I told her it would be hard, but I'd be fine. Said her husband was out of town and invited me to her house for dinner last night. She's remarried." Annie put her coffee on the desk. "I accepted. We did a lot of reminiscing, some crying and laughing too. It was good for me, and I think it was good for her."

Annie wasn't sitting across from me just to shoot the shit. I didn't ask what she and Amanda talked about. "You seem like you're in a better place. I'm glad. It's hard to move on, but sometimes it's for the best."

"What are you talking about?"

I took a deep breath. "Let me ask you the same question. What are *you* talking about?"

"Buster's mother wants to talk to you."

"Why?"

"She wants to hire you to look into Buster's death."

"Did you tell her you'd already been talking to me about her son?"

"Kinda. I gave her your number." Annie stood and headed toward the door. "Gotta get back to work. Talk to you later."

I wasn't happy about the situation, but Amanda Fallon was going to call me, and if she were going to be a paying client, I would listen.

Annie wasn't gone a half-hour when the phone rang. "Casey Quinby, Private Investigator."

"Hello, my name's Amanda Fallon. I'd like to make an appointment to speak with you."

I pretended to check my calendar in a gesture to stall for time. "I'll be available this afternoon at two o'clock or tomorrow morning at nine."

"See you at two." The conversation ended as quickly as it began.

I pigged out on Smartfood popcorn and a Diet Coke while I put together a fill-in-the-blank contract in the event Amanda Fallon became a paying client. My standard up-front retainer is two thousand dollars, then a hundred dollars an hour, plus expenses. I couldn't yet fill in what the actual investigation would be. After talking to her, I'd incorporate it into the contract.

I quickly scanned the reports on Buster's accident I'd gotten from the Barnstable PD. At this point, I had no intention of getting into the files on her ex-husband's case, so I left them in my briefcase.

It was one forty-five when the knock on the door, followed by a quick entrance, startled me.

A petite middle-aged woman dressed in what struck me as designer clothes walked in. "Casey Quinby, I presume?"

I stood. "I am, and you must be Amanda Fallon."

She nodded. We shook hands before I invited her to have a seat across from me. "May I get you a cup of coffee?"

"That would be nice, just black, thank you."

Amanda wasn't at all what I expected. I'm not sure what I expected, but she wasn't it. Thank goodness for my Keurig. Less than two minutes later, I set a cup down on the desk in front of her.

"I'm sure you spoke to Annie," Amanda said as she took a sip of her coffee.

"I did."

"What did she tell you?"

"She told me you had dinner last night, and the subject of Buster's accident came up. She said something about looking into it."

I kept my eyes focused on hers as I leaned forward on my desk, my hands woven together for stability. I wasn't overly comfortable with this meeting, so the next move was hers.

"We talked about Betsy Harper's death, which led us to my son's so-called accidental drowning ten years ago in Wequaquet Lake." She fumbled to get a tissue from her purse. "Annie and my Buster grew up together. I always thought, actually hoped, they'd end up together, but it didn't happen. Instead, he was murdered. That's why."

I sat for what seemed like an eternity, trying to figure out what to say next. I wasn't opposed to taking the case involving Buster, but it appeared to me, Amanda was linking her son's death to Betsy's. And Chief Lowe and Sam told me to stay away from the Betsy Harper homicide investigation.

Amanda wiped her eyes. "Yes, murdered. And I want to hire you to find out who did it. For ten years, I've contained my feelings about what happened. I only expressed myself to my ex— Brian—Buster's father. He listened, then told me I was a grieving mother, and there was nothing to substantiate a finding for anything other than a tragic accident. I can't prove it, and now he's dead. Brian was never the same. We drifted apart and then divorced. It was two years, almost to the day our divorce was final when he supposedly committed suicide."

Why did she say supposedly? Is she here to talk about her son's death or her ex-husband's?

I was walking on eggshells and had to choose my words carefully. "Why did you wait until now?"

"Betsy."

The police are investigating Betsy's death as a homicide made to look like a suicide. I also knew I wasn't about to share or discuss anything involving Betsy's death. "Mrs. Fallon—" I was stopped before I could continue.

"Please call me Amanda."

"Amanda, before we continue, I have to tell you, even if I did hear something about Betsy's death, I'm not at liberty to talk to you about it. I read the papers like everyone else and have the same information you and other readers do. It's an open case, a *new* open case, and I have no business making inquiries into it."

"Annie told me Betsy didn't commit suicide. Betsy stayed close to me after we both lost Buster. I saw her last week. She was excited about her upcoming class reunion. And I won't say more." Amanda took another sip of coffee. "Can we get to the subject at hand? I'd like to get this started."

I pulled up the fill-in-the-blank contract I'd started to prepare for Amanda and read her the list of potential costs and what they covered.

She didn't bat an eyelash. "That's fine."

"Before we complete our agreement, we need to talk about what you want and what you expect me to find."

"Very simple. I want you to find the truth behind Buster's death. I already told you he was murdered."

"I can promise you I'll perform a thorough investigation, but I can't promise you the results you're looking for without any concrete evidence."

"Annie said to trust you. She assured me if there was anything to be found, you'll find it."

"I'll do my best not to disappoint you." I looked at my notes. "Give me a few minutes, and I'll have the contract ready for you to review. If it's to your liking, you can sign it."

Amanda walked to the front window and stared in the direction of the Barnstable County Superior Courthouse. "I'm going to sit outside. Let me know when you're finished."

I filled in the blanks and read it over before I walked out to get her. "Ready?"

She followed me inside, sat down, and fished her checkbook from her purse. "Two thousand … right?"

I nodded. "Read this over first."

Neither of us spoke for at least five minutes. Amanda set the paperwork down on the desk and signed on the line above her name. "I make the check out to Casey Quinby, PI?"

"Yes, thank you."

She took a paperclip from a trinket dish on my desk and attached my retainer to the front of the contract. She didn't mince any words. Her actions spoke for her.

Chapter 14

Watson and I were playing a game of fetch in the yard when Sam rolled into the driveway. The minute the boy saw the man, I was out of the picture. *I might as well have vanished into thin air.* I moved to the steps and sat down to watch.

What would I do without those two? Banish that idea.

I was deep in thought and didn't see Sam throw the ball in my direction. Watson jumped up and caught it mid-air before hitting me in the head.

"Hey, what's with the wild pitch?"

Sam ran over and wrapped his arms around me. "Sorry about that, Sherlock."

I wanted to be mad, but his hugs always changed my mind, and he knew it. "Apology accepted."

"Want to go to Dino's for pizza, or DiParma's for an antipasto and some calamari?"

"I thought we could stay home. I stopped by the market and picked up hot dogs and potato salad."

"You don't want to go out to eat? You're not sick, so what's runnin' round inside your pretty little head?"

"Maybe I want to play an early game of grab ass." I stood with my hands on my hips. "Is that a problem?" I laughed.

Sam's eyes focused on mine. "Not with grab-ass."

I didn't answer, just sashayed into the house. My two guys followed.

Sam filled Watson's water bowl, opened himself a Coors, and sat across from me at the kitchen table.

My briefcase was on one of the chairs. I unzipped the side pocket and slid Amanda Fallon's check from under the paper clip holding it to the signed contract. I held it between my thumb and pointer finger and waved it in front of Sam.

"I'm afraid to ask."

"A retainer from my new client."

"Amanda Fallon?"

"Yep. How'd you guess?"

Sam didn't use his serious voice often. When he did, he meant business. "Our talk last night didn't register?"

"Oh, yes, it did. When we discussed it, I didn't have a client. I had a friend asking for help. But she'd gone beyond help, and I was done. Annie called about a half-hour after I got into the office. She invited herself over for coffee. I'd made up my mind you were right about not sticking my nose into places it didn't belong. I'd convinced myself to tell her I wouldn't do any more snooping into Buster's death. She could if she wanted to. It was her decision."

"And?"

"That's when she told me Amanda Fallon wanted to meet with me to talk about her son's death ten years ago."

"Since you dangled her check for me to see, I assume you've already met with her."

"Yep." I set the check and paperwork on the table in front of Sam. "As of this afternoon, I'm officially conducting an investigation for Amanda Fallon, formally Amanda Adams."

Sam raised his eyebrows and gave me a half nod. "The last word of advice before I give you my blessing …unless Chief Lowe asks … stay away from the Betsy Harper murder probe."

Chapter 15

Thursday

Sam left the house for Bourne at six a.m. He was in charge of recreating the scene of yesterday's fatal school bus accident, so he needed to be at the station early to meet with his team. I got a slap on the ass and a peck on the cheek, followed by a quick see-you-this-afternoon before he ran out the door.

I took advantage of the early wake-up call and dragged myself to the bathroom to shock my body with a cold shower. It worked. I was halfway to the bedroom when my cell went off. With a towel wrapped around my head and a pair of flip-flops on my feet, I dashed to catch it before the caller hung up. I heard a click at the same time I said hello. The caller ID read unknown. I couldn't imagine anyone I knew calling me at six-thirty in the morning.

It was supposed to be a beautiful warm spring day, and I didn't have any formal meetings planned, so I slipped on a pair of jean capris and my new Tom Brady jersey. Since I'd probably be in and out of the office, I hooked Watson to his run and set food and water on the deck. "See you later, little guy."

Instead of going directly to the office, I headed to Wequaquet Lake. When I swung by there before, it was to satisfy Annie and to pinpoint the location of Buster Adams' death. It was a one-time ride-by with no intention of revisiting the site. But now, Buster's *accident* took on a whole new perspective with a client, his mother, paying me to investigate his death.

The lake was calm and inviting. I pulled over and parked near the scene of Buster's *accident.* I took the map, accident reports, and pictures of the scene from my briefcase and laid them out on the passenger seat. I studied the map indicating the exact location where

Buster's car went off the road into the water. It was like time stood still. The foliage, although much denser, was the same as in the pictures ten years ago—mostly wild seagrass, cinnamon ferns, and ground-crawling scrub brush native to the Cape. There was a clearing, about twenty feet wide and forty feet in from the road. It bordered the street on one side and the foliage on the other. It was worn down to the dirt from being used for parking a trailer or truck after launching a boat or for a late-night hideaway to get a piece of ass. Across the street was a smaller clearing, roughly thirty feet from the road to the water, where the boats were launched. According to the map, the closest house was out of sight, about four hundred feet up the road and around a bend, not visible from where I parked.

I held the pictures taken ten years ago and positioned myself to face the lake in the same direction Buster's car entered the water. There was a bend just before the clearing, but judging from a separate image of the tire tracks, he deliberately positioned his car and drove straight in. In the pictures, all I could see was part of the trunk and the rear bumper sticking up. I parked by the water and walked the area, trying to determine how he got up enough speed to fly fifteen feet out before taking a nosedive in the shallow water. Something didn't sit right. I needed to know the slope hidden under the surface. If this happened on dry land, the car would probably have flipped. Instead, it got stuck in the mud, submerged enough for the water to drown any life left in Buster's body—assuming he was alive on impact.

I took a new set of pictures, mimicking the ones in the case file, then some additional ones of the surrounding area. I was standing by the water, trying to recreate the scene when I thought I heard a vehicle approach. I turned to catch a glimpse of a silver pickup, making a quick U-turn and high-tailing it toward the main road.

That's two days in a row I've seen a silver pick-up.

Chapter 16

It was 11:15 when I got to Barnstable Village. I swung by the post office and, since there were only a couple of people in the deli next door, I grabbed a corned beef and Swiss cheese on rye before settling in behind my desk to scrutinize the case reports.

The ME's report found no drugs or alcohol in Buster's system and no bruising. I can't imagine a person driving into a lake and letting himself drown. If someone intentionally drove off a pier into deep water, it would most likely be suicide—particularly with no evidence of braking and figuring once you headed for Davy Jones' locker, you'd be a goner. But Wequaquet Lake isn't that deep in the area where Buster died. There were missing puzzle pieces, and it was my job to find them.

I took a big bite of my sandwich, cleared my desk, and laid the reports from the four police officers out in front of me. One of the versions was longer than the others. I highlighted the date, time, and location in the first report. The other three were the same, as they should be, but I highlighted them too. The scene's accounting was similar except for buzz words that were different but meant the same thing. Reports one, two, and three noted the same make, model, color, and vehicle year. The fourth report included an additional description of the vehicle after removing it from the lake. All the reports noted that the Registry of Motor Vehicles provided the year of the car. All four stated Buster wasn't wearing a seat belt. Three of the reports were damn near copies, but not the fourth report, written by Officer Paul Bishop.

I'd met Officer Bishop on several occasions in my early days with the *Tribune*, but I was sure he left the department some seven or eight years ago. His description of Buster's vehicle was more detailed. The notation regarding the front windows on both the passenger and driver sides being completely open didn't appear on the other reports.

Since it was noted that Buster didn't have his seat belt on, he wasn't trapped in the car. With nothing holding him in place, and an adequate opening for him to use as a means of escape, the 'accident' finding didn't fit. If he intended to commit suicide, the windows would have been up, and he'd be strapped in.

Did Betsy know something?

Officer Paul Bishop—where are you? I could call Chief Lowe, but since he knew I was checking into Buster's death, he'd want to hear what I was up to. Maybe Maloney could find out for me—but he's new with Barnstable PD, so he wouldn't know who to ask. Or, perhaps I should bite the bullet and ask Sam to get me the information.

I tapped my fingers on the desk. "What the hell." I pushed speed dial, then number one.

Sam answered on the second ring. "Good afternoon, Sherlock."

"It may be. I have a favor to ask."

"I should have just said *afternoon*."

"It wouldn't have made a difference. Do you remember Paul Bishop from Barnstable PD?"

"Yeah. He did some training at our academy. Didn't he leave the department about eight years ago?"

"He did. I need to find out where he is. He was one of the four officers who responded to Buster Adams' accident. His incident report was more detailed and different than the other three."

"In what way?"

"I'll show you tonight. In the meantime, do you think you could help me find Bishop?"

"I'll make some calls. My other phone's ringing. See you at home."

Sam wasn't very talkative. There must have been somebody within earshot.

66

One more call to make. It was 2:30. The phone rang five times before it went to voice mail. "You've reached Annie. I'm unable to take your call, please leave a message, and I'll get back to you as soon as possible."

"Annie, it's Casey. If you can, call me back this afternoon. I'd appreciate it." I wasn't sure if she saw me on her caller ID and didn't want to talk or if she was away from her desk. The stress of Betsy's death had gotten the best of her. I was worried, but she wouldn't accept my offer of help.

I settled in to plan a strategy and better acquaint myself with Buster Adams. Annie was my key to unlocking the names of close friends, any romantic relationships, problems that may have caused him to wander out of his comfort zone, his plans after high school—anything to give me insight into Buster. Of course, all this happened ten years ago so that any information would be stale, but it's all I had. Somewhere out there, hidden amongst the comings and goings of his last few days, were clues that would give me the answers.

I glanced at my watch. It was almost 4:00. I packed up my briefcase, closed the office, and headed home.

Chapter 17

Watson was hooked to his run all day, so he was ready to roam free. I reached into my pocket to bribe the boy with a couple of treats. "We'll head for the beach when Daddy gets home."

No sooner did I get settled into my comfy deck chair and take a sip of white zin, my cell rang. Since I'd left word for Annie to call me, I assumed it was her. "You got my message."

"You called me?"

"I thought you were Annie."

Marnie hesitated. "You do know she took a mini-vacation, don't you? She said she wanted to disappear for a few days."

"No, I didn't know," I said. "Where'd she go?"

"Beats me."

"I don't remember the last time Annie went off Cape. She hates to cross the bridge."

"I didn't say she left the Cape. Betsy's death got to her. And, it's not going to get any better, especially working at the DA's office. I caught her looking at pictures taken at the scene. Judging by the expression on her face, she was having a bad time accepting what happened."

I paced the deck. "Not a good thing." I heard a car door shut. "Sam's home. I'll call you in the morning."

Annie's impromptu time-off concerned me, but I wanted to further research it before discussing it with Sam.

"Welcome home. Watson's been waiting for you. He told me he wants to walk the beach."

"So now he talks?"

"Yep." I put my empty wine glass on the table and hooked Watson up to his leash. "Ready?"

"Ready, willing, and able."

The thoughts in my mind were tumbling over each other. I needed to get them in some order before sharing them with Sam.

"You hardly said a word since we left the house. So, what's swirling around in that pretty little head of yours?"

"Nothing." I didn't look at him. Most of the beachgoers had packed up, so we had unhooked Watson from his leash and let him run free. We'd been on the beach for five minutes before either of us spoke. Finally, I broke the silence. "Just daydreaming … watching Watson playing with his seagull friends and thinking of how life would be without a care in the world."

Somehow Sam always knew when I was only giving him half an answer. He put his arm around me and drew me close. "Sad, we'll never be there." He smiled. "But, we've got each other."

I cuddled in close as I could and whispered into his chest. "Annie's missing."

"Again, please, I couldn't hear you."

"I love you."

Chapter 18

Friday

It was quiet in the village. The parking lots at the District and Superior Courthouses were only half full. I parked behind my office and walked to Nancy's Donut Shop for a coffee, sticky bun, and friendly conversation with Nancy.

The bell above the door jingled when I walked in. "Mornin'."

"Half hour ago, I was on roller skates. Now I can sit and enjoy a coffee with you."

I didn't mention the sticky bun, but she automatically brought me one.

"What's my favorite private investigator up to these days?"

"Finished a couple of boring but profitable cases at the end of last week." The *boring* was the truth, but the *profitable* wasn't.

"And ... a new one on the horizon?"

I chuckled. "I hope so. I have to pay the mortgage somehow." I didn't want to get into any particulars since Nancy knew at least one of the players.

"I'm toying with the idea of selling pies. I'll start by doing it for the holidays. Then if it works out, I can add special order requests."

"Nancy, haven't you thought about doing this before?"

"Yes, but I wasn't ready. Now I am."

"And why."

"Just something I want to do before I retire."

"Retire?"

Nancy stood, walked to the coffee machine, and returned with a full pot of coffee. "Just a word. I'll never really retire." She smiled. "By the way, have you seen Annie lately?"

"A few days ago. Why?"

"She's been quiet. Not like her at all. Is she feeling okay? When I asked her, she nodded, took her coffee and donut, and left."

"When was that?"

"Tuesday or Wednesday. Just a mother's instinct. You girls are like my own."

I reached across the table and took Nancy's hand. "Love you."

Sam came through with information on Officer Paul Bishop. He'd left the Barnstable Police Department in November 2008 to take a job with the FBI in Washington, DC. That's where Sam's trail went cold. The person he talked to thought Bishop only stayed with the Bureau for a few years. He didn't return to Barnstable, but Sam's contact said to give him some time, and he'd try to make a connection.

I put Bishop's information in my briefcase, leaned back in my chair, and stared at the ceiling. "Annie McGuire, where the hell are you?"

Annie was an island girl. In the years I'd known her, the only time I knew she went over the Sagamore Bridge was with me when she needed a dress for a wedding. I thought she looked great in several of the ones she tried on, but nothing at the Cape Cod Mall satisfied her. It was a classmate's wedding. She wanted to dress to impress. But, to impress whom, she never said. Annie had been white-knuckled and sweating as we traveled the short span over the Cape Cod Canal. I couldn't imagine her driving off Cape alone.

Annie liked the Lower Cape best because it was still quaint and not commercialized. She loved the National Seashore and was obsessed with the Lady of the Dunes 1974 cold case murder in the Race Point Dunes in Provincetown.

Worried, I called her cell again. This time I didn't leave a message.

Obsessing about Annie wasn't getting me closer to the Buster Adams case that Amanda Fallon was paying me to investigate. I put my thoughts of Annie aside.

Since I didn't have her to talk to, I developed a different plan of attack. The 2003, '04, '05, and '06 Barnstable Red Riders yearbooks might give me some insight into who Buster, Betsy, and Annie hung around with.

I looked up the number for Barnstable High School. The recording directed me to push the corresponding number for the desired department. The library was number five.

My call was answered on the second ring by a live voice. "Library, Miss Sparks speaking. How may I help you?"

"I'm looking for the Red Riders yearbooks dated 2003 through 2006. Are they available?"

"Yes. You can't check the books out, but if you come to the information desk, I'll get the books for you, and you can look at them here."

"Thank you."

I assumed the person behind the computer screen at the information desk was the same as identified by the desk nameplate. "Miss Sparks?"

"Yes."

"I called about a half-hour ago regarding the Red Rider yearbooks from 2003 through—"

"2006. Right?"

"Yes."

"Wait here." Without another word, she turned and exited through a door behind her.

I'm sure she has a complete list of the Dewey Decimal numbers in her head. The room was empty except for one person. I assumed he was a teacher, mulling through an oversized reference book. I eyed a table and waited for *Marian, the Librarian,* to return.

I didn't hear her come up behind me. "Here you go." She leaned forward with the four books I'd requested.

"Thank you. I'll be over at the corner table."

"That one is reserved for Dr. Bennett." She pointed. "Use the one next to it."

I felt her eyes watching me as I headed to my assigned seat.

Libraries were never my favorite place to pass the time.

I started with the 2006 book. Seniors always seemed to reveal secrets just before graduation. Maybe because they figured they'd never see some of their classmates again. I remember and don't want to remember some of the things I wrote in my friends' yearbooks. I made a note to ask Annie and Amanda Fallon if they tucked a copy of the 2006 Red Riders' yearbook away somewhere for safekeeping. Betsy's could prove interesting, but finding hers would be a miracle.

The caption under Annie's picture read:

A quiet girl with love for detail. Highest honors and Annie were best friends. Her voice in the glee club will be missed, and her presence in the art room will live on in the pictures permanently affixed to the walls.

The caption under Buster's picture read:

Always smiling, laughing, and clowning. The master of practical jokes, yet sincere and loyal when called upon by a friend. His love of boats, fishing, and water will follow him in whatever path he chooses to pursue. He was never late for football, baseball, or basketball practice. His athletic abilities helped the Red Riders achieve victory in many Thanksgiving Day football games.

The caption under Betsy's picture read:

73

A leader—A go-getter—A cheerleader—A master with a paintbrush and a pallet of vibrant colors. A friend to all. Queen of the junior and senior proms. What committee hasn't she been on? Usually never seen without her sidekicks Tami, Buster, or Mark. A promising career in the medical profession looms in her future.

I noted the name Tami, then scanned the candid shots of 'most likely to succeed,' 'headed for a career in sports,' 'class clown,' then stopped when I came to 'class sweethearts.' Betsy and Mark Mosley were smiling and posed in their finest as the king and queen of the senior prom. Once Annie surfaces, I'll ask her about the 'Betsy-Mark' relationship.

The rest of the yearbooks spotlighted Betsy and Mark in their areas of expertise. Buster and Betsy also surfaced several times in group pictures from plays put on by the high school theatrical group. In their junior year, Annie, Betsy, and Mark won first, second, and third place in a National Forensics League Tournament held in Lewiston, Maine. Annie for extemporaneous speaking and the other two for debate. It wasn't my favorite, but I had my share of successful debates when I was in school.

Chapter 19

The traffic to the village was unusually heavy. Phinneys Lane can be stop-and-go if you get behind a school bus. After a quick check of my watch, I was too early to get caught up in it. It wasn't even a stop-and-go. It was completely stopped. The problem with having a small car is that you can't see over most other vehicles, especially pick-ups and vans. Ten minutes went by before I got nosey enough to step outside to see what was going on. About eight cars ahead, I saw the reflection of flashing red lights. *Great, an accident*!

With nowhere to go, I called Annie's cell. I didn't expect an answer, but I felt the urge to try anyway. My wait was interrupted by an incoming call. "Hello."

"Where are you?" Marnie's voice was quick and broken.

"Stuck in traffic on Phinneys. What's wrong?"

"How soon can you get to your office?"

"Didn't you hear me? I'm stuck in traffic, and there's flashing red up ahead."

"Call me as soon as you get through." The phone went dead.

I hit my hands on the steering wheel. I couldn't imagine why Marnie was so unbalanced. Another ten minutes passed. Finally, the pick-up in front of me started to creep forward. A tow truck, with its lights spinning, drove past me in the opposite direction, heading toward Hyannis.

I wrapped my fingers around my steering wheel and clutched as hard as I could. It felt like an hour, even though it was only twenty minutes before I drove in behind my office. I grabbed my purse and briefcase, scrambled to unlock the door, and ran to my desk. The message light was flashing. I answered, but it was a hang-up. At this moment, Marnie was my first concern.

I pushed her number on my cell. "It's me."

"I'll be right over."

I unlocked the front door just as she ran across the street and through the open door of my office. She didn't stop to catch her breath before she began talking. "Something's wrong … very wrong."

I steered her to the chair by my desk and waited for her to sit. "What is it? What happened?"

Tears rolled down Marnie's cheeks. "They found Annie's car."

"Where?"

"In Wellfleet."

"Okay. Stop right now, compose yourself and tell me what's going on."

Marnie took several deep breaths. Her expression lacked emotion. She slid her hands under her thighs and rocked back and forth. "They found Annie's car in Wellfleet."

"Maybe it broke down, and she couldn't get a tow."

Marnie slid her hands out from under her, reached up to rub her eyes, then covered her face and started to sob. "Her car … it was destroyed."

"Destroyed?"

"Yeah, like in burned."

You could hear a pin drop.

The silence was interrupted by the phone. "Casey Quinby, Private Investigator." There was no emotion in my voice. Empty words echoed in my head.

It was Maloney. "Hey, Casey, is Marnie with you?"

"She is. Do you want to talk to her?"

"No. I'll be there in a few."

I hung up. "Maloney's on his way over."

Within fifteen minutes, I saw his cruiser pull up and park in front of my office. Since he had an unmarked, I knew something was up—something not good.

Marnie sat like a stone statue. She didn't even turn to look at Maloney when he walked through the front door.

He sat in the chair beside her and addressed me. "I'm heading to Wellfleet. I spoke to Chief Lowe, and he suggested you come with me. You can furnish information about Annie. Information I can't." Maloney turned toward Marnie and took her hands. "Chief said it was okay for you to come with us."

Chapter 20

Maloney drove. It seemed like forever. No one spoke. I figured he might have some sources worth talking to since Wellfleet was his neck-of-the-woods before transferring from P-Town PD to Hyannis PD. Marnie insisted on sitting in the backseat so Maloney and I could bounce theories back and forth.

"I realize I'm not supposed to ask questions about Betsy's death, but Annie's disappearance must be related. And, we don't want Annie to meet the same fate Betsy did."

Marnie sat as still as a department store mannequin. I felt it best to let her veg out.

Maloney, as if he read my mind, nodded. "The last thing Chief Lowe said before I left the station was to be *careful*."

"I understand."

"What I know is Annie's car was burned beyond recognition." Maloney looked at Marnie. "When the Wellfleet PD scoured the area, they found an empty gas can in some brush about twenty-five feet away from the scene. There was a Hyannis Marina sticker on it. Chief Campbell from Wellfleet sent a couple of guys to the Marina to check it out."

I shrugged, "Are they sure it was Annie's car?"

"Yes. They were able to pull a partial plate number and some of the VINs. By running them through the registry using different combinations, they got a hit—Annie McGuire, with a Cummaquid address. "

I checked to see if Marnie was okay. She was still in the same position as when we left Barnstable Village. I had a hard time asking Maloney the next question. "Did they find any human remains?"

"I won't know that until we meet with Chief Campbell. Other than the gas can, the only thing they found within fifteen feet from the car was an almost unrecognizable burnt sneaker." Maloney shook his head. "It belonged to someone with big feet."

"Could mean someone else was in the car with her, or she was never in the car at all. Someone using Annie's car could have been the intended victim."

Maloney stopped for the first of the two traffic lights in Wellfleet. "Definitely a possibility, which opens up more avenues. Is Annie being held against her will? Is she hurt and unable to get help? If she were mobile, I'm sure she would have called or sought help. We'll get more information when we meet with the chief."

Marnie suddenly grabbed the top of my seat. Her voice was elevated and fast. "She's got to be alive. We have to find her."

I swiveled around and put my hand over hers. "We will."

Marnie resumed her original position.

I looked at Maloney. "Annie asked for help when Betsy was found dead. I pretty much said I couldn't—that my hands were tied—but in a roundabout way, she did get me involved."

"How so?"

"By investigating a ten-year-old closed case involving the *accidental* death of a mutual friend of hers and Betsy's. This mutual friend, Buster Adams, may have been the victim of a homicide. With Annie shadowing behind her, his mother hired me to look into it. Frankly, I don't think the accident theory fits. I think it was staged to be an accident, but the player or players were amateurs."

The light turned green. Maloney continued on Main Street. "Do you think Annie was digging where she shouldn't have?" he asked. "Or maybe, she said something to or asked questions of the wrong person?"

79

Chapter 21

Maloney took a left into the Wellfleet PD parking lot. He dropped Marnie and me off at the main entrance then pulled into a space marked for police vehicles only. Once inside, Maloney checked us in with the officer at the duty desk.

Chief Campbell was waiting in his office when the three of us arrived. "Maloney, it's good to see you. How're things going in Hyannis?"

"I like it. Although I miss P-Town, my life has taken on a new perspective." He gestured to Marnie. "I'd like you to meet my new perspective, my fiancé, Marnie Levine."

"Pleased to meet you." The chief smiled. "Take care of this guy. He's one of the good ones."

Marnie nodded. "I agree."

I stepped forward and extended my hand. "It's been years, Chief. I think it was when you hosted the Lower Cape marathon back in 2010."

"That sounds about right. I followed your investigation of the girl found dead in one of the cabins on 6A. Nice piece of work."

"Thanks, chief. Since then, I've hung a shingle in Barnstable Village."

The chief moved behind his desk and motioned for us to sit. "You'll do well." He leaned forward, resting his folded hands in front of him. "Maloney briefly filled me in on your involvement in this case. I understand the vehicle we found belonged to your friend Annie McGuire."

I glanced at Maloney. I was surprised he'd mentioned me to the chief. "I met Annie in 2007, a few years after moving to the Cape. I was the investigative reporter for the Cape Cod Tribune, and she was, and still is, the right hand to District Attorney Sullivan." I motioned in Marnie's direction. "She's an assistant district attorney in the same office."

Chief Campbell nodded. "Sergeants McCoy and Danielson left a couple hours ago to meet with Aaron Harding, the owner of the Hyannis Marina. They've got pictures of the gas can we found near the scene. They should be back anytime now. I've got officers stationed at the scene round the clock."

I hesitated to continue but did anyway. "Chief, not to sound like a smart ass, but anyone could have a gas can from Hyannis Marina. Boats are more popular than cars here on the Cape, and this marina is one of the biggest."

The chief nodded in agreement. "Let me get copies of all our pictures and reports. Be right back."

Maloney watched the chief leave. "He's a real hands-on guy. Wellfleet doesn't see much violence or serious crime. He deals with the influx of over-the-bridge wash-a-shores during the summer, but not nearly as many as Upper Cape does. He'll put his all into finding Annie."

Maloney moved closer to Marnie, drew her close, and kissed her forehead.

I told Annie from the start I couldn't investigate anything to do with Betsy's death. There was no proof Annie went off on her own. But, knowing her, I think she may have. Now more than ever, I'm convinced the ten-year-old Buster Adam's accident that I've been retained to look into and Betsy Harper's weekend death are related. This wasn't the time or the place to bring up theories to Maloney. I just stuck to the facts.

Chief Campbell returned to his office with a folder containing reports and pictures. He spread the photos of the scene and the lone sneaker across his desk.

I perused the pictures starting with Annie's car and ending with several of the sneaker. I closed my eyes. I could smell the burned rubber, seat material, and the vegetation surrounding the car. Whoever did this knew the area was a remote section of Wellfleet and knew the fire wouldn't spread. They must have figured the seagrass would give it enough fuel to keep the flames alive until the car became fully engulfed. Then the sand would contain the fire, and it would burn out—which appears to be precisely what happened.

"Chief," I said, "I have a problem with this scenario. From these pictures, it doesn't appear there was an explosion. If there was, the car rubble wouldn't have been contained in such a small area. It would have scattered parts who knows how far out."

The chief looked from the pictures to me. "You're right. I've got a call into the State Fire Marshal's Office. It's my guess somebody drained the fuel tank. The person, or persons, involved didn't want to take a chance of somebody hearing even the slightest noise. Even though this was in a remote area, a perpetrator would be worried his planned performance could cause local concern."

Maloney picked up the picture of Annie's burnt car. "An expert arsonist did not do this. There are too many sloppy details."

"Exactly what we thought." Chief Campbell stood and paced off fifteen feet from his desk. "The sneaker was found approximately this far from the outer edge of the burnt ring of seagrass. It was badly burned but not destroyed. The person who was wearing it may be sporting a serious burn. In addition to being a large size, it was a high top, so it probably belonged to a male."

"Females wear high-tops too." I picked up the pictures of the shoe. "Chief, do you have a magnifying glass?"

He opened his left top drawer, took out a magnifying glass, and handed it to me. I used it to enlarge the details before I gave Maloney the pictures.

A couple minutes later, I handed the pictures to Maloney. "Take a look and describe what you see."

Maloney studied the images. "It is, or was a large sneaker. Some distinctive markings need to be checked out."

"My officers scoured the area. There was only one shoe and the gas can. The car is being treated as a crime scene. Investigations is handling it, but I told them not to disturb the scene. I want nothing moved until I say so." Chief Campbell swiveled in his chair.

Maloney gave the pictures back to the chief.

I looked at Maloney, then at the chief. "Before I voice my observations, I'd like you to take another look at the sneaker images using the magnifying glass. I reached over the desk and handed it back to him.

Without saying anything, the chief studied them again.

I'd seen something in the pictures I wanted to research. I took out my cell phone and Googled men's red and white high-top sneakers. The names I recognized were Puma, Adidas, Air Jordan, and Converse. Of course, none of the pictures matched our images because of the damage. *Wow, they weren't cheap.*

"Casey, take your time with these pictures. I'm going to check to see if my officers are back from the marina."

Marnie had been quiet since we sat down with Chief Campbell. She was in deep thought.

I reached over and took her hand. "Hey girl, you doing okay?"

She took a breath. "I'm trying to remember if Annie said anything about meeting someone or going off somewhere for a few days. But nothing is coming to me. It's like I'm brain dead."

I looked at Maloney. "We all need to sit and gather our thoughts. When I get back to my office, I'll contact Amanda Fallon, Buster's mother. Maybe she saw Annie before she went missing. If she did and doesn't know Annie's missing now, there would be no reason for her to contact me. I told her I'd call her when I found information on her son's case. So, I'm assuming that's why I haven't heard from her. Then again, Annie may have talked to Amanda about taking a few days off. Everything right now is speculation."

I'd just stood to walk around the room when Chief Campbell came back in.

"My guys aren't back yet. Maloney, when they return, and we finish going over reports, I'll give you a call. In the meantime, if you stumble onto something or you have any questions, don't hesitate to call me. If I'm out, they can always get ahold of me. Earlier, when I talked to your chief, he told me, since you're familiar with this end of the Cape and if we needed more staffing, you're available to assist us."

"I am, and I will. Thank you."

The chief handed a folder of pictures to me and another to Maloney. "Casey, you have ideas regarding the images of the sneaker. Study them and give me your thoughts. The car pictures are also in the folders. Take a closer look. You knew Annie's car before somebody torched it. Maybe you can pick out one little thing that we're missing."

I nodded. "We'll be in touch."

Chapter 22

It was almost 6:30 when Maloney and Marnie dropped me off in front of my office.

"I'll give you guys a call later," I said as I stepped out of the car.

Marnie gave me a weak smile. "We'll be home."

I'd just stepped inside when I heard my office phone ring. "Good afternoon, Casey Quinby, Private Investigator."

It was Sam. "Where've you been? I've been trying to call you."

I reached into my purse for my cell phone. "Oops. Maloney, Marnie, and I were at the Wellfleet PD meeting with Chief Campbell. I shut my cell off and forgot to turn it back on when we left."

"Why were you meeting with him?"

"They found Annie's car burned in a remote section of Wellfleet."

"You've got to be shittin' me."

"No, I'm not. Chief Campbell called Barnstable PD to inform Chief Lowe. To make a long story short, Maloney will help Wellfleet with the case."

"You've danced long enough around the question, I'll ask again. Why were *you* meeting with Chief Campbell?"

"Because Chief Lowe requested I ride down to Wellfleet with Maloney. Instead of talking about it now and having to retell it over dinner, I'm just going to wait till I have a face-to-face audience." I hesitated. "Are you on your way home?"

"I'll be leaving Bourne in about five minutes. I was calling to see if you wanted to eat out somewhere."

"Sure. I'll go home now and take care of Watson. We'll leave when you get there. I didn't have any lunch or coffee since 8:00 this morning, so I'm ready for food and a couple mind-altering wines."

The parking lot at Seafood Harry's wasn't even half-full. Sam pulled into a spot next to the door.

When we walked in, I noticed the corner table, farthest away from the counter, was open. "Looks like there's a place to sit away from listening ears," I said.

"Fried clams, onion rings, and coleslaw with a glass of white zin to wash 'em down?"

"Yep. Don't forget the ice." I went to the empty table and sat down.

Sam walked up to the counter, placed our order, and returned with the drinks. "So, what's happening?"

I knew his questions would start the minute his ass hit the chair. I waited for a question requiring a specific answer. Nothing.

He rested his elbows on the table and cradled his chin. "Are you getting involved in the Betsy Harper investigation? The one you were told to stay away from."

"Only in an indirect way." I shrugged. "But it *wasn't* my doing. Earlier, I mentioned they found Annie's car in Wellfleet. Well, Chief Lowe got a call from Chief Campbell. Chief Lowe called Maloney in to discuss the Annie incident with him. Chief Lowe knew Annie was my friend and knew I was digging into an old case because of her. He felt it could touch upon Betsy's homicide."

Sam shook his head. "You're rambling and got it all in without taking a break."

"Clamp it." I looked away from Sam. "My involvement at this point is finding Annie."

Our food came.

I was partway through my meal when Sam spoke. "I'm sorry. I wish I were with a police department closer than Bourne. And, of course, because I get everything second-hand, I'm frustrated. Annie is my friend too. I know Chief Campbell well, so tomorrow morning, I'll give him a call and offer my help."

I managed a slight smile as I handed Sam my glass. "Can I please have another wine?"

"Sure, be right back."

I took several deep breaths trying to compose myself. I needed Sam's help and, more so, his support. I also realized he was under the same pressure to find Annie.

Sam folded his arms across his chest. "Do you want to tell me what happened today at Chief Campbell's office?"

I looked around. There still wasn't anyone within earshot. "Earlier today, I did some research at the Hyannis Library. On the way back to my office, I got a call from Marnie. She seemed anxious. She said she needed to talk to me. I explained I was stuck in traffic on Phinneys Lane due to an accident, and I'd be in the village as soon as possible. It was like she didn't hear a word I said. I finally raised my voice to get her to calm down."

"Is she the one who told you about Annie's car?"

"Yep. Right afterward, I got a call from Maloney. He was on his way over."

"Tell me about Annie's car."

"It was burned beyond recognition in a remote section of Wellfleet."

"You already told me that."

I twisted my head sideways so as not to look at Sam. "Maybe I did, but I'm telling you again. I have pictures to show you when we get home. Chief Campbell gave a set to Maloney and one to me."

"Is it Maloney who wants you involved?"

87

"It was Chief Lowe. He said I might be able to offer helpful information about Annie."

Sam's expression put him into deep thought. It was a few minutes before he spoke. "This is tied somehow to the Betsy Harper case."

"I agree. I was surprised when I got the call from Maloney to accompany him to Wellfleet."

Sam nodded.

"I don't want to talk about the pictures now. I have some ideas, but I want your take on them." I took a double sip of wine.

Watson was waiting impatiently at the door for one of us to take him out. "What a phony. I took him out when I got home, and we haven't been gone long."

I set my briefcase on the table. "Why don't you guys take a walk around the house, and I'll get the pictures ready for you to look at."

Sometimes Watson understands everything I say, especially the word walk. He darted to the front door and started his *please-take-me-out* cry.

Sam grabbed the leash. "I'm coming … I'm coming."

I took the pictures from my briefcase and set them on the table. I wanted to check further into the sneaker information before talking to Sam, but there wasn't time. It might work better later. I was curious to see if he had a reaction or questions before I voiced my opinion.

I'd just finished when the door opened. "You're quick."

"He was faking." Sam gave Watson the I-know-what-you're-doing eyes.

I smiled, "He still needs a treat." I reached in his doggie jar and swished my hand around to make a noise. "Here you go, buddy. Now, for my big buddy. Do you want dessert or another beer?"

"Got ice cream?"

"I do."

Sam headed toward the kitchen table. I tried to watch him check out the pictures as I half-filled two bowls with chocolate almond chip.

He looked up from studying one of the car pictures. "Wow, what a mess. If there was somebody in the car, they didn't survive. Did they check for human remains?"

"Visually at the burn site or surrounding area, no human remains were found. As you can see, it's burned beyond recognition. Wellfleet doesn't have anyone trained in arson investigation, so the chief's got a call into the State Fire Marshal's Office. Chief Campbell assigned two officers from each shift to secure the area. Their only assignment is to make sure nobody compromises the scene or destroys the evidence."

"I'm going to make a call to Chief Campbell. Tomorrow's Saturday, so I don't need to be in Bourne. I want to meet up with him, take a ride out to the scene, and scout the area."

"How well do you know Chief Campbell?"

"We graduated from the academy together. I haven't seen him for a few years, but we were pretty tight. Not long after I got out of the academy, I took extra courses in arson investigation. I got lent out to area departments to investigate complex arson cases. Then I made detective, and there was enough in Bourne and Upper Cape to keep me busy. Besides, they started teaching it as a required class at the academy."

"You never told me."

"Fortunately, I haven't worked an arson case for years, so there was never any reason to talk about it." Sam smiled. "And that's the rest of the story."

"Take a look at the rest of the pictures and give me your take on them." I watched his expressionless face.

Sam picked up one of the sneaker pictures. After a quick peruse, he leaned forward and picked up the other sneaker picture. "Because of the size and the fact that they're high-tops, I am concluding they belong to a male."

"The chief said the same thing. I mentioned females wear high-tops too. It's true, but these particular ones are costly and large Air Jordans. If a female were to wear expensive high-tops, she'd opt for Michael Kors or Burberry."

"How are you so sure they're Air Jordans?"

My laptop was on the desk in the living room. "Be right back." I returned and set it on the kitchen table. Without saying anything, I opened it and Googled men's high-top-red-and-white sneakers. When the images came up, I turned my laptop so Sam and I could examine them. I laid the two sneaker pictures from the scene on the table beside the computer. "Your thoughts?"

Sam stared at the pictures. "The sneaker is badly burned, but you can still see some red. The white not so much, but I bet if we brushed the soot off, there would be no doubt as to the colors."

It appeared the sneaker was on its side. "Here. See those two dark spots?" I pointed to an almost completely camouflaged marking on what I believed was the bottom of the shoe. "Now look at the computer image showing the sole. There's a silhouette of Michael Jordan swooping in to make a basket." I tapped my finger on the PD picture. "This dark spot is this image. The sole is partially melted away, but you can still see enough to confirm my finding."

Sam's face wrinkled. "Here are my observations. First, the facts. This is a picture of Annie's car. It was torched. And, I agree with you, this shoe belongs to a male with big feet. It may or may not have had anything to do with Annie or her car. We don't know if Annie or the possible unknown male was in the car. Once we resolve the human remains issue, the chief will determine if he's investigating a murder or arson.

"That's it in a nutshell." My eyes welled up. "We still have no idea where Annie is. And worse—if she's alive."

Sam got up and took my hand. "It's late. Let's go to bed."

Chapter 23

Saturday

I caught up with Sam in the kitchen. "Since you called Chief Campbell while I was in the bathroom, I didn't hear any of the conversation. Are we heading to Wellfleet this morning?"

"We are. I told the chief you'd be coming with me."

"He must have wondered why you were in the picture."

"Uh-huh. I gave him a brief explanation. Said I'd fill the rest in later." Sam was ready to get going. "He's going to meet us at the station; then we'll go with him and his team to the site of the fire."

I gathered the pictures still spread out on the kitchen table, along with my notes, and slid them into my briefcase. "You driving?"

He took his keys off the counter. "I am."

"This whole thing is like a movie…scenes change, settings change, and while all this is happening, the player or players, motives, and the good, the bad, and the ugly remain a mystery. The only definites are the burnt car belonged to Annie, and she's missing."

"After we talk to the chief, we'll head to your office and put together an evidence board to see if we can make sense of it."

When we arrived at the Wellfleet PD parking lot, the chief was leaning against a cruiser, talking to two uniformed officers. The chief motioned for Sam to park in the 'police vehicle only' section.

Chief Campbell waved us over. "Morning," he said as he extended his hand to me, then to Sam. "Sam Summers. Long time, no see."

"Too long." Sam smiled.

"Meet Sam Summers and Casey Quinby." The chief stepped aside while we said our hellos to the two uniforms.

"Sam is the lead detective in Bourne. He's well versed in arson investigation. We go back to police academy days."

Sam and the two uniforms exchanged handshakes.

One of the guys snickered.

The chief at him looked over his glasses.

The snicker turned to a smile. "I was thinking of the movie, Chief."

Sam looked at me. "You're up."

Chief Campbell nodded. "Casey is a private investigator out of Barnstable Village. She holds a master's degree in criminal justice from UMass, has been through the police academy, paid her dues, and is more knowledgeable than some cops I've worked with."

"That's a stretch, but I'll take it." I shook their hands.

"My youngest recruit, David Horton, has been with us for about six years. Kind of reminds me of you, Sam. Gung ho, taking every specialty class offered. Especially when the department paid." The chief turned toward the other officer. "Mitch Cabral, his partner, joined us two years ago. He came down from Fall River PD."

Officer Horton, who seemed to be in deep thought, looked up. "Casey Quinby, I've heard the name. Didn't you have something to do with a murder case out of P-town about five years ago?"

"I did. Sometimes it's good to enjoy a reputation, and sometimes it's not. I've tried to stay on the good side."

The chief opened the driver's door of his cruiser. "Sam, let's get this show on the road. You and Casey ride with me. Cabral and Horton will follow. We'll check out the scene, come back to my office, hash out our observations, and brainstorm." The chief waited for comments. "Anything could be helpful, so don't hesitate to speak up."

I looked at Sam. I knew the last sentence the chief recited wasn't for our benefit but for his officers. I liked Chief Campbell. He wasn't a hard-ass but expected professionalism.

"Sam, I don't imagine you're familiar with the Wellfleet flats, the small hidden beaches, or the abandoned family cottages or properties tied up in probate. You're not alone. We don't have much crime around here, but these areas could produce stuff that could be the makings of a movie." The chief shook his head, then continued, "Casey, you've helped P-town PD on several investigations, so I'm assuming you are somewhat familiar with what I'm talking about."

"I am."

We hopped into the chief's car—Sam in front and me in back. "I've had two officers per shift securing the site as soon as we were notified of the situation early yesterday morning. Since we don't have a designated arson squad, I requested help from the State Fire Marshal's Office." We were not quite twenty minutes from the station when he turned onto a roughly paved road. "Hold on. This area is better traveled with an ATV. Whatever blacktop is left ends around the next bend." A moment later, we were riding on crushed shells and sand.

I smiled. "Better your tires than mine."

About a mile farther in, we found ourselves on what appeared to be a rarely used dirt road.

Sam looked around. "Judging from the healthy covering of beach grass, this isn't well-traveled."

"There are many places like this in and around Wellfleet, Eastham, and most of Lower Cape. We're almost there," The chief said.

"Back to the fire marshal," Sam said. "He's a good friend of mine. I know they're stretched out. They've got a class going, but that's not going to help you. If it's okay, I can call him, explain the situation and do the arson part of the investigation myself. Your investigations division can handle the criminal side. I understand Maloney will also be helping."

"Sam, thank you. Immediate attention to details will make a huge difference in solving this case."

Seeing Annie's car wasn't going to be easy. I can handle most crime scenes without a problem, mainly because it was part of the job. This time it was personal.

We rounded a bend. There it was. A charred buffer of beach grass quickly gave way to a blackened blanket of sand cradling the remains of Annie's car. Crime scene tape surrounded the area.

The Chief pulled over and stopped well away from the scene. Cabral and Horton parked about eight feet behind him.

Sam opened my door. "Casey, you okay?"

Without looking up, I took a deep breath. "I will be."

He took my hand. I got out and leaned against the chief's car. It seemed like forever before voices broke the silence.

Officers Horton and Cabral already had booties over their shoes and stood outside their cruiser.

The two officers assigned to securing the site were parked another ten feet out. They joined the rest of us for a briefing.

Chief Campbell took three sets of booties from the trunk of his vehicle. We put them on then joined the other officers.

"It's a puzzler. Sam, I didn't want them to disturb anything until you checked it out. As you can see, the matching tire tracks are marked with different colored flags. And the shoe and footprints are also marked with different colored flags. I wanted you to see it before we take it to the garage for further examination."

Sam took a notebook from his pocket and stepped closer to Officer Horton. "Where did you find the sneaker and the gas can?"

Horton brought Sam to both locations. Sam took pictures of each area.

I followed Sam, being careful not to compromise the scene. I looked out over the area, then back to Annie's car.

Annie, where are you?

Along with taking notes, Sam visually scanned, then snapped pictures and made sketches of the area. "Those four darkened circles appear to be areas where there was a concentration of accelerant. The charred beach grass was to finish the job and make it look like it was only one fire when I think several little ones of different degrees resulted in the one big one."

The chief moved around to the driver's side of the car where Sam was standing.

Without looking away from the site, Sam asked the officers if they had a rake with them.

Officer Cabral responded, "In the trunk." He went to his cruiser, returned with the rake, and handed it to Sam.

I watched Sam gently scrape the ashes from various areas of the burnt car. It seemed like forever, but within a matter of minutes, he stepped back and surveyed the results of his work. "If there was a body or were bodies in Annie's car, we would have seen bones under the ashes in the areas I raked. My appraisal is that this car was driven here by an unknown somebody trying to create a diversion in Annie's disappearance."

I stared at the blackened rubble. "Your assessment of all this feeds right into the Betsy Harper murder and the ten-year-old Buster Adams case. Somebody is going to great lengths trying to alter the truth. Annie poked around too close to home. She riled somebody's feathers. I believe that Annie is still alive but in grave danger."

"When we get everything back to the garage, we'll scour it with a fine-tooth comb." The chief said.

Sam slowly moved around the perimeter of the scene. "In a vehicle fire, a car can be burned beyond repair in ten minutes. And because of the rubber, fabric, and plastic, a car can be reduced to just the metal in less than an hour."

Sam had the podium. "This fire was intense. It didn't burn farther into the beach grass because it was controlled, but by whom, and why? Annie or any other human wasn't in the car." He turned to Officers Cabral and Horton. "We need to get samples around the outer edge of the circle. I believe an amateur or amateurs, a careful one or ones, did this. The beach grass fire was more than likely put out with a common extinguisher. That would allow the arsonist to control it."

Cabral went to his cruiser and returned with evidence bags. He took samples from different areas around the car, handing them to Horton for recording.

Sam stepped away to talk to the chief. "The sneaker may also check positive for an accelerant. If it does, my first instinct would be that it belongs to one of the people involved. We know the sneaker caught on fire. My take is the owner ripped it off his foot and threw it aside. That person is more than likely nursing a serious burn and may require medical attention."

The chief shook his head in agreement. "If someone was burnt enough to require medical attention, the only place around here is Outer Cape Health Services in Provincetown. On the other hand, if the person lived around Hyannis, they'd go to Cape Cod Hospital."

"Chief, if you check Outer Cape Health, I'll take care of the hospital," Sam said.

These amateurs knew enough to start the fire and stop it. Even though the scene is way off in no-man's-land and there aren't any residents around, the smoke could have attracted attention.

I fought to keep my mind on what we were doing. I'd had enough of looking at Annie's destroyed car. The real questions are, where is Annie? Is she still alive? Could the burnt vehicle provide clues? Could those clues help us find Annie and who took her? "Do you think the gas tank was emptied before the fire was started?" I asked.

Sam faced me. "Yep."

Chief Campbell lowered his head to a sudden gust of wind then walked back to talk to the two officers from the patrol team. "Did either of you walk up around the burn site?"

"No, sir," they answered in unison.

"We pulled beside Towner and Myers. They directed us not to go near the site. We'll pass that information on to our replacements."

Chief nodded and walked back to his cruiser where we were standing.

Sam spoke up, "We need to walk the perimeter of the burn very carefully. This area is not widely traveled. There have to be tire tracks from Annie's car and the vehicle following her car."

Cabral signaled Horton to join him. "We'll check around near where we found the sneaker."

Sam stopped making notes. "When you find the tire tracks, look for shoe prints."

Officers Cabral and Horton worked as a team. Sam worked alone, and I went with the chief.

Twenty minutes into our search, Cabral called us from about twenty-five feet out on the opposite side of the burnt area. Horton stepped behind him. "David, wait before you come any closer. I may have found something. Get the camera from the cruiser."

We didn't want to compromise the area, so we moved out a good ten feet and circled until we were beside Officer Cabral.

Cabral was crouched down, studying his find. "There are both tire tracks and shoe and footprints. One set of tracks is from Annie's car. The other set of tracks stops here, backs up, then turns to exit the site." He got up and followed the second set towards the road about another twenty feet. "And, there is a set of shoe prints, then a single shoe print and a footprint."

I made notes while Sam took pictures.

Officer Cabral continued, "There's a set of shoe prints coming from her car heading toward the follow-up vehicle. I believe they're from the person who drove her car to the designated area then torched it. It appears that during his mission, he spilled some gas on his sneaker. It caught fire and burned his foot. We know this because before the person reached the follow-up vehicle, he kicked off his burnt sneaker—from that point on, there's a footprint and a shoe print. It'll be a miracle, but we can check for DNA on the sneaker."

"The second set of prints, consisting of two shoes, presumably belonged to the driver of the follow-up vehicle," Sam said. "That person walked halfway up to the burn site, turned around, and walked back to where his car was parked." Sam took out his cell phone and videoed the follow-up driver's route. "There must have been some discussion between the two because it appears that the person belonging to the second set of shoe prints stopped and scuffed his feet. Fortunately, he left a couple of prints still intact."

Chief Campbell nodded. "We've got one dangerously nervous perpetrator and one scared accomplice."

Horton followed Sam and took another set of shoe prints and footprint pictures along with additional sets of tire pictures.

Sam checked his watch. "We need to get castings of the tire tracks and shoe prints. Be sure to take a mold of the footprint."

"I have kits in the trunk." Cabral sprinted to his cruiser.

This whole thing with tire tracks brought me back to a case I worked in Bourne. It was a hit and run, resulting in the death of a sixteen-year-old girl. The tire tracks led us to the person who did it.

In the Bourne case, the tire tracks were much more defined, though.

Chief Campbell watched as Horton and Cabral took the impressions. "Sam, is there anything else you need to do here at the scene?"

"We'll take all the castings we need, and I'll do one more check around the car again to see if there's something I missed. When you get everything back to the station, we'll take a closer look at the evidence we gathered."

I watched Sam bend down and pick up small pieces of something and some paper stuff, then drop them into evidence bags he'd taken from his pocket. Not the time to ask. I'd find out later.

After Horton and Cabral finished taking the castings, they packed up their kits and secured them in the trunk of their cruiser.

The chief took a deep breath before he walked over to the two officers assigned to the round-the-clock team securing the scene. "We're heading back to the station. Be here same time tomorrow unless I notify you of a change. I plan on moving the car back to the garage late morning or early afternoon, but not sure of the time."

He walked over to his cruiser where Sam and I were standing with Officers Horton and Cabral. "We'll go back to the station, get the evidence logged in, then talk about our next move."

Once out on the main road, the chief turned to Sam. "This isn't going to be easy. If you've got nothing pressing in Bourne, I could use your help. It's been years since I've worked arson investigation, and none of my officers have the training to work this case. I know we're waiting for the State Fire Marshal's Office, but they're stretched out all over the state. You've got the expertise."

"I don't see any problem, but before I commit, let me run it by my chief. I'll call him from your office. We need to get moving while the evidence is still fresh."

"Thanks, Sam."

Chapter 24

When Chief Campbell filled the water reserve in his Keurig, I figured we were going to be working or at least brainstorming for the next few hours.

Sam called his chief in Bourne, explained the situation, and, as expected, was given the okay to work the Wellfleet case for as long as Chief Campbell needed him.

When Horton and Cabral returned to the station, they opened the cruiser's trunk, put its contents on a dolly, and went to the chief's office to report in.

"We have the box of evidence bags and castings of several different tire tracks, the shoe prints, and the footprint." Horton set them on a table in the corner of the office.

Officer Cabral moved closer to Chief Campbell's desk. "I sketched the area." He handed his drawings to the chief. "As Officer Horton said, we numbered the impressions, and I numbered my sketches to correspond to where each was found."

"Good job." Chief Campbell got up from his desk, walked over to the table displaying everything gathered from the scene, then turned to face his officers. "I'll see you guys in the morning."

We all shook hands, and they walked out the door.

The deep breath I took didn't go unnoticed.

"Anyone need a coffee?" The chief had already popped a K-cup into the Keurig.

Sam walked over to where the chief was standing. "Yeah, I could use one."

I waited for the chief's and Sam's coffees to finish, then made one for myself.

"Before we take a look at the castings, I'd like to look at the evidence bags." Sam reached into his pocket. "I have three more to add. One I find very interesting." He handed it to the chief.

The chief put it on the table and, without emptying it, gently spread it out to view the contents. "It's six cigarette butts. Two different brands." He examined them closer, then shook his head. "And, a roach."

Sam moved the contents around again. "Two roaches, to be exact," he said.

The second bag Sam handed to the chief contained three candy wrappers.

"Where did you find these?" the chief asked.

"When we were doing the perimeter walk, I noticed a hint of color lodged beside a clump of seagrass maybe five feet out from the burned circle," Sam said. "What I think happened is that one of the arsonists had some candy, threw the wrappers away, and a breeze blew them into the grass. The density of the long narrow seagrass leaves traps anything that flies into them. You know, like what the spider said to the fly. The web is the trick, and you are the treat."

The chief smirked, then picked up the bag to closely examine the wrappers. "Sam, these aren't just any candy wrappers. They're penny candy wrappers. They're Atomic Fire Balls and Mary-Janes. There's a store on Main St. known for their penny candy. I know they sell these because I've stopped on more than one occasion to buy some."

"We'll check that out. Maybe the clerk will remember somebody they know or somebody out of the ordinary coming in and making a purchase. We're pulling at straws, but right now, that's all we have."

The chief agreed.

"Chief, I have a third bag. I found the content of this one also in the seagrass about four feet from the candy wrappers. My theory is that this bag's content was accidentally pulled out of one of our arsonist's pockets at the same time the candy was. And, like the candy wrappers, because it dropped in the seagrass, the person didn't notice it fell from their pocket. And, since the third object is an unopened condom packet, I'm going to suggest at least one of our arsonists is a male."

The evidence bags Horton and Cabral brought in mostly contained samples of burned debris. I figured Chief Campbell would send them out for possible identification of the accelerant used and or identify what scraps of the burnt objects might be. None of this was going to give us answers overnight.

I watched Sam again look over the bags he'd entered as possible evidence. I knew the look. He was in deep thought, especially when he held up the third bag. "Chief, I'd like to dust this condom packet for prints. The packet hasn't been opened, so we might luck out and get a clean print."

"Give me a minute, and I'll grab a kit." The Chief headed out his office door.

"Sam, you've got something on your mind. Do you care to share it with me?" I waited for a reply.

"I can't put my finger on it, but there's something about that condom packet. I've seen one like it before."

"You were in CVS the other day. Maybe you walked by the display and stopped to take a look."

"Why would I look at condoms? I don't use them."

"That's true." I smiled.

"I'm going to take a picture with my phone. I need to study it more."

I knew he was trying to zoom in on something, so I took my coffee and went back and sat in the chair beside the chief's desk.

A few minutes later, the chief returned with a fingerprint kit.

He handed it to Sam. "You're more of an expert than I am."

I got up from my chair and joined Chief Campbell next to the table where he'd put the kit.

Sam opened it. "Chief, I need a couple pieces of plain white paper." While he waited for the chief, he took out a pair of gloves and the fingerprint powder. Since the condom packet was light in color, he chose the black powder.

"Here you go, Sam." The chief handed him the pieces of paper.

The chief and I stepped back from the table so as not to bump or distract Sam.

He operated like a surgeon—put on gloves, then gently cradled the edges of the condom packet, removed it from the evidence bag, and laid it on a piece of white paper. He transferred a small amount of the dusting powder into the lid then dipped the tips of the fingerprint brush's bristles into the powder to retain a small amount. Before he continued, he gently tapped the brush on the edge of the container to return any excess powder.

I was mesmerized. When I was in the police academy, we had a detective come in and demonstrate the art of fingerprinting. That was almost fourteen years ago, and he was not as precise as Sam.

It was amazing to see a couple of prints materialize. Sam stopped dusting so he wouldn't overdevelop them. He carefully applied the tape, pulled a perfect set of prints, and transferred them onto a square white card he'd taken from the kit.

"I'll be right back," Sam said. "I need to make a phone call."

I had no idea what Sam was up to. He was all business, and something significant had taken over his mind.

"Barnstable Police Department, how may I direct your call?"

"This is Detective Sam Summers from the Bourne PD. Is Chief Lowe available?"

"Let me check."

Within seconds Chief Lowe answered. "Sam, what's up?"

"I'm in Wellfleet with Chief Campbell helping him with the Annie McGuire car arson case. I'll explain later. Right now, I need to know if you got any prints from the condom packets you found in Betsy Harper's room at the Sheridan? And, the brand of the condoms."

"Let me check. Can you hold on?"

"Yes."

Not even five minutes went by, and the chief was back on the phone with Sam.

"Detective Maloney was at his desk. He said they have one good full print and a real good partial. He submitted both of them to the FBI's database, but IAEFS came back with no match. The condom brand is Okamoto 003. A white package."

"Thanks, Chief. I'll swing by tomorrow and explain what's going on."

"Sounds good. Even though it's Sunday, I'll be here most of the day. I'm working on some new training policies and procedures for the academy starting in a few weeks. Call me if you need something else before then."

When Sam came back into Chief Campbell's office, the chief had just finished telling me how glad he was to have Sam's help with Annie's arson case. He praised Sam and his skill level. "Sam was always an overachiever at the academy. He's the best."

I knew that Sam's mind was preoccupied with something, so it didn't appear he'd heard
anything Chief Campbell said.

Sam got himself another cup of coffee. "Are you going to have the remains of the car brought into the garage tomorrow?"

"I was planning on it. Right now, the garage is empty, so we can spread out if we have to. Plenty of space to do some recreating." The chief leaned back in his chair. "Are you coming back out tomorrow?"

"There are some things I have to check out with Barnstable PD first. Then I'll be here."

"That will give me time to get the car moved."

Sam took a couple more swallows, then threw his cup in the basket. "Sounds good to me."

Chief Campbell put his hand on my shoulder. "Casey, you're welcome to come back tomorrow if you'd like."

We said our goodbyes, then Sam and I headed back to Hyannisport.

Chapter 25

It had been a long day. I was exhausted. "I don't feel like cooking or going out to eat. Besides, Watson's been in the house all day. He needs a little walk and some cuddle time. How about we call DiParma's for a pizza."

Sam smiled. "I like the way you think."

I pulled up the number on my cell. They picked up on the first ring. "I'd like to order a mushroom, pepperoni, and artichoke pizza, thin-crust well done. We'll be there at 6:30. The name's Casey."

"Now that the important stuff is out of the way, who did you call when you stepped out of the chief's office?" I asked.

"I called Chief Lowe. Remember I said that the condom we found today looked familiar."

"I do."

"Well, the two opened condom packets they found in Betsy Harper's room at the Sheridan were the same brand. I asked the chief if they had done fingerprint tests on them. He checked, and they had. They got one good partial and one okay full print. I want to swing by Barnstable PD and take their prints out to Wellfleet to compare them with the ones we got today. The problem is, when they ran them through IAEFS, there was no match."

"Sam, do you think there might be a connection between Betsy's murder and Annie's burned car?"

"What the connection is, I don't know yet, but the answer to your question is yes."

"I'm going to make a statement, then wait for your reply. Let me add one more thing. Right now, all I want is a simple reaction. I don't want a lecture to follow. At least not until we've talked."

"I'm afraid to hear what's brewing in your ever-so inquisitive mind." Sam sighed. "Go ahead."

"I have a theory. Well, maybe not a theory, but an inkling. Hear me out. I think the Buster "*accidental*" death, Betsy's murder, Annie's arson case, and the fact that she's missing are all related."

At least five minutes went by before Sam acknowledged my conversation. I figured he was trying to find a way to tell me I was wrong.

"My little Sherlock. What am I going to do with you?" Sam kept his eyes on the road but kept talking. "What I'm going to say doesn't mean I agree with you, but tonight we need to do some talking— some brainstorming. There are too many things that overlap. I want to start the evidence/murder board. I don't deny these three cases are linked. What bothers me is the way they're linked doesn't justify the end. There's one more link that I think is the driving factor in the three cases. And, it's one we don't yet know about. That's the one that scares me the most."

Right on time, it was 6:30 when we drove into the parking lot at DiParma's. I went in while Sam waited in the car.

A few minutes later, I was back. "Boy, this smells good. When we get home, you walk Watson around the yard, and I'll set up for our 'pizza party'— get you a beer, me a glass of white zin, and put out the 'fine' china. How's that sound?"

Sam leaned over and kissed me. "That's my girl."

Chapter 26

We wolfed down our pizza with only two slices to spare. I'd just poured myself another wine and gotten Sam another beer when there was a knock at the front door.

Sam answered it. He motioned Marnie and Maloney to come in. "What are you guys doing out so late?"

"You're turning into an old man. It's only 8:30." Marnie laughed. "We went to a movie at the Cape Cod Mall and thought we'd swing by to see if you two were home. Maloney said the Red Sox are playing a night game and figured you'd be watching."

"I forgot it was a night game. Casey will be thrilled."

I came out of the kitchen. "Did I hear Miss Marnie's melancholy voice?"

"You did. I called you earlier about the movies but got no answer." Maloney stayed in the living room with Sam, and Marnie followed me back to the kitchen.

I took my phone from my purse. "No answer because I had it on mute." I shrugged. "We were in Wellfleet all day. It was disturbing."

Marnie brought a beer and a piece of pizza to Maloney, then came back into the kitchen. I handed her the other slice of pizza and a glass of white zin.

"I told Sam about our trip with Maloney to Wellfleet. I didn't know that Sam and Chief Campbell were good friends. Nor did I know that Sam has specialized training in arson investigation. Anyway, after Sam's conversation with the chief, we decided to take a trip to Wellfleet this morning. I think Maloney knew we were there because Sam called Chief Lowe about comparing some fingerprints he recovered on unopened condom packets found by Annie's car with open ones found in Betsy's hotel room. I know tomorrow's Sunday, but Sam's going into Barnstable PD to meet with the chief. After he leaves Barnstable, he's going back down to Wellfleet. Tomorrow they're bringing the remains of Annie's car to the police garage. I figure Maloney will go. Anyway, I'm sure Sam's running that by Maloney as we speak."

"Other than the prints, did they have anything new since we were there yesterday?" Marnie asked.

"Well, they scoured the area around the car, and Officers Cabral and Horton took impressions of tire tracks and shoe and footprints. But nothing that brings us closer to finding Annie. I feel so helpless. Because I was told to stay clear of Betsy's case, I think Annie went rogue and tried to do a little snooping on her own. I don't know if she knew more than she was telling us or if she discovered something that's put her in danger. I will tell you this, though, there's some stuff in Brian Adams's court records that I want to do more research on. The stuff doesn't pertain to Attorney Adams himself, but rather one of his cases."

"Is there anything I can help you with? We're not on overload at the DA's office, and I'm sure Mike will let me do some research if it helps find Annie. He's upset about her disappearance. Maybe you should talk to him."

"Before I do that, I'd have to run it by Sam. I want to help, but I don't want to hinder—if you know what I mean."

Marnie nodded. "I do."

I could feel my emotions trying to take over. I took a deep breath. "I think whatever is happening to Annie and what happened to Buster and now to Betsy are all related. There's a common thread, especially in the Buster and Betsy cases. Annie may have stumbled onto that thread of evidence that caused her to be suspicious about something—maybe even another person. You know that working in the DA's office is like living in real-life murder mysteries. Annie saw everything that ran through the office. Maybe she picked up on something and didn't want to tell anyone until she checked it out.

And, if there is another somebody involved, Annie could be in danger, especially if she's walking around with bits and pieces of evidence she may have uncovered. I'm afraid she might try to confront this person."

"I understand what you're saying, but I don't think Annie would go out on her own."

"I hear you, and normally I'd say you were right. The underlying problem is that before Annie steps forward with what knowledge she thinks she has, she will do some checking. And, if she opens the wrong closet door, she might find a deadly skeleton."

"Are you going with Sam tomorrow?"

"No. I want to sort through my notes and start an evidence/murder board. We were going to work on it tonight, but it's too late. I'll be in the village if you want to come over and help me. We can bounce ideas back and forth, make notes, and hopefully link things together. Annie didn't disappear on her own. That's not her thing. My fear is that time isn't on her side. And, if her disappearance is tied more to Betsy's death than we think, she's in serious danger."

"What time do you want me at your office?"

"Let's plan on meeting at nine."

"I'll be there."

It had been a long day. I was ready for bed. Maloney and Marnie left in the seventh inning.

"Is Maloney going to Wellfleet with you tomorrow?"

"Yeah, he is. Are you coming?"

"No, since we didn't work on the evidence/murder board tonight, Marnie and I are going to head over to my office around nine and get it started."

"The Sox are seven runs ahead, so I don't care about watching the rest of the game. Let's call it a night." Sam stood in front of me, pulled me up from the couch, and wrapped his arms around me. "What would I ever do without you?" As he leaned down to kiss me, Watson started to whimper.

"Look who's jealous," I laughed and knelt to ruffle his fur. "Daddy will take you outside while Mommy gets ready for bed."

Chapter 27

Sunday

It was 7 a.m. when the alarm clock on my side of the bed rang. I must have fallen into a deep sleep at some hour of the night because I didn't hear Sam get up. He was already dressed, and in the kitchen making coffee.

I swung my legs over the edge of the bed and rocked back and forth a few times before standing up. The nightmare continues. I wish I were going to Wellfleet with Sam, but Marnie and I need to sort through everything we know regarding Annie's disappearance.

I threw on a pair of jeans and a long-sleeved jersey and headed to the kitchen. Watson greeted me with slurpy dog kisses on my bare feet. I leaned down and patted him. "Hey, boy, I'm going to hook you to the run today. We'll do a beach walk when I get home."

"I came up behind Sam, cuddled into his back, and hugged him. "What time are you leaving for Wellfleet?"

"I'm going to the station at 8:30 to meet with Chief Lowe and Maloney, then Maloney and I will head out. The chief may want to come. When I talked to him yesterday, I got the feeling he's linking the Annie arson to the Betsy murder."

"Marnie and I are going to my office and brainstorm. It will be a good head start. And depending on when you get back, you guys can take a look at the evidence/murder board. I know both you and Maloney have the blessings of your chiefs in assisting Wellfleet with their case."

While Sam poured us each a coffee and put a couple day-old donuts on a plate, I went to the bedroom and put on my deck shoes. He was already sitting at the table when I got back.

"I forgot what time you're meeting Marnie?"

"I told her I'd be there at nine. Since I'm up and you'll be leaving soon, I'm going to get an early start. I can get everything that I have into piles and label them. That's busy work that we don't need to waste time on. I also want to scan through the copies of Attorney Adams's court cases. I remember, but I don't remember, something I read in one of them." I looked at Sam for a reaction. He didn't answer right away, so I continued, "Do you know what I mean?"

"Since that came out of your mouth, I completely understand." He laughed. "Scary, isn't it."

"Alright, alright, don't be a wise guy."

"It's five after eight. I'm going to take off." Sam stood, then leaned down to kiss me. "I'll give you a call during the day to let you know what's going on. Don't turn your phone off. If you need me, you know where I'll be."

I walked him to the door. "Love you."

"Love you too, Sherlock. Don't you and Marnie get into any trouble."

No sooner did Sam leave, my cell rang. Marnie's name appeared on the caller ID. "I'm figuring that Maloney just left for the station, and you're chomping at the bit to get started."

"I've always said you do good detective work."

"I keep asking if you want to join me. The other desk in my office has your name on it."

She chuckled. "I keep thinking about it. But I don't know if Barnstable Village could handle two female investigators. Let me change that … two nosey female investigators."

"Well, you've got a point there. Anyway, I'm ready if you are. I'm leaving in about ten minutes. I'll swing by Dunkins' and pick us up coffee and donuts."

"Ok, bye." Marnie's usual abrupt ending.

Chapter 28

Since it was Sunday, there wasn't much activity in the village. Marnie hadn't arrived yet. That gave me time to get settled and get my cork board out of the storage closet. It took me a while to find it. Just as I walked out of the closet, Marnie came in through the back door.

"I've been in there ten minutes looking for this thing. One of these days, I need to do some housekeeping." I set the board on the counter, leaning against the upper cabinets. "You're early. I was going to try to organize paperwork into related piles before you got here."

"Well, I'm here. We can sort and talk at the same time. Four eyes are better than two, and spontaneous conversation sometimes can evoke meaningful paths of interest."

I chuckled. "Oh my, aren't we philosophical this morning."

"Yep. That sounded damn good. Don't you think?" Marnie took a coffee and donut off the counter, sat at the kitchen table, and stared at the blank evidence/murder board.

"Before we get started with the board, let's hash some things out." I took my coffee and donut and sat across from Marnie. I cradled my cup between my hands and rested my arms on the table. "First of all, I have a general comment. This whole scenario started with the *accidental* death of Buster Adams. Then ten years later, Betsy Harper was murdered. And days after, their mutual friend Annie McGuire went missing. Those statements are factual."

Marnie took the upper body pose of The Thinker. "I know Amanda Falon, Buster's mother, hired you to look into her son's death. Why, after ten years?"

115

"Because Amanda thinks that Betsy was murdered for the same reason Buster was."

"Casey, do you think that somebody at the class reunion panicked?"

"Possibly. I don't think the person panicked, but I think someone with a deep dark secret felt threatened."

"Threatened enough to kill?"

"Well, think about this. Betsy and Buster were good friends— sometimes considered *friends with benefits*. I think it went far beyond that. I think Buster was Betsy's confidant. My gut feeling is that whatever Betsy told Buster, and I'm assuming it was the same night he died, he acted on it."

"Are you saying that Betsy manipulated Buster?"

"From what I understand, Betsy was into herself and had been known to be quite promiscuous. Buster knew that but still stood by her as her protector. Whatever Buster heard that night is what killed him. And, what it was, we'll never know unless we figure out who the other player was."

"Casey, have you run all this by Sam?"

"Um, not really. But, now, with Annie missing, it's time I discuss my theories with him."

"We can talk while we go through your paperwork. Once that's done, we can start the evidence part of the board."

It was almost noon before we finished sorting the contents of my briefcase. The piles consisted of my notes, the copy of the Barnstable PD file on Buster Adams, pictures I'd taken of the area where Buster's car went into Wequaquet Lake, Annie's burnt vehicle, and copies of certain Attorney Adams's court cases.

"Your portable file cabinet's empty." Marnie smiled.

I stood and stretched. "It was getting heavy. Let's grab a water and sit out front for a change of scenery."

We both sat and looked around. Almost simultaneously, we started to laugh.

"Look at us," Marnie said. "The sky couldn't be any bluer. There's a warm, gentle breeze dictating the climate, and the smell of the ocean is begging us to take a walk on the beach. But here we sit, on a Sunday, working. You, the private investigator, and me, the lawyer. Not really what I bargained for. How about you?"

"Nope."

For the next half hour, we sat outside and made small talk. It was a much-needed distraction from the conversations we'd shared for the last two hours.

"Well, girl, now that we've solved the problems of the world, we better get back to the problems inside my office awaiting our expertise."

Marnie stood. "I'm right behind you."

I took the Attorney Adams's court cases I'd copied and handed them to Marnie. "You're the lawyer. Can you peruse these and see if you find anything interesting or questionable? I'll look at the Barnstable PD reports on Buster's accident. I've looked at them a couple times already, but I've got to be missing something. After we're done with the cases and reports, I want to show you my notes from my Buster investigation."

I fired up the Keurig and made each of us another cup of coffee. Marnie took the court case files and her coffee, went out to the front office, and sat at the desk I teased was hers. I spread the PD's reports over half the kitchen table. Before I started, I made myself a note to ask Sam if he'd heard any more about Officer Bishop's whereabouts.

I laid the pictures from the PD, the ones I'd taken, and the sketch I'd drawn of where Buster's car entered the lake, down in front of me. The original scene was ten years ago. A lot can change with vegetation and waterfront in ten years. The pictures from the PD showed sparse vegetation. The plant life in mine was much denser but still offered an opening from the road to the water. My guess is that the area in question, being somewhat remote, was and still is probably used by the younger set for late-night shenanigans. I judged

117

the angle the vehicle entered the water to that of a person making a perfect dive—about thirty-three to forty degrees. Barnstable PD sent an officer from their dive team to measure the depth from the surface to where the vehicle hit bottom and became embedded in the muck.

The sketch I made didn't show any measurements for the distance from where Buster's car may have started to move towards the lake to where he entered the lake. To determine his approximate speed, I needed to find those measurements. I also considered it was more like hitting a wall than a cushion when his car hit the water.

I leaned my elbows on the table and opened my hands to cradle my face. The more I thought about Buster's death being *accidental*, the more my instincts told me it wasn't. The problem is there are lots of unanswered questions. Answers to these questions died with Betsy, are hiding with Annie, and being covered up by another individual who at this time remains nameless and is walking among us.

I glanced at my watch. Marnie and I had been scrutinizing paperwork for almost an hour. It was time for a break. She must have had the same idea because if I weren't paying attention, we would have collided in the doorway between the two rooms.

Marnie laughed, "Attorney Adams was quite the lawyer. Keeping company with people who are known to break bread with South Boston's well-known slime boss."

"Yeah, I saw that." I shrugged. "Now that you've read some of the pages, I'll give you my overall opinion."

"Before you start, let me get my notes." Marnie was back a minute later with Adams's files and her notepad.

We stayed in the kitchen.

"Marnie, I'm going to start because I want to paint the picture that's trying to fill the canvas in my mind."

Marine nodded and sat back in her chair with paper and pen in hand to take notes if needed.

"Don't stop me because it will jam up my train of thought. Jot down any questions or comments, and we'll discuss them after I'm done."

"Got it, boss." She smirked.

"This is no walk in the park. I don't think Attorney Adams's legal practice had anything to do with his son or has anything to do with Betsy's death. I know, you're going to say Brian Adams died long before Betsy did, so, of course, he didn't factor into the deadly equation."

Marnie nodded.

"I think Attorney Brian Adams did have a shady side, but I think it's isolated from Buster's *accidental* death and Betsy's murder. And, I'm sure Annie's disappearance wasn't by choice. But I do believe that Annie's disappearance is related to the Buster and Betsy deaths. I'll bet my bottom dollar she went rogue, found some incriminating information on our unknown individual, and is in trouble. My thinking is that we don't know the person, but Annie does." I felt a wave of emotion come over me and started to cry.

Marnie got up, came around the table, and hugged me. "She's strong and very street savvy. She's learned to conjure up a defense from working at the District Attorney's Office."

"Annie's strong when it doesn't involve her. But, not so strong when it does. You know what I mean?" I said.

"I do."

"The day after the reunion when she came to your house?" I asked. "Annie said that Mark Mosley called her that morning to tell her that Betsy was dead. He was at the hotel when the police arrived. They asked Mark a lot of questions about Betsy. He was their class president, so they felt he might give them insight into Betsy's goings and comings. Annie also told us that she and Mark assumed murder because of the nature of the questions."

"I've never seen Annie so upset. She was a mess."

119

"We're at a loss not knowing what questions the PD asked Mark. When Sam and Maloney check-in, we need to ask about those questions, and if anyone from the Barnstable PD has talked to Mark since the morning Betsy was found dead."

I sat back in my chair and took a deep breath. "For the time being, I want to put Attorney Adams to bed and work on the mystery surrounding Buster Adams."

"I agree. Not having seen any of the reports surrounding Buster's death, I can't offer an opinion about the whys and hows he died. But, judging from what you've told me, something isn't kosher."

"Absolutely. Buster's death would remain an *accident* forever if it weren't for Betsy. It's like she's talking from the grave. And, I, for one, am listening."

Marnie lifted her cup. "I could use something stronger than coffee, but I don't need anything brain-altering to add to the mystery."

I smiled. "Ok, two coffees coming up." I slid the police reports across the desk. "Start reading." I wanted Marnie to scan all she could, so I took my time at the Keurig, then came out of the kitchen and joined Marnie at 'her' desk.

Marnie sipped her coffee. "Interesting reading. And, I've only touched the surface."

"You've got that right." My head began to bob slowly. "My general overview is that the person or persons who murdered Buster and the person or persons who murdered Betsy are one or two in the same."

"That's where we're going to have a problem. Because you were told to stay away from the Betsy Harper case, and the only person who might be able to fill in the gaps is missing, you're screwed."

"Somehow, I need to talk to Mark Mosley without rattling Sam's feathers." I gave Marnie my best I-need-you look.

"I don't think I want to hear what you're going to say."

"Of course you do." I smiled a phony smile. "You're already in too deep to back out."

"Alright. Talk to me."

"You haven't read my Barnstable class of 2003 through 2006 Red Rider Yearbook's notes yet. Since I can't take the books out of the library, I need to go back there and go through them again. You're going to be my second set of eyes. If we both agree there's something hidden between the lines or in the shadows of the pictures, Betsy's would probably provide the most information. Annie's might be able to add something to the mix, but until I have something more concrete to share about her whereabouts, I don't want to ask her parents for her's."

"What about Mark Mosley's? Since he was their class president, some of the written memories in his might prove interesting."

"Point taken. After we see the library copies again, we'll make a decision."

A light bulb went off in my head. "I've got an idea. I know I have all my yearbooks from Shrewsbury High School. I'm sure Barnstable PD has or will be going through Betsy's apartment. Maloney will know that. I used to take my books out and relive those years before going to one of my reunions. She lived alone, so maybe we'll get lucky. And, if she still has them, she may have relived those years like I did, remembering the good times and suppressing the bad. It's *the bad* we need to know about."

"That's it!" Marnie stood and started walking and talking, shaking her finger as though she was making a point to a jury.

Her spontaneous burst of energy took me by surprise. "Who are you addressing?"

"My jury."

"What jury?"

"My imaginary jury. I use it to invest myself in a situation. It's my way of wrapping my thoughts around a crime, or in some cases, a testimony given by a witness."

"Does that mean you've found something interesting?" I grinned.

"Working on it."

I shook my head. "We make a dangerous pair."

Marnie raised her eyebrows. "Dangerous, but good."

My cell rang. The screen read unknown caller. I looked at Marnie then answered the call.

It was Sam. "Hi, buddy. Are you still in Wellfleet?"

"We just left. Is Marnie with you?"

"Yep. We're about ready to call it a day."

"Do you girls want to meet us at Seafood Harry's?"

"I'm sure I could convince her."

Sam knew there wouldn't be a problem. "Unless the traffic picks up, we'll be there in a half-hour."

"See you then."

Chapter 29

As I turned into Harry's parking lot, I glanced in my rearview mirror. Sam was right behind us. Marnie and I got out of the car and walked over to where the guys were waiting.

"Good timing, Sherlock."

I kissed Sam. "Productive day?"

He nodded. "You might say that. How about you and Marnie? Any progress?"

"Yes and no." But…." Before I could get anything else out, Sam jumped in.

He looked at Maloney. "You'll get used to this. Whenever Casey says but and hesitates, I'm afraid of what's coming next."

"And they're not even married." Maloney laughed. "I'm hungry. Let's go inside."

Our favorite corner table for four was available. The guys took our food and drink orders then went to the counter to place the order.

Marnie looked at me. "They seem to be in a good mood. That should be to our advantage."

"Cross your fingers," I said just as Sam put my wine on the table.

"What does Marnie have to cross her fingers for?"

"Stop eavesdropping. It doesn't become you."

"Eavesdropping is part of my job, and I'm darn good at it." He pretended to wag his finger at me. "Don't you forget it."

Our bantering was good for a laugh. I gave our favorite toast. "Here's to it, those who get to it, and don't do it, may never get to it, to do it again." We clicked our glasses and took a sip of our beverages.

"So, who's going to start?" Sam looked from Maloney to Marnie and smiled when he got to me. "Looks like you've got center stage."

I took a deep breath deciding where to begin. "Let's see. We had a busy day. Marnie worked at 'her' desk in my office, and I took up residency at the kitchen table. We each had an agenda. Marnie scanned the Attorney Adams's Superior Court cases I'd copied. And I reviewed the Barnstable PD reports on Buster Adams's *accidental death*."

Sam got serious. "Did you find anything worth mentioning?"

"At this point, nothing more than we've already talked about. But I did do some research over the internet. I tried to recreate the Wequaquet Lake scene before, during, and after the *accident* occurred. I feel I'm getting closer to some valid scenarios explaining Buster's accident. But the whys are still a couple of hand lengths away from my grasp. The whodunit is walking around and could be dangerous if he or she gets wind of our investigation."

Maloney leaned forward and rubbed his chin. "You're talking about a ten-year-old murder that was deemed an *accidental death* by the medical examiner, and the case was closed."

"You're right," I said. "That's true. But, now, Buster's mother and Annie have expressed concern about his death not being an accident. As you know, his mother, Amanda Fallon, has employed me to look into it. They both feel his death and Betsy's murder are very much related."

Sam looked at Maloney and shrugged.

I put my hand on Sam's shoulder. "When I get everything in order, I'll fill you in."

"We also believe that Annie went rogue trying to get answers regarding Betsy's death," Marnie tilted her head. "Casey and I are afraid she's in trouble."

Everything got quiet. Before we could resume the conversation, our food came.

There were still a couple hours of sunlight left when we got home. Plenty of time to take the boy for a beach walk. Sam drove into the driveway right behind me. When I got out of my car, I could see Watson in the backyard peeking around the corner. I looked at Sam. "Can you please hook the boy up to his leash? I need to change my shoes."

"No problem." Sam always had treats for Watson in his pocket, and the boy knew it. Sam knelt, snuggled him, and teased him with a couple of milk bones.

I didn't feel like taking a walk, but the boy had been on his run all day, and I'd been sitting most of the day, so a bit of exercise wouldn't hurt. It would also give us some time to throw questions back and forth, trying to make answers fit.

"Okay, I'm ready," said Sam.

"How did it go in Wellfleet today?"

"Depends on the way you look at it." Sam looked at me, then continued. "The fingerprints I lifted off the condom packet I found near Annie's car match the prints on the condom packets in Betsy's hotel room."

I stopped dead in my tracks. "So, the person or persons is or are the same. I don't like those odds."

"Neither do I. The only possibly good thing to come out of this is, as we suspected, Betsy's murder and Annie's disappearance are definitely related."

I wanted to sit down, roll up in a fetal position, and cry. The sea wall was about ten feet in front of me. It was the most challenging ten feet I'd ever walked. "Sam, I've gotta sit."

Only a few people were sitting on or walking the beach, so Sam let Watson run with his seagull friends. We sat like two strangers, not saying a word for what seemed like ten minutes.

"Sherlock, we'll find her." Sam put his arm around me and hugged me tightly. "She's going to be okay."

"Something is missing. Or, should I say, we're missing something."

"When we get back to the house, we'll come up with some direction...some names...some ideas. Develop some hypothetical situations. Ask why and where, and how. These are things we do in the bureau. Of course, the players and the circumstances don't hit home most of the time. Believe it or not, sometimes it's harder to see the big picture when you're dealing with *family*."

I nodded. "I've got to keep a clear head."

Sam stood. "Let's go home." Watson came running on the first whistle. "Good boy." Sam gave him a quick pat, a couple of treats, and hooked up his leash.

"We've both had a trying day. Let's start fresh tomorrow morning. I think it will be more productive."

"Agreed."

Chapter 30

Monday

Sam was in the kitchen. He had the Keurig ready to go, Honey Chex with blueberries on the table, and the newspaper unfolded and divided into two sections.

"You going to Bourne this morning?" I asked.

"No, I called my chief, and he said to do what I had to do, but to keep him informed."

"I was awake most of the night. The last time I looked at the clock, it read 3:15. I was afraid I'd wake you, so I went to the living room and watched television."

Sam reached across the table and took my hands in his. "You've got to take care of yourself. If you get sick, you're no help to anyone. Annie wouldn't want that." He got up and made our coffees.

I let out a deep breath. "You're right."

Sam nodded.

"Let's throw out ideas. Maybe some of them will overlap, and we can start to put things together." I took a few spoonful's of cereal. "Something's been bothering me. The day Annie came to Marnie's house, she mentioned Mark Mosley. I came across the name Mosley somewhere in my research, but I can't remember where. I'm going to go through my notes. It has to be there."

"Hold that thought. I forgot to feed the boy." Sam took Watson outside, gave him a couple of treats, then filled his bowl. "Keep talking."

"Okay, back to Mosley," I said. "Did Maloney say anything about trying to contact Mark Mosley? Or did Maloney show you a police report from when they questioned Mosley at the Sheraton the morning after the reunion?"

"I met Maloney at Barnstable PD. We talked to Chief Lowe about our plans for Wellfleet. We didn't talk much about Betsy. The only thing we did discuss was the fingerprints match on the condom packets. Although that indicates the two cases may be connected, most of our concentration was on Annie. You got your paperwork with you, or is it at your office?"

"It's in the living room." I got up and went to get my briefcase.

Sam cleared the table so we could group my pages into related piles.

I handed Sam the police reports on Buster's case, and I took Attorney Adams's case files.

"Casey, I thought you wanted to concentrate on one thing at a time?"

"I do, but before we can do that, we need to find the reference to Mark Mosley. I've got to check my notes. You look at the ones I gave you. I'm going to look at the court case files. Working together, we should be able to find the reference to Mosley pretty fast."

Not even a half-hour later, I stood up, waving a wad of paper in front of Sam. "I found it. I knew I read the name Mosley. The only problem is the first name is Peter, not Mark."

Sam took a mouthful of coffee. "Mosley isn't an overly common name. The first thing we have to do is give him an identity."

"Before we do anything, please read why his name was even mentioned in an attorney's caseload. And not any attorney's caseload—but one belonging to Attorney Brian Adams."

Sam took the file from me and, without hesitation, started to read it.

Fifteen minutes later, Sam closed the file, leaned back in his chair, and crossed his arms over his chest. "Sherlock, I think, no, I know, that your super-sleuth intuitions have opened up a can of worms. And, here's the biggest dilemma. If Annie hadn't asked you to look into the Buster Adams *accidental death,* none of this would have come to light. The two cases probably would never have been connected. I'm going to call Chief Lowe. We need to run this by him today."

While Sam was on the phone, I got ready to head to the station.

"Chief will be waiting for us. He's going to call Maloney in. I told him we'd be there within a half-hour."

I put all the paperwork and reports back into my briefcase.

"Watson is set for a while. He's got food and water. I figure we'll be back well before dark."

"Sam, a ten-year-old *accidental death*, a seven-day-old murder, and a missing person … all who knew each other. But, not just knew each other, were connected in one way or another."

"We need to know more about Betsy Harper. She had secrets. Secrets that probably only a few people knew. She's dead. That's a fact. Somebody who knew about those secrets tried to make sure they went to the grave with her. Buster may have known the secrets. That may have been what caused his *accidental death*."

"If that's true, then these so-called secrets happened more than ten years ago." I stood. "Let's get going."

Chapter 31

I followed Sam. We took a couple back roads, turned onto Phinney's Lane, then left into Barnstable PD's parking lot.

The officer behind the desk knew Sam. He buzzed us in. "Chief's waiting for you."

"Thanks, buddy." Sam motioned for me to walk in front of him.

Chief Lowe's door was open. He was on the phone, but when he saw us, he waved us in. He held up a finger to let us know he'd be right with us. He shook his head, rolled his eyes, and nicely but abruptly ended his conversation.

"Glad I'm done with that one." The chief stood to greet us, then gestured for us to sit in the two chairs in front of his desk. "Make yourselves comfortable." He shook his head. "My neighbor. Just because my wife and his wife are best friends, he thinks he's my neighborhood snoop and needs to report dog poop from an unknown source on his front lawn. He must call me three times a week with stuff like that."

Sam snickered.

"Hey, don't laugh. You think it's easy being chief?"

"Better you than me."

Chief Lowe picked up his phone and dialed the duty officer. "Please call Detective Maloney and tell him we're about to begin our meeting. Also, unless it's an emergency, hold all my calls." He nodded as though the officer could see through the phone.

Sam slid another chair up for Maloney.

I took my files from my briefcase and set them on the desk in front of me. I figured this was the best way to keep the paperwork sorted, and the conversation concentrated on each aspect of the discussion.

It wasn't five minutes later when Maloney knocked on the door and came in. He took the seat beside Sam.

Chief Lowe turned his attention to me. "Casey, I want to start with you. You told me that Amanda Fallon hired you to look into her son Buster's ten-year-old death. Is that correct?"

"Yes. But, before Amanda, Annie McGuire asked me to do the same thing. Amanda said something about Betsy didn't believe Buster died in an accidental death."

"So Amanda was still in contact with Betsy?"

"She was…with both Betsy and Annie."

Sam leaned forward in his chair. "Chief, as you know, Casey was looking into Attorney Adams's cases. I'll let her continue."

"Please do." Chief Lowes's voice was firm.

I flipped through my paperwork 'til I came to the attorney's case files. Two packets into the pile was the case regarding Peter Mosley. I handed it to the chief. "I've marked certain sections with sticky notes. I'd like you to look at those areas first."

Silence filled the room as the chief followed my suggestion.

Minutes passed before he spoke. "Officer Maloney, the name Mosley was in a report taken by one of my officers the morning we were called to the Sheraton regarding the death of Betsy Harper. Please get that for me. In fact, bring the entire file."

"Yes, sir, be right back."

"Casey, you're very astute in recognizing meaningful facts and those that are not. After reading your noted areas, I'm concerned. The records show that Attorney Adams represented Peter Mosley in a rape case. The case never mentions the female's name, and it never went before the court. It appears it was dismissed."

Maloney knocked on the door and walked in. "Here's the file."

"Thanks." The chief flipped through the pages until he found the four-page report. "The person interviewed is a Mark Mosley."

Casey looked at Sam. "We're guessing that Peter is Mark's brother."

131

"We ran their names and found that the residential address listed for Peter and Mark are one and the same as of a year ago., but Peter doesn't appear on the current Barnstable County Census. That doesn't mean he's not there. Who knows— he may have moved off Cape." Sam leaned forward in his chair. "We didn't run a state census or DMV inquiry."

"We need to do that." The chief nodded. "There's nothing in the report from the Sheridan to indicate a problem with Betsy. It was their ten-year class reunion, so I figured there was a lot of drinking going on, both in the bar and in the rooms. The report doesn't indicate they found any alcohol in the girl's room. But there could have been and whoever was there with her took it out when he, she, or they left."

I had so much I wanted to say, but I had to choose my words carefully so as not to mix my thoughts. "The morning after the reunion, Annie showed up at Marnie and Maloney's house. She was beyond upset. Marnie and I tried to calm her down, but she got worse as she told us about Betsy's death. She said Mark Mosley showed up at her house earlier that morning and told her what had happened." I took a deep breath then continued. "He didn't know the details, but whatever Mark said to her, they both assumed Betsy was murdered."

"Officer Maloney, we need to bring Mark Mosley into the station today. I also want confirmation that Peter is or is not his brother." The chief sat forward, resting his folded arms on his desk. "I also want him to repeat the story he gave to the officers at the hotel. After comparing the two reports, we'll decide our next move."

"Chief, do you think Amanda Adams, AKA Fallon, would know anything about her late husband's cases?" I asked. "If so, she may know who the rape victim was."

"Casey, I know you're doing some work for her regarding the death of her son, Buster. Does she know that you looked into her husband's cases?"

"I didn't tell her. I didn't think there was any need for her to know at this time. Furthermore, I didn't think the case in question had anything to do with Buster's death." I shrugged. "Now, I'm not sure."

The chief sat quietly for what seemed like forever. "I don't want you to ask Amanda anything about the cases. We'll take care of that when the time is right. We'll also take care of the Mosley brothers. If either one tries to contact you, I want to know immediately. Other than with Sam and Maloney, I don't want you to discuss any particulars of the case with anyone else."

"I won't. My biggest concern right now is finding Annie. I'm afraid for her life. She's not a traveler. She hates going over the bridge to the mainland. She's shut down all contact with Marnie and me. She hasn't been to work or hasn't called in. I don't know about her family. She may have given them some cock and bull story that she needed some alone time. If so, they may believe that. I don't. I've known her for a long time. I think she's figured some things out about Betsy's murder and went snooping. There's no doubt in my mind she's in trouble."

Sam watched the interaction between me and the chief, then spoke up. "My chief has given me carte blanche to work the Wellfleet case involving Annie's car. Since I believe her disappearance, Betsy's murder, and Buster's ten-year-old murder are all connected, I'd like to work alongside Barnstable PD too."

"Absolutely." Chief Lowe reached across the desk to shake Sam's hand.

"Mark, having been the class president, may have been the person who had the most contact with the Sheraton in setting up the reunion. I'd like Maloney and me to visit their banquet coordinator. Hopefully, we'll get contact information, especially Mark's phone number, be it a cell or landline. We can pull records from the phone company and, with any luck, match up names with numbers. Once we get those, we can meet with Mark."

The chief looked from Maloney to Sam to me. "We have to speak to Annie's family. The guys need to handle that for the time being. And, I want that done by tomorrow. Time is not on our side. Casey, I want you to keep an open line between my personal cell number and yours." He wrote his number on the back of his business card and handed me a pen and 3 x 5 to give him my information.

"Thank you," I could feel my emotions starting to well up in my chest. I took a deep breath. "I'll keep you informed."

Chief Lowe stood. "Officer Maloney, you and Sam head to the Sheraton. If you get that information, swing by Mark Mosely's house. I'll have one of the guys take Casey home."

"No, I'm all set. I drove myself here this morning. I'm going to head to my office."

Chapter 32

It was almost noontime when I got to Barnstable Village. My head hurt. There was only one Tylenol left in the bottle. "Shit," I said out loud, knowing I wouldn't get an answer.

I didn't feel like talking to anyone, so I didn't open the shades or unlock the front door. I just sat, closed my eyes, folded my arms on my desk, and rested my head on them.

Please, God, help me find Annie.

My mind wasn't thinking correctly. I needed to focus. I had to take the personal out and make this one of my for-hire private investigator cases. My French vanilla coffee didn't even sound good, but water—I needed a water.

I took a fresh pad of paper and a new pen from my top desk drawer. I made sure running out of paper or ink wasn't an option to stop writing.

I began by making a bio page for Annie. Name, address, phone number, physical attributes, place of employment, friends, hobbies, and left room for anything else that came to mind. I thought I knew her better than I did. I knew very little about her youth and her teenage years. Those things never seemed important. Sometimes we'd talk or laugh about something we individually did as a kid, but those conversations didn't get stored in my memory file. During our talks, Annie may have mentioned places special to her. If she's hiding in one of them, I know she'd find a way to let me or Marnie know. Annie's bio page didn't even fill one whole side of the paper.

I knew she hated to go over either the Bourne Bridge or the Sagamore Bridge that connected Cape Cod to the mainland. And that she loved lower Cape. I stared at the framed map of the Cape that hung on the wall between my front door and picture window.

Then, there was Betsy. I didn't know anything about Betsy Harper. I never heard her name until it was time for Annie's ten-year class reunion.

Sam and Maloney need to talk to Annie's family. The guys have to search Annie's house for any hint of where she might be. Maybe they'll let me come with them for that. I also want to see if she has or her parents have her yearbooks. I'll talk to Sam tonight.

My thoughts were interrupted when my office phone rang. 'Name unavailable' flashed on the screen. "Casey Quinby, private investigator." Nothing—I upped my tone and repeated my greeting. "Casey Quinby, private inves..t..i..g.." The call went dead before I could finish. The next thing I heard was my cell. The caller ID read 'name unavailable'...same as the previous call. This time I answered, "Hello."

A raspy, muffled voice, unrecognizable as male or female, whispered. "Mind your own business. I know what you're up to, and I know where you are." Again, the call went dead.

Now it was time to go from a pad of paper to a notebook. My heart was racing. I couldn't let my nerves get the better of me. "Stay calm," I muttered. I jotted down the date and time then made notes regarding the two calls. There wasn't much to write, but what little there was might come in handy further down the road.

A few pages in, I created a legend for a to-do list. It was my list but also included things others were doing. To keep it simple, I used colored checkmarks and small circles. I topped the list with a red checkmark. Sam, Maloney, and Marnie were green, blue, and pink checkmarks, respectively. The Barnstable PD was a black circle, and the Wellfleet PD was a purple circle. Annie was an orange circle. Since there were so many variables and people involved, I knew I needed to organize my part of the Annie investigation, including the *accidental death* of Buster Adams.

There was no doubt in my mind that the paths leading to answers in Buster's death, Betsy's murder, and Annie's disappearance are all connected. My problem is that Buster's case is a closed case that his mother, Amanda Fallon, has paid me to look into, so I'm good with that one. Betsy's murder and Annie's disappearance are open cases that I'm supposed to stay clear of.

I knew nobody would answer, but I called Annie's cell anyway. It went straight to voice mail, the same way it did at least a dozen times before.

I needed to talk to Sam.

He answered on the first ring. "Sherlock, you alright?"

"I am. Where are you?"

"On my way to your office. Are you there now?"

"Yes."

"I'll be there in five minutes."

I'd finished my water and was making a cup of coffee when Sam came in through the back door. He hugged me.

"You sounded anxious when you called. I hope you're going to give me some good news."

"Well, maybe it could be." I put my coffee on the table and made another one for Sam. "Let's sit here in the kitchen. There's more room if we need to spread out." I sat in the chair closest to the back door, leaned forward, and tented my folded hands on the table.

"You look like you're getting ready to pray," said Sam.

"Trust me, I am," I said.

"When Maloney and I left the station, we went to the Sheraton. Fortunately, the banquet manager was there. He said that he and Mark discussed everything except room reservations. Those were made months in advance directly by the guests through the front desk."

"Did he give you Mark's contact information?"

"Yes. Two numbers—home and work."

"Where does he work?"

"A moving company out of Hyannis." Sam flipped through his notes. "Boyd Movers. The office is on Kidd's Hill Road, and the warehouse is near the airport."

"Where does Mark live?"

"Tide's Path in Dennisport. Maloney and I went to the house. It was a small cottage type—the worst on the street. We knocked several times, but no answer. Maloney identified himself as Barnstable Police. Nothing. We walked around the house. A piece of electrical tape was over the front doorbell, and a piece of cardboard, secured from the inside, covered a broken pane in the door. We couldn't see inside because the shades on both the front and back doors were closed, as were the shades on all the windows. If there hadn't been a relatively new grill and two bikes beside the back door, I'd say nobody lived there."

"Did you call his cell?" I asked.

"We did—it skipped voice mail and went right to the 'mailbox full message." We went back to the station. Maloney's going to set up a meeting with Annie's family. When he does, I'll go with him."

"Sam, before you called, I tried to call Annie's cell again. Annie is never—let me emphasize—never without her cell phone. I've been calling it since she went missing, hoping she'd answer. We both know she hasn't and more probably won't. Annie's now goes directly to the *mailbox full message* too."

Sam nodded. "I think they're together."

I took a deep breath, "So do I."

Neither of us spoke for a couple minutes.

I broke the silence. "Before you called, I started to do some research on cell phones. I should have thought of doing this before. Don't tell me I've been watching too much TV crime. But isn't it possible they can tell what tower or towers her phone, and now his, last pinged from?"

Sam didn't let me continue. "Yes and no. I believe it varies by the cell provider and the cell tower owner. Depending on who their providers are, I may be able to help. I have a friend on the Boston PD who I know has used cell tower data to track people. In fact, he spoke about cell phone tracking at a conference I went to last year. I recall him talking about having to subpoena tracking data from AT&T and Verizon. He mentioned some other names, but these are the ones that come to mind. I don't remember if either of them were legally obligated to do so."

"In Annie's case, that's easy. We both have Verizon. I know this because about four months ago, we went to the Verizon store, changed our plans, and upgraded our phones to the Samsung Galaxy S7." I rubbed my hands over my face. "Mark's is a different story. We have no idea who his provider is."

Sam took his cell from his pocket and scrolled through his contacts. "Here we go." He pushed the button for Lt. Larry Tucker. "Casey, we'll start with Annie's. Then we can run Mark's. Maybe we'll get lucky."

I slid my pad of paper and pen over in front of Sam. "In case you need it."

Lieutenant Tucker answered on the second ring.

"Lieutenant, Sam Summers here."

"A voice from the past. Detective Sam Summers, how the hell are you?"

Sam managed to get a half-smile out. "Well, Larry, since you ask…things could be better."

"I'm assuming this isn't a social call."

"I wish it were, but you're right, it's not." Sam shrugged. "I need your help. I'm working on a missing person's case with Barnstable and Wellfleet PD's. It may involve two people—a female and a male—the female being a friend. She works for the DA's office here in Barnstable. We believe they may have information regarding a murder that took place last Saturday night at the Sheraton in Hyannis." Sam hesitated, then continued. "At this time, we have no suspect or suspects in custody or on the radar screen."

"I saw the incident you're talking about. It came over the wire Sunday morning. Here in Boston, unfortunately, we're more exposed to violent crimes than the Cape and Islands. So, it stands out when something like this comes over the wire. Wasn't it during a class reunion?"

"Yes, it was."

"You know if I can help, I'm here for you."

"Thank you," said Sam. "Last year, when I attended the Boston PD Communications Conference, you gave a presentation regarding cell phone tracking. I recall you discussed finding missing persons by checking if their cell numbers pinged off certain towers. You said you were successful in many of your tries. I've never done it before, and I know you're the expert. That's why I'm reaching out to you."

"Sam, I need names and numbers." Lt. Tucker didn't even pause to think about an answer. "If you've got the information in front of you, I'm ready to write. Also, give me the provider's name or names if you have them."

"Thanks, Larry."

I handed Sam the information I had, and he gave it to Lt. Tucker.

"My caller ID shows restricted, so give me your number."

Sam rattled it off. "Call me any time of the day."

"You'll hear from me soon."

"Thanks, Larry." Sam ended the call and turned towards me. "You okay, Sherlock?"

"Not really, but hopefully, Lt. Tucker will be able to get us the cell phone data information."

"Casey, the other thing we need to do is concentrate on finding Peter Mosley. He could be the key to this whole thing." Sam hit speed dial for Barnstable PD. "I'll have them run his name through records and the DMV. Right now, we have absolutely no information on him except for the dismissed rape case. I did check the address listed in the court records, but he's not there. It was a rental property, and the current resident never heard of him. I had hoped to find him living with his brother. He may be. Remember I said there were two bikes outside at Mark's address. But, then again, Peter, as I said before, may be living off Cape."

140

Things were moving fast. Sam had already given Peter's name to an officer at Barnstable PD. "We should get an answer, if there is one, within the next few minutes."

"Can you check with Maloney about visiting Annie's parents and getting into her apartment?" I asked.

"As soon as the station calls me back with Peter's information, I'll give Maloney a call to see if he set something up."

"And, I don't think I mentioned it, but, if possible, I'd like to see Annie's yearbooks. They may be at her parent's house, or she may have taken them when she moved. One way or the other, it might give us a clue about relationships with people she graduated with. Those were the people she was with Saturday night. And, not to change the subject, but we need to find Betsy's yearbooks too. If they're still around, they'd have to be in her apartment."

Sam stood and walked around the kitchen, then leaned back on the counter. "What kind of clues could you find in a ten-year-old yearbook?"

"Understand what I'm going to say. I've looked back in mine many times, and my yearbooks are more than ten years old. It's the things people wrote. Those thoughts, ideas, ambitions, and relationships may help us find missing puzzle pieces. It's not just classmates that revealed their utmost inner secrets, but sometimes, it's a teacher. Someday I might show you mine." I smiled.

"A teacher?"

"Yeah, a teacher. I had a couple of teachers that I looked up to. Believe it or not, math was one of my favorite subjects. I was pretty good at it. I was even in an after-school math club."

"A numbers nerd." Sam made sure he wasn't within arm's length.

"Yeah, I was. This teacher I worshiped got fired because of a gambling problem that spiraled out of control. It voided his effectiveness as an educator. I thought the sun rose and set on this guy. He was like my idol. He wrote in my yearbook. He praised me and put me on a pedestal. You'd have to see the way he expressed himself to understand."

"Did he abuse you?"

"No. Not me, but there were rumors. Sam, all I'm saying is we have to check all avenues. Does that make sense to you?"

"Well, let's put it this way. We're pulling at straws right now, so anything that we can find a reason to dig into, we should be doing it."

"That's why I want to see Annie's and Betsy's yearbooks. It may be nothing, and then it may prove interesting."

Chapter 33

I'd just finished my sentence when Sam's phone rang. "It's Maloney." Sam put him on speaker. "Yeah, I'm at Casey's office."

"I was in the radio room when you called about running Peter Mosley through records and the DMV. Records show many incidents— a few DUIs, suspected of being involved in a street robbery, several other offenses, but not enough evidence to arrest him, and one shy of ten fingers for disturbing the peace but none within the last six years. These are what's on file. I have no doubt there are more, but nothing noteworthy. He was a punk."

"What do records show as his last known address?"

"General Patton Road in Hyannis. I looked it up on the census, but he's not listed as living there now. The current resident's last name is Bonner. They've been registered as residents since February 16, 2011."

Sam shook his head. "What was the last known address from the DMV?"

"The last address Motor Vehicles had for him was the same as his brother's— Tide's Path in Dennisport. The DMV shows his license expired three years ago and never reissued."

"It's like he dropped off the edge of the earth. See if you can find a social or get his expired DMV number. Let me digest this, and I'll get back to you." Without saying anything else, Sam ended the call.

"Is there any way you can check to see if he has a working cell phone?" I asked.

"When Lt. Tucker gets back to me, I'll ask if he can do that without a social or any type of identification. This Peter Mosley doesn't fit the description of a boy scout, so my guess is if he has a phone, it's probably a burner. Then we're shit out of luck."

"Sam, speaking of cell phone calls—I got a call before you got here. Actually, I got two calls in a row. The first one was on my office phone. The screen read, 'name unavailable.' I answered with my usual greeting. You know—the Casey Quinby, private investigator spiel. Nothing. The call went dead before I could finish repeating myself. About thirty seconds later, my cell rang. The caller ID read the same—name unavailable.' I answered with a hello. This time the caller told me to mind my own business, that they knew what I was up to and knew where I was. And again, the call ended."

"What you just told me cements the fact that we're dealing with a dangerous person. Was there anything distinguishing about the voice?"

"It was raspy and muffled. I couldn't tell if it was a man or a woman."

Sam jotted down another note next to Lt. Tucker's name. "When I talk to the lieutenant, I'll ask if incoming calls can be traced."

I didn't want to tell Sam, but I wasn't comfortable with the Mosley brothers. From what Annie said, she's friends with Mark, but she never mentioned Peter. He was older, so he probably didn't move within her circle of friends.

"Sam opened his recent calls list and pushed the button beside Maloney's number. "I forgot to ask Maloney if he called Annie's parents.

Maloney answered on the first ring.

"Did you get a chance to call Annie's parents?"

"I did, but there was no answer. I left a message for them to return my call. That was two hours ago. Let me try again. I'll call you right back."

"Wait a minute. Before you hang up, I thought of something else. Can you try to pull up an address for Mark and Peter's parents? How about a voter's list or the town census? Since Betsy, Annie, Mark, and Buster were all from the Hyannis/Centerville area and all went to Barnstable High School, we should be able to find it." Sam checked his watch. "Another idea. With a little luck, there may be somebody still in the office at the school department that can do a computer or records search for any addresses associated with the Mosley family ten or more years ago."

"I'm on it, boss." Maloney ended the call.

My head was spinning. Nothing was falling into place. We had feelers out but no hard evidence of the who, the where, and the why. My earlier unknown name-caller made me aware that someone was watching me—watching us. Things were moving fast but staying still at the same time.

"I'm going to have another coffee. Want one?" I walked to the counter and popped a K-cup into my Keurig.

Before Sam could answer me, his cell rang. "Lieutenant, that was quick. Any good news?"

"I contacted my source at Verizon. He will work with his people and ping the towers from Boston to Cape Cod. Usually, we'd need a subpoena, but I explained the circumstances and that it could be a matter of life or death." Lt. Tucker hesitated, then continued, "My source told me it could pop in a few hours, or it might take a day or two."

Sam glanced to see if I was watching.

I was. I quietly told him to tell the Lieutenant that the last time I or anybody else had seen or talked to Annie was Thursday, five days ago.

Sam shared the information then continued, "Lieutenant, I have another question. Is it possible to data track an incoming call? I ask because my fiancé, Casey Quinby, has received several questionable calls from a 'name unavailable' caller since this whole scenario started. She's not only one of Annie McGuire's best friends, she's a private investigator out of Barnstable. Right now, she's working on a case involving a person or persons with connections to the Betsy Harper murder. The last caller said to mind her own business—that they knew who Casey was and what she was up to. Casey couldn't determine if it was a male or female because the voice was altered."

I was speechless.

"Give me Casey's last name and number, and I'll see what I can do."

After Sam gave Lt. Tucker the information he requested, they ended the call.

I stood and walked back to the counter. "Now I need something more substantial than cream to put in my coffee. Your fiancé?"

"Well, you are—aren't you?" Sam smiled, got up, wrapped his arms around me, and gave me a mind-altering kiss. "I love you, Sherlock."

Before I knew what was happening, Sam reached in his pocket, took out a little box, and got down on one knee. "Casey Quinby, will you marry me?"

Oh my God—was this really happening? I dropped to my knees and wrapped my arms around Sam's neck. My mouth opened, but nothing came out.

Sam laughed. "I've never known you to be at a loss for words."

My heart felt like it was beating right out of my chest. Tears rolled down my cheeks. "I love you too. And, yes, yes, yes—I am your fiancé, and I will marry you."

We froze in the moment—until his cell rang.

Sam smiled. "The perks of the job."

146

Chapter 34

"**S**am, it's Larry. If Casey is there with you, put your phone on speaker."

"Done."

Lt. Tucker continued. "I checked back with my guy at Verizon. He's going to work on Casey's incoming calls. He said he should be able to get something. The other thing is, if it was a burner phone, law enforcement agencies are supposed to be able to get information. I've never tried. There is a way you can block unknown or name unavailable callers if you want to. You use either *57 or *69. I'm no expert on it, so Casey, you should call or, better still, go to the Verizon store and ask them how to do it. The only problem is numbers like Sam's and mine that fall under restricted would also get blocked."

Sam took his phone off speaker. "Thanks, Larry. Talk to you later."

"We're no further into finding Annie. Unless Lt. Tucker can work wonders with the cell provider, we're screwed." I'd just finished voicing my disappointment when Sam's phone rang again.

It was Maloney. "Sam, I just got a call back from Annie's mother. She and Mr. McGuire are home. I told them we'd be right over. Is Casey coming with you?"

"She knows them well. I think it would be a good idea. Besides, I don't want her to be alone right now. I'll explain later."

Sam ended the call and slipped his phone into his pocket. "Casey, Maloney just got off the phone with Annie's mother. He's on his way to their house. We'll meet him there. Like I told Maloney, you know them well. It may give them some comfort if you're with us."

"Thank you." I grabbed my notebook and a pen from my desk and locked the front door.

Sam was already out the door and had the car running. "Let's get going. You know the way," he said.

Annie's family lived in Centerville off Phinneys Lane, several houses down from Amanda Fallon's. Mrs. McGuire was sitting on the front porch. Maloney pulled in just before us.

I walked up in front of the guys. I could see she'd been crying, so my first move was to comfort her. She stood when I got close.

"Casey, I'm so glad you're here."

I had all I could do to hold back the tears. "I'm glad I'm here too. Let me introduce you to the guys." I turned first to Maloney. "Mom McGuire, this is Detective Maloney from the Barnstable PD." Then, I turned to Sam. "I think you've met Sam, but let me reintroduce you. Sam is my better half most of the time." I tried to eke out a smile. "He's the lead detective out of Bourne. Right now, he's working with Detective Maloney to find Annie."

Mom McGuire reached out to shake the guy's hands. "Please call me Theresa. Let's go inside. My husband is waiting for us." She opened the screen door, and we followed.

Dad McGuire stood and gave me a hug that I didn't think would quit. Annie was his baby. I had to stay composed. Before we sat down, I introduced him to Maloney and Sam.

A few seconds felt like a few minutes before anyone spoke. Dad McGuire sat forward on his chair. "Annie loved her job at the DA's office. She'd come home with unbelievable stories of cases that passed through her hands. Please don't take me wrong. She didn't share any information that she wasn't supposed to. It was after the cases were over or with information that had already made it to *The Tribune*." He folded his arms and rested them on his knees. "Never did I think my Annie would be the subject in a missing person's case." He went quiet.

Maloney spoke up. "Our entire department is dedicated to finding Annie. Sam has some information to share and questions to ask."

"Mr. and Mrs. McGuire…" I could feel the emotion in Sam's voice.

"Please call us Theresa and Henry." Annie's father looked at each one of us. "Mr. and Mrs. are for strangers, and we consider you family."

"Thank you." Sam continued, "Theresa and Henry, I'm working with a friend of mine in the Boston PD, who has extensive experience with cell phone tracking. When was the last time you received a phone message from or spoke to Annie?"

"It was Friday afternoon. We went shopping. It was a message. We didn't talk to her. Neither one of us had our cell phones with us. When we got home, both our phones had a couple of messages, but only one from Annie." Theresa picked up her phone, searched back through her messages, and played the one from Annie. The time was 7:10 p.m. *It's me. I won't be home tonight. I'll call you later."*

Henry did the same. Annie's message was the exact wording as the one on Theresa's phone. The only difference was the time. Henry's noted time was 7:13 p.m.

I moved my eyes slightly sidewards to see Sam's reaction. I could read his mind. The words weren't Annie's. They were too scripted. Not only that, Annie didn't live with them. She had her own place. *What was Annie trying to say?*

"Please, can I see both your phones?" Sam reached forward to get them. "You said there were a couple other calls but no messages. He scrolled back to Annie's, then moved forward. Both Theresa's and Henry's phones showed two more. The caller ID on both read unknown, and both were hang ups. The time was minutes of each other—the first 7:18 p.m. and the last 7:24 p.m.

While Sam made notes regarding the phone information, I took the opportunity to ask a couple questions. "Mom, knowing Annie, she has Barnstable Red Riders yearbooks since her freshman year."

Mom McGuire spoke up before I could ask a question. "She certainly does. I remember the first one. She was so excited. They had a pretty tight class. Most of her friends that wrote in her 2003 book wrote in all four. The entries were fun to read. It brought back memories of when I did that. Some things don't change."

"No, they don't," I said. "Do you have the books here?"

"I do. We sat down about a week before the reunion and looked through all four of them. Annie was going to take them to her house, but we put them aside, sat down for dinner, and she forgot them. I was going to drop the books off but didn't get around to it."

I needed to see those books, so I mentally crossed my fingers and asked, "Mom, do you think I could take all four home? I want to go through them."

"Casey, of course, you can. And, if you need Henry or me to answer any questions, please don't hesitate to call us. Let me get them. I'll be right back."

I got what I needed. Now it was Maloney's turn. "Henry, I'd like to see Annie's house. I understand she's renting in Cummaquid."

"She is. I hated to see her leave. But it was time." He sucked his bottom lip in and turned away. "She came back here at least three, sometimes four, times a week. Theresa's a great cook. I think our Annie was still adjusting to living alone."

Maloney didn't want to go down that road, so he didn't comment but returned to finish his original request. "Can we meet you there tomorrow morning?"

Henry nodded. "Whatever time is good for you, we'll be there."

"How about 9:00."

"That works. Casey, will you be there too?" Henry asked.

I knew Sam would keep me pretty close to the vest for a while. "Dad, I'll be there. Do you have my cell number?"

"I don't think so."

I took a business card from my purse and noted the number on the back. "Front is the office number, and back is the cell. You can always reach me on the cell. Don't hesitate to call if you need me or just plain want to talk."

"You're a good friend, Casey. You and Annie were like sisters." Henry teared up.

"And we still are. She'll be home soon." I hugged Henry.

Theresa walked back into the living room carrying Annie's four yearbooks. "Here you go, Casey."

"I'll take good care of them."

"I know you will."

"We're going to meet you and Henry at Annie's house tomorrow morning at 9:00. We'll talk some more then." I gave Mom and Dad McGuire a kiss.

Maloney and Sam thanked them for meeting with us, and we headed out the door.

"Maloney, if you and Marnie aren't doing anything tonight, why don't you come over for supper. I'll throw burgers on the grill and pick up corn at Lambert's. I think the Silver Queen is ready." Sam smiled. "Besides, I know Casey wants to talk to Marnie about something."

I covered my left-hand ring finger with my right hand. Since Maloney hadn't said anything earlier, I knew he hadn't seen my newest piece of jewelry. It was a guy thing, but I was glad he hadn't noticed.

"We'll be there around 6:00."

Sam patted Maloney on the back. "I'll have a cold one waiting for you."

Chapter 35

We stopped at Lambert's for the corn. Sam picked out twelve ears of Silver Queen while I checked the deli. A fresh batch of homemade potato salad was calling my name.

"I love this place," I said.

"I think I have enough beer, but I'm going to pick up another six-pack anyway."

"It won't go to waste." I laughed. "I'll meet you at the checkout."

The ten-minute ride home was filled with non-stop conversation.

"Casey, while we're all together, let's brainstorm," Sam said. You, me, and Maloney were with the McGuire's today. Because Marnie wasn't with us, I want to run some things by her and get her take on Annie's behavior since the reunion. Marnie's with her all day at work. She might recall Annie having said something or, because she's so predictable, displayed some unusual body language. It might not be anything, but one little bit of fresh information could open up a new lead or leads as to her whereabouts."

"The other thing is the yearbooks." I glanced at Sam. "I gave you my take on them. That was a generality because I haven't looked them over myself, but I believe they could be significant. If four sets of eyes and four inquisitive brains don't come up with anything, then I'm out in left field. I don't believe that's going to be the case. There's one for each of us to start with. We'll rotate them and make notes as we go. When we're through, we'll compare the notes and talk about our findings."

Sam turned onto Old Town Road, then right onto Bayberry Lane, and left into our driveway. We could see Watson was patiently waiting for Sam to set him free from his backyard run. I didn't quite make it to the door before the boy jumped up to greet me. My hands were preoccupied with grocery bags, so I couldn't grab the rail and almost went flying off the open side of the steps.

"Yo boy, take it easy. You almost knocked your mama over."

Sam unlocked the door and took the bags of corn from me. "I'll meet you on the deck."

I brought Sam a pot for the corn and a bag for the husks. "Be right back. I want to get Annie's yearbooks from the car."

I looked at the books as I set them on the table. *Please talk to us.*

Watson was curled up at Sam's feet but quickly got up when he saw me come out the door with his food bowl. "Good boy. Here you go." The bowl barely made it to the floor before he had his nose in it. I laughed. "You might think we starve you."

"We've got a couple hours before Marnie and Maloney get here. Sit down and relax for a few."

"Works for me." I leaned over Sam's shoulder and kissed him. "Who are you kidding? You want me to help with the corn."

"That's why I call you Sherlock. Can't get anything by you." He handed me a few ears to shuck.

"What are you thinking about?" I asked.

"Nothing in particular." Sam brushed his hands together. "The corn's ready. I'll bring the pot inside, and then I'm going to get a beer. You want wine?"

"A wine and a little music would be nice. The James Taylor CD is already in the Bose."

"You've got it, my lady."

I moved to the chaise and leaned back. I lifted my left arm, bent my wrist, and stretched it out in front of me. I was engaged. I was going to be Mrs. Sam Summers. I smiled as a couple of tears rolled down my cheeks. What a day—a beautiful blue sky dotted with puffy white clouds and a gentle breeze. I could hear James Taylor singing *"How Sweet it is to Be Loved by You."*

Sam slid the screen door open, handed me my wine, then sat down beside me and started to sing.

I raised my head at the same time Sam leaned over. There were no words, just a kiss that I knew would last forever. "Not bad, Sweet Baby James."

It was exactly 6:00 p.m. when Marnie and Maloney pulled into our driveway. Sam had just fired up the grill, and I was in the kitchen getting the burgers ready.

"Anybody home?" Marnie called.

"I'm in the kitchen, and Sam's on the deck."

Marnie joined me, and Maloney walked around the house to where Sam was.

"Have you ever met Annie's parents?" I asked

"Her mom stopped by the office a couple of times, Annie introduced me to her, but I've never met her dad."

"They're great people. I felt so bad. They're scared. And, I don't blame them. I wished I could reassure her parents that everything is going to be alright."

Marnie nodded. "We have to stay positive."

"Yes, we do." I rubbed my eyes, then ran my fingers through my hair—catching my ring on a few strands. "Ouch."

"What's the matter?"

"Um … My ring got caught up in my hair," I said.

Marnie's face wrinkled. "What ring?"

I pretended I didn't hear her and quickly reached around with my right hand to loosen the strands. I wanted to break the news with a toast of wine and beer when we were all together on the deck.

"Here. Take these beers out for the guys. I'll be right behind you with our pink shit and ice."

I joined them with the two glasses of white zin, making sure my left hand was carefully placed around her drink so that when I handed it to her, she couldn't see my ring.

Sam put his arm around me, held up his beer, and started the toast. "Here's to it, those who get to it, and don't do it, may never get to it, to do it again."

He leaned over and kissed me. "I'd like to introduce the future Mrs. Sam Summers."

We clicked glasses, sipped to seal the moment, and embraced in a giant hug.

I held up my left hand and turned it slowly to reveal my newest piece of jewelry. I couldn't curtail my emotions. "I'm so happy to share this special moment with two of our best friends." Tears rolled down my cheeks. "And, we'll do this again when Annie comes home."

Marnie wrapped her arms around me. "I'm so happy for you. Just think, now we can open the *Mrs. and Mrs. Private Investigators of Barnstable Village.*"

I put my hands on Marnie's shoulders and gently pushed her back a step. "Does this mean you're going to take the desk next to mine?"

She shrugged her shoulders and smiled. "I've been giving it serious consideration."

"Consider no more. Decision made."

"Hey girls," Sam waved us over, "The burgers are almost ready to come off the grill."

Sam and Maloney were in charge of the burgers and beers, and Marnie and I went inside to get the corn, potato salad, and wine.

"We're ready out here," Sam called from the deck.

"On our way," I said. I handed Marnie the bottle of wine and the potato salad. "One of you grab the door."

I put the plate of corn, the butter dish, and the salt and pepper shakers on a tray. "Here I come, ready or not."

"We're ready." Maloney took the tray from me. "Everything looks so good."

I looked around for Watson. "Where's the boy? He's not begging for people food."

Sam laughed, "That's because he has his own burger. I figured it was a special day, so why not let him be part of it."

I shook my head. "You're an old softy."

"Wait till you guys have kids." Maloney glanced from me to Sam. "They'll be spoiled rotten."

"Well, not to change the subject, but …

I piped in before Sam had a chance to finish. "Good food—good meat—good God, let's eat.

We've got other things on the agenda for tonight. Let's briefly talk about what's been done to date. I think we can eat, drink and talk about what we want to accomplish tonight."

"I'll start," Sam said. "I'm not going to talk about Annie's car now. What I want to do is talk about a couple other things. Make a mental note or interrupt me if you have something to add." Sam looked at Marnie. "As you know, Maloney, Casey, and I went to speak to Mr. and Mrs. McGuire today. They, like us, haven't heard from Annie since last Friday. They didn't have anything to help us find the missing puzzle pieces. We're going to meet them at Annie's house tomorrow morning at 9:00. Their next-door neighbor is driving them. Maloney's taking a fingerprint kit with him. I also want to look at her computer. It's a long shot, but maybe, hopefully, it's turned on and not passworded since she lives alone."

"Sam, I'll look through her clothes and toiletries. I can't imagine she planned a getaway, but we have to consider everything. It could have been a getaway that went bad. And, as much as I don't want to think about it, she may have gone rogue trying to get answers regarding Betsy's death." I looked at Sam and raised my eyebrows. "She can be more pigheaded than me."

"Does she have a landline?" Maloney asked.

"No, just a cell phone," I said.

"Speaking of a cell phone," Sam leaned forward on the table, "I've contacted a Lieutenant. in the Boston PD who is well associated with data tracking. I gave him information regarding incoming or outgoing calls on Annie's cell. He's working with the service provider to ping the towers, amongst other things. Casey also got some hang-up calls that concern me, so I'm having him check those out."

"What's the Lieutenant's name?" Maloney asked.

"Terry Tucker," I said.

Maloney smiled. "My father and Terry worked together for years. In fact, they graduated from the police academy in the same class. They're the best of friends."

"Small world. Maybe they'll tag-team if the need comes up."

"I know they would."

"Hey guys, I have another theory. I call it the yearbook theory. Marnie, let me ask you—did you buy a yearbook every year from your freshman year to your senior year?"

"Of course, I think almost everybody did ... especially the girls."

"And, did you have people write little tell-tale or goofy things in them?"

"I did. And, I wrote stuff in theirs. Many times, I've looked back at my books and either laughed or cringed at what I read."

"Marnie, let me ask you something else. Did any of your teachers write in your books?"

"Sure—but only the ones I liked—the ones I wanted to remember."

Maloney listened, then spoke up, "Casey, I know Mrs. McGuire gave you Annie's yearbooks today.

"She did, and that's what we're going to look through tonight. There are four of them and four of us. We'll each start with one and pass them around. I want each of us to read and, if necessary, write notes on some of the scripture. Also, the pictures could prove

157

interesting. Look at the clubs, the sports, the candids—everything. Read the names associated with each group. Note the ones that Annie or Buster or Betsy or Mark belonged to. Peter Mosley was older than Mark, by I don't know how many years, so you might find something on Peter in Annie's freshman or perhaps sophomore or junior books. Anything—any hint—any clue."

Marnie looked around the table. " Since we're all done eating, we might as well go inside and get this show on the road."

Sam and Maloney cleared the outside table and brought the dishes inside.

"Just put them in the sink. I want to get started with the yearbooks." I held up a K-cup. "I'm going to have a coffee. Anyone else?"

The guys and Marnie raised their hands.

I laughed. "I feel like a fourth-grade teacher asking the kids if they're ready for snacks."

Maloney sat straight up in his chair. "Mrs. Summers, does that mean we're getting snacks?"

"Wiseguy," I said. "Maybe, if you're good."

I had already gone through the 2003 to 2006 yearbooks when I visited the library. But those were clean copies with generic captions and no deep personal connection. I did get some helpful information, but now I was looking for encrypted messages with possible subjective insinuations to help solve two murders and bring Annie home.

I started with the class of 2003—Annie's freshman Barnstable Red Riders yearbook. "Wow … they taught cursive back then. It looks like nobody paid attention. Some of these "little tell-tale tidbits" are hard to read."

Sam didn't look up but asked, "Did you ever think that maybe they did it on purpose so teachers and nosey private investigators can't figure out what they wrote?"

"Hmm, is that what you did, Sammy?" Marnie chuckled.

I finished reading the inside front cover and first two pages that initially were purposely left blank in anticipation of being filled with classmates' autographs and words of life, love, and wisdom. There were lots of hearts, X's and O's, and ninth-grade puppy love stuff. I thought back to one of mine. *Have fun with Jerry over the summer.* I quietly smiled. Then I came to the dedication page.

The class of 2003 dedicated their yearbook to the newest addition to the faculty, Mr. Arthur "Artie" Richardson. He was also their class advisor, so the yearbook committee wrote a little administration-approved bio on him. He graduated from the University of Massachusetts in 1990 with Bachelor's and Master's degrees in Art Education. He then, in 1992, earned another Master's degree in Fine Arts from the Massachusetts College of Arts and Design. He started his career at Barnstable High School in 1997 when the former head of the art department, Stanley Goodman, retired. Mr. Richardson was young and handsome. I might have paid more attention in art class if I had a teacher that looked like him.

I looked around the table. My cohorts were engrossed in their respective yearbook. Marnie was making notes. Sam was reading student captions, and Maloney was looking through group pictures.

I flipped to the back of the book. Again, there were more written reminiscences between classmates. Nothing stood out until I flipped to the back inside cover. In the top right corner was a parting summer wish written by someone named Artie. *'Caress the grass, paint the skies, and dance in the flowers. See you in September.'*

Why did that name sound familiar?

Then it hit me—the art teacher. I took my cellphone out and snapped a picture.

On the bottom, left corner was a short, barely recognizable two-line entry. It looked like somebody tried to erase it, but I could still figure out what it said. 'Hey, freshman, ready for beach party bingo with the graduate?' It was signed PM. I went to the senior class headshots that began with an M. Halfway through my search. It jumped out at me—Peter Mosley.

The caption under Peter's picture read:

Ladies to the left—Ladies to the right. The football field was his favorite 'classroom.' PM came to life when the sun went down. On Valentine's Day, his artistic skills and romantic prose overtook the art room. Andy Warhol was his idol, and his unique script defined his identity. A career in the art world may be in his future.

Before I said anything, I ran through all the M's. The only match was his.

Something wasn't right. Annie only spoke about Mark Mosley. I'd never heard her mention his brother.

"Hey, guys. Check to see if anyone named Artie wrote in the yearbooks you have." Since Peter Mosley graduated in 2003, he wouldn't be in Annie's other yearbooks. I'll mention the Peter thing when we start brainstorming.

Marnie spoke up, "I saw that name. I made a note to ask you about it. Stuff you write in a yearbook can be a little crazy, but this person wrote—*Caress the grass, paint the skies, and dance in the flowers. See you in September.*"

My stomach started to churn. "You've got to be shittin' me. What year do you have?"

"2005." Marnie brought it over to show me.

I took the 2005 book and opened it to the inside back cover. "Here it is. The top right corner—almost like it was rubber-stamped. It's written in the same spot. "Guys, top right corner on the inside back cover—what's there?"

Sam took a deep breath, then slowly let it out. "Grass, skies, and flowers by the famous Artie."

Maloney repeated Sam's findings.

I looked at Sam, Marnie, and Maloney. "We need to find Betsy's yearbooks."

"Maloney, tomorrow morning, find out from Chief Lowe if anyone's searched Betsy's apartment yet," Sam said. "If not, get the address, and we'll head over there after we meet with Annie's parents."

"I'm going to get another wine. Do you want one?" Marnie asked.

I handed her my glass. "Thanks."

Two minutes later, she was back. "Here. Did I miss anything?"

"Nope." I turned toward Sam. "Did you see anything odd or that might cause concern?"

"The four of us made notes." Marnie shook her head. "But we haven't compared them yet. Most of what I read seemed harmless—straight out of a *Stupid Things to write in a High School Yearbook for DUMMIES.*"

"Maybe you should send them the idea." I laughed. "I know it's not funny, but it just came out."

Sam leaned back in his chair. "Casey, what am I going to do with you?"

"I don't know. That's your problem now." I laughed. "How about something written by Mark Mosley?"

I knew I hadn't seen any written blessing signed by someone named Mark. Sam, Maloney, and Marnie said they hadn't either.

"Okay. Nothing signed by a Mark. Since I have the 2006 yearbook, let's look at his graduation picture." I flipped through the pages until I came to it. I read the caption below out loud.

Mr. Personality or MM—he answered to both. 'It wasn't me' was his favorite reply whenever asked what happened? Loved to live through travel magazines. Said traveling, meeting people, sampling food and drinks, and never growing old were his life's ambitions. Class President since his freshman year, he held his head high in anticipation of leading the class of 2006 into their graduation commencement. Always seen walking the corridors with Betsy—of course, they had a pass.

"Annie said she was friends with Mark." I sighed. "Recheck the other three."

Sam held up his hand. "Got it." 'Maybe one of these days, we'll get over the bridge. There's a whole new world out there.' "It's signed, MM."

Marnie looked up. "He wrote the same thing in 2005."

"Same in 2003," said Maloney

Sam nodded. "Ditto in 2004."

Chapter 36

Tuesday

My mind was on overdrive all night. It felt like I'd just fallen asleep when the alarm went off. I hit the snooze button and rolled over to hug Sam. He wasn't there. I knew the eight-minute snooze wouldn't make me feel any better, so I mumbled, "the hell with it," and got up.

When I walked into the kitchen, Sam pointed to his phone and mouthed Maloney. "We'll meet you and Marnie at Annie's house."

I made a coffee then sat down at the table, waiting for Sam to finish his call.

"Maloney got Betsy's address. We'll head over there after we leave Annie's." Sam looked at me. "Better down that coffee. We're meeting the McGuires and Marnie and Maloney at 9:00."

I looked at the digital on the stove. "Shit, it's 8:04. Don't talk to me. I've got to get ready." Fifteen minutes later, I rushed back into the kitchen, grabbed my coffee, and poured it into a travel mug. I'm ready." I glanced around the room. "Where's Watson?"

"All taken care of. He's hooked to his run and has food and water. He'll be fine." Sam laughed and handed me my purse, notebook, and a pen. "Let's go, Sherlock?"

Mom and Dad McGuire, Maloney and Marnie, were already at Annie's house when Sam and I pulled into the driveway. "Have you been inside?" Sam asked.

"No. We didn't want to go in before you got here." Dad McGuire reached into his pocket, pulled out a set of keys, and handed them to Sam. "Our neighbor drove us down." Dad McGuire pointed to a car on the other side of the parking lot. "He said he'd wait and take us home when we were ready."

I turned to Mom McGuire. "Have you been here since Annie went missing?"

"No. Until we got the call about her car being burnt, we didn't have any reason to think anything was wrong. We didn't talk every day. Sometimes she'd come over for Sunday dinner, but since the weather's been nice, she was doing some serious bike riding."

Sam asked the questions, and I took notes. "Was she biking alone? Did she go with a group? Did she mention any names?"

"A couple weeks ago, she and Mark Mosley rode down to Harwich to get an ice cream at Sundae School. I remember asking her if they could have found anything closer. She just laughed and said it was good exercise." Mrs. McGuire took a tissue from her pocket and wiped her eyes. "Maybe you should talk to Mark. Before the reunion, they saw each other two or three times a week. I figured they were working on stuff that pertained to the reunion."

Maloney suggested that Annie's parents take a seat on the front porch while the rest of us looked around. Marnie and I took Annie's bedroom, Maloney stayed in the living room, and Sam headed for the kitchen.

"I'm going to look through her desk. Why don't' you start with her dresser drawers." There were three piles of paper neatly arranged on the left side and one on the blotter in front of her chair. The one on the blotter appeared to be recently paid bills. I thumbed through them. One was for a new bike helmet and two backpacks purchased from Browns Sporting Goods in Dennisport dated three days before the reunion. *Why two backpacks? Maybe one was for Mark.* I took a picture with my phone. The other bills were for utilities, nothing noteworthy. The top center drawer held the usual pens, paper clips, scissors, sticky notes, and 3x5 file cards. The contents of the two remaining drawers didn't offer any clues or scraps of interest in Annie's outside-the-office life. I tried to open her computer and tried to get into her files. It was passworded. I tried a few words that I thought she might have used—nothing.

"Marnie, find anything worth talking about?" I asked.

"There are a couple of new dresses and three pairs of dress pants—all with the tags still on them—hanging in the front. I figure Annie bought some new clothes for the reunion but couldn't make up her mind which ones she wanted to keep, so took them all home to decide."

When I glanced around the room, I noticed a Vera Bradley overnight bag beside her bed. I walked over, lifted it off the floor, and set it on the bed. I knew it had more than a change of underwear and nightclothes in it. "Interesting," I said.

Marnie joined me. "What's so interesting?"

"Annie's overnight bag has enough clothes for three days. And, not only clothes but toiletries too." I took a deep breath. "Did she say anything to you about a mini vacation?"

"Not at all. She's got a lot of time on the books, but I don't think she put in for any vacation days."

I looked at Marnie. "I don't want to talk to the guys about this find in front of Annie's parents. I do, however, want to ask them if they have a spare key at home and can leave this key with me in case we have to get back in. I don't think it'll be a problem."

Marnie knelt to look under Annie's bed. "She's got a platform bed, so there's nothing here to look at."

"Marnie, the bathroom is between the bedroom and the kitchen. Take a look in the medicine cabinet and under the sink. I'm going to check out her toiletry bag. I wonder if Sam and Maloney found anything of concern in the living room or the kitchen?"

"Don't know, but I saw Maloney head to the kitchen about five minutes ago."

"You do the bathroom, and I'll meet you in a couple."

Annie's toiletry bag had shampoo, conditioner, hairspray, hand cream, toothpaste, toothbrush, and a small hairbrush. I was about to zip it back up when I noticed a small plastic pouch. I opened it. There was a travel-size container of Tylenol, a little bottle of eye drops, and a prescription card of birth-control pills. My mouth dropped. Just as I was about to call Marnie, she came through the door.

"I found these in the medicine cabinet." She held up two full and one half-empty card of birth control pills."

I thought I knew most of Annie's personal life's comings and goings—not that it was any of my business. But with Annie missing, I'm making it my business.

"Do you know if Annie was seeing anyone?"

Marnie shook her head. "Last time I knew she was dating someone, it was like six or more months ago. It was one of the ADAs. And, I thought it wasn't anything serious. She'd say it was like being with the brother she never had."

I took one of the pill cards, checked the date on the script, and did the math. "Annie filled this two weeks ago." I closed the closet door. Marnie and I went to the living room to meet Sam and Maloney.

"Casey, did you find anything?" Sam asked.

"We found a couple things of interest. I'd rather wait until Annie's mother and father have left before we get into that conversation." I glanced out the front window. The McGuires were sitting on the porch swing, barely rocking and staring out over the front yard.

I put my hand on Sam's arm. "Come out with me."

Marnie and Maloney stayed inside.

Maloney had brought two fingerprint kits from the station. "While Sam and Casey are talking to the McGuires. I'm going to dust for prints. It's a crapshoot. I'll take some in the living room and kitchen. See if you can figure out which side of the bed Annie slept on. Maybe we'll get lucky, and whoever she's sleeping with touched the nightstand or headboard. Also, I want to check the bedsheets for semen stains.

I walked over to Mom and Dad McGuire and crouched down in front of them. "We may need to come back for another look. Do you have an extra key to Annie's house?"

"You can take this one. We do have another one at home." Dad McGuire handed me the keyring with three keys on it. I knew one was for Annie's house, one looked like a car key, and the other could have been a key to the office. It wasn't the time to ask. I took their hands in mine. "Thank you for helping us today. I don't see a reason for you to stay any longer. I'll keep you informed as we get new information. And, in turn, if you think of anything that may help us or if somebody tries to contact you, please don't hesitate to call me."

Sam and I walked with the McGuires to their neighbor's car. We assured them that everything that can be done to find Annie is being done. The guys shook hands, and I got hugs from Mom McGuire. I watched as the neighbor backed out of the driveway then headed toward 6A.

I sat on the porch swing and braced my feet on the floor so I wouldn't move. "Life sucks, and then you die," I whispered.

"What?" asked Sam.

"Nothing." I took a deep breath. "Did you guys find anything?"

We walked back inside the house.

"There are some photo albums on the shelf in the coat closet," Sam said. He opened the door and reached up to get them. "It's two photo albums and one scrapbook. I didn't want to take them down while her parents were here."

He handed them to me. "We'll take them home. Right now, I want to go to Betsy's apartment."

Maloney was finishing up with his last set of prints. "Give me five minutes, and I'll be done here. I'll take more at Betsy's."

Chapter 37

It was a twenty-minute ride from Annie's house in Cummaquid to Betsy's apartment in West Dennis. Maloney and Marnie led the way. Sam and I followed.

Sam glanced over at me. "What's going on in that pretty little head of yours, Sherlock?"

"I'm trying to put two and two together, but it's not adding up. Marnie and I found a supply of birth control pills in Annie's bedroom. The script was filled a couple of weeks ago. Half of one of the cards is empty."

"Do you think she's involved with someone?"

"Yeah, I guess that's what I'm trying to say. But what concerns me is Annie, and I are pretty tight. She usually tells me everything that's going on in her life." I shrugged. "Maybe I know who it is, and for some reason, she thought I wouldn't approve."

"Okay big sister. You're overthinking the situation. We'll talk more about that later."

"I want to find something concrete—something that will give us a clue as to where Annie is. Time isn't on our side. She's so predictable and not good at keeping secrets. Sam, my gut is telling me she's in real trouble."

"Casey, what we all need to do right now is stay level-headed. When we go through Betsy's apartment, we need to use gloves. I know it's not the actual crime scene, but whoever murdered her may have been at her apartment. If you or Marnie find something, I don't want either of you to touch it unless you've got your gloves on." Sam hesitated. "Do you understand?"

"Of course I do. You're talking to me. Neither Marnie nor I would do anything stupid to compromise possible evidence."

"I know that. I shouldn't have said anything." Sam sighed. "I think we're all so close to Annie that we need to realize what are facts and what are maybes. The maybes might turn into facts, but we don't want them to interfere and send us looking in the wrong direction. Maloney's going to dust for prints at Betsy's like he did at Annie's.

I could feel my eyes starting to well up. Now was not the time to let my emotions take over.

"We're at Betsy's." Sam pulled in the lot and parked in an empty spot three away from Maloney.

Maloney and Marnie got out of his unmarked and waited for us to join them.

"Do you have evidence bags with you?" Sam asked.

Maloney held up a canvas bag. "Evidence bags, tape, markers, and anything else we might need." He handed the bag to Sam. "I spoke to the resident superintendent earlier. As far as he knows, nobody has been there since Betsy's death. He's going to give me a key to get in. It's apartment number 16. I'll meet you there."

"Nice area," I said. "Since there aren't many cars in the lot, I'm assuming most of the residents are working people. We should check to see what the approximate age group is. And, I bet the super knows who Betsy was friendly with."

"Point taken." Sam nodded. "Usually works that way."

Apartment 16 was on the first floor. The main sidewalk, with small runways leading to the front doors, ran the entire length of the building. The landscaping for each unit was tastefully planted with a mixture of flowering and ornamental shrubs. Since it was meticulous, I assumed the apartment complex maintained it.

"Casey, do you have a notebook with you?"

"Now, Sam, you know I always have one in my purse." I smiled.

"Here we go." Maloney dangled the keyring as he walked up to the door. "The super wanted to know if we needed his help. I nicely told him we were all set but knew where to find him if we had questions."

Betsy's apartment was a one-bedroom, good-sized living room and an eat-in kitchen. It appeared very neat and clean. There was no evidence of a roommate. A quick check of the bathroom and the bedroom closet should confirm that she lived alone for the most part.

Maloney took gloves from his bag and handed us each a pair. "Casey, you and Marnie check out the bedroom and bathroom. Sam and I will start with the living room then head to the kitchen. The super did tell me that all the apartments have a small storage unit in a building at the end of the parking lot." He held up the keyring again, noting a second key. "We'll deal with that once we finish here."

Sam watched Maloney as he delegated duties to each of us. Maloney's father, Big M, was a friend and a lieutenant in the Boston Police Department. He was disappointed when his son decided to join the Provincetown PD instead of Boston. But Big M couldn't have been prouder when Chief Lowe hired Maloney away from Ptown PD to fill a Barnstable PD detective bureau position.

I took the closet, and Marnie started with one of the nightstands.

I opened the closet door. "I should be so organized," I said. "There are twelve shoeboxes on the top shelf and sixteen more pairs on a shoe rack." I shook my head. "And next to the shoeboxes, there are nine pocketbooks of various colors and sizes."

"I'm still on the top drawer." Marnie smiled. "There are six little piles of receipt size papers clipped together, a small stack of envelopes under an elastic, a roll of tums, a blister-pack of Benadryl, and an open box of condoms."

"A box of condoms?" I asked.

"Yep, that's what I said."

"What brand?"

Marnie picked up the half-empty box. "Okamoto 003."

"You've got to be shittin' me. That's the same brand of condoms found in Betsy's room at the Sheridan and near the burnt remains of Annie's car. Bag them." Casey walked over beside Marnie. "Bag those clipped papers and envelopes too. We'll lay them out on the kitchen table and examine them after we finish going through the bedroom."

The second drawer had pairs of rolled-up socks and a box of tissues. And the third had three five by eight and one eight by eight transparent plastic catchall cases. "Betsy was certainly was a neatnik. I'll take them out so we can check the contents," Marnie said.

I went back to closet duty. "Betsy sure liked her clothes—at least liked buying them. About a quarter of her tops still have the tags attached." I shook my head. "And, not just that. She was a designer diva. Would you pay $82.00 for a Michael Kors T-shirt or $275.00 for a small Coach swinger shoulder bag, then just let them take up space in your closet? Even when I was making a good salary at the *Tribune*, I didn't like putting out $30.00 for a pair of regular Levi's."

"Betsy liked to dress to impress. When the PD figures out the 'who' she was trying to impress, they might discover who murdered her—or not." Marnie shrugged.

"There are four stacked bankers boxes tucked in the deepest part of the closet. I'll take them down. You pull them out." I moved her clothes to the other end of the closet and slid the top box off the stack.

Marnie pulled it out to make room for the second box.

Because the first box wasn't very heavy, I assumed the others would be the same. Wrong. "What the hell. This box feels like it's full of rocks."

Marnie reached over to help. "You're not kidding."

The last two boxes were the same as the first.

I called to Sam, "Can you guys please help us?"

"Be right there."

When the guys came into the bedroom, I asked them to take the four boxes into the living room. "Since Betsy has a platform bed as Annie did, nothing is under it, so we just have the dresser and bathroom to go through, then we'll join you."

Marnie took a few plastic bags and headed to the bathroom. I started on the dresser.

The top drawer had two jewelry boxes, one sporting her initials on the cover. I took the two boxes out and set them on the dresser. The first one had a swing clasp to keep it closed, but the second box was locked. *Interesting—Now to find the key.*

The first jewelry box was filled with what appeared to be costume jewelry. All the jewelry in one section was somehow associated with things relating to arts and crafts. There was a pair of earrings with tiny dangling paintbrushes. Another set resembled artist's pallets. There was also a pin made to look like a canvas with her name written in a fancy script and a cluster of hearts painted in one corner. In the same box, there was a pressed red rose and a picture of a female, who I figured was Betsy, and an unknown guy. It was sealed between two pieces of laminate. May 14, 2010, 'Love you,' and the letter A was written in script on the back. It didn't appear that it was taken by a professional, but probably from a stranger being a good samaritan. It looked like one taken when you boarded a cruise ship. The guy wasn't looking at the camera. He was looking down and off to one side. My mind went into overdrive. *He didn't want to be recognized.* These were more than just things. They had to be attached to something memorable in Betsy's life. I stood with my arms folded across my chest, staring at my find.

In the back right side of the drawer was a pink and white striped soft drawstring bag. I carefully untied the ribbon and gently removed the contents, setting them on the bed. There was a hospital picture of a newborn baby, a pink nursery cap, and a set of pink beads with HARPER embossed on them. I figured they must have been Betsy's, and her mother gave them to her just like my mother gave me mine.

My mother considered them a family heirloom.

I looked at the picture—cute baby. But when I turned it over, there was a hand-written date, and the hospital's name stamped on the back.

"Casey, you got something?" Marnie walked over beside me.

"I do." I pointed to the jewelry in the drawer and the bag on the bed. "There's a theme to the jewelry and a story to go with the contents of the bag." I handed Marnie the baby picture. "Look at the back."

She shrugged. "What am I looking at?"

"The picture's dated November 14, 2010. That's almost two and a half years after Betsy graduated from Cape Cod Community College. It also says South Shore Hospital in Weymouth.

I remember Annie telling me that after Betsy graduated from CCCC, she worked for a doctor in Yarmouth, then near the end of the summer of 2010, she moved just outside of Boston to Weymouth. Supposedly for employment at another doctor's office.

Marnie looked puzzled. "I thought Annie and Betsy weren't close friends."

"From what I understand, they weren't close friends … only acquaintances. They grew up together but didn't share the same values. Their strongest link was Buster Adams, and he died ten years ago."

"Casey, didn't Annie mention his name when she came over to my house the day after their ten-year reunion … the morning after they found Betsy's body? I'm confused."

"Yes. I'm seeing a big triangle involving Buster, Betsy, and Annie. Two of the points on the triangle are dead. The third one is Annie, and she's missing."

I took the baby picture back from Marnie. "This is a picture of Betsy's daughter."

Marnie moved over and sat on the edge of the bed.

"Time to share what we've found with the guys," I called for Sam and Maloney to join us.

Sam came in from the living room and walked over beside me. "Maloney will be right in. He's labeling items he wants to take to the station." Did you and Marnie find anything of interest?"

"I'm afraid we did. Annie may be in more danger than we thought." I handed Sam the baby picture and the picture with Betsy and the unknown male.

"Who's baby?" asked Sam.

"I think it's Betsy's."

"And, the unknown male?"

I shrugged my shoulders. "It could be just someone she knew or knows. My guess is he's the baby's father."

Maloney came into the bedroom and walked over beside Sam. "What baby?"

"Casey found some interesting things in the dresser draw." Sam handed Maloney the pictures.

Maloney studied the picture of Betsy and the unknown male. "This dude doesn't want to be recognized." Maloney walked over to the window to catch more light. He tapped the picture. "There's something about this guy. First of all, he looks older than Betsy. I know that doesn't mean anything. Younger girls do keep company with older guys, and this guy isn't old, just older."

Sam took the picture from Maloney. "You're right, he does look older, but there's something else. I can't put my finger on it."

Maloney pulled out a couple evidence bags. "I'll bag it along with the other things Casey and Marnie found."

"Are you girls done in here?" Sam asked as he looked around the bedroom.

I walked over to the window and pulled the shade down. "We're done in here for now. Everything we found is Betsy related and could be significant in solving her murder. But, there's nothing to indicate that Annie was here."

Sam walked to the living room. "Casey, you and Marnie go through the boxes. Maloney and I are going to check out the storage unit."

"Will do," I said.

Three of the boxes had seasonal clothes, and the fourth was books. Marnie and I snaked our hands around the clothes but came up with nothing out of the ordinary.

"I think we should take the books out and fan them to see if there's anything hidden between the pages." I handed a couple to Marnie and took a few for myself.

We were down to the last six books. I gave Marnie two Mary Higgins Clark books. When I started to lift the remaining four out, I realized we might have hit paydirt. I held two up in each hand— "Betsy's yearbooks."

Chapter 38

Maloney and Sam went to Barnstable PD to file a report, and drop off the evidence bags and yearbooks they'd taken from Betsy's apartment. Marnie and I went to my house in Hyannisport.

"I wish we could have gone through Betsy's yearbooks before Maloney entered them as evidence. We need to look at Annie's books again. The only difference is who wrote and what they wrote. When I think about my yearbooks, some people wrote well-worn overworked canned idioms just to say they wrote in your yearbook. It's the original jargon that I want to compare. If I can convince Chief Lowe that they might offer clues to find Annie, I'm sure he'll let me look at them."

I pulled into my driveway. As soon as I opened the car door, I could hear Watson barking for attention. "Better go give the boy a treat. I'm going to take him for a short walk. Then we can get started with our 'homework'.

Marnie smiled. "I'll go with you."

"I welcome the company. I think we might be working well into the night, so we'll order pizza when the guys get here."

Usually, when I take Watson for a walk, my stress levels go down. Not today. I looked at Marnie. "The things we found in Betsy's apartment give us some insight into the person she was. It was like she lived a double life. I think that's what killed her."

"Casey, I'm trying to follow you, but not sure where you're headed," said Marnie.

"I need to recheck Annie's yearbooks, but if I remember correctly, one year Betsy and Mark Mosley were the king and queen of their prom. So, at some point, they were an item." I looked at my watch. I pushed the number one on my cell. "I'm calling Sam to see if they're still at the station."

Sam answered on the first ring. "Casey, you okay?"

"Yeah, I'm as good as can be expected. Are you still at the station?"

"We're just getting ready to leave. What's up?

"Please ask Chief Lowe if you can take Betsy's yearbooks and return them tomorrow. I need to compare them with Annie's."

"He's standing right beside me. I'll ask him." Sam hesitated. "Gotta go. Call coming in from …."

The call ended before he could finish. I looked at my cell. "Sam cut the call short."

Marnie looked puzzled. "Why."

"He got a call from someone, somewhere. It must have been important."

My mind kept flashing a neon sign reminding me that Annie and Mark are missing and Betsy is dead. There is no doubt in my mind there's a connection between the missing and the dead scenarios. Right now, the clock is ticking, and time is not our friend.

"I want to work with the whiteboard. I need to write stuff down. Like I said before, Buster Adams's "accidental" death, Annie and Mark missing, and Betsy's murder are separate incidents but related. What we're lacking is the why. This whole thing started ten years ago with Buster. My thinking is that one person is responsible for this entire mess."

We didn't do much talking on the walk back to my house. Marnie hooked Watson to his run, filled his bowl with Kibbles 'n Bits, and brought him some fresh water. I went inside to get the whiteboard set up, then we both moved to the deck, sat, and continued discussing our thoughts while waiting for Sam and Maloney to show up.

"Have you found anything new on Buster's case? Marnie asked.

"No. With everything that's happened, I haven't worked it as much as I should have. That's going to change. Buster *needs* to talk to me." I took a deep breath. "He *is* the star witness."

We both sat back and vegged out. The quiet felt good, but I knew it wasn't going to last.

Watson jumped up and ran to the corner of the house. Sam and Maloney were pulling into the driveway.

I laughed, "Wish my hearing was half as good as his."

When I heard the car door shut, I called out to tell the guys we were on the deck.

Instead of walking to the backyard, they cut through the house, stopped at the fridge to get a beer, then joined us.

Watson sat outside the door, waiting not so patiently for a head tussle. Sam didn't disappoint him. "Hey, good boy, did momma take you for a walk?"

I smiled. "Momma and auntie did."

I pointed at Sam's bottle. "No glass?" I asked.

"Not this time around." Sam raised his arm. "I don't see any wine. You girls on the wagon?"

"Very funny," I said. We were busy. Besides, we didn't want to get a head start on you two."

Sam and Maloney pulled the other two chairs on the deck closer to us.

"We've got some work to do tonight." Sam sat forward and rested his hands on his knees. "I told Chief Lowe you wanted to compare Annie's yearbooks to Betsy's. At first, he was hesitant. It took some convincing, but he said to go ahead but to have them back within a couple days."

"I can handle that," I said.

"Something else. You know my phone rang, and I had to cut our conversation short." Sam took a deep breath. "I don't want to get anyone's hopes up, but it was my friend, Lt. Tucker, from the Boston PD."

My emotions were on the verge of a breakdown. I wanted to hear but was afraid of what Sam had to say.

"I filled Maloney in on Lt. Tucker on the way over, but I want to give Marnie a little backstory." Sam stood, walked over, and leaned against the railing. "Last year, I attended a Boston PD Communication Conference taught by Lt. Tucker. One of the things he discussed was finding missing persons by pinging off towers. It was a shot in the dark, but I asked for his help. I gave him all the information we had on Annie and Mark, and he told me he'd get right on it."

"Did … did he … ?" I couldn't finish my sentence.

"He's still working on it but wanted to let me know his progress so far."

Marnie pulled her chair over beside mine and took my hand in hers.

"There had been activity on both her and Mark's cell phones since they went missing. We know Annie's provider is Verizon. Lt. Tucker said he should have a printout of her activity tomorrow. He said Verizon doesn't have any record for a Mark Mosley with a Dennisport, MA address. He is checking other providers."

"Does he know if any of the activity on Annie's phone was from off Cape locations?" I asked.

"From what I understand, calls can ping from more than one tower. Or bounce from tower to tower to get from where the call originated to where it ended. I went to the conference but have never had to deal with cell pinging and communication. So, to answer your question, I don't know. The Lieutenant is going to call me back tomorrow. Hopefully, we'll have more answers."

I checked my watch. "It's four-thirty. We need to move inside and get working on those yearbooks. Sam, can you and Maloney go pick up a couple pizzas. We'll call them in. We can eat and work at the same time. I think it would be more productive if we worked together. That way, we can ask questions, discuss possibilities, and bounce ideas back and forth to get positive feedback."

Chapter 39

Marnie ordered two fourteen-inch thin crust, extra crispy pepperoni, cheese, and mushroom pizzas while I prepared the table, then set both sets of yearbooks on the counter, ready for us to go through. My whiteboard was propped up, leaning against the cabinets. Several colored markers and a dry erase eraser were in a box to one side of the board.

I stepped back. "The *war room* is ready."

"What?"

"That's what we called it at the newspaper when discussing certain stories for print," I said. "We've got thoughts, ideas, fragmented storylines, and some facts. If we weave them together and come up with one concrete piece of evidence as to Annie's location, we may be able to move forward. Right now, time is not our friend. The minute hand is advancing the hour hand way too fast."

Marnie pulled a chair out, sat down, and folded her arms on the table.

Without saying a word, I walked over to the whiteboard and picked up red, blue, and black markers, then started to make a diagram in the upper left corner. Buster, written in red, topped the chart. I put the month and year he died beside his name. I wrote *accidental* in black. Next line down, I did the same for Betsy. The only difference was I changed *accidental* to *murder*. Under Betsy's info, I wrote Annie and Mark's names, left a space, and wrote Peter's. The month and year I associated with them was September 2016. Annie and Mark were noted as missing and Peter's involvement was questionable. The last notable individual or individuals were unknown murderers and kidnappers.

Marnie shook her head. "How much crime show television do you watch?"

"We did a lot of "what if" and "whodunit" role-playing when I was in college." I shrugged. "Since my ultimate goal in life was to be a detective, crime investigation studies and my degree in Criminal Justice were a big part of my future. After my police academy accident put an end to my dream, I never thought stuff like this would surface from the bowels of my brain."

"Was drama your minor?" Marnie smiled. "Only kidding. The whiteboard puts things in a visual perspective, almost like an outline."

I walked over and sat beside Marnie. "Exactly."

"Interesting." Marnie stared at the whiteboard. "I have some ideas, but rather than repeat them, I'll wait till the guys get back.

Not five minutes later, I heard car doors close. "Looks like they've returned. I'll get the wine and beer. You get the plates and napkins."

"Sounds good to me."

Sam opened the front door.

Maloney followed, carrying the pizzas. "Anybody hungry?"

"Does a bear shit in the woods?" I laughed and motioned for him to set the boxes on the counter next to the plates.

Sam glanced at my whiteboard. "Looks like Sherlock has been busy."

"I think we're in for a long night." Maloney smiled as he plated himself a slice of pizza.

Sam opened a couple beers for him and Maloney, and I poured a glass of white zin for Marnie and one with ice for me, then held up my arm for our usual toast. "Here's to it, those who get to it, and don't do it, may never get to it, to do it again."

"That's my girl," Sam said as he took a swallow of beer. "Are we eating first, or are we talking and eating?"

"I've got a pad of paper and a pen beside me, so if we eat and banter back and forth without a lot of thought, something helpful

182

might slip out. I remember one of my professors telling our class that too much deep thinking can cloud or alter an incident or an idea."

Sam grinned, "Was that investigation 101 or 102?"

"Smartass," I smirked. "Okay, seriously, let's rehash. This chart helps me keep things in perspective. We know that Buster died *"accidentally"* in 2006. I say accidentally because that's what the ME listed as the cause of death. You know I've been retained by his mother to investigate that finding. She believes he was murdered."

Sam piped in, "For the record, his mother, Amanda Adams, came to you on a recommendation from Annie. And, if I'm not mistaken, Annie also believes Buster was murdered."

I looked around the table. "Correct."

"And, this all came up after Betsy Harper, their classmate, was found murdered the day after their ten-year class reunion," Maloney added.

"Yep," I said. I took a couple of pizza bites and washed them down with a swallow of wine. "Sam, you look thirsty. You ready for another beer?"

"Very Sherlock of you. I'll get it." He stood and walked to the fridge. "Maloney, you ready?"

"I could use one," Maloney reached over between Marnie and me. "Thanks, buddy."

"Let me sum up my whodunit diagram. We have a mixture of names and titles. The names, all except for Peter, were all friends. Two were murdered, and two are missing. The only thing we know about Peter is that he's Mark's brother." I took a deep breath, then continued. "I don't' know for a fact, but I don't think he hung with the same crowd as Buster, Betsy, Annie, and Mark. In my opinion, that makes Peter a missing person of interest. He may be completely innocent of committing a crime but knows who did. In my book, that makes him just as guilty."

Sam walked up to the whiteboard and waved his hand across the list of names. "I agree with everything you said regarding our known players. I don't believe whoever orchestrated the murders and possible kidnappings was a stranger. And, it's possible that Buster's murder, assuming he was murdered, and Betsy's murder may have been done by more than one person."

Maloney leaned forward on the table. "In a nutshell, the person or persons responsible for the missing and the dead is or are still walking around ... a dangerous person that could strike again."

"Betsy is dead. Annie and Mark are missing. We don't even know if they're together." I tried to hold back my tears, but it wasn't going to happen. "My biggest concern is finding Annie."

The mood was somber. We knew we had a night's worth of work still ahead of us. Sam helped me clear off the kitchen table, and Marnie and Maloney went to the living room to get Annie and Betsy's yearbooks.

I made coffee and plated some Oreo's. Sam and Maloney took Betsy's books. Marine and I each took two of Annie's. "If you see or read something that doesn't sound right, or is out of sorts, share it with the rest of us. Since these four were close, I'm sure we'll find duplicate writings. But, on the other hand, we might find interesting "personal" scriptures from mutual *friends*."

"We've examined Annie's before, and, I believe, we've missed something. Now we have Betsy's," Marnie said. "We have to study, scrutinize, and dissect them. Any little concern, we need to look at."

Maloney looked at Marnie. "That's the lawyer coming out, but she's right."

I had both 2003s. Sam, Marnie, and Maloney split up the remaining six. Marnie and I spread out on the kitchen table, and Sam set up a folding table in the living room for himself and Maloney.

"My strategy is to go through both books, comparing them page by page. Disregard the canned sayings. It's the original writings we need to dissect." I laid Annie and Betsy's books side by side. "The other thing we need to pay attention to are the pictures. If either girl is in a picture, note the names of the others."

For the next forty-five minutes, the only noise was when I coughed, and one of the guys slid their chair out to make a bathroom run.

I had a couple pages to go when Sam stood. "I've finished. I'm going to take Watson for a short walk then bring him inside. Be right back."

Five minutes later, the rest of us were done and waiting for Sam to return. "I need a coffee. Any takers?" I asked.

"I'll have another wine," Marnie said.

Maloney shook his head. "Nothing for me."

"Maloney, why don't you move into the kitchen with us," I said. "The table is bigger, so we'll be able to spread out a little more."

Sam returned from walking Watson, gave the boy a treat, and joined us in the kitchen.

Marnie and I closed our books and straightened out our paperwork to make room for the guys. I made my coffee and got Marnie her wine.

"Sam, you want a beer?" I asked.

"Yeah, sure. Thanks."

I got a Coors from the fridge, handed it to Sam, and settled in, ready to start.

"I know we've gone through Annie's yearbooks already," I said. "Before, when we read and talked about things, nothing screamed danger. Now, by comparing Annie's and Betsy's books, I hope something jumps out and yells at us. Something is hiding between the covers, and we have to find it."

I'd marked pages of concern with small tabs of sticky notes. When I glanced at the books in front of Marnie, she'd done the same. "Great minds think alike," I said.

Marnie gave me a puzzled look. "What's that all about? Did you find something?"

"No, not really." I tapped on the books in front of me, then reached across the table and ran my fingers over her sticky notes. I couldn't help but smile. "It's trivial but a much-needed break in our concentration."

Marnie nodded. "Gotcha."

Sam glanced at Maloney and raised his arms in an I-have-no-idea gesture. "Where in the world did we get these two?"

Maloney shook his head. "Beats me, but I think we'll keep them around."

I put Annie's 2006 yearbook and Betsy's 2006 yearbook one above the other and opened the front covers to reveal different ink colors, writing styles, and mostly unrecognizable mini-drawings. "I'll start," I said. "But before I do, why don't you arrange and open the books you have the same way I have the 2006's ." I felt like the teacher my mother wanted me to be.

"I'm going to read names. It's a long shot, but I want to see who they were both friends with throughout high school. I'm trying to establish a close circle of friends. My thinking is that one or more of these persons could offer insight into the personal lives of Annie and Betsy."

For the next hour, we made a list of names, clubs, and their members, teachers, and advisors that appeared to share an attachment with Annie and Betsy. We discussed the journalistic prowess, or lack thereof, displayed by the names listed.

I leaned back in my chair and folded my arms over my chest. "Betsy wasn't a wallflower. And, it appears that Annie, even though she was active in various groups, was more grounded."

"Pray tell. How did you come up with those assumptions?" Marnie asked.

"Back to Criminal Justice 101. It's the study of facial, body, and gestural expressions. Also, group associations, to include gender ratio."

Sam smiled. "I have to give you an A+ for paying attention in school."

"Thanks," I said. "I have more to add. We've scoured these books and are no closer to finding Annie or finding Betsy's murderer. I'm not saying that we've wasted our time. I'm saying that we need to file this information and move on."

Maloney stood, stretched, and walked around the table before sitting again. "What are you suggesting?"

"I'm suggesting we look beyond their fellow students and acquaintances. Many of these people have probably moved on. They could be living anywhere on or off Cape. Most females are probably married, resulting in a name change."

"Meaning that we're beating a dead horse." Sam sighed. "Casey, I agree with you and can see where you're headed. The teachers."

I nodded. "Yep, the teachers. The teachers probably haven't changed much in the ten years since Annie, Betsy, and crew graduated from Barnstable High. Most of the time, teachers knew what was going on between students, in groups or clubs, and even in outside school activities."

Marnie shook her head. "Casey's right. I confided in my teachers many times. My father was, and still is, a lawyer. For most of my early years and continuing through high school, he was very busy first building then maintaining a very successful law practice. My mother was involved in many outside-the-home activities, some involving my father's business. I was an only child, so I had no siblings to confide in. A couple of my teachers became my surrogate parents."

"Point made." I thought back to my school days. "There was no doubt that a couple of my teachers knew me better than my parents."

Sam looked at his watch. "We've got a good hour, hour and a half left before we call it a night. Can I interest anyone in a coffee?"

The three of us raised our hands.

Sam set our coffees on the table, opened the fridge, and took out a bottle of Baileys Irish Cream. "Any takers?"

I looked at Sam. "Do you need to ask?"

We held up our cups.

Ten minutes and little conversation went by before we started back to work.

"Okay, let's get going. Before we put the yearbooks to bed, our next move is to note the teachers who were advisors for the groups Annie, Betsy, and Mark belonged to. Let's collaborate to make sure we got them all." I took my notes and flipped to the page where I'd written down the names of the clubs that Annie belonged to. "Here's what I found for Annie—the Community Empowerment and Leadership Club, the Drawing and Design Club, the Recycling Club, and the Glee Club."

Marnie held up her hand. "Betsy was a member of the Photography Club and the Drawing and Design Club."

"Mark belonged to the B28 TV Club. It was for students interested in video production." Sam smiled.

I looked at Sam. "What's that smirk for."

"Nothing, just thinking back to the day. They didn't have clubs like these when I was in high school."

I smiled. "I'm not even going to ask what they did have."

"Betsy was also a cheerleader," Marnie said.

"Let's make sure we add Buster to the mix. He was a real jock, and coaches seem to know their players sometimes better than their parents do. Peter Mosley was also a jock. Since he graduated in 2003, anything on him would only appear in the 2003 yearbooks. Besides the sports pictures, Buster was in the theatrical group picture." I took my pad of paper and divided it into sections representing the groups our persons of interest belonged to. "I'll read the group's name, and you guys give me the name listed as the advisor."

Since we'd already flagged the group pages, it was easy to compile a list of advisor names. All but a couple were the same for the entire four years.

"I need to change the subject before I forget what I'm thinking. Sam, I know we don't know for a fact that Mark Mosley is missing.

188

Let me rephrase that. We know he's missing, but we can't prove it. We are ninety-nine percent sure he's with Annie, but we can't prove it. You've tried to find family. We only know about his brother, Peter, and we can't find him either. Somehow, we need to get into Mark's house."

"Maloney and I will talk to Chief Lowe tomorrow. I've pulled search warrants on missing persons in Bourne when we couldn't find a family to confirm the person's whereabouts. We pretty much think that Peter Mosley is involved in what's happening but have no proof. His last known address is the same as Mark's. That house may very well be securing much-needed evidence in Annie's disappearance and Betsy's murder. In Mark's case, he's suspected of being in danger, and in Peter's case, he may be the victim of criminal activity. We'll plead our case to the chief."

"Interesting," said Maloney. "When Sam and I talk to Chief Lowe tomorrow, besides the search warrant for Mark's house, we'll stress the need to interview the aforementioned advisors. I don't expect any problem getting an okay for the interviews."

Marnie put her paperwork into a neat pile, folded her hands in front of her, and leaned back in her chair. "My head can't handle any more tonight. Let's close up shop and get a fresh start tomorrow."

"Ditto," I said.

Sam and I stood in the doorway and waved as Marnie and Maloney backed out of the driveway. We let Watson run around the yard a few times before heading inside.

"We looked at a lot of 'stuff' tonight. My gut tells me there are definitely clues between the pages just waiting to be found. We're getting close, but time isn't on our side," I said. "Let's go sit on the deck, enjoy the star-studded sky, and try to relax a little before we go to bed."

As we walked through the kitchen, I took my half-full glass of wine off the table, and Sam grabbed a fresh beer from the fridge. On the way out to the deck, I reached into the jar on the counter and tried to sneak a few doggie snacks into my pocket. From the look on Watson's face and the non-stop wagging of his tail, I knew I had gotten caught.

Sam stretched out in one of the lounge chairs. I laid back in the other one, and Watson curled up between us. Sam reached over and took my hand. Nothing was said.

I looked up at the sky and closed my eyes. *Twinkle, twinkle little star, Annie, tell us where you are.*

Chapter 40

Wednesday

The last thing I remember about last night was getting into bed and kissing Sam goodnight. I was too tired for anything else.

I knew when it was morning because the sunlight was framing the window blinds, and I could smell the inviting aroma of coffee brewing. I heard muffled conversation, hesitation, then more conversation. Since Sam's voice was the only one I heard, I assumed he was talking on his phone. I rolled over to check the time on my alarm clock. It was 8:12. I slid my legs out from under the covers and sat up.

"Ok, we'll meet you at Casey's office at 9:30," Sam said as he walked around the corner into the bedroom. He ended his conversation and put his cell in his pants pocket.

"Who are we meeting at my office?"

"Marnie and Maloney."

"What's the plan?" I asked.

"Maloney talked to Chief Lowe this morning. He's calling Judge Mathews about the search warrant for Mark Mosley's house. The chief figures there won't be a problem, and Maloney will be able to pick it up at the courthouse this morning."

"What about the advisor interviews?" I asked.

"Since the high school is close to the station, Chief Lowe will drive over and talk to Principal Walters directly. The chief doesn't expect a problem but doesn't want to offer too much information about why we want to speak to the advisors." Sam nodded, then continued, " I agreed. At this point, we are trying to see if any of the group advisors can give us insight into Betsy, Mark, Annie, and

Buster's relationships with other group members or students they may have associated with throughout high school."

"Let me get ready so that we can get going." I looked at the piles of papers on the kitchen table. "Can you please put an elastic around those piles and slip them into my briefcase?"

"I'm on it."

I took my coffee and headed to the bedroom to get ready to meet Marnie and Maloney. "Also, please feed Watson and put him on his run."

Sam smiled. "I haven't even said 'I do,' and I'm getting the 'to-do' list."

I stuck my head out the bedroom door and gave him the raised-eyebrow, eyes-wide-open look. "Yep."

It was 9:20 when Sam and I pulled into the parking space behind my office. I'd just turned the key to unlock the door when Marnie and Maloney pulled in and parked beside him.

"Marnie, my briefcase is on the floor behind the passenger seat. Can you please grab it for me?"

"Sure."

Sam and Maloney were already inside talking.

"I'm going to run over to District Court. Judge Mathews is expecting me. Be right back." Maloney headed across the street.

Sam took a deep breath. "Getting that search warrant, and so quickly, is a biggie. We'll make a plan of action, then get started. We'll take my cruiser. I've got plenty of evidence bags, gloves, and my camera. I've also got a fingerprint kit—all detective standard supplies or should be."

Marnie went back to Maloney's car to get her purse.

I looked at Sam. I'd never seen him so removed from the moment. His mental checklist became verbal.

"Casey, we're going to find Annie." He put his arms around me.

Sam had stayed strong for me. Now we had to stay strong for each other. I forced a smile. "I know we will."

Marnie came in the back door just as Maloney walked in the front door. He waved the search warrant in the air. "Judge wants us to keep him informed."

Sam nodded. "That we will do."

"Give me a minute." Maloney took his cell from his pocket. "I told Chief Lowe I'd call him when I got the warrant."

Maloney pushed the speed dial connecting him to the chief. "I just picked up the warrant from Judge Mathews. He asked to keep him informed. I told him we would." Maloney gave us a thumbs up. "We're about ready to head to Mark Mosley's house on Tide's Path in Dennisport. We'll keep you apprised of our progress. If we need assistance, I'll let you know." Maloney ended the call.

Sam, Maloney, and Marnie headed toward the back door. "Let me lock up, and I'll be right there."

Marnie got in behind Maloney, and I sat behind Sam. Since most of the summer tourist crowd had left, Sam figured the traffic wouldn't be bad, so he took 6A to Route 134 to Route 28, then made a left on Depot Street and a hard right onto Tide's Path. Sam pulled into the driveway. Since Sam's car was unmarked and the guys were plain-clothes detectives, our arrival didn't make the neighbors stand up and take notice.

I looked around. "Certainly not an up-and-coming neighborhood. The other day I ran this address through Google. There's a couple of properties that went for over four hundred thousand dollars just around the corner, and one property two houses down that went for over five hundred thousand. That's Cape Cod real estate for you."

193

Maloney walked up to the front door, and Sam went around the house to the back door. Marnie and I stayed beside Sam's unmarked. Both guys knocked, identified themselves, and when there was no answer, they repeated the drill. Again, with no results.

"The bikes are still here. It doesn't look like they've been moved," Sam said. "Let's go in through the back door. The backyard is surrounded by some thick vegetation, so we shouldn't have any peeping toms per se."

"You two stay by the car and note any curious gawkers that might appear. Sam and I will go in through the back. When we're sure it's safe, we'll come get you."

Since I had a license to carry, I'd taken my 9mm from my bedroom safe and put it into my purse before we left to meet Marnie and Maloney. I opened the back door on the driver's side, reached into my purse, took out my gun, and secured it under my shirt, between my belt and the waistband on my jeans.

Marnie caught wind of what I was doing. She cocked her head to one side and, without saying anything, put her hands up in a what-are-you-doing gesture.

I shook my head and waved her off. "Between us girls."

She didn't have time to give me a rebuttal. No sooner did I 'request' her silence, the front door opened, and Maloney called us to join him and Sam.

Before we got to the door, Maloney stepped down to greet us. "I want to forewarn you. There's been nobody here for a while. The stench is nauseating. It took us time to make sure there wasn't a decomposing body. We've opened the back door and some windows, but it's not going to do much good."

The front door went directly into the living room. I cupped my hand over my nose and mouth, walked in, and looked around. It didn't appear that anything was out of place. I was sure it wasn't, but it looked staged. "Where's the smell coming from?"

Maloney pointed to an archway leading to the kitchen.

I walked over to check it out. "This is definitely the source of the stench. Except for half-empty Chinese take-out boxes, an open bottle of milk, a sink full of dirty dishes, and a wastebasket full of trash, this place is somewhat picked up." I shrugged. "Two guys live here?"

Sam came out from what appeared to be a bedroom and joined us. "I'll be right back. I've got to get evidence bags, etc."

Maloney held his handkerchief over his nose and mouth. "When Sam comes back in, we'll figure out where to start. Don't touch anything until you get a set of gloves. I'm not saying this just for evidence's sake. I'm mostly saying it for safety's sake."

I couldn't believe my eyes. There's no way anybody has been in this house for days. I walked to the room Sam came out of. "What the hell …."

Marnie joined me, her sleeve still covering her nose.

"I don't understand," I said. "This room is neat as a pin." The bed was made, and no clothes were strewn on chairs or piled on the floor. The curtains and shades appeared clean and looked relatively new. The walls were white beadboard. A dresser and one nightstand with a nautical-themed lamp sitting on a white doily. A navy-blue tufted headboard was attached to a full-sized frame. I recognized the quilted bedspread. It was navy and white stripes and came from the Christmas Tree Shop.

Marnie headed back to the living room. I followed her. On the opposite wall, a closed-door indicated either another room or a closet. Since two males were supposedly living at this address, I assumed another bedroom was behind the closed door.

"Maloney, did you or Sam look to see where this door leads?" I asked.

"We did. It's a bedroom if you can call it that. It's a pigsty, the exact opposite of the room you and Marnie just saw. Sam said not to touch anything, then went to get his camera, the fingerprint kits, and evidence bags." Maloney hadn't finished speaking when Sam came through the front door.

"Here." Sam opened a plastic bag and handed us each a face mask. "Might help a little." He opened a small folding table he'd brought in from the trunk of his car. "Everything we need is here on the table. I don't want to compromise any evidence we might find on other surfaces." He handed Marnie a notebook and pen. "I'd like you to take notes and label the evidence bags as needed."

"Maloney, I'm going to dust for prints in the unknown room. Once I get inside, we'll see what we're up against. You take the other kit and dust the first bedroom for prints." Sam turned to face Marnie and me. "I want you two to step away from the door."

When I was going for my degree in criminal justice, I got involved in an extracurricular role-playing class. The reality of the scenes and the actors was chilling. The situation was beyond realistic, and the experience was eye-opening. I had no idea what we were about to experience.

Marnie and I put our facemasks and gloves on.

"What the hell," I shivered. "This is like a scene from a horror movie. The bed wasn't made. The shades were pulled down as far as they'd go, leaving an inch of the window exposed. There were piles of clothes, crumpled-up McDonald's bags, open cans of beer, a box of condoms, moldy smelling towels on the bed, a dog leash hanging on a clothes hook, an open package of zig-zag papers, a fishing license issued to Peter Mosley, and a picture torn into tiny pieces, along with remnants of a smoked down roach, in an ashtray on top of the dresser.

I looked around the room again and stopped when I came to the bed. The blanket was jammed between the mattress and the footboard; the top sheet was rumpled and pushed more than halfway down. I saw a brownish-red stain peeking out from the edge of the top sheet. "Sam, I don't want to touch anything, but I think you should look under this sheet." I pointed to what appeared to be dried blood.

Sam walked over to where I was standing. "I'm going to move the blanket and pull the sheet down some more."

Marnie wrote as Sam talked.

"Bingo. It looks like the person who occupied this bed had a serious foot injury. Not only are there bloodstains, but there are black flakes and a black residue ground into the sheets." Sam took a series of pictures, then looked at me and nodded. "We'll take samples back to the lab and have them checked for blood, dead skin, and soot residue from a fire."

I didn't say a word, just stood up and walked towards the closet, opened the door, and froze. "Sam, you need to see this." I backed away. I didn't have to say anything else. Sam reached down and picked up a dirty red and white partially burnt Air Jordan high-top sneaker.

Sam called to Maloney. "Hey, buddy, can you bring me one of the extra-large evidence bags and four small ones."

"Yeah, sure," Maloney called back.

Marnie and I moved away from the bed so the guys could collect what evidence they needed to bag. My mind needed a time-out. I looked around the room, then glanced at the stuff piled on top of the dresser. My eyes stopped—the condom box—it was the same brand as the packets found in Betsy's room at the Sheraton and those found in the seagrass near Annie's burnt car.

"Sam, check this out."

"What?"

"The condom box. Look familiar?" I asked.

"Ah…yep." Sam looked at Maloney. "Call Chief Lowe. We've got to get a team out here.

This location is now part of an active crime investigation."

Sam walked around the outside of the house while Marnie and I sat on the front steps waiting for Maloney to finish his call to Chief Lowe.

A few people, we assumed to be neighbors, walked by to see what was going on. Curiously, none of them stopped to ask questions. I looked at Marnie. "If you lived here and saw people walking around checking out a house either next door or a couple houses away from yours, wouldn't you want to know what's going on? I mean, think about it. To me, Sam and Maloney give off the persona of being a cop, but in reality, they're not in uniform, so in somebody else's mind, they could be Joe Schmo. If I lived around here, I'd want to know who they were."

Marnie shrugged, "I'm sure they'll know soon enough. Mark Mosley may have been a good tenant, but I'm assuming his brother may not have been."

Maloney finished his call and walked back to Marine and I were sitting. "Where's Sam?" he asked.

Before I could answer, Sam appeared from around the corner of the house. "What did the chief say?"

"He's already talked to the chief in Dennisport. Since Chief Lowe has available personnel, Barnstable PD will provide the security teams. I told him we bagged some things we want entered as evidence in Betsy's murder and Annie's disappearance. I also told him we'd taken pictures to substantiate the relationship between the evidence and observations we found regarding the murder and disappearance." Maloney stopped talking and turned toward the street.

Sam folded his arms, backed up a few steps, and did a visual once over of the house and the yard. To avoid any conversation with the streetwalkers, he avoided making eye contact. Instead, he looked at me, raised his eyebrows, cocked his head, and quietly said, "that's why we need a uniformed team here round-the-clock."

Maloney gestured for Sam, Marnie, and me to join him at Sam's unmarked. "Chief Lowe told me he'd have a team here within the hour," Maloney said. "I told him we'd brief them, then head back to the station. The chief is going to wait for us. Meanwhile, he'll get a schedule together so there will be round-the-clock surveillance at Mark Mosley's house."

Marnie and I stayed by Sam's car while the guys walked down to the street to introduce themselves and dismiss the small crowd that had gathered. It took a few minutes and repeated instructions to move on before the streetwalkers decided it was best they heed the detective's request. One couple lingered behind, waiting for the others to leave before they asked to speak to Sam and Maloney.

"Detective, um … my name is Dan Weston, and this is my wife, Mary. We live next door."

Mary pointed to a nicely appointed Cape-style house visible through a sparse hedge of blue rhododendron bushes.

"Are you here about the problems we've been having with the occupants of this house?"

"Problems?" Sam asked.

"Yes. We've lived next door for four years. As we understand it, the house belongs to an off-Cape real estate office that deals in rental property. We don't know the name of the outfit. When we moved in, only one person lived. His name was Mark Mosley. We talked occasionally but never struck up a friendship. About a year or so ago, another person moved in. Mark told us it was his brother."

Even though Sam knew the answer to his next question, he asked anyway, "Do you know his name?"

"He was introduced to us as Peter Mosey, Mark's brother," Dan said.

Mary Weston spoke up. "From the start, I didn't feel comfortable with him. He didn't seem quite right."

"What she's trying to say is that it appeared he was on some kind of drugs. He was spacey if you know what I mean." Dan looked back at Mark's house. "I don't want to be talking out of school, but there were problems between the brothers. Occasionally, when Mark wasn't home, a guy who appeared completely out of Peter's league would come by, stay for an hour or so, then leave. He wasn't dressed in business suit attire, but rather as a model for Ralph Loren."

Maloney walked to the front door of Mark's house, then turned a quarter way around to face Weston's house. He glanced up and down the hedge, nodded, then walked back beside Sam. "You do have a good vantage point from your house to Mark's," Maloney said.

"We do, and not only that. We have a dog who barks when there's any activity in or around our yard," Dan stopped, then continued. "The reason you don't hear him now is because I put him in the house. It wasn't as bad in the beginning, but lately, our dog has had barking episodes all different times of day and night. It was Peter coming home. I didn't want to get involved, so I never said anything to him or his brother. But I will tell you that on most of those occasions, he had to be mixing the alcohol and the drugs. He could barely speak and hardly stand. He'd call his brother's name, and Mark would come out and get him."

Mary took a deep breath before speaking. "The brothers argued one night. I heard Mark tell Peter to get his stuff and move out." Mary looked at her husband, then down at the ground. "Please don't think I was eavesdropping, but my windows were open, and I couldn't help but hear them."

Sam looked at Maloney before addressing the Weston's. "Thank you." He hesitated when he saw the Barnstable PD cruiser pull up. "We've got uniformed security teams from Barnstable assigned to monitor the house and property occupied by Mark Mosley."

Maloney pulled a small notepad and pen from his jacket pocket. "You've both been very accommodating. Since we've got more questions to ask, we'll need you both to come down to the Barnstable Police Department on Phinneys Lane in Hyannis. I'll take your contact information, and we'll be in touch."

After Sam and Maloney briefed the security team, Maloney locked the house down, and Sam walked over to where we were standing. "The chief is waiting for us at the station. We'll fill him in on our findings and drop off the evidence bags," Sam said, then continued, "I want to talk to Chief Lowe about having the Weston's come to the station if we need to run more questions by them."

"Time isn't our friend," Sam said. "I'm going to drop you and Marnie off at your office. Maloney and I will go over to Barnstable PD, fill Chief Lowe in, and discuss our next move. My suggestion is to get the interviews with the school advisors out of the way."

"I'd like to be in on those interviews. Could you call the chief and see if Marnie and I could sit in with you and Maloney? We can observe and maybe add something useful that a female's intuition might pick up on—if you know what I mean."

Sam made the call, and Chief Lowe had no problem with Marnie and me in on the interviews.

We swung by my office so Maloney could get his car. Marnie rode with Maloney over to Barnstable PD. I rode with Sam.

"I hope you don't mind me wanting to sit in on your interviews," I said. "I don't intend to say anything unless, of course, you want me to. But I'll be able to observe the advisor's body language. If they've got nothing to hide, there shouldn't be a problem. On the other hand, if they get fidgety or stumble over words, I can note that. I'm sure Marnie has had some observation training in law school so that she could do the same thing with Maloney. It's your decision," I said.

"As long as the chief is okay with it, so am I."

We met up in the PD parking lot. "Chief said that Principal Walters is expecting us."

We got into Sam's car and headed to Barnstable High School.

Chapter 41

I checked my watch. It was 1:22. "I don't know what time school gets out, but usually, the teachers and administrators are there for at least a couple more hours. Most of the clubs are after school, so if it's meeting day, we may get lucky." I opened my briefcase and took out the list of clubs and the advisors associated with each one. "I made this list from the information we found in the yearbooks we went through. Since the most recent book is ten years old, it may not be entirely accurate. We'll soon find out."

Principal Walters was in his office waiting for us. He stood when we walked in. After Sam introduced us, Mr. Walters sat behind his desk and motioned for us to sit in the four chairs he'd put in front of his desk.

He nodded. "Please call me Paul. Chief Lowe called and briefly filled me in on why you're here. He said you'd like to talk to several of my teachers, who are also advisors to some of the extracurricular clubs offered here."

Sam chose his words carefully. "That's correct. We're investigating a couple of cases involving former students at Barnstable High School."

"Chief Lowe and I go way back. He did tell me that he wasn't at liberty to get specific as to the whys you needed to talk to certain members of my staff. I respect that and will help in any way I can."

"Thank you," said Sam. "What I can tell you is that we're trying to get to know more about four former students. Maybe who they were friendly with, what circles they ran with, their outside interests, or their dreams and goals after graduation. Using two of the former student's yearbooks, we've determined clubs they belonged to throughout their four years at Barnstable High. It's a shot in the dart, but any information the advisors can furnish us could benefit the outcome of our cases."

I took the list we'd composed and gave copies to the principal, Sam, Maloney, and Marnie. "Mr. Walters, I mean Paul. First I'd like to say I'm impressed by the number of clubs and the variety of subjects they cover. Sure has changed since I was in school." I smiled.

"We pride ourselves in offering life experience and community-based involvement clubs to stimulate students outside 'readin', 'writin' and 'rithmatic'. Actually, there are more groups than you have listed."

"I did see that when we were looking through the yearbook, but none of the four students in question belonged to them," I said.

Mr. Walters picked up his list. "Let's get started. The clubs meet fifteen minutes after school ends and usually are in session for an hour to an hour and a half, depending on the curriculum of the day. Today is Wednesday, so Community Empowerment and Leadership Club, Mr.Leonard, advisor; Photography Club, Mr. Bonner, advisor; and Drawing and Design Club, Mr. Richardson, advisor, are scheduled to meet. They meet in rooms 105, 201, and 207, respectively. The Glee Club meets during school hours. Students do not receive core credits for being in the Glee Club but can receive extra credits."

"What time do you leave?" Sam asked.

"I'll be here until 4:30. Because this happened so quickly, I haven't briefed the advisors in question, so they'll have no idea you're coming. It's 2:10. Let me run into each room and tell them you're coming and that you'll explain your visit when you get there." Mr. Walters nodded. "How does that sound?"

"Works for us," Sam said.

"You can wait in my office. Classes end at 2:30, so I'd be outside their doors at 2:25. Let me get going. I'll see you before you leave."

Sam stood up and shook Paul Walters's hand. "Thank you."

I looked at Sam. "What's the plan?"

"We've got three interviews today. Maloney, you and Marnie go to Community Empowerment in room 105. Casey, you go to Drawing and Design in room 211, and I'll go to Photography Club in room 207. Let's get going. We'll find our rooms, do our interviews, then meet back here in Mr. Walters's office when you're finished."

"Sounds good to me." I picked up my briefcase, and we followed Sam out of the principal's office.

I had about seven minutes before I was about to meet the infamous Arthur "Artie" Richardson. Although he didn't say so, I knew Sam had a reason for assigning me to the art teacher interview. I positioned myself just outside of his room so that when the last student exited, I'd immediately walk in. Because Principal Walters visited his classroom, Richardson knew someone would be coming to talk to him. And, in my opinion, he knew exactly why. I didn't want to give him time to organize his thoughts or form a game plan. Then again, I could be all wrong. I knew I had to be impartial. I wasn't here to question him about Betsy's murder or Annie's disappearance or have him explain how to '*caress the grass, paint the skies, and dance in the flowers.*' I was here to get information about groups or circles the girls and Mark were involved with and people the three were close to back in high school.

I knew Sam was down the hall in room 207 and was sure his interview with the advisor to the Photography Club was going to be short. If I could make Richardson believe my reasons for conducting the interview and keeping him talking, I knew Sam would join us when he finished in 207.

At exactly 2:30, the bell rang, signaling the end of the school day. I moved across the hall to stay clear of the exiting students.

The last person to exit 211 was Mr. Arthur "Artie" Richardson. It appeared he planned to continue walking but stopped when he saw me standing across from his room. He walked over beside me and extended his hand to shake mine. "Are you the person here to interview me?"

"I am." I introduced myself, making sure to keep eye contact. "If we can step back in your classroom, I have a few questions. It won't take long." I had the feeling he felt too comfortable with me. Almost like he knew me. I thought back to the voice-disguised telephone call to my office. The person who called said, 'I know what you're up to, and I know where you are.' There was something about the voice coming out of the person standing in front of me and that disguised telephone voice—smooth and proper.

He pulled a chair up for me beside his desk. Before we sat down, he walked to the back of the room and closed the door. I wasn't comfortable having the closed door to my back. *Stay calm.*

"Principal Walters didn't say why you were interested in talking to me. I'd feel more comfortable if I knew what was going on."

"I'm not a liberty to disclose why I'm here. I can tell you that I'm here at the request of the Barnstable Police Department to help conduct interviews that will hopefully give them insight into a couple of cases they're working on. You aren't the only person being interviewed. We're trying to connect with friends or acquaintances of two students who graduated from Barnstable High School in 2006. We're beginning with the school clubs they belonged to. People tend to bond with members and advisors of those respective clubs, sometimes more than their fellow students."

Without hesitation or batting an eyelash, Richardson asked, "Who are the students you're speaking of?"

"Betsy Harper and Annie McGuire." I didn't say another word. I wanted him to be the first to speak.

I tried to imagine what was going through his mind. He slid his chair back, stood, and turned to face the blackboard. "What do you want to know?" he asked as he picked up an eraser and cleared the assignment he'd previously written on the board.

I was bull-shit. "First of all, I'd like your undivided attention. I won't take up much of your time if you answer my questions. But, it's up to you. I can sit here until the janitor comes to clean and lock your room—your choice." I knew Sam wouldn't let me be alone with Richardson much longer. I sat back in my chair and crossed my arms over my chest.

Arthur "Artie" Richardson gently put the eraser back in the tray and slowly turned to face me. His eyes were dark and daring.

I was scared but couldn't let him know. "I'm trying to establish a group of people that Betsy and Annie were close to in high school and may have continued that friendship after they graduated."

As if by a wave of a paintbrush, Richardson's persona changed. His eyes softened, and the tension vanished from his body. "They both were very talented. Up until a few years ago, I had pictures Betsy painted hanging on my display wall. I still may have them in my storage closet."

"What about Annie? According to the write-up under her graduation picture in the 2006 yearbook, she also had pictures affixed to the walls in the art room." I leaned my elbow on his desk. I wanted to call him out. I wanted to interrogate him as a suspect, but it wasn't my place to do so. We had no positive proof that he was involved in Betsy's murder or Annie's disappearance. But, there was no doubt in my mind that he was.

Richardson moved away from the blackboard and took a couple of steps closer to me. "Um, I believe Annie took her paintings home just before graduation."

I needed to change the way this interview was heading. "Mr. Richardson, we got sidetracked. Let's get back to the reason I'm here." I knew my next question was overstepping my authority, but

206

the climate was perfect for getting a reaction that could prove interesting in finding Annie. "As I'm sure you know, Betsy Harper was murdered." I didn't go any further. I was trying to get him to add to my sentence.

He turned, moved a few steps away from me, then said without demonstrating any emotion, "I read it in the *Tribune*."

"I've looked at the yearbooks from 2003 to 2006—Betsy's to be exact. I'd say that you were one of her favorite teachers." I smiled. "Some of the teacher and fellow students scripted scribblings reminded me of mine some twenty or so years ago."

Richardson was like a stone statue. Without moving anything but his eyes, I watched as he glanced at the wall clock hanging over the door leading to the hallway.

I had to keep going. "I also read the verses in Annie McGuire's yearbooks. You wrote the same thing in hers. Something about *caressing the grass, painting the skies, and dancing in the flowers.*"

There was a chill in the air.

Before I could say anything else, the door below the clock opened, and Sam walked in.

"Sam, I'd like you to meet Arthur Richardson. He's head of the art department and the advisor who leads the arts and design club here at the high school."

Sam knew I was playing a game. He fell right in step and walked over to shake Artie Richardson's hand. "One of my favorite classes in school. I contemplated going into design, but as good as I thought I was, I really wasn't. Instead, I went into law enforcement."

"That was two totally unrelated fields." Richardson smiled.

Sam looked around the room and stopped when he got to me. "Casey, are you finished talking to Mr. Richardson?"

"I am." When I looked at the art teacher, something flashed in my mind. "Thank you," I said. "If there's anything else, Detective Summers will contact you." I didn't shake Richardson's hand, just walked past Sam and out the door.

Sam gave the teacher a nod and followed me out.

I waited until we got three rooms away from 211. "Sam, he's hiding something. I can't put my finger on it, but give me time, and I'll figure it out."

"Hey, you weren't in there to interview him. You were there to get information on close contacts that Annie and Betsy had in high school—friendships that both girls may have kept up after graduation."

"I know, and I tried to get him to furnish that information. He didn't."

"So, if he didn't furnish any information, what were you two talking about for the last three-quarters of an hour?"

"Oh, was it that long? Let's meet up with Maloney and Marnie so we can all sit down and talk without repeating everything."

Sam stopped, but I kept walking. When he got behind me, he tapped me on my shoulder.

I turned to look at him. "What?" I asked.

He shook his head. "You know what. You pushed the envelope, didn't you?"

"Well, maybe a little. There's something about that guy that rubs me the wrong way. I jotted a few things down. When I caught him trying to see what I wrote, I stopped and turned the recorder in my mind on." I smirked. "He didn't like that."

Before Sam could respond, his cell rang. "Hello." The ID read restricted. He motioned me to follow him as he walked to the end of the hallway. "Hi, Larry."

My breathing quickened. *Please have information on Annie.*

"I'm in the hallway at Barnstable High School. We just finished some interviews. I'm with Casey. We're meeting up with Maloney and heading back to the PD. Can I call you back in fifteen minutes?"

"I'll be waiting. I've got some information."

Sam ended the call and punched in Maloney's number.

He answered on the first ring. "What's up?"

208

"I just got a call from Lt. Tucker. He has information and questions regarding Annie and Mark's disappearance. Are you finished with your interviews?"

"We're finished and waiting for you in the front office," Maloney said.

"Be right there."

I heard Sam tell the lieutenant. that he'd be back to the PD in fifteen minutes, so I didn't engage in conversation.

Maloney and Marnie were waiting for us at the door.

"Meet you at the station," said Sam. "Call Chief Lowe. He needs to be in on this."

Even though we were only minutes from the station, Sam turned on his siren.

Chapter 42

The duty desk officer directed the four of us to go to Chief Lowe's office.

The chief was sitting at the head of the conference table at the far end of his office. He motioned us to take seats. "Sam, you've got the floor."

"I received a call from Lt. Tucker. As you know, he's been working on getting cell phone information on Annie and Mark's cell phone numbers." Sam continued as he dialed the lieutenant's number, "He has information ...."

Lt. Tucker answered on the second ring.

"Larry, it's Sam. We're back at the station, and Chief Lowe has joined us. What have you got?"

I took a pad of paper from my briefcase to take notes.

The lieutenant began. "We ran the cell numbers for Annie McGuire and Mark Mosley that you furnished us. It appears they were in contact with each other many times long before they went missing. There was no contact between them since they went missing. I'm assuming it's because they're together. Since I had Casey's cell number, I noticed that she and Annie were in frequent contact with each other. Mark Mosely's phone records reflect calls from a burner phone, and as I said before, he and Annie had a history of back and forth phone calls."

Lt. Tucker hesitated, so I spoke up. "I haven't talked or seen Annie since last Wednesday. I've tried to reach her via her cell, but she never picked up."

"That's about right," Lt. Tucker said. "I say about because her phone pinged off towers around the Duxbury, Plymouth, and Hanson area last. There also wasn't any activity on Cape Cod towers. But, not only her phone, Mark Mosley's too. It appears they were together and off Cape. Then, after that Wednesday, there wasn't any activity on either phone."

I looked up at the ceiling and rocked back and forth. I didn't want to hear that.

"Can you fax me a copy of their phone records?" Sam asked.

Chief Lowe wrote his fax number on a Post-it Note and handed it to Sam.

"Lieutenant, here's the direct number to Chief Lowe's office."

"I'm sending the fax now. You should have it momentarily," said Lt. Tucker.

"Got it," said Sam.

"Thanks, Larry. We'll get to work on this. I'll get back to you."

"You're welcome. You know where to find me if you need help." Lt. Tucker ended the call.

Marnie and I looked at each other. I knew we were on the same wavelength. Annie hated to go over the bridge connecting the Cape to the mainland.

The chief took the report from Sam, made two additional copies, then gave one back to Sam and one to Maloney.

"Sam, this can't be happening," I said. "If I've told you once, I've told you a thousand times—Annie McGuire hated to go over the Bourne or Sagamore Bridge. This phobia isn't anything new. It goes way back. For some reason, she's paranoid about crossing over the canal."

Sam glanced at Maloney. Then they looked at Marnie and me.

Sam spoke first. "Because of her phobia, there had to be a compelling reason for her to make the trip. That is, of course, if she made the trip willingly. If she had no control of the situation, she could have been forced to leave the Cape."

Maloney nodded. "Either way, it appears she's, or at least her phone is, on the mainland."

I felt helpless. "Duxbury, Plymouth or Hanson. I've never heard Annie mention knowing anyone who lived in any one of the three towns. I've never been to Duxbury. When I was at the *Tribune*, I did go to Plymouth for an Ice Cream Sundae Harbor Cruise with a few people from work. I've never been to Hanson, but the name sounds familiar for some reason."

"This is my take of the over-the-bridge situation." Sam leaned forward on the chief's desk. "First, we know that Annie didn't drive over the bridge. I think she and Mark were taken over the bridge by somebody who had a part in setting Annie's car on fire. I don't know about Mark, but we all know Annie wouldn't have gone willingly. And I don't believe Mark would have let any harm come to her. They may have been drugged and didn't know what was happening. As far as phone records showing calls from Annie's phone to Mark's phone to and from the off Cape locations I mentioned, somebody besides Annie and Mark could have orchestrated those calls to throw us or anyone looking for them off course."

"Larry, thank you for your help. I'll be in touch," Sam ended the call.

"We need to take a trip over the bridge," Sam stood and paced the floor. "Chief, we need a plan of action before we go off Cape. And, since it's almost 6:00, I suggest Maloney, Casey, Marnie, and myself work on that tonight and head out tomorrow morning. If that's okay with you, I'll give you a call before we leave."

The chief got up from his chair and walked over to Sam. "I'll agree but only if you agree to call me, even with the slightest bit of information or concern. I don't want you going rogue. If you need backup from one of the local departments, I'll make the call."

"Duly noted." Sam reached out to shake Chief Lowe's hand. "We're a team."

We said our goodbyes and collected our good-lucks as we left the chief's office.

"We've got work to do," Sam said. "Why don't you guys come over to Hyannisport. It's closer. We'll throw some dogs on the grill and start hashing out our plans for tomorrow."

Marnie looked at Maloney, then nodded. "Right behind you."

Chapter 43

Sam and Maloney took Watson for a walk while Marnie and I scrambled to get a quick supper together.

"There's so much running through my head that I don't know where to start. We're heading into unfamiliar territory, which will be challenging. Sam is probably the most familiar with the area," I shrugged. "My brain has been running so many scenarios that they're starting to overlap. I'll take copious notes, then go back and highlight what stands out most to me."

"We're up against a bomb that could go off at any time. The biggest thing we have going for us is Annie." Marnie took a deep breath. "She's been around *crime* for enough time to know how to keep her cool."

"You're right. As long as Annie can disguise herself as a player and distance herself from being the subject, I think she'll hold up," I said. "She's strong. I'm counting on her to build that wall and not let her abductors break through."

Marnie glanced over at me. "Since we don't know Mark, his actions could convey a different story. Plus, we don't know who they're keeping company with—if anyone."

I walked to the refrigerator and took out the fixings for supper.

Marnie took them from me and set them on the counter. "I'll get the dogs ready if you go outside and start the grill."

"I'm on it," I said as I went out to the deck.

It wasn't two minutes later when Sam, Maloney, and Watson walked around the side of the house.

"Doing my job?" Sam smiled. "I'll hook Watson to his run, then take over."

"It's all heated and ready to go. We'll eat inside tonight." I turned to go in just as Marnie was carrying the plate of dogs out.

Marnie handed the plate to the guys then joined me back inside. The guys stayed on the deck.

I looked at the table. "You found the potato salad. I've got some chips too, but I think there's enough salad."

"You get us some wine, and I'll grab the guys a couple beers," Marnie said. "Meet you on the deck."

I brought Marnie her wine and took a sip of mine. "I'm going back inside."

The copy of the report Lt. Tucker faxed to Chief Lowe's office was on the kitchen table. I set my glass down and picked up the report. It was two pages with information on cell towers—what they are and how they're used in an investigation, along with two more pages describing what pinging a cell phone refers to. At a quick glance, I assumed this might have been part of the package the lieutenant used at one of the conferences where he spoke. I shuffled through the rest of the report. The fifth page addressed Annie and Mark's phone records. There have to be clues hiding between the lines, and we need to find them before heading over the bridge in the morning. Just as I set the pages back on the table, Sam, Maloney, and Marnie came in from the deck.

Sam put the platter of grilled dogs on the table. He watched me move the lieutenant's report to the counter. "Did you find it interesting?" he asked.

Marnie and Maloney had already taken a seat. Sam pulled out a chair for me, then sat in the empty one between Maloney and me.

"All I did was skim the general information part." I shook my head. "This is going to be like cramming for a test." I reached over, took a hot dog from the platter, and a scoop of potato salad.

I glanced at Marnie and saw her eyes move from watching me speak to waiting for a reaction from Sam. There was none.

The silence was killing me.

I ate the last bite of my hot dog, then stood and walked around, trying to gather my thoughts. I took my laptop off the counter and handed it to Sam. "Can you pull up maps of Hanson, Duxbury, and Plymouth and list places of interest in and around the towns? I know I went on a class trip to Plymouth to see the big rock." I sighed, "that was too many years ago, but let's give it a try."

Marnie cleaned up the kitchen, Maloney took care of the grill, and I made copies of Lt. Tucker's report while Sam did some computer research.

Ten minutes later, we were all sitting around the table, ready to delve into the report, discuss our options and make plans for our trip off Cape.

"I'll start," said Sam. "Plymouth and Duxbury list museums, beaches, one has a concert venue, and, of course, Plymouth has the *rock*. Hanson has even less. They have a brewing company, a bowladrome, a private company that offers helicopter rides and several hiking trails."

"That's all you found?" I asked.

Sam nodded his head. "Yep."

"You said there were several hiking trails. Were any of them connected to campsites?" I leaned back in my chair, trying to find something useful in what little information Sam had to offer.

"It appeared that although there were six trails mentioned, only four are still used. Those four are connected to an active town-owned campground. The other two don't exist anymore. The land they were on is now part of a housing area known as Camp Wampatuck," Sam said.

"I've never been to Hanson, but for some unknown reason, the name Wampatuck is trying to talk to me. I need some thinking room. I'm going outside for a few." I picked up my pad of paper and a pen, then without saying anything else, went out on the deck, moved one of the chairs to face away from the house, sat, and stared out over the backyard. I kept writing the word Wampatuck over and over again. I closed my eyes and rocked back and forth. "Talk to me," I whispered. "Camp Wampatuck … Camp Wampatuck … Camp Wampatuck." I jumped up and ran inside.

Sam stood. "Casey, you okay?"

"I am. And, I know why the name Camp Wampatuck is familiar." I paced the kitchen as I talked. "My mother …my mother went to Camp Wampatuck. It was a summer camp for girls. I remember her stories. She loved it. She wanted me to go. Every summer, for about five years, she'd tell me the stories and try to convince me how much fun I'd have." I smiled. "I wanted no part of it."

Marnie raised her eyebrows and, without moving her head, looked from Sam to Maloney, then back to Sam. "Am I missing something? Casey, where are you going with this?"

"Think about it. Plymouth, Duxbury, and Hanson are, for the most part, quiet bedroom towns. They're all a straight shot down Route 3. You have to veer off Route 3 for a short distance, but that's nothing when you're coming from Boston." I took a deep breath, then continued, "Duxbury and Plymouth are more populated than Hanson."

Sam nodded. "I think I get where Casey's headed, but before we start concentrating our sites on one particular place, let's look at Lt. Tucker's report. Hopefully, we can tie the cell phone information he's furnished us with areas of interest I pulled from my computer search."

It was 7:30. It had been a long day, and we still had work that was going to take us hours into the night.

Sam picked up his copy of the report. "Let's get started. Maloney, I don't know about you, but I haven't had hands-on experience regarding cell towers affecting the outcome of a case. I've read about, studied, and used information gathered from others but never was involved in the initial process."

"Other than from Lt. Tucker, I think my father has. On several occasions, he talked about how the Boston PD established the location of a homicide he was investigating, but I don't recall the details. It actually might be a case he worked with Lt. Tucker."

Sam nodded. "Good to know. We may need to tap into that pool of information. What I do know is that sometimes it can take up to 12 pings to close in on the exact position of the phone. When a cell phone is on, its signal is received by two, three, or more wireless towers. When the cell phone user makes or receives a call, the cellular network analyzes the phone's position. It determines which tower, or cell, is best positioned to provide the wireless service. Because of this overlapping service coverage, any mobile phone that is turned on maintains connections with several nearby towers."

"You paid attention at the conference," said Maloney.

"Is that the reason both Annie and Mark's phone show contact with Duxbury, Plymouth, and Hanson towers?" I asked.

"It's a strong possibility," said Sam. "The other thing is that the phone does not have to be actively engaged in a call to be connected to a tower, but it must be turned on."

Maloney leaned forward on the table. "If that be the case, their phones are or were turned on."

Sam shifted slightly in his chair to face me. "Casey, didn't you say you and Annie got new phones not too long ago?"

"I did. We got Samsung G7s from the Verizon store in Hyannis."

"That means you both have smartphones. I believe a smartphone is constantly communicating with cell phone towers to find the strongest signal. The tower that communicates with the cell phone has a limited range. Therefore, if records show that a specific cell

218

phone was communicating with a specific phone tower, then the police will know that the cell phone was within the geographical limits of the tower."

I picked up my copy of Annie's and Mark's information. "We know this report indicates their phones pinged off a tower in Plymouth, a tower in Duxbury, a tower in Hanson, and a few times off a tower in Bourne." I shrugged. "Does that mean that Annie's and Mark's phones pinged off Plymouth, then Duxbury en route to Hanson? Cause according to this report, the last location off Cape is the Hanson tower."

Sam took his cell phone from his pocket. "Google, how many miles is it from Bourne to Plymouth?" Google reported twenty-six. "How many miles from Plymouth to Duxbury?" Google reported twelve. "How many miles from Duxbury to Hanson?" Google reported fourteen miles.

"If I understand this tower stuff, the pinging, and the trail from tower to tower, then Hanson is the end of the line. Lt. Tucker didn't indicate there was any communication closer to Boston." I tapped my fingers on the table. "My suggestion is that we start in Hanson."

"I agree," said Sam. "Maloney ... your thoughts?"

Maloney nodded. "We don't have a lot to go on, so we have to start somewhere."

"Alright." Sam put the report back in order. "We should leave here around 7:00 a.m. I'll give Chief Lowe a call in the morning. He said he'd call the chief in whichever town we wanted to start in. From what we just observed, I want to start in Hanson. I'll ask Chief Lowe to give the chief in Hanson a brief explanation of the situation and let him know we're on our way up to meet with him."

I looked at my watch. "I don't know about you guys, but I'm beat. Let's call it a night."

"I'm with you." Marnie rubbed her face. "I'm exhausted, and it's not going to get any easier tomorrow ... mentally or physically."

I walked with Marnie and Maloney to their car while Sam took Watson for a jaunt around the house. "See you guys in the morning." I waved as they pulled out of the driveway.

Sam was waiting on the front steps. Watson curled up at his feet. "Sherlock, I'm tired. Let's get to bed." He opened the door, took my hand, and guided Watson and me inside.

Chapter 44

Thursday

The alarm went off at 6:00. I wanted to pull the pillow over my head and pretend I didn't hear it. I reached over and shut it off, then rolled back to wake Sam up. He wasn't there. "Hey, buddy, where are you?"

He came around the corner, still in his Joe Boxers and holding his toothbrush. "I was in the bathroom."

I managed to form half a smile. "You almost done, or do you want to share half the sink?"

He laughed. "It's all yours. I'll get dressed, then take Watson out, but I'm not going to make coffee. We'll stop at Dunkins' at the Sagamore rotary."

"Yeah, yeah, yeah … whatever."

I slipped on a pair of jeans and my Patriot sweatshirt. Sneakers were the footwear of the day in case we ended up off-road exploring. Sam was still out with Watson, so I took the time to gather my notes from the night before, the report from Lt. Tucker, a fresh pad of paper, and a couple of pens.

I was about to head out the door to see where Sam was when I heard a car pull into the driveway. It was Marnie and Maloney. I greeted them at the door. "Come on in. Sam took Watson for a walk. He should be back momentarily."

Five minutes later, Sam knocked on the back sliding door. "I'm ready. The boy is hooked to his run. He'll be fine till we get home."

"Ready to get this show on the road?" I asked.

Sam took his phone from his pocket and dialed Chief Lowe's number. When the chief answered, Sam put him on speaker. "Morning, chief. We're five minutes from leaving for Hanson."

"I'll call Chief Marshall, give him a briefing, and let him know you'll be there within the next hour and a half. Give me a call either when you have something to report, or you're on your way back."

"Will do." Sam ended the call.

I gathered my stuff and followed Marnie and Maloney to his cruiser. Marnie and I sat in the back, and Sam rode shotgun. I felt anxious and scared both at the same time. We had bits and pieces of information but nothing concrete. And, worst of all, time wasn't on our side.

Maloney rode through the Dunkins' drive-thru for coffee, then continued over the Sagamore Bridge and onto Route 3 north. Traffic was mild, certainly not like the summertime on and off Cape fiasco.

I thought of Annie and how much she hated the fourteen-hundred-foot ride over the water. Halfway across the bridge, I reached over and took Marnie's hand. *Annie, where are you?*

It was 8:20 a.m. when we pulled into the parking lot at the Hanson Police Department. The four of us walked into the lobby. Marnie and I stayed in the waiting room while Sam and Maloney checked in with the duty officer.

The guys walked back to where we were standing.

"Chief Marshall is expecting us," Sam said. "The duty officer said the chief is finishing up his morning meeting and will be with us in about ten minutes." Sam walked over to the opposite wall to look at a glass-enclosed showcase filled with pictures, accolades, and trophies earned by the department. There was also a section depicting youth-related activities sponsored by the PD.

222

Maloney joined him. "Have you ever been in a fishing tournament?"

"Not one dedicated to youth. I was never much of a fisherman. Baseball, football–no basketball—Baseball and football were my *vices*. How about you?"

Maloney laughed, "The only fishing I did was off the end of my uncle's wharf at his summer camp on Rocky Pond in Boylston. I was so excited when I caught a kiver. Then I felt sorry for the fish, threw it back in, and watched it swim away."

"Looks like it's kinda a big deal for the kids around here. They've got four different tournaments, all dated this summer, featured in the case."

"Small towns can do things like that." Maloney nodded. "Remember, I grew up in Boston."

"Yep, you're right," Sam said.

The guys walked over to where we were sitting. Before they could say anything, the duty officer motioned us to come to his desk. "Chief Marshall is ready to see you now."

We followed the officer to the chief's office.

"Thank you," Sam said before addressing the chief. "Chief Marshall, I'm Sam Summers, lead detective for the Bourne PD, but because of this case, I'm working with Barnstable." Sam turned toward Maloney. "Detective Russell Maloney is with the Barnstable PD." Sam moved to his right between Marnie and me. He held out his right hand. "Casey Quinby is a private investigator from Barnstable, a former investigative reporter for the *Cape Cod Tribune*, and a 'friend' and off-the-books investigator for most of the Cape's PDs. Marnie Levine is an Assistant District Attorney for the Barnstable DA's Office."

Chief Marshall stood, came out from behind his desk, and reached out to shake our hands. "I received a call from my buddy at Barnstable PD. Chief Lowe gave me a very brief overview of why you're here. He said you'd fill me in on the details." Chief Marshall motioned for us to sit in the four chairs in front of his desk as he walked behind it and sat down facing us.

Sam took the lead. "A week and a half ago, Betsy Harper was found murdered in her room at the Sheraton in Hyannis."

Chief Marshall nodded. "I remember reading about that."

Sam continued. "She was at the Sheraton celebrating her ten-year class reunion from Barnstable High School. Annie McGuire, the administrative assistant to Mike Sullivan, the Cape and Islands District Attorney, was also a class member. The class president, Mark Mosley, and Annie McGuire are now missing. Both were at the reunion. And, to add fuel to the fire, a ten-year-old case involving the death of Buster Adams, another member of the class of 2006, could be the underlying reason creating this whole scenario. The ten-year-old case was deemed accidental. In looking into the case, it may have been murder." Sam took a deep breath. "Also, Annie's car was found burned in a remote section of Wellfleet. We've conducted a full fire investigation, searched Betsy's, Annie's, and Mark's residences, and have linked evidence found in each place together." Sam leaned forward on the chief's desk. "Why are we here? I have a friend on the Boston PD who's well versed in cell tower tracing. Before Annie's and Mark's phones went completely dead, they pinged off towers from Bourne, over the bridge to Plymouth, Duxbury, and Hanson."

The chief was taken in by the information. "Fortunately, I've never had to, and hopefully will never have to use that technology. So, please continue. You named Plymouth, Duxbury, and Hanson. Why did you choose Hanson first?"

"We researched the three towns and surrounding areas looking for a somewhat remote but accessible place where two people, two kidnapped people, could be kept without causing notice to the general public." Sam took out his notes. "I did a computer search of places of interest and things to do in the three towns. There were six hiking trails listed in Hanson. The site said four trails are still active and located in the Camp Kiwanee campgrounds. The other two don't

224

exist anymore. They were on land now occupied by a housing area known as Wampatuck Estates." Sam looked at me and nodded.

"When Lt. Tucker's report named the three towns, I, of course, recognized Plymouth and Duxbury. I'd heard the name Hanson but couldn't remember why," I said. "When Sam told us about the hiking trails and Camp Kiwanee and Camp Wampatuck, I asked him to look up Camp Wampatuck. He found a Camp Wampatuck memories website. It was a summer camp for girls. My mother went there. I remember her talking about the cottages with Indian names. I think the girl's camp closed in the 1990s, but maybe one or two of those cottages could still be standing."

Chief Marshall shook his head. "Any of the cottages not taken down by humans have deteriorated over the years and fallen on their own. The only thing left standing is an abandoned cottage on a small island in Wampatuck Pond. The island is privately owned, and at one time, the owner started to refurbish it. But, as I understand it, there was some sadness in the family, and he stopped working on it. The other thing is, it's only accessible by boat. We haven't had any problems with parties or squatters in the cabin. Sometimes one or two fishermen will pull up on the island and fish, but we haven't had any complaints, so we let them be. Besides, years ago, so I've been told, the fishing in Wampatuck Pond was great, but today not so good. I'm not a fisherman, but my friends that are don't like to fish there. They said the fish are too small. As a result, there isn't much going on."

"Is there a boat ramp?" I asked.

"Yes, there is. A ramp and a parking lot for six cars and boat trailers."

"Does the department have a boat?" Sam asked.

"Because we have a considerable number of ponds and lakes in and around Hanson, we do."

Sam's face wrinkled. "Do you think we could go out to the cottage while we're here? I'm probably being over-cautious, but that's the detective in me. I want to be sure it's empty."

"I'll go out there with you, but I'm not qualified to operate the boat. Give me a minute to make one of my officers available." The chief got up from his desk and left his office.

We waited in the lobby for the chief to return.

He was back in less than ten minutes. "I'll ride in the truck with my officer. You can follow us. It's literally five miles away." The chief glanced out the window. "Here he is now."

We all walked outside and got into our respective vehicles to make the short trip to the pond.

I looked at Maloney and Marnie before I spoke. "Sam, do you think we might find something or somebody inside that cottage?"

"I don't know."

Chapter 45

It may have only been five miles to our destination, but it felt like an eternity to me. There was only one other car and trailer in the parking lot. Marnie and I stood beside Maloney's unmarked while the guys walked over to the truck. The officer backed the trailer up until it was partially in the water, then cranked down the line holding the boat until it started to float. He handed the chief the rope.

"I'm going to pull the truck and trailer over to the space in the corner."

Sam stood beside the boat, giving it the once over. "Do you have many calls where you have to take the boat out?"

The chief nodded. "Mostly in the summer. We've got our share of recreational water sites for a small community. As far as this immediate area, not so much. Many of the houses in King's Landing and the Wampatuck Estates have pools. Also, Wampatuck Pond is pretty murky and muddy in spots."

Marnie and I took in the scenery. "This is beautiful," I said. "My mother always wanted me to spend a couple of weeks at Camp Wampatuck—like she did." I watched the ripples in the water as the officer leveled the boat for us to climb in.

The boat had seating for six people, plus the operator. There was also a little door that I assumed led to a small galley. I wasn't in any mood to ask if I could look below deck. I sat staring at the small island directly in front of us. Under other circumstances, I'd welcome the adventure, but not today. I folded my hands in front of me and fiddled with my fingers trying to divert my thoughts away from our destination. It didn't work.

It appeared our pilot knew the area well. He headed for a partially hidden opening that housed a not-so-well-maintained dock. But then, the island and the cottage had been abandoned for years, so I imagined that nothing had been maintained. The foliage was extremely overgrown, but the path to the house was pretty worn down.

We stood beside the boat until the officer finished securing it to the dock. When he finished, he did an eyeball survey of the area.

"Do you have any problems here?" I asked.

"No, not really," he said. "Just a precaution." He led the way. The chief, Sam, and Maloney followed. Marnie and I brought up the rear.

The windows were all covered on the inside with cardboard or plastic. Between the glass and inside coverings on four windows were bright yellow signs with bold letters screaming **NO TRESPASSING**.

"When was the last time anyone was inside?" Sam asked.

The chief walked over to what appeared to be the front door. He stood back, looking the door up and down.

"Something wrong, chief?" asked Officer Bisbee.

"I'm not sure. You're usually the person who does the property checks—right?"

"Yes, sir, I am."

"When was the last time you were here?"

"About two weeks ago."

The chief folded his arms. "Is there anything about this door that is cause for concern?"

It didn't take the officer long to reply. "There certainly is. The padlock is new. That wasn't the one on the door the last time I was here."

Chief Marshall unlocked his holster, took out his 9mm, and backed away from the door. Sam, you stay here with me. Officer Bisbee, you and Officer Maloney go around to the back of the house. Use your radio and signal me when you're there. I'd bet money on it that you'll find the same kind of lock on the back door." Maloney and

228

Officer Bisbee followed the chief's direction and readied their weapons.

Within seconds, Officer Bisbee reported that the back door was a carbon copy of the front door.

Marnie and I stepped back away and tried to take some cover behind a huge oak tree. My heart was pounding.

Sam stood on one side of the door, and the chief stood on the other. The chief whispered into his radio, "On the count of three, shoot the lock off. If there's no return fire, kick the door in. We'll do the same."

I felt like I was on the set of *Blue Bloods*, and Mark Wahlberg was going to come running down the path with a camera crew behind him. No doubt I was scared shitless, and I was sure Marnie felt the same way.

The only shots fired were friendly fire. The guys ran into the cottage from both the front and rear doors. Once we were given the okay, Marnie and I joined them.

It was like stepping back in time. The only light was from the open doors and the flashlights we'd taken from the boat. Most of the furniture was covered with sheets. It reminded me of my grandmother's house. I did a quick look around the room. I saw a kitchen, an open door leading to a bathroom, and three other closed doors that I assumed were bedrooms.

Nobody spoke. All communication was done with hand or facial gestures.

The chief put his finger to his lips, signaling us to be quiet, then motioned Marnie and me to move closer to the door we'd just come through.

Again, Sam and Chief Marshall cradled one of the doors, and Maloney and Officer Bisbee took another one. That left one unmanned, closed door. I reached behind my back and pulled my gun from my waistband. I didn't plan on using it, but there was one door that nobody was guarding.

The chief raised his left hand and mouthed *on the count of three* and held up three fingers, then pointed to the door. Marnie and I ducked behind the couch. I put my hand on Marnie's shoulder and gestured for her to stay down. With gun in hand, I raised myself just enough to watch the guys.

It was showtime. The chief looked around, nodded, then one at a time held up three fingers on his left hand and mouthed go. The two doors they flanked went flying open. Nothing. Then there was one.

It may have been my imagination, but I could swear I heard a noise indicating movement ever so slight coming from behind the last closed door. I caught Sam's eye, tapped my finger on my ear, and pointed to the door. I nodded, then repeated my hand message.

Maloney stood on the left side of the frame. Sam on the right. They made eye contact, then Sam nodded. The door flew open. Sam flashed the light into the room, then called for the chief.

I knew something was going on but stayed clear of the room search. A few minutes passed before the chief exited the room. He took the radio from his belt and moved outside. Something was happening, but from my vantage point, I couldn't hear what was being said or see what was going on in the room. Without notice, Officer Bisbee ran across the floor and out the front door in the direction of the boat. Not two minutes later, he ran a beeline back into the room where Annie and Mark were.

"Marnie, wait here," I whispered as I moved out from behind the couch. I took four small steps towards the center of the living room. Just as I went to take another step, Sam walked out of the third bedroom. The look on his face scared me. "What's wrong.?" I wanted to ask more questions, but nothing would come out.

"Casey," Sam took a deep breath. "I want you and Marnie to sit down."

Marnie came out from behind the couch, and I moved back to the couch. We sat facing Sam.

"We found Annie and Mark."

Marnie froze.

I tried to stay strong, but the tears started to roll down my face.

"There's no doubt they've been drugged—*with what* needs to be determined. There were two hypodermic needles on the floor," said Sam.

Officer Bisbee gave both Annie and Mark a shot of Narcan.

Chief Marshall went outside to call the paramedics.

They also were handcuffed to the bedframe. They're alive, but barely. It's going to be challenging to get them back to the mainland," said Sam. The chief and Officer Bisbee have water rescue training. Maloney and I will help with lifting and moving. There will be two ambulances waiting to transport them to the hospital."

I looked at Sam. "Can I see Annie?"

"Both you and Marnie can go in for a couple of minutes. Don't be upset if she doesn't recognize you. And, watch your emotions." Sam scanned the room. "The chief also called the station to have two fingerprint kits and a camera brought over. You guys go with Officer Bisbee to the mainland when he goes ashore to get the paramedics and two stretchers. Once Annie and Mark are secured for water transport back to the mainland, they'll be taken by ambulance to South Shore Hospital in South Weymouth. Officer Bisbee will pick up the equipment the chief requested, and we'll scour the inside of the cottage."

"There's probably not much Marnie and I can do here. So, unless you think you need us, we'd rather go to the hospital and be with Annie," I said.

"That works," said Sam. "Now, go in and see her cause Officer Bisbee will be leaving momentarily."

Marnie and I slowly walked into the room that had been Annie's and Mark's prison for who knows how long. They looked like two lifeless bodies posed in a fetal position. I went over to Annie's side of the bed. Her eyes were closed. I stared at her chest and prayed for even the slightest sign of life. Marnie stood behind me.

I knelt, so I was face to face with Annie. She was pale. Her lips were cracked and peeling. Her hair was knotted and unbrushed. I whispered, "Annie … it's Casey. Can you hear me?" I moved back a couple inches and watched her eyes. They didn't open but moved ever so slightly. "Annie McGuire, it's time to go home. We've come to take you home."

Marnie bent down beside me and gently took Annie's hand in hers. "You need to come home to help with my wedding plans." Marnie tried to smile. "Besides that, you missed the fitting for your dress." Marnie's voice started to crack. "Yep, that's right."

I looked at Marnie. "What's right?"

"Annie was answering me. She heard me cause she moved her hand." Marnie turned away and wiped her eyes.

I leaned over and kissed Annie on the cheek. "We'll ride with you to the hospital."

Marnie pushed Annie's hair back and softly spoke into her ear, "Love you."

Sam came in and stood behind us. "The ambulances are here. Officer Bisbee is ready to move Annie and Mark to shore. We'll catch up with you at the hospital."

I nodded. Marnie and I moved outside.

We watched as Maloney and Sam helped secure Annie and Mark on the police boat.

Chief Marshall waited with Marnie and me until Officer Bisbee came back to get us.

I rode in one ambulance and Marnie in the other.

Officer Bisbee went back to the island to join the chief, Sam, and Maloney.

Chapter 46

Maloney and Officer Bisbee took the two fingerprint kits and the camera from the boat. Chief Marshall and Sam walked around, first the outside of the cottage, then back inside.

"I'm having a problem establishing a timeline for how long these two people were held hostage here," the chief said. "I don't see any food boxes or water bottles or bags of junk food."

"Officer Bisbee said he'd been here less than two weeks ago, and there weren't new padlocks on the doors then. So, we can assume at that time, Annie McGuire and Mark Mosley weren't here either. Whoever kidnapped, drugged, and held them against their will must have been somewhat familiar with this area." Sam reached in his pocket. "I had gloves on when I undid the handcuffs. I know it's not a big surface, but hopefully, we can pull a good print—or at least a good partial."

The chief looked around. "I don't remember if I gave you any history on this cottage."

"You mentioned it was being refurbished. Then because of something that happened in the family that owned it, the project was never completed," Maloney said.

"That's it in a nutshell," the chief said. My point is the cottage was never lived in after the renovations were started. Look around. There are countertops, windows, bathroom fixtures—a toilet seat, faucets, etc. Great surfaces for an unsuspecting killer to leave fingerprints."

Sam picked up one of the kits. "There's two of them and two of us. Maloney and I will divide the area and start working."

"I had Officer Bisbee bring me extra evidence bags before he left." The chief gave Sam and Maloney half the bags and two sets of gloves.

"There are two empty beer bottles in a bucket in the corner next to where a stove should be." Sam bagged the bottles, noted where he found them and set the bag on the table. He walked to the kitchen sink and opened the cabinets below. "Interesting," Sam said. He took out a plastic Home Depot bag. There's a bubble pack that, at one point, contained four padlocks like the ones on the two outside doors. I'll dust the package for prints. Not only are there two locks left, there's also a receipt." Sam took it from the bag. "It was a cash sale made twelve days ago. I know the Home Depot stores have cameras recording activity at their registers."

"What's the store address?" the chief asked.

Sam looked at the receipt. "You've got to be shittin' me." He shook his head. "It's the Home Depot in Hyannis."

Chief Marshall spoke up. "Sam, we're not dealing with an ordinary person. It appears the person did a lot of planning. The person wasn't stupid, but that person was also not a killer. This was a crime from bits and pieces taken from television cop shows. A seasoned criminal or deranged individual would have more than likely killed Annie and Mark then hid their bodies. The Webb Island cottage was an ideal spot. Your would-be killer did his research and knew this was a prime location."

"Thinking along those lines, our would-be killer had to be familiar with the area." Sam pivoted around, taking in any sights that might be of interest.

"I'm back." Officer Bisbee called as he rounded the bend halfway up the trail leading from the water to the cottage.

Maloney spun around. "I didn't hear you pull the boat in."

"Come back someday, and I'll introduce you to investigative boating." Officer Bisbee smiled. "As quiet as I was pulling in, I can make the engine sound like troops storming the beach. The ponds in and around Hanson are my assigned beats."

"Are you a Hanson native?" Sam asked.

"Yes, sir, born and brought up here. My grandfather and father were both members of the Hanson Police Department. I decided it was my calling to follow in their footsteps."

Chief Marshall spoke up. "He forgot to mention that his grandfather, my mentor, was the chief for many years." He nodded. "Okay, let's get back to work."

Maloney took out a notepad and a pen. "To review, Officer Bisbee, have you noticed any activity on or around the island in the last month? Since I don't believe this was a spontaneous event, unless somebody knew the area, the person who kidnapped Annie and Mark and left them to die had have done some hands-on research."

"During this time of the year, I'm not out on the boat very much. That doesn't mean that I'm not out canvassing the area. I respond if we get a call regarding a problem from a concerned resident whose house borders or has water access to Wampatuck Pond. The boat is always hooked up to the truck, ready to go. Usually, the trucks and trailers parked at the boat landing belong to fishers. Over the years, I've become friends with a lot of them. Pleasure boats cruising the lake in September and October usually come from private boat docks. The summer is a different story. And, as far as Webb Island, we've had very few nosey *visitors* over the last twelve years that I've been on the job, and never a serious problem."

"Sam, as you can see, if somebody was trying to be incognito on Webb Island because of the dense vegetation, it could happen," Chief Marshall added.

Sam glanced around and nodded.

"Chief's exactly right. During the summer months, I've pulled the PD boat behind pond plants and bush-like trees to observe the lake boaters. In fact, at the beginning of the summer, I do some pruning, so I always have a hiding place available."

235

Sam made notes, then took a deep breath. "Maloney, will you please take pictures of inside and outside the cottage. I'm going to call Chief Lowe and ask him to get ahold of the manager at Home Depot about their surveillance cameras."

Sam moved away from the cottage to call, and Maloney took pictures.

After Sam hung up with Chief Lowe, he walked over to Chief Marshall and Officer Bisbee. "Guess it's time to get going. We're going to head over to the hospital. I haven't heard from Casey, so things must be stable. In all the confusion, I didn't get the hospital's name. Also, I'll need directions."

They're at South Shore Hospital in South Weymouth. It's about ten miles from the station. We're going to drop the boat off and get my cruiser. Why don't you come back to the station, then follow us to the hospital? There's road construction going on. If we encounter congestion or a detour, I'll use the siren."

Sam held up the evidence bag that contained the opened bubble pack with the two remaining padlocks. "Chief, you'll need these to lock up."

"Thanks." The chief took them from the bubble pack and handed them to Officer Bisbee

"We'll get going as soon as my officer secures the cottage."

Chapter 47

Sam and Maloney followed Chief Marshall and Officer Bisbee into the Hospital Personnel Only parking lot.

"I forgot to tell you. I assigned an officer to Annie and one to Mark. Annie is in a private room on the fifth floor, and Mark is in intensive care. I cleared Casey and Marnie to be allowed into Annie's room. Because Mark is in intensive care, the hospital frowned on letting anyone other than staff into the room. I radioed hospital security and told them we were on our way. The Director of Security is going to meet us in the lobby."

Sam walked beside the chief. Maloney—Officer Bisbee followed. They weren't ten steps into the lobby when a man in a navy blue blazer, white button-down shirt, blue and white striped tie, and perfectly pressed khaki pants greeted them.

"Sam, Maloney, and Officer Bisbee, I'd like you to meet Tom Flanigan, Director of Security for South Shore Hospital." Sam reached out and shook the director's hand—the other two followed.

"Sam Summers is the lead detective with the Bourne Police Department, Rusty Maloney is a detective with the Barnstable Police Department, and you know Officer Bisbee. The two people transported here by ambulance from Webb Island are the subjects of a missing person's investigation. The female, Annie McGuire, is the administrative assistant to the Cape and Island's District Attorney. The male, Mark Mosley, is an acquaintance of hers."

Sam stepped forward. "Director Flanigan, before we get into the particulars, Maloney and I would like to go up to Annie's room. I understand it's on the fifth floor, but I don't have the number."

"No problem. I'll be right back." Director Flanigan walked over to the information desk.

"Sam, we won't come up with you, but I want to talk to you before we leave. I've still got unanswered questions," Chief Marshall said.

"Give me about a half-hour. Then I'll meet you in the coffee shop," said Sam.

Chief nodded, "Sounds like a plan. I'll radio the officer assigned to Annie and let him know you're on your way up."

"Thanks, chief."

The director returned to where Sam and Maloney were standing.

"Annie is in room 504. I called the nurses' station and told them to expect you and Maloney." The director pointed to the elevator across the lobby.

Sam thanked the director, then turned toward Maloney. "Ready?" he asked.

Maloney didn't verbally respond, just moved in step beside Sam.

When the elevator opened on the fifth floor, Sam could see the nurses' station and a uniformed officer standing beside the half-closed door to the room across from the station. Sam and Maloney walked down the hall, stopped briefly to acknowledge the police officer, then went to the counter to check-in per the director's instructions. The nurse checked their credentials, had them sign in, then went with them to Annie's room.

I was sitting on one side of the bed and Marnie on the other. Annie lay lifeless, hooked up to all sorts of monitors. We turned slowly as Sam and Maloney came into the room. My eyes were glazed and red. Sam walked up beside me and leaned over. "We're here now," he said as he put his arms around me and pulled me close.

Maloney moved a chair beside Marnie. She tried to talk between sobs, but nothing came out. He took her hands and whispered, "She's going to be alright."

The Hanson police officer opened the door and slid his chair over beside Sam. "I'll get another one."

"Thank you," said Sam. The officer turned to leave when Sam held up a finger. "Have you been on duty since Annie they brought in?"

"Yes, sir," he said.

"I'll be right out. I want to run a few things by you." Sam dipped his head and shared a casual salute.

"Casey, do you know what's happening? Have they communicated anything to you about her condition?" Sam was careful not to push too hard.

"The only time we haven't been in her room since she's been here is when the medical staff was conducting bedside evaluation or administering treatments. It was apparent Annie was drugged. I don't know if they have determined with what. They asked me questions about any medications she might be on. When we went through her house, I remember seeing Losartan and Simvastatin. They stuck in my mind because I take them too." I shrugged.

"Has she come to at all?" asked Sam.

Marnie spoke up, "I thought I saw her try to open her eyes, but nothing. When I was rubbing the back of her hand, I did feel it move slightly."

"Keep talking to her … quietly and slowly …. Keep rubbing her shoulders, her arms, and her hands. Maloney and I will speak to the officer outside her door and the nurse in charge. Push the call button if you need us before we get back."

Sam leaned down and kissed Casey on her cheek. "I love you, Casey Quinby."

Sam and Maloney stepped out of Annie's room. The officer had procured another chair and was sitting guard. He stood as the guys approached him.

Sam looked at the Hanson police officer's name tag attached to his uniform shirt pocket. "Officer Abbot, let me formally introduce myself and my partner. I'm Sam Summers, a detective with the Bourne PD." Sam motioned in Maloney's direction. "This is Rusty Maloney, a detective with the Barnstable PD."

Officer Abbot reached out and shook hands with Sam and Maloney. "I've been with the Hanson PD for six years. Next month I'm taking the sergeant's exam. My ultimate goal is to be a detective. Being with a small department makes it more challenging, but I won't give up."

Sam smiled and patted him on his shoulder. "You'll do it."

"We'd like to ask you a few questions." Sam looked around. "But, I don't want you to leave your post."

"This isn't my first hospital assignment. During the day, this floor is pretty quiet. At night can be a different story. But, we should be good," Abbot said.

"Alright," said Sam. "Have you been here since Annie came to this room?"

"Yes. I started my watch in the ER. Then, I escorted her to the fifth floor."

"Have you noticed anyone who might be taking an interest in this room?" Maloney asked.

"Not any more than usual. You're always going to get the overcurious wondering why a uniformed police officer is stationed outside a patient's room. In all the times I've done this type of assignment, I've only had a handful of people ask questions."

"I know I don't need to, but I'm going to ask anyway—have you observed a *visitor* or *visitors* walking by more than usual?"

"No, I have not."

"Is this floor used primarily for a specific type of patient?" Sam asked.

"This is primarily the surgical floor. Usually, it's full of patients who've just had surgery. Occasionally, depending on the doctor and the care level the patient needs, others are assigned a room here. This floor also is home to a rehab hospital operating within a hospital. If you walk down to the end of this corridor, corridor A, go right and another right and come up corridor B. Patient rooms occupy half of corridor B, then the rehab hospital takes over."

Sam glanced at a person slowly strolling by Annie's room and, without taking his eyes off him, asked, "Is this rehab hospital open to the public?"

Officer Abbott turned his hands, palm up, and shrugged. "From what I understand, the rehab hospital is a continuation of treatment of existing patients. But don't hold me accountable for that statement. So, yes, I do believe it's open to the public."

"Maloney and I are going to explore the fifth floor." Sam tilted his head in the direction he wanted to proceed. "We're supposed to meet with Director Flanigan in ten minutes. We'll be back to check on the girls before we head downstairs. What time are you here 'til?"

"I work a twelve-hour shift. Today I'll be here until 7:00 p.m. Then I'll be back at seven in the morning."

Sam and Maloney went into Annie's room. "Casey, we're going to do some exploring, then we have a meeting downstairs in ten minutes. We'll be back as soon as possible. If you need us, we'll be in Director Flanigan's office."

The guys left Annie's room, didn't stop to talk to the officer or nurse, just hand gestured a quick good-bye and started down corridor A.

"Nothing jumped out at me," Sam said. "It's set up like any other hospital."

Moans and groans came from several rooms, and the red call lights were blinking outside others. There was very little corridor traffic other than from hospital personnel.

Corridor B was set up the same as Corridor A, except halfway down, double doors led to the rehab hospital. There was more traffic in that area than on the rest of the floor.

"I'm impressed," said Maloney. "It's like a baby Spaulding Rehab, but not as intense."

The elevator door at the end of the corridor opened. Sam and Maloney sprinted to catch it before it closed. They rode it to the first floor.

Chief Marshall and Director Flanigan were waiting for them in the coffee shop. They'd found an empty table in the far corner, away from the take-out counter. They both had a full cup of coffee in front of them.

"I could use one of those right about now." Sam pointed to their cups. "Maloney, how about you?"

Maloney motioned Sam to sit down. "The first one's on me."

Sam looked around. "There's nobody nearby. We can talk and move away only if we have to."

"Okay with me," said the chief.

Sam took a sip of coffee. "I needed that," he said. "I'll address the first part of this conversation to Director Flanigan. Chief Marshall

242

is aware of our investigation of a murder that happened seven days ago at the ten-year class reunion of the Barnstable High school class of 2006."

"I read about it in the Boston Herald," said Director Flanigan.

"It wasn't pretty." Sam shook his head. One of the girls, Annie McGuire, the patient on the fifth floor, was a member of that class. Mark Mosley, a patient in your ICU, was also a member of the class of 2006. There's a whole backstory to this case, but to quickly catch you up to date, I'll give you the highlights."

Sam leaned forward on the table. "Betsy Harper, the girl murdered, led a somewhat promiscuous lifestyle beginning back in high school. It finally caught up with her. We think she may have threatened to reveal one of her secret 'relationships'. The who, how, and why haven't surfaced yet, but we're closing in. Annie McGuire has two approved visitors upstairs with her now. Casey Quinby works with local police departments on Cape Cod and is a private investigator in Barnstable Village, and Marnie Levine is an Assistant District Attorney in Barnstable County. Marnie works with Annie, and Casey is one of her best friends. Not to mention that Maloney is engaged to Marnie, and I'm engaged to Casey."

Sam continued, "Six days after the reunion where Betsy Harper was murdered, Annie's car was found burned beyond recognition in Wellfleet. It was then the PD discovered that Annie and Mark were missing. There's a joint effort from PDs on the Cape to combine their manpower and expertise to find the person or persons responsible for both the murder and the kidnapping with intent to commit murder. There's also a possibility that a ten-year-old death that was deemed an accident involving another member of the class of 2006 was, in fact, a murder."

The silence was broken when somebody dropped a tray full of food. Sam jumped up and looked around, then sat back down. "That's why I always try to sit with my back against a wall."

The three other guys looked at him and smiled.

"I learned that the first week in the academy." Chief Marshall nodded. "I drive my wife crazy when we go out to dinner. You'd think she'd be used to it by now."

"Back to business," Sam said. "Director Flanigan, can you please check with the lab to see if they've isolated the drug used to knock Annie and Mark out? Also, can I get both emergency room reports with the doctor's initial evaluation?"

"Give me another half hour. Then we'll meet in my office."

"In the meantime, can you okay me to do a visual of Mark in ICU?" Sam asked.

The director took his beeper from his pocket, punched in an extension, then, at the beep, he entered his cell number. His cell rang. He answered. "Marilyn, Director Flanigan here. I'm sending Detective Summers and Detective Maloney to ICU to see you. Please take them to Mark Mosley's room and let them do a visual. Also, has there been any change in his condition since he was admitted?"

"Not really. We're giving Mark fluids. He was dangerously dehydrated. We're waiting for the lab results regarding drugs found in his system. He's on eyeball watch. Do you want me to inform you of any changes?"

"Yes, please." The director ended the call.

"Marilyn is expecting you. Chief, why don't you come with me. I'll work on getting the other reports and see you two back in my office in a half-hour. If I get those reports before you're back, the chief and I will look at them."

Marilyn was waiting just inside the entrance to the ICU. "You must be the detectives that Director Flanigan told me about."

"Yes, we are. I'm Detective Sam Summers from Bourne, and this is Detective Rusty Maloney from Barnstable. This has become a nasty case involving innocent people. I'm sure you see more like this being so close to Boston. Fortunately, Cape Cod has been spared. The person you have here in ICU is one of the innocents."

"He's in rough shape. Not only are drugs involved, but he was also severely beaten. He's got a couple of broken ribs and took some serious blows to the stomach area."

"Has he regained consciousness?" asked Sam.

Marilyn looked down and took a deep breath. "No, he hasn't. He'll be lucky to make it through the night. Follow me."

Mark was in a room two doors down and, like Annie, directly across from the nurses' station. Even though the general public isn't allowed to access the ICU, Chief Marshall had an officer posted outside Mark's door.

Sam glanced at the officer's name tag and introduced Maloney and himself to Officer Wilkins. Marilyn explained the order from Director Flanigan, permitting Sam and Maloney to conduct a visual of Mark Mosley. The officer stayed his post while Marilyn, Sam, and Maloney went into the room.

Sam walked to the end of the bed. It wasn't a pretty sight. Mark lay helpless, breathing with the help of a ventilator. Sam turned to face Maloney." I've seen a lot of shit on and off the job, but this sucks. We'll find the bastard or bastards who did this to Mark and Annie. And when we do, you'll have to hold me back." He turned away and lifted his hands to rub his face. "Judging from those injuries, Mark was defending Annie."

Marilyn nodded.

"I agree," said Maloney.

Sam's phone rang. "Detective Summers."

"Sam, Chief Lowe here."

"Hold on." Sam turned toward Marilyn. "I need to take this call. Can I meet you in your office when I'm finished?"

"Absolutely," Marilyn said as she moved out of the room, closing the door behind her.

Sam moved over beside the window to ensure phone contact. "Go ahead, chief."

"I have a copy of the Home Depot security footage taken on the date and at the time noted on the receipt. I'm going to send you a copy via your cell phone. Check it out and give me a callback."

"Will do," Sam said before he ended the call.

"Chief Lowe?" Maloney asked.

"It was. He's sending me a video from the Home Depot security cameras. Should be here momentarily."

Maloney walked over to where Sam was standing.

"We need a break. I'm hoping someone of interest makes their movie debut." Sam stared at his phone. "Here we go." The buzz indicated something was coming through.

Sam and Maloney moved away from the window to a small table with two chairs in the corner of the room.

"Call complete. Let's take a look." Sam laid his phone on the table between him and Maloney, opened the message from Chief Lowe, and pushed the button to start the video. "Since this is labeled section one, I'm assuming because the front of the store is so big, we'll probably end up with four or more sections. They also have a nursery section with two registers. In fact, if we're not dealing with a stupid criminal, the person would realize once you pay at the nursery register, you're immediately out the door."

The video had just started when Sam pushed the stop button. He reached into his back pocket and took out a notebook. "I took a picture of the receipt. I also noted the address of the Home Depot and the date the item was purchased." Sam flipped to the middle of his notebook. "It's dated September 24. That will narrow down our search.

"I want to run it through once to make sure we have it all. Then go back down to the director's office and scrutinize it section by section. We have no idea who we're looking for, so it's going to take time. Also, the director may be able to transfer it from my phone to a computer screen."

"Good idea." Maloney got up, walked to the window, then turned around to focus on Mark.

Sam stood, went over beside Maloney, and put his arm on Maloney's shoulder. "Ready?"

"As ready as I'm going to be," Maloney said quietly.

Sam looked at Mark and gently tapped the back of his hand. "Hang in there. Annie needs you. We'll be back to take you home."

Officer Wilkins was talking to Marilyn as Sam and Maloney left Mark's room. They reached out to shake the officer's and Marilyn's hands.

"I'll call Director Flanigan to tell him you're on your way down," said Marilyn.

"Thank you. Thank you for all you do," said Sam. "We'll be in touch."

Chapter 48

Since ICU was on the third floor, Sam and Maloney decided to take the stairs down. They didn't feel like getting into an elevator with other people. Chief Marshall and Director Flanigan were waiting for them in the Director's office.

"Hate this part of the job," Sam said.

"I was just about to get a couple of coffees from the coffee shop. Would you both like one?"

"Yes, we would. Thank you." Sam and Maloney took the two empty chairs in front of Flanigan's desk.

"Be right back." The director left Chief Marshall, Sam, and Maloney to gather their thoughts.

"Rough day," Sam looked up at the ceiling and rotated his head, trying to relieve the stress. "Mark isn't good. Whoever's behind this did a number on him. They're not sure if he's going to make it."

No one else spoke until the director came back with the coffees. "They're all black, but I brought some creamers and sugar packets."

Sam fixed his with cream and sugar. "I needed this."

Maloney nodded in agreement.

"Director, before we move on, did you get the lab results yet?" asked Sam.

"No. Let me give them a call." The director pushed the numbers for the lab. "Director Flanigan here. Do you have the lab results that I requested earlier?"

Sam assumed he was still connected to a person on the other end because he nodded several times before speaking again.

"In twenty minutes. Okay, I'll be waiting."

"Is there a problem?" Maloney asked.

"They're running a couple extra tests to determine if more than one type of drug was administered. The technician had Annie's done but not Mark's. They assured me I'd have the report in twenty minutes. You heard me repeat that to them."

"We did," said Sam.

The director took another sip of coffee. "In the meantime, let's move on."

Sam rested his arms on the desk. "Chief Marshall is familiar with most of this. To give you some backstory—at the cottage on Webb Island, we found a Home Depot bag with an open bubble pack that originally contained four heavy-duty padlocks. When we found it, there were only two. The other two had recently been used to secure the front and back doors of the cottage. Chief Marshall had instructed his officers to shoot the two locks off to gain entrance. That's where we found Annie McGuire and Mark Mosley. Also in the Home Depot bag was a receipt for the locks. They were purchased at the store in Hyannis. Chief Lowe from the Barnstable PD called me to let me know he got a video from the security cameras at the aforementioned Home Depot.

About fifteen minutes ago, I got a text from Chief Lowe." Sam leaned back. "It's the video from the Home Depot. I can pull it up on my phone, but I wondered if you could take it from my phone and put it onto your computer? It would make the people images much clearer and, with any luck, recognizable."

"I can do that," said Director Flanigan. "We had some problems with employee/vendor theft, and because of security cameras, we were able to determine who was involved and press charges. I'm not versed on the *how's* of the operation, so let me give Jim Bower a call. He's our technical guy."

Not five minutes after the director hung up, there was a knock on the door. "Come in," said Flanigan. "

A young man wearing jeans and a T-shirt that said *I'm a member of the tech world* walked in. Director Flanigan introduced him to

249

Chief Marshall, Sam, and Maloney. They shook hands then went back to their seats. Jim Bower slid another chair up and sat to the side of the desk.

"Sam, why don't you explain to Jim what you need," the director nodded.

Sam smiled. "I don't know any of the technical terms, so I'll put it as clearly as I can in laymen's language."

"Shoot," said Jim.

A pun on words to a policeman, Sam thought. "I have a video on my phone that I need to send to Director Flanigan's computer."

"That's easy. Do you have an iPhone?" Jim asked.

"I do." Sam handed his phone to the techie.

"Good. That makes it even easier."

Out of the corner of his eyes, Sam glanced at Maloney, who wiped his hand over his mouth, trying to hold back a smile.

The director stood and motioned Jim to sit in his chair instead of moving the computer around. The techie's fingers flew over the keyboard as his head bobbed quickly up and down, from Sam's phone to the computer screen.

"Do you want me to turn the screen so you can all view the video?" asked Jim.

"Please do," said the director.

Jim got everything into place, then turned to Sam. "So that you know, I took a copy of the video. You still have the original on your phone."

"Thank you. I appreciate that," said Sam. "I want to run through the whole video first, then go back and look at specifics. Are you able to freeze a frame and get a close-up if we need to?"

"Absolutely. Stop me if you want a close-up of something or someone. I can run the whole video in slow motion." Jim looked at the director.

The director nodded.

"That works for me." Sam sat back in his chair, took his notebook and a pen from his pocket, and fixed his eyes on the computer screen. "I do know the video is divided into sections. I assume that corresponds to the cameras in the front of the store. We'll figure that out as we go along." Sam held his hand up in a stopping motion. "Director, before we start, I'd like to have Casey Quinby and Marnie Levine here to view the video. They're very involved in this investigation and, together or individually, may be able to identify a person of interest."

Director Flanigan and Chief Marshall agreed.

The director picked up his phone. "I'll call the fifth-floor nurses' station and have them tell Casey and Marnie to join us."

Chapter 49

Marnie had finally given in to exhaustion. I was right behind her but wanted one of us to be awake when Annie opened her eyes. I found myself rocking back and forth to the rhythmical beeps of Annie's heart monitor. Every once in a while, the machine would hiccup, indicating a slight involuntary movement. I studied Annie's heart rate on the monitor behind her bed when Nurse Sampson came into the room.

"I just got a call from Director Flanigan. He wants you and Marnie to come to his office for a meeting." Nurse Sampson said.

Marnie didn't bat an eyelash.

I stood up and stretched. "It's been a difficult day. I'll wake her up, and we'll head down to his office."

I tapped Marnie on her shoulder. She didn't budge. I leaned down, slightly moved her arm, and spoke her name in a voice above a whisper.

She moaned. "What?" she said.

"Hey, girl, we're being summoned to the director's office."

She abruptly sat up. "Why ... what's wrong?"

"Relax. Nothing is wrong," I said. "Stand up, get your bearings, and let's go."

Marnie went into the bathroom in Annie's room to splash some water on her face. "Okay. I'm ready."

We grabbed our purses and headed to the elevator. It was empty when we got in but half full by the time we reached the first floor. We could see Maloney and Chief Marshall standing outside the director's office when we crossed the lobby.

Maloney gave Marnie a much-needed hug. She'd been a trooper all day, but the stress was starting to wear on her.

252

"What's up?" I asked.

"Sam got a video on his phone from Chief Lowe. It's footage from the front-end security cameras at the Hyannis Home Depot," said Maloney.

I felt like the *wow* emoji from my phone escaped and affixed itself to my face. "Have you guys seen it yet?" I asked.

"No. Sam wanted you and Marnie to see it with us. You two may recognize somebody we don't. Two more sets of eyes will never hurt." Maloney stepped aside and gestured for us to go into the office.

The director had moved three more chairs from the lobby into his office. We sat in a half-circle, encompassing the sides and front of the desk. Sam and I sat on one side of the desk, Marnie and Maloney were on the other side, the director and Chief Marshall were in front, one on the left side and one on the right, and Jim Bower was in the middle.

Jim had the computer set up so we could all see the screen. Director Flanigan's screen had to be at least twenty-four by fifteen inches.

"This is like being in a mini-movie theater," I whispered.

The director heard me and chuckled. "It works great for meetings. People can't complain about not being able to see my presentation. Sometimes Jim puts it up on a riser. There's only six of us, so we should be able to see the screen without a problem."

Jim started the video. 'Section 1' appeared in the center of the screen. "You want me to play the whole video first, then again in slow motion, right?"

"Yeah, let's start with that," Sam said. "Also, if something stands out, can stop the video and zoom in on a particular frame?"

I pulled my chair as close as I could to the screen.

Jim signaled to the director he was ready to start. The director flipped the switch for the lights as Jim pushed the button to begin the show.

I'd never seen a store video that security cameras had recorded. I was impressed. I whispered to Sam, "Remind me not to scratch my butt or something worse while standing in a check-out line."

I got the look.

It was fascinating, but at regular speed, it was hard to mentally zoom in and identify the facial or body characteristics of the shoppers. I was glad, however, that we watched the video with normal movement first.

When the first video ended, the director turned the lights back on. "Wow, I've never needed to observe security camera video on this scale. It's fascinating. The next time I go into a big box store, it's the first thing I going to think about."

Jim got the video ready to play again in slow motion. "These security cameras are high quality. I've seen some that are useless. They're very grainy, and the pictures aren't crisp. Of course, we're talking Home Depot here. The money they invest in their systems saves them thousands of dollars in theft." Jim looked around. Any questions before I start the video?"

"I have one," I said. "If we want to zoom in on a frame, do we just say stop?"

"Exactly, yes," Jim said. "Okay, with no other questions or comments, I'm ready to get started."

Again, I was glued to the screen. Jim was right to show the real-time video first. It made it easier for me to concentrate on the people checking out.

We were about halfway through the first section when Sam asked Jim to stop. "Can you zoom in on this frame?"

"Sure," said Jim.

Sam moved closer to the screen. It was strange because you felt like the people were right there—Right in front of you.

I looked at the screen. "Sam, what or who are you looking at"?

"Register two. Look at the items on the screen. Does the package beside the box of screws and the two packages of light bulbs look like a bubble pack of padlocks?"

Maloney, Marnie, and I got closer to check it out.

"It does," said Maloney.

Jim stopped the video and enlarged the frame. "That's what they are," he said.

"Can you back this up, rerun it without stopping, and continue until this customer pays?" Sam stepped back for a minute, rubbed his eyes, then went back close to the screen.

"Yep." Jim followed Sam's directions. He stopped the video when the customer handed the cashier a credit card to pay the bill.

Sam sat back on his chair. "This guy's in the clear. Our guy paid cash."

"I'll start back up where we left off," Jim said.

Nothing in the remainder of the section one video appeared to match our person of interest. Jim moved on to section two. Sam had Jim stop the video a few times to take a closer look at several of the patrons. I recognized a couple of attorneys with offices in the village but no person of interest.

We were about three-quarters through section three, with not even a sniff of a match.

"Let's take a break from the videos and do some brainstorming. We know the locks used on the Webb Island cottage came from the Hyannis Home Depot. That's a fact. And, the person who bought them paid cash. That's a fact." Sam abruptly stopped talking and paced the floor.

"Sam, what's up?" I asked.

He waved me away and walked to the other side of the office. He took his phone from his pocket and pulled up the pictures of the Home Depot receipt. "That's it," he said as he walked back to the desk where we all were waiting. "The receipt has a register number on it." He held up his phone with the picture of the receipt on the screen. "The transaction took place at register eight."

"Jim, please bring up section three again and see if register eight is in that section."

We watched as Jim followed Sam's directions. Jim's eyes were glued to the screen. He studied every change until he froze the video and announced, "Here you go … register eight."

Sam took a deep breath. "Now, can you magnify the video? If we see another bubble pack of padlocks, can you move the image down to see the face of the person buying them?"

Jim worked like a surgeon, carefully moving around the screen, observing every detail. He slowed the video down as much as possible to avoid missing anything. His finger hovered over the stop button. About six minutes into the video, Jim pushed the button.

Sam and Maloney looked at the computer screen.

Maloney moved closer. "There no doubt. Those are the same locks."

"Good work, Jim," Sam said. "Let's take a look at this person's face."

Slowly Jim moved the image down until it appeared on the screen.

My heart stopped. I looked at Sam. "That's Arthur Richardson, the art teacher at the high school. You know—the one who wrote the same flowery message in each of the girl's yearbooks—the one that I interviewed the other day." I had to sit down. I knew he was a jerk, but a murderer?"

"Casey, are you sure?" Sam studied the picture some more. "Another person is standing real close behind him—they might be together. Can you move the video around and try to get a shot of his face?"

"I'll give it a try," Jim said as he painstakingly went to work. It took a couple of minutes before Jim said, "The second guy is looking away, so that's the best I can do."

"Okay. I'll take it anyway. Another question. Can you give me printouts of these two faces? Then, can you also go back and give me a picture of the money exchange between the person paying cash for the locks and the cashier? I want to see his hands."

"I can." Jim walked over to the director's printer to make sure it was on. "Give me a minute, and I'll have them for you.

"Since you're able to print them, may I please have three copies of each?" asked Sam

Jim gave Sam a thumbs up, "No problem." He sent the facial images and the one of the money exchange to the printer, made the copies, and handed them to Sam."

Director Flanigan turned toward Sam. "Do you need Jim for anything else?" He asked.

"Not today," Sam said. "Thanks, Jim. Great job."

Jim smiled, shook Sam's hand, then left the office.

Director Flanigan got a call from the lab. "Okay, I'll be right down., he said, then turned to us. "That was the lab. They've got the reports ready. I'll be back in ten minutes."

Sam, Maloney, Marnie, and I walked over to the small conference table in the far corner of the office. Sam rested his elbow on the table and cradled his chin in his hand. Maloney and Marnie sat without making conversation, waiting for the director to return. And, I studied the printouts Jim had retrieved from the Home Depot video.

"Before we start, I want to call Chief Lowe to tell him what's going on." Sam checked the time on his phone, then made the call.

The chief answered after the first ring.

"Reporting in." Sam cut right to the chase. "I need you to send somebody over to the Barnstable High faculty parking lot. Hopefully, the teachers, or at least some of them, should still be there. "Tell them to look for a pick-up truck with a boat hitch on the back. I know there's probably more than one, but run all the plate numbers and let me know who they belong to. Also, throw in the make and color."

"Whatever you need, I'll get it started, then call you back," said Chief Lowe.

Sam ended the call.

"Let me see the picture of the other person and the one of the money exchange," I said.

Sam handed them to me.

I checked out the facial image first. The person had a baseball cap on backward. From the angle of the picture, I could see an embroidered image of a panel truck on the front.

"What are you seeing," Sam asked.

I pointed to the image. "Can you read the name on the cap?"

Sam looked at it, then handed it to Maloney. "Got any ideas?"

"No idea," he said. "Let me think about it." Maloney set the pictures on the table.

I reached over in front of Sam and picked up the picture of the money exchange. "It's not Richardson paying. It's the baseball cap guy. Check out his hand. He's sporting some heavy-duty bandages."

Sam took the picture from me. Maloney slid over beside him to get a better look.

"Peter Mosley," said Sam. "The name on the cap is Boyd. That's the name of the moving company where Mark worked."

"Yep," Maloney and I said in unison.

"So Richardson is the puppeteer, and Peter Mosley is his puppet," I said.

Chapter 50

Ten minutes later, Director Flanigan was back in his office. He put two folders on the table, then took the seat next to Sam.

"Let's start with Annie," Sam said. He reached over and picked up the folder labeled Annie McGuire. "Director, I'll need your help dissecting the information from the lab results."

"You've got it," he said. "I know you want to start with Annie, but I want to give an overall finding first, then we can separate the particulars. Is that okay with everyone?"

We nodded.

"Thank you. It will make it much easier." Director Flanigan took both Annie's and Mark's folders, opened each one, and put them on the table in front of him. "You already knew that both Annie and Mark were drugged. Do you know if either one of them did recreational drugs?"

I spoke up. "I've known Annie for years, and I can say with complete confidence she never did drugs. She even hated to take an aspirin. She participated in some counseling programs sponsored by the courts to educate at-risk youth about the dangers of drugs and addiction. Did she use drugs? Absolutely not."

"The test they conducted found fentanyl in her system."

"Then it was forcibly introduced," I said.

Marnie waited until I finished, then spoke, "I've worked with Annie in the District Attorney's office for almost five years. In these times, we see many cases come through that involve drug usage and the drug trade. Annie saw firsthand how drugs ruined people's lives. She wanted no part of them. They disgusted her."

The director took a deep breath. "Fortunately, she wasn't given enough to cause her to overdose. It's common for addicts to mix fentanyl with heroin. It increases the potency. The lab didn't find any trace of heroin in her system. They're treated her at the scene with Narcan. She will probably have some side effects and may have to be under a doctor's care for a while, but the prognosis is she should make a complete recovery."

I was having a hard time controlling my emotions. I knew if I looked at Marnie, I'd lose it. Sam sensed I was having a hard time and reached over and took my hand.

The director closed Annie's folder for the time being and opened Marks. "Mark Mosley isn't as lucky as Annie. How much do you know about him?"

Sam looked at me then answered the director. "We don't know him at all. He was a close friend of Annie's. We think they were dating or maybe just hanging out as friends, but we're unsure. We know that they have known each other since high school, maybe longer. He was their class president all four years."

"I never heard Annie talk about him at work," Marnie said.

"And, as long as I've known Annie, I never heard her mention his name," I said.

"I gave you the backstory regarding Webb Island and how we found Annie and Mark. There's more leading up to that story. Twelve days ago, there was a murder at a hotel in Hyannis. A friend of Mark and Annie was killed. The Barnstable Police Department is conducting the investigation. We think Annie and Mark tried to do some detective work on their own and got too close to the truth. They found her car burned down to the frame in a remote section of Wellfleet. They didn't find any bodies at the burn site. But, Annie or Mark went missing until we found them in the cottage on Webb Island."

"Do you have any idea of who brought them or how they got there?" the director asked.

"We had our suspicions but needed proof. Because of the information your tech, Jim Bower, pulled off the security camera footage, we feel confident we know the who. It's a matter of picking up the two individuals we feel are involved and making our accusation stick. I'm waiting to hear back from Chief Lowe."

The director closed Annie's folder and opened Marks. "Let's get back to Mark Mosley. Not only did Mosley have fentanyl in his system—but he also had heroin. And, as you know, he has broken ribs, and his stomach was somebody's punching bag. They're trying to stabilize him, but it doesn't look good. His body is more black and blue than flesh color. He was beaten real bad. I would surmise it was easy for his abductor or abductors to inject him with the drugs. Strange though, they never hit his face. It was like they wanted him to watch what they were doing to him or Annie. Almost sadistic. Fortunately, she didn't suffer any physical or sexual abuse. The drug abuse is bad enough."

I needed a break. "I'm going to check in on Annie. Marnie, do you want to come with me?"

She nodded.

We left the guys in the director's office and took the elevator to the fifth floor. I checked in with Officer Abbot. "Any abnormal curiosity?" I asked.

"It's been quiet. A couple of gawkers, but nothing noteworthy."

"When does your shift end?"

"We're working twelve-hour shifts. I came in at seven this morning, so I'll be relieved at seven tonight. Officer Kimball and I have been assigned to this room for the duration."

I glanced inside. Marnie had already curled up on the chair beside Annie's bed. Her eyes were closed. I didn't want to startle her, so I made a soft coughing noise as I walked in the door.

Her eyes opened, then closed them again.

261

"You okay?" I asked as I walked over and crouched down beside her.

She sat forward on the chair and rubbed her face. "Listening to the director downstairs—I felt so helpless. I can't fathom how this all happened."

"None of us can. Talk to her, watch her—see if you get a flinch or eye movement—anything that might indicate she knows we're here. I'm going to check with Nurse Sampson to see if there have been any changes in her vitals. I'll be right back."

Nurse Sampson was sitting at the desk at the back of the station. The nurse staffing the front desk looked and asked if she could help me. Nurse Sampson heard her, looked up, and said she'd handle it. She came around the counter to talk to me. "Let's take a walk down to the dayroom at the end of the corridor. We can talk privately there."

I nodded and followed her into the dayroom. Fortunately, there wasn't anyone else there, so we were free to talk. There was a small table and two chairs in the back corner. We walked over and sat.

"Any change?" I asked.

"Not really. I talked to her on and off, hoping she'd hear me and try to open her eyes. She didn't. Her vitals haven't dropped or spiked. She's been regular. That's good. She was given a dose of Narcan before she got here. That probably saved her life."

"I've heard of it, but can you please bring me into your world and explain its use?" I asked.

"Sure. Narcan blocks or reverses the effects of opioid medication, including extreme drowsiness, slowed breathing, or loss of consciousness. They use it to treat a narcotic overdose in an emergency. There are different levels of consciousness. We monitored her from the nurses' station, but when you and your friend left for a meeting with the director, we sat beside the bed and talked to her. We didn't detect any movement, but it's still early in her treatment. Her breathing is good. And that's important. If there's a change, it will flash on our screen and set off an alarm."

"Both Marnie and I will be here all night. Detectives Summers and Maloney are still with the director. I'm going to sit with Annie and Marnie for a while, then head back downstairs." I stood. "Thank you," I said.

We left the dayroom and walked back to the nurses' station. Annie's nurse went back behind the counter, and I went into Annie's room.

Marnie looked up. "The nurse at the front desk brought me a magazine. I was sitting over at the table flipping through it when I thought I heard Annie make a noise. I went over to her bed, leaned down, and whispered her name. I repeated it a couple of times." Marnie shook her head, "Nothing."

"Sam will let us know when he hears back from Chief Lowe. Right now, I think it's better if we sit here and talk to her. Even if we talk to each other, it's familiar voices, and maybe her brain will react."

Marnie tried to talk about her upcoming wedding plans but couldn't get through more than a few sentences. "Can't do it," she said, then reached over and picked up the TV remote.

"That's okay," I stood and did a couple of circles around the room. "Any voices are better than silence." I was just ready to sit when my cell rang. I answered without looking at the caller ID. It was Sam. He'd heard from Chief Lowe.

Marnie didn't look up. "Was that Sam?" she asked.

"It was. I'm going down to the director's office." I took a deep breath. "Can you stay with Annie? She needs one of us here with her."

"Of course. Let me know what Barnstable PD found out. I'll let you know if anything changes here." She stood and hugged me.

Chapter 51

I knocked on Director Flanagan's door. He motioned me to come in. I took the chair beside Sam. "You said you heard from Chief Lowe?" I asked.

"I did," Sam said, then continued. "The officer he sent over to the high school to check the faculty parking lot found four pickups with a boat hitch. He ran the plate numbers, but none matched our person of interest."

"Did the chief check to see if Richardson was at school today?" I asked.

"He did. And, no, he wasn't."

I was frustrated. In my book, Arthur Richardson was a calculating, conniving murderer. "Did he call in sick? Or was he out for a meeting?"

"Called in sick," Sam said.

"So now we've got a problem. If Richardson called in sick, he might have taken a ride to Webb Island and ...."

Sam didn't let me finish. "Chief Marshall, could you have your officer, the one who took us out to the island, check to see if there's a pickup with an empty trailer in the boat lot?"

Chief Marshall didn't take any time for conversation. He called the station and got Officer Bisbee on the line. "As we speak, I need you to take the PD boat to the boat lot for the Webb Island area. Have two available officers follow you in an unmarked. If there is a pickup or pickups in the boat lot, run the plate number or numbers. If one comes back registered to an Arthur Richardson, I need to know immediately. He's a person of interest in the murder in Barnstable and in the intended murder of the two people we found inside the cottage." The chief shook his head. "If there is a name match to the plate number or if something doesn't look right, take the PD boat out for observation. Do not go back to the island. He may be armed and is considered dangerous. Circle the island, but use extreme caution. Call me to report your find."

I looked at Sam. "If Richardson gets wind that we're on to him, there's no telling what he might do. The other thing is Peter Mosley. Also, if Richardson is spooked, he's liable to make sure Peter Mosley is permanently unavailable for questioning."

Sam nodded. "Not to mention that Richardson and Peter Mosley probably are the disguised voices behind the threatening phone calls you received. If either of them is backed into a corner with no way to escape, one or both of them will be looking for you."

My stomach was in knots, but I didn't want Sam to know.

"Have you heard any more on Mark's condition?" I asked.

The director shook his head. "No, but ICU has instructions to let me know of any change whatsoever."

"There's nothing more I can do here. I'm going back up with Annie," I said.

Sam took my hand and walked me to the door. "Maloney and I will be up shortly." He hugged me and whispered, "Hang in there."

The elevator was packed and stopped at every floor until it reached the fifth. Marnie was standing to the side of the door, waiting for it to open. She was doing her happy dance, so I knew something positive was happening. She didn't even wait until I was firmly planted on the floor before she took my hand and pulled me aside.

"What's happening," I asked, half-scared and half-excited.

"Annie moved. When I leaned over to acknowledge her movement, she opened her eyes. Mind you, it was ever so slightly, but she was trying. I took her hand, hoping she'd react to the attention." Tears formed in Marnie's eyes. "She didn't. But, she's trying."

We walked up to the door to Annie's room. I acknowledged Officer Abbot, then Marnie and I went into the room. We stood at her bed, one on each side. Marnie held one hand, and I held the other. I leaned down and quietly said, "Annie girl, Marnie and I are both here. The three musketeers are together. Why don't you give us a smile?" I had all I could do to compose myself, but I had to stay strong for both Annie and Marnie—and me, for that matter.

I was so into watching Annie that I didn't notice Nurse Sampson come in. "You've heard the good news," she said. "A baby step in the right direction. This may be the first indication that she's, to some degree, starting to receive and process sounds. I'm encouraged that she opened her eyes, even if it was just a little bit. Gradually she'll be able to keep them open for longer periods of time and be awakened from "sleep" easier—at first by pain, like a pinch, then by touch, like gently shaking her shoulder, and finally by sound as in calling her name."

"Thank you. It's hard when you're so out in the dark as to what's going on." I went back to my spot beside Annie.

Director Flanigan called the coffee shop and asked to have four coffees delivered to his office. "I figured you could use one. I know I can."

"Much appreciated," said Sam.

The other two nodded in agreement.

"Sitting and waiting for an hour feels like five hours," said Sam. He stood and walked over to the window that overlooked the lobby.

"My take is Richardson murdered Betsy the Saturday night of her class reunion. I think he carefully planned it. Or, at least he thought he did. If we knew the why, we could get inside his sick mind and figure out his next move. His biggest mistake could be his hookup with Peter Mosley. But he needed a puppet and, it looks like he found one."

Maloney tapped his fingers on the desk. "In my opinion, Richardson knows something in his plan went wrong, and now he's fumbling around trying to figure out how to divert attention from himself to Mosley. If the officials think Mosley was the mastermind and now feels threatened, then a carefully orchestrated suicide would take the heat off Richardson."

"That's entirely possible," said Chief Marshall.

"Not only is it possible, but Peter Mosley might also already be Richardson's latest victim." Sam turned to Chief Marshall. "I know you told Officer Bisbee not to pull up to Webb Island, but if there's no other boat docked at the island, I think he should take a look." Sam cocked his head to the side and shrugged. "There may not be a boat now, but if Richardson were there earlier and discovered the locks had been changed, he'd know he'd been made. So, there may not be a boat, but there may be a body. Richardson might not think so, but Peter Mosey could do a lot of talking from the grave."

"I agree with Sam," Maloney said. "In my opinion, Richardson is sweating the outcome."

Chief Marshall took a deep breath and looked down at the floor. "That makes him even more dangerous. Let me call Bisbee back and tell him if there's no boat on the island to check it out."

"Director, can you distribute to your security personnel and post a picture of Arthur Richardson in locations throughout the hospital? I don't know how he'd find out that Annie and Mark are here, but I don't want to leave anything to chance."

"Absolutely, get me the picture, and I'll distribute it."

Sam took out his phone and dialed Chief Lowe. "Chief, I need a picture of Arthur Richardson sent to my phone ASAP. Director Flanigan is going to post it here in the hospital." Sam put his phone on speaker. "One more thing, I forgot to ask, since he wasn't at work today, could you send an unmarked by Richardson's house to see if there's a pickup with a boat hitch parked in a driveway or somewhere around his property?"

"I'll call Principal Walters. I have his home number if he's left for the day. I'll get the address and send an unmarked by Richardson's house. As far as the picture, I don't need to be a middle man. He can send that directly to you. Let me know when you get it. I will, however, give you a call back as soon as I get information on the vehicle."

"Thanks, chief." I ended the call and turned my attention to the director. "You heard him. Okay, both those things are in the works."

Chapter 52

I took the remote off the table across from Annie's bed and turned on the TV. "Marnie, you haven't eaten anything but vending machine junk. Why don't I call Sam and have him ask the director where we can call to get something delivered. I could use some food myself, and I'm sure the guys could too."

"If you want to, it's okay with me," Marnie said.

I called Sam. "Could you check with the director about where we can call to get some food delivered?"

"Anything in particular?" he asked.

"Maybe pizza," I said.

"Okay. I'll find out, then order the usual. When it comes, Maloney and I will join you in Annie's room," Sam said.

"See you when you get here."

"What are we getting?"

I knew she was in la-la land when she asked what we were getting. She was sitting beside me when I talked to Sam. "Pizza," I said.

It was four o'clock. Channel 7 Breaking News flashed across the screen. My head snapped around when I heard the reporter say Webb Island. A male, presumed to be in his early to mid-thirties, was found dead an hour ago on Webb Island on Wampatuck Pond in Hanson. My phone rang before the story finished. It was Sam.

"Sam, I've got the TV on in Annie's room. Channel 7 Breaking News reported finding a body on Webb Island."

"Slow down," Sam said. "Chief Marshall just received a call from Officer Bisbee, who was assigned to check the island. Apparently, two guys who'd never fished Wampatuck Pond before were fishing near the island, got curious, and went over to check it out. They were the ones who found the body and called the Hanson PD. Officer Bisbee and the two additional officers assigned by Chief Marshall had just pulled into the boat launch lot when Bisbee received the call from the station regarding the body. They proceeded to the island, checked it out, and questioned the two fishers. "

"Do the officers know who it was?" I asked.

"Chief Marshall said it was a male and that he had no identification on him," Sam said. "Officer Bisbee took a picture and sent it out for facial recognition. Somebody staged the scene to indicate suicide. Our John Doe was shot in the head. Chief's hoping that won't alter the image, making it impossible to identify the deceased. Our John Doe had a gun in his hand. But, his finger wasn't near the trigger, and there was no powder residue. Our John Doe did not shoot that gun. And, since there were no reports of a gunshot, the shooter had to have muffled the sound. Chief's waiting for a callback. Gotta go, I've got a call coming in."

"Sam, Chief Lowe here. Your man Richardson has a gray pickup truck. It wasn't at his house, but his neighbor was out mowing the lawn, so our officer asked him about the truck. The neighbor confirmed that Richardson does drive a gray pickup, and his wife, Marsha, drives a Hyundai Santa Fe. Then added that three days ago, the wife told Mrs. Neighbor, she and the two toddlers were leaving to visit family in New Hampshire. Our officer then asked if Richardson owned a boat. The neighbor told him the make and model and said it's usually parked behind the house, but he thought Richardson must have taken a day off to go fishing because he saw him pull out around 9:30 this morning with the boat in tow."

"Thank you, Mr. Neighbor," said Sam.

"I'm going to send an unmarked over to Richardson's neighborhood," said Chief Lowe. We need to find this guy. Casey is with you, right?"

"Yes, she is. She and Marnie were already planning on staying at the hospital tonight to be with Annie. This guy, Richardson, isn't stupid. We don't know what he, and I'm assuming, Peter Mosey talked about. We don't know what Richardson knows about Annie and Mark. I think it's a good idea if Maloney and I stay the night also."

"I was just about to suggest that. As soon as I get any more information, I'll call you. And, if you hear anything else, I don't care what time it is, give me a call."

"I will. Someone is trying to text me." Sam ended his call with Chief Lowe and opened his text messages. There was a message from Principal Walters with three pictures attached. "Yes." Sam made a fist and pulled his elbow in.

The text read—*Sam, I took these pictures from the newest yearbook. They're crisp, clean, and very recognizable. Let me know if you need anything else.*

Sam texted back—*These are great. We'll get them circulated throughout the hospital. I don't want this son of a bitch getting anywhere close to Annie and Mark.*

Sam asked the director for the telephone number to the nearest pizza place that delivered. Sam made the call and ordered two pizzas, gave them his credit card number, then Maloney's cell number so he could meet them in the lobby. They said they'd be there in forty-five minutes.

"Director, I have three very recent pictures of our person of interest. Believe me. I'm being kind, referring to him like that when I know the son of a bitch is the murderer. We can transfer the pictures from my phone to your computer, print them off, and get them circulated."

Director Flanigan made twenty copies of each picture. "I'll get these distributed, and if I'm not back before you go upstairs, I'll meet you guys on the fifth floor. I also want to make some heads-up calls."

Maloney and Sam waited in the director's office for the delivery person to call. "I know the Cape Cod Hospital like the back of my hand. Here, I'm lost. I should have asked the director if he had a printed schematic of the layout. Sam walked to the door of the outer office. Director Flanigan's secretary was at her desk. "Maybe we'll get lucky."

Sam walked to her desk, glanced at her name plaque, then asked, "Do you, by any chance, have a schematic of the hospital, and if so, could I have a copy?"

"We have a binder that's at least a hundred pages of prints from the boiler room to the patient rooms on the sixth floor. It includes everything. The director told me he was meeting you on the fifth floor in about a half-hour. My suggestion is to ask him if there's something that would be more helpful for you."

Sam nodded. "Thank you. I agree."

"Sam, hear me out." Maloney stood and paced while he talked. "First of all, we're 99% sure the body found is that of Peter Mosey. There is no doubt that Richardson played him and, before he killed him, got all the information he needed to figure out where Annie and Mark might be. A hospital would fit into the category of a *might be* location."

Sam searched his phone for hospitals in the area, other than South Shore Hospital. "There's Beth Israel Deaconess, Brigham and Women's, and Mass General, to name a few. But they are at least six miles farther than South Shore."

"And, as you get closer to Boston, there's much more traffic. In an emergency, as this was, the patient or patients would be transported to the closest hospital equipped to handle the situation." Maloney added. "So, in Richardson's mind, if Annie and Mark were taken to a hospital, it would likely be South Shore."

Maloney's phone rang. They met the pizza delivery girl in the lobby then headed to the fifth floor.

The only other person in the elevator got out on the second floor. Sam sighed. "Maloney, I have a thought I want to share. Richardson is an art teacher. The word creative just came to mind. We have pictures of what the real Arthur Richardson looks like, and those are the ones we're distributing, but think about this. What if he got creative and disguised himself, so he didn't resemble his real identity?" Sam rubbed his chin and let his eyes wander around as though he was studying an evidence/murder board.

Maloney shrugged. "I don't see how he could have completely changed his persona from when he allegedly killed Peter until presumably now."

"Remember, he called in sick this morning, and his wife and two small children are off Cape with family. So, he had plenty of time to change his appearance. I'm willing to bet the farm he did just that—knowingly creating a problem for us."

"Whoa. We need to have extra details stationed on both Mark's and Annie's floors. I have a suggestion to run by Chief Marshall and Director Flanigan."

The elevator opened on the fifth floor. Sam and Maloney stepped out.

"Before we head to Annie's room, hear me out," said Sam. "My suggestion is to have two female police officers disguise themselves as nurses. Both Annie and Mark are directly across the hall from the nurses' station. We'll use his tactics by having an armed female PO disguised as a nurse and the officer stationed outside their rooms, watching and waiting for our perp."

"I like it. Let's run it by the director so we can get started."

Maloney and Sam acknowledged the officer outside Annie's door, then walked in. The director was there waiting for them.

Maloney set the pizza and a stack of napkins on the table. The director had already gotten a few cans of Diet Coke, water, and ginger ale from the kitchenette across from Annie's room.

Sam walked over to the door leading to the hallway and closed it. "We can eat and talk at the same time. Maloney and I have something worthy of discussion that, if implemented, needs to be done immediately."

The director motioned for Sam to continue.

Sam recapped the disguise scenario that he and Maloney had talked about then continued, "We're dealing with a desperate, dangerous person who has no regard for human life. I've spoken with Chief Lowe. He agrees that Maloney and I should stay at the hospital tonight with you girls. As we know, Casey was threatened several times. We don't believe those were idol threats. Richardson is desperate. He knows we're on to him, and I think he's working scared. Casey, in particular, has introduced a death that happened ten years ago. The cause of death recorded then was accidental drowning, but now it's looking like it should have been murder. And, the person of interest, in that case, is none other than our Arthur Richardson."

Director Flanigan sat forward in his chair. "I'm in. Let me give Chief Marshall a call." The director moved to the other side of the room, called the chief, explained the situation, and briefly outlined the action plan. He hung up and returned to where the rest of us were sitting. "He's calling in a couple of his female POs to meet us here. We have uniforms that will provide good cover. He said he already had one foot out the door and would be here in fifteen minutes. He also added that he was taking his personal car and wearing civilian clothes. He's not going to stop in my office. He's coming directly up here."

Marnie and I stepped away from the guys and moved over beside Annie. I stared at the machine monitoring her heartbeat. It wasn't jumping up and down sporadically. It appeared regular. I held my hands together and silently prayed that she'd be okay, then reached down and took her hand in mine. "Annie," I whispered. "We're all here for you and will be until you're up walking around and can come home." I felt a couple of tears roll down my cheeks. "Hang in there." I turned to find Sam standing right behind me.

"You okay, Sherlock?" he asked, then wrapped his arms around me and hugged me tightly.

"I will be," I said and burrowed my face into his chest.

Chapter 53

Richardson's motel room

Arthur Richardson stood in front of the mirror in his room at the Surf Side Motel in Duxbury, admiring his transformation into a person even he didn't recognize. "Not a bad job, not bad at all—Artie boy." He smiled. It was 3:30. In his mind, he had plenty of time to introduce the old Arthur Richardson to the new Artie Richardson. He emptied the two Walmart bags full of new clothes onto the bed. The third bag contained toiletries and a fourth one, a new pair of Nikes, and a couple packages of underwear. He surveyed his purchases, then nodded. "This should be enough to get me through the better part of two weeks."

He stripped down to his underwear, sat on the edge of the bed, propped the pillows up against the headboard, then sat back against them and turned on the TV. The 4:00 news came on. The lead story reported a body discovered in Hanson near a cottage on Webb Island in Wampatuck Pond. He smiled smugly, acknowledging his accomplishment. "Perfect," he whispered out loud.

His blood-stained old jeans lay on the floor beside the bed. He reached over and pulled his wallet and a bank envelope of money from the back pocket and his cell phone from the front pocket. He looked at the phone. "Shit, I forgot to take the charger." He grimaced. "Note to self—pick up a charger." He checked for messages. There were none. He knew that Marsha should be well-settled in by now at her parent's house in New Hampshire. Things hadn't been good between them ever since their last child was born. Things hadn't been good for a lot longer than that. In his heart, he knew she wasn't coming back. There were no messages, and he didn't care.

Chapter 54

Fifteen minutes to the second, Chief Marshall walked into Annie's room, and five minutes after he came in, the two female POs showed up. We were introduced to Officers Moore and Curtis before they were whisked away by the charge nurse to change into the uniform of the hour. Not even ten minutes later, they returned in uniform with stethoscopes around their necks, pen holders in their pockets, official name tags pinned to their shirts, and clipboards with mock orders and information.

I looked at Sam, then back to the costumed officers. "They'd fool me. Are they carrying?" I asked.

"They are, and we are—and you better not be."

"I'm not, but I wish I were."

The director and Sam went out to the hallway to talk to Officer Abbot. They instructed him to knock once to let them know he was coming in, twice to have one of us come out, and three times if he wanted Sam and Maloney both to come out. The director had procured scrubs and a jacket usually worn by an orderly. "We'll make this quick and get into place. We have no idea of his timeline or if he's going to show at all," said Director Flanigan. "So we're going to play the waiting game."

"He'll recognize Maloney, Marnie, Casey, and me. So we can't let him see us. We were at the high school doing interviews, so he definitely knows who we are." said Sam. "One of your female POs can be in the room and the other at the nurses' station alongside Director Flanigan. Just hospital personnel doing their job. It won't look like anything out of the ordinary. Casey, you, Marnie, and Chief Marshall stay in the room at the back of the nurses' station. There's a curtain—make sure it's pulled all the way across."

276

"Where are you and Maloney going to be," I asked.

"In the bathroom in Annie's room.," Sam said. "Officer Abbot is going to signal us."

I looked over to Annie. "This is for you, girl," I whispered.

"Listen up. Richardson isn't going to look like the pictures we circulated earlier. When you go back behind the counter, look at that picture. But, concentrate on the facial features—his eyes, nose, mouth, and even cheekbones. He may be wearing glasses or some kind of skin-altering makeup. I would bet he changed his hair color and to what, who knows. So, that's why the facial features have to be the center of your focus. We can't afford to make a mistake." Sam nodded. "Any questions?"

There were none.

"He's cocky and, in my opinion, overconfident. He's a charmer. But don't lose sight of the fact that, first and foremost, he's a killer. Do I want to see him dead? For what's he's done, I'm not going to lie. Of course, I do. He belongs in the grave. But, unless he initiates it, we don't have that choice. Does everyone understand?" Maloney looked around. "If there are no concerns, let's take our places."

"One other thing. I want everyone to silence their cell phones. A ringing noise could spook Richardson, and there's no telling what he might do." Sam watched as we all heeded his directive.

I felt like I was in the middle of filming the TV show *The Rookie*. We didn't know if Richardson would show, but we had to be ready if he did. My heart was pounding. All sorts of scenarios were running through my mind. I mean—here's a teacher—a teacher. Someone who kids look up to—someone they idolize and want to be like when they grow up. I sat in my chair, staring at the pulled curtain. More than I knew, I wanted this to be a filming of The *Rookie* because when it was over, we'd all laugh, shake hands, and maybe head out to the local watering hole for a drink—and I wanted to be in this line of work. Why? I took a deep breath, then slowly let it out.

Marnie and I stayed back away from the window. The second hand on the wall clock kept moving, but the minute hand seemed to remain still.

Marnie leaned over and rested her head on my shoulder. "Do you think he'll show?" she asked.

"I don't know. I don't think anyone knows. Richardson has no idea what Annie's condition is. It's 7:15. We've been in here almost a half hour. Visiting hours are over at 8:00 p.m.—not that the time makes any difference. But, Richardson might think that having people around him will make him just part of the everyday visitor's movement. We'll find out soon enough." I wanted to be on the other side of the curtain. I could identify him, disguise or no disguise, but he would also recognize me, then all hell would break loose. "Hey, Marnie, I have a question. How would he know what room Annie is in?"

"In my earlier years, I worked as a Candy Striper at the Cape Cod Hospital. The local florists would deliver flowers to the front desk for patients. They already had room numbers written below the patient's name on the envelope, so I'm assuming the florist called and got that information."

"So, it's possible that Richardson called South Shore pretending to be a florist to get Annie and Mark's room numbers."

"Yes. But, with Mark being in ICU, those patients are not allowed to have flowers or visitors."

"Hence, a cog in the wheel of his *plan*. Although, if Mark's in ICU, he's not in good shape and, chances are, won't make it out of there." I shrugged. "I'm not saying that's what's going to happen, but I'm hoping that's what Richardson is counting on."

"That means, if he shows, he'll come here, and it'll be showtime." Marnie leaned forward and rested her arms across her knees.

Chief Marshall stood and started pacing the floor. "In my thirty years on the department, I've never dealt with anything like this," he

278

said quietly. "That little lady across the hall and her friend in ICU didn't ask to be here. Thirty years ago, there were bad people, but nowadays, they're not only bad, but they're sick bastards."

I wanted to move the curtain just enough to see the door to Annie's room, but that wasn't in the cards. I had to wait. We all had to wait. I thought I heard some movement. Then nothing. I decided it was my mind playing games with me. Games I didn't want to play.

I closed my eyes and let my mind drift back to happier times. I visualized Annie's smile, dancing freckles, and natural red hair. I chuckled softly. "I remember the time we went to the Melody Tent to see Chicago. That was in, let me think—um, July 2013. We sang and hummed the lyrics to *Saturday in the Park* for weeks after. Then Frankie Valli and The Four Seasons in July 2014." I looked at Marnie. "You were with us for that one. Remember—we bounced around in our seats laughing and singing to *Big Girls Don't Cry*."

Marnie leaned over and hugged me. "The three of us are going to do it again."

I had to compose myself. "Yes, we are."

All of a sudden, we heard a thud. I held my breath. No gunshots, just the sounds of objects being moved or thrown. I didn't know what was going on. Then came the voices. I recognized Sam's and Maloney's. I walked up close to the window but didn't move the curtain. Chief Marshall and Marnie moved up beside me.

The noise stopped. The voices stopped. I looked at the Chief and mouthed, "What do we do?"

He shook his head and rested his hand on his gun. "Nothing yet," he mouthed back.

I nodded.

Marnie stayed in the corner. The look on her face said it all.

I put my finger up to my lips.

She nodded.

Five minutes went by. The chief walked to the far end of the curtain and moved it just enough to get a visual of the nurses' station. He signaled for me to join him. The director and the head nurse were standing against the wall looking in the direction of Annie's room. The door was halfway open, but we couldn't see if anything was going on inside.

The chief tapped on the window to get Director Flanigan's attention.

Director Flanigan walked over and opened the door. "It's over," he said.

My body felt like a jar of jelly. So much for my staying strong. I took Marnie's hand and guided her out of our safe room. Sam or Maloney was nowhere in sight. I could hear muffled voices but didn't know where they were coming from or who they belonged to. I thought it was from Annie's room, but I wasn't sure.

I looked at the cardiac monitors lining the desk. The room numbers were in bold letters above the screen. Annie was in room 504. The monitor for room 504 was silent. The line that normally reflected the patient's heart rate was stagnant—no line—no noise— nothing. I moved aside, so Marnie didn't realize what I was looking at.

I was functioning in slow motion at a loss of what to do next when Sam walked out of Annie's room. Behind him was Arthur Richardson cuffed and in shackles, escorted by Maloney and Officer Abbot.

Sam nodded. "It's over," he said.

"And Annie?" I asked. I was afraid to hear what he had to say.

"She's next door in room 506."

Richardson wasn't as smug as he was when I interviewed him at the high school. I knew he couldn't get to me, so I walked right up in front of him, looked him square in his eyes, and said, "Artie Richardson, don't forget to *caress the grass, paint the skies, and dance in the flowers.* But as far as anyone *seeing you in September,* not going to happen. Your calendar is about to change drastically— better get used to it. You should also consider changing your hairstylist. You don't look good as a dirty blonde. And, by the way, Buster Adams sends his regards."

"You'll never prove anything," Richardson spouted.

I looked him straight in his eyes. "I'm sorry. Prove what?" I smiled. "We'll meet again."

Sam knew Richardson was getting aggravated. I didn't care, but when Sam tilted his head in the direction of room 506, I knew exactly what he meant.

Marnie and I gave the teacher one more look of approval of his new wrist, and ankle jewelry, then moved down the hall.

Even though I now know Annie wasn't connected to the 504 cardiac monitor, I was relieved when we walked into room 506 and saw the line movement and heard the noise indicating a regular heart rate. Marnie stood on one side of the bed, and I stood on the other.

We still didn't know what happened while we were behind the curtain. Obviously, Annie had been moved. But, if there wasn't a body in room 504, why did Richardson go in?

Marnie must have read my mind. "What's going on?"

"I was trying to figure that out, but I've hit a stone wall." I just finished my sentence when Maloney walked in.

"What happened here today?" I asked.

"There was a change of plans. One of the female officers did a costume change. She became a patient—Annie—the patient in room 504. They quickly hooked the officer up to the monitor and disguised her enough so, at a glance, she resembled Annie. Since Richardson was in a hurry to get the job done, he didn't pay attention and assumed Annie was the person in the bed. It worked."

"I'm going down to the coffee shop to get some coffees. Do you girls want one?"

"Yes, please. I could use one right about now. Marnie, why don't you go with him. A change in scenery might help."

Marnie smiled and nodded. "You're right."

I rested Annie's hand in mine and rubbed the back of it. "Annie, everything is going to be alright. You'll be home before you know it. We got lots of things to do. Remember, Marnie's getting married and we're both in the wedding. We've got showers to plan and, of course, she'll need our advice on her gown and the reception. Although, I'm not sure if it will be on Cape or in New York. Either place, we're going to have a ball."

I'd been looking at Annie's hand the whole time I was talking and only looked up when I felt it move. "You heard everything I said, didn't you?" I kissed her hand and touched her cheek. "Love you."

Along with the two Hanson POs, Sam escorted Richardson down to a waiting squad car. "We'll hold him tonight, then have him arraigned on kidnapping, murder, and attempted murder. Chief Marshall might have him transferred to Plymouth County House of Correction." The officers secured the teacher in the backseat. "Thank you for your help in apprehending this bastard. We'll be in contact."

Sam shook the officers' hands and watched as they drove away.

It had been a long day, and it wasn't over yet.

Chief Marshall and Director Flanigan were waiting for Sam to return before deciding on a plan of action.

Maloney was in Annie's room with Casey and Marnie.

Sam stopped at the nurses' station before heading to room 506. He glanced at the monitor recording Annie's readings and looked at the head nurse. "She'll never believe this story when she wakes up."

He smiled. "I'm going to check in with Maloney and the girls. Then I'll be back."

There was a cup of lukewarm coffee in Annie's room waiting for Sam.

"I'd go down to the coffee shop to get another coffee, but they were getting ready to close when I was there. So I know they're closed now," I said.

"I think I saw a microwave in the room we were in," said Marnie.

"Nope, I'm fine. It could be stone-cold, and it would still taste good." Sam flipped the tab and took a drink.

"About tonight?" I asked. "Marnie and I would like to stay. I've already asked Nurse Simpson, and she said it was fine. The problem is we have only one car. Would you be able to come up tomorrow to either pick us up or bring up a change or two of clothes? Both Marnie and I think we should be here when she regains consciousness. She has no idea what's happened to her and doesn't need to be surrounded by unfamiliar people. The other thing is, we know Mark is teetering on the border of life or death. If she remembers any of what happened, she'll ask about him. It has to be one of us that tells her. Not a stranger in a strange place."

"Both Maloney and I will be here tomorrow. Maloney will take care of Marnie, and I'll take care of you regarding clothes for at least four days. It will be late when I get home, so I won't go over to Mrs. Martin's house to get Watson. I'm sure she's wondering what's going on, but I'll talk to her in the morning and see if she'll watch the boy till one of us is back full time. All I'm going to do is give her a little snippet. Then you can fill her in further if you want to."

"Sam, I'll stop by the station before I come over to your house to let Chief Lowe know what transpired today. He'll have to call Chief Marshall to decide what happens where first." Maloney walked to the window and stared out into the darkness.

Marnie walked up behind him, wrapped her arms around his waist, and leaned her head on his back. "I'm going to be proud to be Mrs. Maloney."

"We got a ride ahead of us, and we have to make a stop at the nurses' station before we go, so let's say our goodnights now, and we'll see you sometime tomorrow morning." Sam moved over beside Annie's bed. "Hey girl, we're counting on you to get up and back running the DA's office." He smiled. "See you tomorrow."

I could see the emotion in Sam's face and knew he was trying hard to control it. I hugged him, kissed him goodnight, then watched him and Maloney head down the hallway.

Marnie and I sat quietly and finished our cold coffee. We were exhausted, but neither one of us was ready to call it a night. There was one recliner in Annie's room that made into a bed and a futon, so all we needed were sheets, blankets, and pillows.

I wanted to sit and veg out. I was exhausted, but my mind was working overtime. "Ok, if I turn on the TV?" I asked.

"I was going to ask you the same thing." Marnie turned the TV on and flipped through the channels until she came to a repeat of *Chicago Med*. We immediately looked at each other. She flipped through seven more channels and stopped at *New Amsterdam*. "That's it," she said. We've had enough real-life hospital drama today to last a lifetime. I'm putting *Beat Bobby Flay* on."

Chapter 55

Friday

It was 7:50 a.m. when Sam and Maloney individually pulled into the Barnstable PD parking lot. They had an 8:00 meeting with Chief Lowe to walk him through the happenings of the day before and discuss their next move.

"Have you heard from Marnie?" Sam asked.

Maloney shook his head. "No. I was about to ask if you've heard from Casey."

"As Casey always says, *no news is good news*, so I'm assuming it was an uneventful night. I'm sure they would have called if there was any change one way or the other with either Annie or Mark." Sam looked around. "I'm all set to travel back to South Shore when we finish up here."

"So am I. I packed up a small suitcase for Marnie."

"Ditto for Casey."

"The chief will be waiting, so let's get going," said Maloney.

Sam and Maloney checked in with the duty officer and proceeded to Chief Lowe's office.

"Morning." The chief walked around his desk and shook the guys' hands. "Have a seat."

He went back to his chair, and Sam and Maloney sat in the two chairs in front of the desk.

They proceeded to describe yesterday's events from the time they arrived at the Hanson PD to when they left South Shore Hospital last night to drive home.

"I sent a cruiser to Arthur Richardson's house in Mashpee at 7:00 this morning." The chief leaned back in his chair. "It was a setup since we knew his family was supposedly in New Hampshire. I was relying on the nosey neighbor to make an appearance. He did. He walked over to ask the officer if there was a problem. Said he was concerned because another police officer was at the house yesterday asking questions about Richardson's truck and if he owned a boat."

"Did this neighbor think there was something wrong? Did this neighbor feel it was his civic duty to offer additional information regarding Richardson or his family?" Sam asked.

The chief nodded. "Nosey neighbors can be annoying, but in this case, this neighbor might furnish helpful information into the Richardson's comings and goings—starting with the wife's."

Sam leaned his elbow on the desk and cradled his chin in his hand. "Okay, how does she fit into the story?"

"We know, per the neighbor, the wife is in New Hampshire with the two kids 'visiting' her parents. We need to find out where the parents live. Since the husband is in custody, she has no reason to be afraid." The chief took a deep breath. "On the other hand, she may know nothing about his life outside their marriage."

"Our Mr. Neighbor did indicate that there appeared to be, as he put it, a little turbulence on the home front," Chief Lowe said.

"I believe," said Sam, "that Mrs. Marsha Richardson could be the star witness at her husband's trial. But since they are still married, she could refuse to testify against him, claiming spousal privilege. Even though he's a piece of shit and should be put away for life, we have no idea what she'll do."

"You're talking about the current charge. Richardson will also be charged with Betsy Harper's murder and the ten-year-old, now considered, murder of Buster Adams. He'll never see the light of day again. No fishing, no consensual sex as he knows it now, no authority—I could go on. She'll testify," Maloney nodded.

Sam's cell phone rang. He reached in his pocket, took it out, and checked the caller ID. It was Casey. He stood up and walked to the back of the chief's office. "Hey, everything okay?" he asked.

"Encouraging," I said. "At least for Annie. She hasn't completely opened her eyes, but every once in a while, it looks like she's trying to. Marnie noticed her lips move as though she was trying to blow out some air. The nurse came in and physically checked her vitals. She was optimistic. The doctor is due to be here within the next hour. I'll try to ask questions without being too pushy."

"Have you heard anything about Mark's condition?" Sam asked.

"No. I don't know if Mark has the same doctor, but I'll find out." I hesitated, then continued, "I don't want to call Annie's parents and tell them what happened over the phone. If I were home, I'd be at their house now. So, I need you to please go over and talk to Mom and Dad McGuire. It won't be easy, but they need to know. After you speak to them and explain the situation, let me know, and I'll give them a call. I'm sure they'll want to come up to see her. But, we'll deal with that when I talk to them." I wanted to wave a magic wand and have this nightmare disappear. "I love you," I said. I could feel myself starting to choke up. "Is Maloney with you?"

"He is," Sam said and handed Maloney the phone.

"I'm handing my phone to Marnie."

"Hi, babe," said Maloney. "You hanging in there?"

Marnie nodded. "It's not easy, but I am. I miss you."

"We'll be leaving here within the hour, so I'll see you soon. Kiss Annie for me."

"Yep." Marnie handed me back my phone, walked over to Annie's bed, and took her hand.

Maloney ended the call. There was no reason to call back. I knew I'd be talking to Sam soon, so I laid my phone on the bedside table and walked over beside Marnie.

"Maloney said they'd be leaving within an hour. I heard you ask Sam to talk to the McGuires before the guys leave to come to the hospital. That's going to be hard."

"It is," I said, "but it has to happen." I leaned over and kissed Annie's cheek, then whispered in her ear, "Hey, girl, want to listen to some music?" I was hoping for even a hint of recognition, but I didn't see any. Annie loved James Taylor. I took my phone from the table, opened the Pandora app, typed in James Taylor, and opened his playlist. I turned the volume down low, hit the play button, and laid my phone on her pillow.

Marnie stood, "I'm going down to the coffee shop to get a coffee and a donut. Want one?"

"Sure, why not." I smiled.

I grabbed my pillow and curled up on the end of the futon closest to Annie. "Sam and Maloney will be here in a few hours." I closed my eyes. The next thing I knew, Marnie was back with my much-needed coffee.

"That tasted good. Thanks." I got up and walked to the window. Without turning around, I said, "The outside looks inviting. I'm going to take in some fresh air. Will you stay with Annie? I won't be long." I pointed to my phone resting on Annie's pillow. "I've got James Taylor songs playing."

Marnie nodded. "Good idea."

Before I ventured down to the lobby, I stopped by the ICU. Officer Wilkins was at his post outside Mark's room. "Good morning," I said.

"Have you been here all night?" he asked.

"Yep. These futons are so comfortable." I smiled. "I certainly will appreciate my mattress when I get home." I peeked into Mark's room. He was in the same position as he was the last time I saw him. I glanced over to the nurses' station. "Is Marilyn here today?"

"She was there a little while ago. She may be in the back."

"And, she may be busy," I said. "I'll stop by later."

The first floor was active with uniformed hospital personnel, housekeeping, drivers making floral deliveries, and people sitting in the lobby gawking around or reading the newspaper waiting for visiting time to start. I walked outside. The fresh air felt good. There were eight park benches in a grassy area close to the entrance. Most of them were empty. I walked over to the first empty one I came to and sat down. I looked up at the white puffy clouds that dotted the robin egg blue sky and closed my eyes. "If you can hear me, please bring our Annie back," I whispered. I sat with my back against the bench, then put my hands up over my face and began to rock back and forth. When I slid my hands down, a little girl was standing there watching me.

"Hi," she said. "Are you a nurse?" she asked.

"No, I'm visiting my friend," I said.

"Is she a little girl like me?" She smiled.

"No, she's a big girl like me," I replied.

She made a half circle and pointed to a lady sitting on the bench two down from where I was sitting. "Me and my mommy are visiting my Grammy." She looked down and scuffed her foot back and forth a couple of times.

"She will be happy to see me."

"I know she will."

"My name is Linsey. What's yours?"

"I'm Casey."

Before she could say anything else, her mother walked over and took her hand. "I'm sorry if she burned your ear off. She's a little Chatty Cathy."

"No problem, I enjoyed it."

"Linsey, say goodbye to the lady."

"Her name is Casey," she said. "Goodbye, Casey."

Her mother smiled. "Thank you."

"No," I said, "thank you."

Linsey took her mother's hand and skipped alongside her until they got to the entrance of the hospital, then looked back at me and waved.

I stayed another ten minutes, just sitting and thinking about nothing, then got up and headed back to Annie's room.

Chapter 56

Marnie was watching TV, and I was talking to Annie. I put down the safety railing so I could sit closer to her. "Did you like listening to James Taylor? Remember riding down 6A—slipping a James Taylor disc in the player, opening the windows, and singing at the top of our lungs. We belted out song after song from when we left Barnstable Village until we pulled into Scargo Café's parking lot. Most of the time, we sat in the tavern. We'd split an order calamari and sweet potato dippers, And, of course, a wine or two to wash them down." I held Annie's hand in mine. "We were full, but there was no way we were leaving without splitting a lobster roll." I leaned in closer. I need my Scargo fix, but I can't get it unless you're with me." I took a deep breath. "So, what do you say. You ready to blow this joint and head back to the Cape?"

I felt my eyes fill up. A couple of my tears fell onto her hand.

Marnie walked over behind me and put her hand on my shoulder. She smiled. "Can we make that outing for three instead of two?"

"What do you say, Annie?" I watched her face as I talked. Can we introduce Marnie to the Scargo Café?" I gently squeezed Annie's hand. "We'll make her a real cappie out of her yet."

"Marnie, did you hear that?"

"Hear what. There's only you, me, and Annie in this room."

"It was a sound a person usually makes when they sleep with their mouth open. If it wasn't you and it wasn't me—we both looked at Annie. "Annie, are you trying to talk to us?" A rush of adrenalin ran through my body. "Annie, try to open your eyes," I said as Marnie walked around to the other side of the bed.

"Marnie, can you please get a facecloth from the nurses' station? I want you to rub it across her forehead and gently dab her eyes, then pass it over her lips."

"Be right back," Marnie said.

With my free hand, I started playing with her fingers—lightly massaging them while talking to her the whole time. I felt a slight twinge. I slowly closed her hand, then opened it. I repeated the process over again until Marnie came back into the room.

Marnie looked at me. "What's up with you. Suddenly, for lack of a better word, you look bubbly."

I got up and told Marnie to sit where I had been sitting. I recreated the scene putting Marnie in my place. I took Marnie's hand and showed her what I'd been doing to Annie. I explained to Marnie that I felt movement when I massaged Annie's fingers. "I want to see if you feel something too."

While Marnie played with Annie's hand, I ran the facecloth under cold water, scrunched it up, ran it softly across her forehead, passed it over her lips, then lightly dabbed her eyes. I repeated the process several more times.

"I'm going to put the James Taylor music on again." I shut the TV off, opened the Pandora app, went to his playlist, and started the music.

Marnie and I continued with Annie's mini spa treatment until the nurse came in. "The doctor called. He's running late but will be here in about twenty minutes." Nurse Sampson looked over at Annie and then at the stats being recorded on the cardiac machine. "Her heart rate and blood pressure are perfect. I'll introduce you to Doctor Menard. He's also Mark Mosley's doctor."

"Thank you," Marnie and I said in unison.

Doctor Menard showed up a half-hour later. Nurse Sampson introduced us. Director Flanigan had briefed him earlier on the relationship between Annie and us and permitted him to discuss her case with us. The doctor was pleased with the progress she'd made so far. Not knowing anything about medicine, I had to agree with the professional. His evaluation of Mark's condition wasn't as encouraging.

Doctor Menard backed away from Annie's bed, walked over to the table and chairs in the corner, and motioned for us to join him. "To rehash the situation, as you know, both Annie and Mark were injected with the drug fentanyl. We also found heroin in Mark's system. So, the injection he got was heroin mixed with fentanyl—in many cases, a deadly combination. They were also severely dehydrated and hadn't eaten in some time. Mark must have put up a great fight to protect both himself and Annie. He has two broken ribs and numerous black and blues. Fortunately, the ribs didn't puncture his lungs, and the punches didn't induce internal bleeding. He's still not out of the woods, and I can only give him a 75% chance of regaining consciousness. If or when he does, he'll have a long road to recovery."

I looked over at Annie—glad she couldn't hear what the doctor just said.

"The person who did this to them is facing time for a list of violent crimes, this one being the most recent. He's in custody and will never see the light of day." I took a deep breath before I continued. "Marnie and I will be here round the clock for whatever time needed until Annie regains consciousness. We don't want her to wake up and be alone."

I told Doctor Menard that both Marnie and I talk to her, massage her hands and fingers, and play some of her favorite music. "It may have been my imagination, but I thought I heard her making a low, moaning noise. I know I felt her hand and fingers move slightly."

"I don't want to discourage you, but the hand movement could be a nerve twitch," the doctor said. "I'm not telling you to stop. Hopefully, the more attention she gets and the familiar voices will trigger something in her brain to react. It's going to be a matter of time." The doctor stood and walked back over to Annie's bed. He reached in his pocket, took out one of his business cards, returned to the table, and handed it to me. "If you need to talk, don't hesitate to call. If you reach my answering service, Nurse Sampson knows how to get ahold of me." He shook our hands, nodded in Annie's direction, and left.

It was just after noontime when Sam and Maloney showed up at the hospital—Sam carrying my small suitcase with one hand, a canvas bag over his shoulder, and a drink holder with four drinks in his other hand. Maloney followed with Marnie's suitcase and two McDonald's take-out bags.

They emptied their hands, gave us each a hug, and walked over to Annie.

"Any change?" Sam asked.

"I think so, but I'm not the doctor. I felt her hand move, and she made a noise," I said. "The doctor warned us about false positives. Not his exact words, but I know that's what he meant."

Marnie turned to face the guys. "We're leaning on the side of encouragement. False positives aren't part of our vocabulary."

We moved over to the table. Sam went to the nurses' station to get another chair while Maloney took the burgers and fries from the bag.

"Did you get any news about Mark's condition?" Maloney asked.

"We did. We'll run all that by you, but first, I want to know if you guys went to see Annie's parents? Sam came through the door just as I finished asking Maloney about seeing the McGuires.

Maloney nodded in Sam's direction. "Casey asked about the McGuires."

Sam took a deep breath and slowly let it out. "When we first went in, they were like stone statues, not wanting to be a part of the scene.

We all sat down. I said that we found Annie and Mark, and they're both alive. Without going into exact details, I said they were both in the hospital under the doctor's care. I lied a little bit and suggested they come here until the doctor has determined the extent of their injuries and the plan of treatment." Sam glanced in my direction.

"Did they accept that?"

"I went on further to tell them that you and Marnie are here and will be staying at the hospital monitoring Annie's condition. I also went out on a limb and said you'd keep them informed as to her progress."

"I'll call them. Dad McGuire can't drive off Cape, and Mom McGuire gave up her license a few years ago. You or Maloney can bring them up if they need to be here."

"Definitely," Sam said.

"Marnie, you haven't been outside since we got here. It's nice out. Why don't you and Maloney sit on one of those benches by the entrance and share some hand-holding time? I'll finish my shake and fries, then take a corridor walk with Sam."

"Thanks, buddy," she said.

After Marnie and Maloney left, Sam walked up to and sat beside Annie's bed, leaned down, and whispered, "I know you hate McDonald's burgers, so I didn't bring you one. So that you know, your first Raw Bar lobster roll is on me." He took her hand in his. Not a minute later, he suddenly turned and looked at me. "She just moved her hand." He leaned over and again whispered in her ear, "I'll even buy you sweet potato fries." Sam pulled his lower lip in between his teeth and looked up at the ceiling, then back at Annie. "Your mom and dad said to say hi."

I rubbed his back. "Thank you."

Chapter 57

Two days later - Sunday

Two days had passed since Marnie, and I *moved into* Annie's hospital room with her. In my mind, the constant interaction between the three of us was a significant step in her recovery. She still wasn't completely out of the woods but well on her way.

It was almost 5:30 in the morning. The sun was trying hard to peek through the blinds. The bells and whistles in the hallway had kept me up most of the night. Marnie and Annie were still sleeping. Remind me never to buy a futon. Just as I sat up to roll my head and get the kinks out, Nurse Sh came in to take her vitals.

"Good morning," she whispered.

"And a good morning to you," I replied.

She finished in no time. "The doctor ordered a liquid and soft foods breakfast for Annie. Since she's been able to get some water down and keep it down, he wants to see if she can handle some soft food."

"Do you want me to try to feed her?" I asked.

"Not the first time. When food services bring the tray in, I'll be right behind them." She looked at her watch. "They should be here within a half-hour. If you want to try to wake her up, that will help."

I nodded. When Nurse Sampson left, I walked over beside Annie's bed, lowed the guard rail, and sat down on the edge of the mattress. "Good morning, sunshine," I whispered. I didn't expect a response. I took her hand in mine, rubbed her palm, and played with her fingers. "Annie, it's time to wake up. Your breakfast will be here soon." I smiled as though she were watching me.

Marnie hadn't flinched. No need to wake her up until Annie's food comes.

"Annie, time to wake up." I kissed her forehead.

Her eyes opened almost halfway.

"Annie, girl, can you give me a smile?"

Her lips moved, but nothing came out.

"You talking to me?" Marnie asked.

"No. Annie just opened her eyes partway and moved her mouth."

Marnie jumped up and hurried across the room. "Annie, it's me, Marnie. Nod if you can hear me."

Within seconds Annie's head moved slightly up and down.

"Oh, my." Tears welled up in Marnie's eyes. "She's going to be okay."

I held Marnie's hand. "Yep, she's going to be okay."

I knew Annie's breakfast would be here soon, so I slowly raised the back of her bed about ten inches and moved her tray table beside the bed. "Your breakfast is on its way." I pointed to the sink in her bathroom. "Marnie, can you get me a wet facecloth. I want to give her the face, lips, and eyes treatment."

Marnie was back within seconds. "Here you go."

I wiped her face, then gently dabbed her eyes.

The softest little 'yes' came from her mouth, and again her eyes opened partway.

Annie's breakfast came. Nurse Sampson followed them in. I told her that Annie tried to speak—that she actually said *yes* after I washed her face.

Annie's nurse smiled and raised the bed a little higher. "Let's get some food in her."

I watched her being fed—almost like a baby. She was eating. Nurse Sampson held a sippy cup of juice to her mouth and slowly tilted it until some of the liquid hit her lips. She slowly swallowed.

"She's doing great. Doctor Menard will be pleased." Nurse Sampson smiled. "Do you want to try to feed her?"

"I do." I positioned myself beside the and mimicked what I had just watched. Annie took a couple more small tastes of applesauce, then made it apparent she didn't want any more. She was still hooked up to the intravenous, so she got the needed nutrients.

Nurse Sampson gave her a sponge bath and changed her bedclothes. For the first time since this whole ordeal started, Annie looked like she was sleeping and would wake up at any time.

Annie's nurse looked at Marnie, then at me. "She has some special friends."

Chapter 58

"Marnie, I'm going to go down to get a coffee, then to ICU to check on Mark. Wanna come with me?"

"Yeah, sure, let me get my phone," she said.

We stopped at the nurses' station to tell them where we were going if they needed us.

It was early, so we were the only occupants. We headed to the coffee shop. The smell of a just-baked coffee sweet bun took over my nose. "I don't know about you, but one of those buns is calling my name. Want one?" I asked.

"You think I'm going to sit here and watch you eat alone—not going to happen. I'll get the table. You get the food and coffee," Marnie said as she walked to the table in the corner by the window.

I'd just sat down when my phone rang.

"Morning, Sherlock."

I looked at Marnie and mouthed *Sam*. "Morning to you. Are you guys coming up today?"

"That's the plan. Watson's having a ball at the Martin's. They said not to worry. He can stay as long as he needs to."

"I miss him."

"Trust me—he misses you too."

"What time are you planning on being here?"

"I'm going to pick Maloney up in an hour—so probably around 11:00."

"Annie has made some progress. She's been reacting to Marnie and me. This morning they gave her liquid and soft foods for breakfast. And she ate some."

"Marnie and I are having coffee, then stopping by ICU to check on Mark. After that, we'll be back on the fifth floor."

"I'm going to call Annie's parents and give them a carefully worded progress report."

"Okay, we'll see you later. Love you," Sam said

"Love you too."

Marnie and I checked in with Marilyn at the nurses' station in the ICU. She asked about Annie. We gave her the short version of what we knew. She was happy to hear about Annie's progress.

I looked across the hall to Mark's room. "Marilyn, did Chief Marshall pull the security detail for Mark?" I asked.

"Yes. As of this morning," she said. "Because they captured the person who they believe to be the mastermind of the operation, he didn't feel Mark needed the security detail any longer."

"Now that you mention it, there wasn't anyone posted outside Annie's door this morning either," I said.

Marilyn came from around the counter. "I was about to do a check on Mark. Why don't you two come with me."

I nodded.

"He's still listed as critical because there are serious problems that still require intensive medical care and monitoring. Mark is being fed intravenously until the doctor determines that his digestive tract can adequately accept food. His breathing has improved slightly, and his vital signs are also starting to show progress, but Mark's not ready to come off the ventilator. Doctor Menard has me icing down where X-rays showed two broken ribs. This morning when I did that, he flinched. I noted it in the report. The doctor will be here soon for morning rounds. But, until Mark regains consciousness and everything is functioning on its own, he'll remain in ICU."

"I don't know how you do it. You have a calling." I looked at Marilyn and smiled.

It was just after 11:00 when Sam and Maloney walked into Annie's room.

"You guys are a welcome sight," I said.

Sam walked over to where I was standing next to Annie's bed. "I've got some good news to share. Let's sit at the table to talk."

I moved to the table. "Let's hear it."

Maloney stayed by the window, and Marnie sat beside me.

"The judge issued a warrant for Maloney and me to search Richardson's truck. Chief Lowe is working on getting a search warrant for his house."

My heart raced. "What did you find?"

Sam took a deep breath. "You'll know if you let me finish."

I nodded. I knew better than to interrupt Sam when he was in detective mode.

"Maloney found a .38 Special—the same type used to kill Peter Mosley," Sam said. "It's been sent to the lab that has the bullet for testing. There's no doubt in my mind they'll issue a finding matching the bullet to the gun." Sam looked at Annie. "And, as soon as our key witness can make a statement implicating Richardson, he'll be taking up permanent residency probably at Souza-Baranowski Correctional Center in Lancaster."

"He won't be teaching anyone there—his fellow inmates will be teaching him from a curriculum developed within the prison community known as prison culture." Maloney shook his head. "Either he'll learn the art of not betraying his fellow inmates by colluding with prison officers, or he'll find himself walking barefoot through hell's embers with Peter Mosley."

Chapter 59

The four of us were still sitting at the table when food services brought Annie's tray. The nurse followed them into the room and checked to make sure the kitchen had followed the dietary instructions given by Dr. Menard. She held up a slice of white bread and looked at us. "This is why I have to check. She's not allowed to have this. I understand she's not feeding herself yet, but since it was on the tray, somebody helping her eat wouldn't know not to give this to her."

I felt the nurse's frustration. "I'll start to feed her. Then, if you want to, you can take over."

"I can do that," I said.

The nurse tended to Annie while the four of us continued our conversation.

"Sitting here, I've had time to do a lot of thinking. There's no question about Richardson's role in the kidnapping and attempted murders of Annie and Mark and the actual murder of Peter. My problem goes much further back—ten years to be exact, back to Buster Adams. Here's my take, Richardson was responsible for Buster's death. Annie had it figured out but needed to prove it before speaking up. She dug till she found something, then confronted Betsy. I think Betsy had too much to drink, got melancholy, and confided in Annie about a secret she'd be harboring for years—ten to be exact. Remember, after the reunion, Annie came to me asking to look into Buster's death.'

"And you told her you would," said Sam.

"That's correct." I looked at Sam. "I did tell her that until you told me not to get involved."

"Then, Buster's mother, on Annie's suggestion, came by my office and retained my services to look into his death."

302

"There's a lot of ifs and unanswered questions," Sam said.

I nodded. "Betsy had a secret that she kept for ten plus years. That secret involved her, Buster, and, I think, Richardson. Our problem is that Betsy's dead, Buster's dead, and Richardson isn't going to offer any information that would make him the third player in this threesome."

Sam walked to the window, leaned on the sill, and looked out over the parking lot. "Annie figured out the connection, and before she could tell anyone of us, Richardson had to get her and Mark out of the picture."

"Why Mark?" Marnie asked.

"Because he didn't know if Mark knew the *secret* and couldn't afford to speculate one way or the other," said Sam.

"Casey," said Nurse Sampson, "Annie is eating little bits like she was this morning. We know she hears you because she reacts to your voice, so talk to her and feed her the way you did before. If you need me, I'm right across the hall."

The guys stayed at the table, and Marnie and I moved up with Annie.

"Hey girl, you've got some applesauce and a little cup of vanilla pudding. Wanna give it a try?" I asked as I put a little dab of pudding on the tip of her spoon. I reached over and gently touched the edge of the spoon to her lips. My legs got wobbly when I noticed her tongue peek out from between her lips and lap the pudding.

Marnie smiled, "Taste good?" she asked Annie.

Sam and Maloney didn't want to crowd the space next to Annie's bed, so they stayed at the table and watched as Marnie and I tried to interact with Annie.

She'd eaten about a third of the pudding and drank a little bit of juice when her nurse came back in to check how Annie was doing. "I know it doesn't seem like she's eaten much. It's okay. She's trying to eat something. And remember, she's also being fed intravenously. So she's getting needed nutrients. It's a slow process, but it's moving in the right direction." The nurse took the tray with the rest of Annie's food, then went back to her station.

A couple minutes after the nurse left, Annie whispered she was tired and wanted to rest. I put her bed down, covered her arms, and told her to get some shut-eye—that we'd be here when she woke up.

Marnie and I walked back to the table and sat down with Sam and Maloney.

"I've got a theory," I said. "This unknown *secret* we've been throwing around, I'll bet dollars to dimes that Peter Mosley knew what it was. And maybe it came out during a discussion he might have had with Arthur Richardson. That might be the reason he killed Peter Mosley."

"That's strictly speculation," Sam said.

"And, to go one step further, Buster Adams probably found out about the secret. Remember the rape case that I found when I went through Attorney Adams's cases at Superior Court?"

Sam nodded.

"Do you recall that the person named with committing the rape was Peter Mosley?" I sat back in the chair and folded my arms. "The charges were dropped. I think somebody paid Peter to take the fall— somebody named Arthur Richardson, a reputable teacher in the Barnstable School System. Peter wasn't charged because the DNA in the rape kit didn't match his."

"How does Buster fit into this?" Manie asked.

"Buster and Betsy were friends with benefits. From what I understand, he looked out for her. My take is Betsy and Richardson were having an affair, and she told Buster, thinking it would get him jealous. She was a tease." I took a deep breath, then continued.

"When we went through Betsy's apartment, we found a picture of a newborn baby. It was a hospital picture. There was also a baby's beaded identification wrist bracelet with the name Harper. We found a picture of Richardson and Betsy on a Boston Harbor party boat dated around the same time as the baby's picture. So Richardson is married, would lose his job if the school department found out about the affair, would most likely end his marriage—I could go on and on."

"A real-life soap opera," Sam said. "Betsy told Buster. Buster confronted the teacher. Richardson panicked, killed Buster, and made it look like an accidental drowning. Peter Mosley could have been Richardson's sidekick in Buster's and Betsy's deaths, and almost Annie's and his brother's."

"That's how I see it," I said.

Sam shook his head. "So, the Saturday night of the class reunion, Richardson knew Betsy had been drinking and figured she was an easy make. I don't think it went the way he'd planned. He figured a quick wham, bam, thank you, ma'am, then walk away. When she got belligerent and threatened to rat him out, he killed her."

"We'll need more proof. Marsha Richardson will be able to provide that proof and then some." Maloney stood, walked over to Annie's bed, and took her hand in his. "Annie McGuire, we need your help to put the finishing touches in place."

Annie's head moved slightly to face Maloney. He motioned for us to join him. Her eyes opened halfway, and she tried to shake her head to let us know she heard us. "Mmmm," she murmured as she formed a half-smile with her lips.

Her water tumbler was on the bedside table. I picked it up and tilted it slightly to touch her lips. She opened her mouth enough for me to let some liquid dribble in. "Before you know it, we'll be toasting with a glass of white zin and ice." I smiled.

Chapter 60

A week later – Sunday

It was 7:30 a.m. when food services delivered Annie's breakfast tray. Marnie had gone down to the cafeteria to get us coffee and donuts.

I was sitting on the edge of the futon when Nurse Sampson came in. "Annie, are you ready to sit up and eat your breakfast?" she asked. "This will be the last day you'll be waking up to my cheery morning voice." She smiled. "I'll miss you, my friend."

"I'll miss you too," Annie whispered. "You can come to Cape Cod and visit me."

"I just might do that," she said. "Casey, will you help Annie with her breakfast? Then we'll get her up, washed, and dressed. I'm sure you're going to miss the *designer* johnny."

We laughed—even Annie.

Marnie walked in with our food. "Did I miss a good joke?" She smiled.

"Yep," Annie said slowly.

"I understand you're going to take up residency at Spaulding Rehab Hospital Cape Cod. They're the best. They'll have you up doing the Irish jig before you know it," her nurse said.

Annie nodded slowly.

"I can attest to that," I said. "I went there for rehab resulting from a fall while at the Shrewsbury Police Academy. The staff is amazing." I looked at Marnie. "Besides, Annie and I are bridesmaids in Marnie's upcoming wedding. And, if Annie thinks I'm getting up and making a fool of myself dancing the macarena without her, she's got another thing coming."

"I want a video of that," the nurse chuckled.

"I'll see that you get one," I said.

"Doctor Menard is scheduled to be here around 10:00. He'll give you instructions, but since you're not going directly home, they really won't pertain to you. I suggest you read them over and keep them handy if you have questions."

"Sam and Maloney should be here around 10:00 also. From here, we'll go right to Spaulding so she can get settled in."

"Let's get her dressed and ready to rock and roll."

Annie smiled. "Yes."

It was almost 1:00 when we crossed the Sagamore Bridge. I looked at Annie. She had her eyes closed. I wanted to joke about it but decided it wasn't the time or place to do so. I'd razz her later.

Sam pulled up to Spaulding's main entrance. I went inside, walked to the information desk to get a wheelchair, then came back to Sam's waiting car.

Marnie and I got out of the car and moved aside, so Sam and Maloney could help Annie get into the wheelchair. Maloney pushed Annie inside the building, Marnie and I followed, and Sam went to park the car.

The three of us waited in the lobby for Sam.

Chief Lowe's friend was the director of admissions. The chief had called and made arrangements for Annie's stay. As per the chief's instructions, Sam went on ahead and asked for Tom Hopkins.

Marnie and I sat outside the admissions office while Sam and Maloney got her checked in. A half-hour later, they took her to a room on the second floor. The guys rode with her, and Marnie waited for the other elevator to reach the first floor, then headed on up.

As we walked down the corridor to Annie's room, my mind wandered back to when I was a patient here. It brought back

307

memories. "When I came to Spaulding," I said, "I didn't know if I'd ever walk normally again." I smiled to myself. "If you didn't know about my accident, you'd never know how badly I was hurt. They worked wonders."

The receptionist for the section Annie was in suggested we sit in the dayroom at the end of the hallway, and they'd get us when she got settled in. A half-hour passed before Sam and Maloney came to say she was ready to see us. They told us to have some girl-time, and they'd be back soon. I had a feeling they were going back to admissions to fill Tom Hopkins in on Annie's situation.

Annie had been awake for almost the entire ride from South Weymouth to Hyannis, so I expected her to be tired. Instead, the attendant had raised the back of her bed to create a semi-seated position. I was surprised but happy to see her alert.

"You can't keep a good woman down." She tried to laugh but instead started to cough.

I moved over beside her. "Take it easy there, *good woman.* You'll be up kickin' ass in no time."

Annie moved her hand in my direction. I reached out and took it.

Trying to brighten up the conversation, Marnie spoke up, "I have exciting news and have waited 'til the time was right to tell my two best friends."

"I know. I know." I laughed. "You're pregnant."

Marnie put her hands on her hips but couldn't resist laughing. "You're an ass. Not yet, Auntie Casey."

"Maloney and I have made a decision. We're getting married on Cape Cod."

Annie did a thumbs up. "Yes," she whispered.

"That's great news. What did your parents say about that?" I asked.

"Well, it took some sweet-talking, but they finally understood," Marnie said. "I explained that although I still have friends and, of course, family in New York City, Cape Cod is my home. I also told them that I wanted a beach wedding."

I looked at Marine. There were still words floating in her head, waiting to come out. "To change Paul Harvey's words around, *What's the rest of the story?*"

"We're going to the Big City for our honeymoon. My father has a client who owns several luxury condos overlooking Central Park. The guy uses them to house, wine, and dine prospective investors. And before you ask, I have no idea, and I am not going to ask what kind of investments the guy has."

"Okay, Annie. We've got our work cut out for us. If the girl wants a beach wedding, a beach wedding she's going to get."

Annie slowly pointed to Marnie and smiled. "You're in trouble."

"Have you set a date?" I asked.

"We've got a couple in mind, but nothing is set in concrete yet. Besides, I need both your input before we pick a beach."

"Laying here, I'll have time—to think," said Annie softly. She slowly lifted her hand to her lips to blow Marnie a kiss.

The nurse assigned to Annie came in and introduced herself. "Miss Annie McGuire, my name is Mary Walsh. I'll be your nurse while you're a guest in our facility. McGuire and Walsh—an Irish duo. We'll have this floor hoppin'."

Marnie and I looked at each other and couldn't resist a thumbs up.

"If you two ladies will excuse us, I need about thirty minutes of Annie's time to get her vitals and change her into our newest line of fashionable sleepwear."

"We'll head downstairs to find our other halves, grab a coffee and come back in about forty-five minutes," I said.

Nurse Walsh nodded. "We'll be best friends by that time."

Annie smiled.

We took the stairs one floor down to the first floor. Sam and Maloney were just leaving the director's office.

"They're getting Annie settled in. We met her nurse, and we approve." I laughed. "If Nurse Walsh doesn't have Annie up telling her Cape Cod tales within the next week, I'll be surprised. They're a match made in heaven."

Marnie looked across the lobby. "Where's that coffee/gift shop you mentioned?"

"We're getting a coffee. You guys with us?" I asked, then motioned them to follow me without waiting for an answer.

"Since we haven't eaten anything, I'm hungry. They used to have freshly made sandwiches and small salads. I'm up for a sandwich. And, by the way, Maloney and Marnie have something to tell you." I hummed *Here Comes the Bride.*

"I have no idea what song I'm supposed to recognize." Sam shook his head. "You never could carry a tune."

Maloney and Marnie laughed, and I gave Sam my *you're a jerk* look.

Sam, Maloney, and I ordered a ham and cheese sandwich with lettuce, tomato, and mayonnaise, and Marnie ordered a salad. Maloney sprung the *surprise* announcement to Sam about his and Marnie's wedding plans.

"So you're going through with this new life of marital bliss?" Sam laughed. "No, really, I'm happy for you guys."

Maloney stood, faced Sam, and went down on one knee. "Will you be my best man?" he asked.

Sam went right along with Maloney by hugging him and saying, "Of course, I will." Then kissed him on the cheek.

When he finished, the other eight people in the cafe, including the two behind the counter, were clapping and laughing.

When the four of us got back to Annie's room, she and Nurse Walsh were sitting on the edge of the bed. Annie looked a little scared, but Nurse Walsh had the situation completely under control.

Annie nodded slowly. "Look at me," she said barely loud enough for us to hear—then smiled.

"That's my girl," I said. "How are you feeling?"

"Tired but excited." Her words were slow but encouraging.

"We haven't stood yet," said Nurse Walsh. She wanted to, but I explained about taking baby steps. Sitting up is a huge positive. I ordered her a nice supper. She's going to have chicken, mashed potatoes, and butternut squash. We're going to stick with water for a couple of days, but for dessert, I ordered a dixie of vanilla ice cream."

"Annie, I know you've got two muscular guys here but no standing yet. I've got to check something at the nurses' station, so I'm going to excuse myself for about ten minutes."

Maloney chuckled, "We'll keep her in line."

While Marnie was talking to Annie, I took the opportunity to follow the nurse to her station and ask about bringing her parents up to visit. As far as Sam was concerned, it was okay, but he wanted me to check with the nurse before mentioning it to Annie. I agreed.

"I didn't want to bring this up in front of Annie, but do you think she's up for a parental visit?" I asked.

"Do her parents know her condition?" Nurse Walsh asked.

"As far as I know, they weren't told how serious of her injuries were."

"How well do you know them?"

"Well enough to call them Mom and Dad."

Nurse Walsh looked at me. "Right now, Annie is on a physical and emotional journey. They may be okay to visit her, but Annie might not be okay to see them. My suggestion is that they wait a few days. We'll address it then and decide what's best."

"I understand," I said. "What time are visiting hours over?"

"They're technically over at 8:00, but Mr. Hopkins said you could stay a little longer if you wanted to."

I sighed, "It's been a very long day. She looks like she's comfortable and hopefully will get a decent night's sleep." I checked my watch. "We'll stay another hour, and if all's well, we'll head out. What time tomorrow morning is good for Marnie and me to come back?"

"They'll do a rehab plan in the morning, so anytime around 10:00 would be good."

I nodded, "Then that's when we'll be here."

I walked back to Annie's room but stopped outside the door to compose myself. I caught Sam's attention and motioned for him to join me in the hallway

"I talked to Nurse Walsh. She suggested we wait a few days before bringing Annie's parents up to see her. She thinks it may be more emotionally challenging for Annie than her parents. She feels that Annie needs some space to deal with her inner feelings before dealing with her parent's thoughts of almost losing her. Right now, we're her strength. And it's that strength that will get her through this horrible ordeal. Nurse Walsh said our support will be a considerable part of her rehab."

"You'll need to talk to the McGuires. If you want, I'll come with you," Sam put his arms around me. "It's not going to be easy."

"I know it won't be, but yes, I'd like you to come with me. I'll give them a call later and set something up."

Sam and I walked back into her room. Annie was resting in bed, Marnie was beside her, and Maloney was standing looking out the window.

312

"Nurse Walsh said you were having a gourmet dinner tonight."
I licked my lips.

Annie smiled.

"We'll stick around until your dinner comes—should be here in less than an hour. I looked at Marnie and Maloney. Then, I don't know about you, but Sam and I are going to grab a sub at Stop and Shop, take Watson for a walk, and hit the hay. I'm tired."

Sam looked at me, then at Maloney. "I don't know what she's talking about. There's a Red Sox game on tonight, and I'm watching it."

We all, even Annie, chuckled.

I turned on the TV and flipped through the channels until I found a rerun of *All in the Family*. Annie gave me the okay.

We all watched for about fifteen minutes, then Nurse Walsh came in, moved Annie up to a sitting position, and slid her tray table over the bed just before the girl from food services came in with her dinner. "I'll feed her tonight so that I can monitor her food intake. Tomorrow you can help."

"Speaking about tomorrow, I looked at Annie. Marnie and I will be here a little after 10:00. Do you want us to bring you anything in particular?" I asked.

"The newspaper," she said, then looked at her food tray. "Gourmet?"

Nurse Walsh laughed. "She going to be just fine."

Chapter 61

Monday

Sam and I were both up early. Watson had already done his run around the house and was back inside, waiting patiently beside the cabinet where we kept his food. "I know, I know," said Sam. He filled the boy's bowl, unwrapped the newspaper, made coffee for both of us, and sat reading when I joined him in the kitchen.

"Are you going to Bourne today?" I asked.

"No, Maloney and I are going to meet with Chief Lowe and go over the happenings of the last few days."

"Can you, or have Chief Lowe, contact Director Flanigan to get a status report on Mark? It's just a matter of time before Annie starts asking questions."

Sam nodded. "I'll do that."

"Be sure to thank Chief Lowe for getting her into Spaulding. I was encouraged by her progress yesterday."

"She's back on the Cape. I think that makes a world of difference."

"You're right. She's home." I smiled.

"I heard you tell Annie that you and Marnie would be at Spaulding around 10:00. Are you planning on staying a good part of the day?"

"I'm not sure. I'll let you know."

Sam and I cleaned up the kitchen and got ready to leave. I called Marnie to tell her I'd pick her up around 9:00. I got my good-bye hug and kiss, then Sam brought Watson outside, hooked him to his run, waved good-bye, and pulled out of the driveway.

An hour later, I was on my way to Marnie's house.

She was sitting outside when I pulled up. "I'm a little early. I figured we could stop by Dunkins' on the way."

"You don't have to twist my arm."

We left Dunkins' and headed to Spaulding. It was just after 10:15 when we pulled into the hospital parking lot.

My cell rang. It was Sam.

"Casey, I just left Chief Lowe's office. He wants me to stop by Spaulding to see if Annie can answer questions regarding Richardson and Peter Mosley. I told the chief I would, but I wouldn't push the issue if the doctor didn't feel she could respond without triggering an emotional breakdown. I know she's meeting with the rehab staff this morning, so I won't plan on being there until after lunch. I'm going to rely on your observations and recommendations before I do anything."

"Oh boy, Sam. Why the hurry?"

"I'll explain further when I get there."

I didn't have the phone on speaker, so Marnie didn't hear any of Sam's side of the conversation.

"Are you going to tell me what that was all about?" she asked.

"You aren't going to like it. Chief Lowe wants Sam and Maloney to ask Annie some questions regarding Richardson and Peter Mosley. I know I can't stop it, but I can voice my opinion. Sam said he'd explain further when he gets to Spaulding." I shook my head. "I'm not going to mention this to Nurse Walsh until I know the whys behind the expedited need to know."

I was a little taken aback when we walked into Annie's room. The bed was made, and everything was in its place as though the room was ready to accept a new patient.

We looked across the corridor to the nurses' station. A girl dressed in scrubs sat at the desk furthest away from the counter, but no sighting of Nurse Walsh. I walked over to the counter. "Excuse me," I said.

The girl looked up. "Can I help you?"

"Yes, we're here to visit Annie McGuire."

She shuffled through a few papers on her desk then walked up to the counter. "Annie is still working with one of the therapists. She should be back in about fifteen minutes."

"Is Nurse Walsh available?"

"She's with a patient. Can I tell her who's asking for her?"

"No, I don't want to bother her. We'll catch up later," I said.

"If she does come back before you get here, can I tell her you were looking for her?"

"Sure. My name is Casey Quinby." Not wanting to engage in a conversation, I turned, looked at Marnie, and we quickly headed toward the stairs.

I shrugged. "She's a *something* in training, I guess."

Marnie laughed. "Let's get some fresh air."

There was a walking trail that snaked around inside a large grassy plot. Several sets of people were slowly maneuvering the walkway. I assumed one of the persons in the duo was a patient, and this was part of their rehab. We decided not to get in their way, so we sat on one of the benches at the beginning of the trail.

"Until Mark regains consciousness, Annie's is the sole source of information against Richardson. Fortunately, she didn't suffer physical abuse. But in my estimation, mental abuse is as bad if not worse. We only know half, maybe not even half, of the story."

"You're right," Marnie said.

316

"Richardson's first victim was Buster Adams—his second was Betsy Harper—and his third was Peter Mosley. Mark is still alive, but barely. For Annie's sake, he has to make it."

"What do you think Richardson's wife knows?"

"My guess is she found something and confronted her husband. He may have threatened her, and that's why she left, taking the children, and went to her parent's house in New Hampshire. Barnstable PD is going to have to find out exactly where she is. The sad part about it is there are two young children involved." I shook my head.

Marnie sighed. "The only good thing is that he can't hurt her. His wife can tell the authorities everything without fear for herself or her children."

I checked my watch. "We've been gone a half-hour. Let's see if Annie's back in her room."

We got to Annie's room just as she rounded the corner at the other end of the hallway. She was using a walker, but she was walking. The therapist had a safety belt around her waist but wasn't holding onto her. She was basically on her own. When we got closer to her room, she looked up and stopped when she saw us heading in her direction. She held on to the walker with one hand and gave us a wave with the other.

I melted. "Annie, look at you."

"Come on in," she said slowly.

"After you," I said.

Annie sat in the armchair next to her bed, and Marnie pulled up two chairs from the table.

"You ready to run the Boston Marathon yet?" I smirked. "You'd probably beat both of us."

Annie turned to look at Marnie. "The only marathon I want to be a part of is the walk down the aisle at your wedding."

"Now I know you're feeling better," Marnie said.

"Can one of you please get me a bottle of water or a juice cup?" Annie asked.

Marnie stood. "Sure, be right back."

Annie watched Marnie walk out into the hallway. "Casey, how is Mark? It seems you guys are avoiding the subject. I don't even know if he's still alive." Annie looked at the ceiling and started to rock back and forth. "Please tell me the truth. I need to know. They beat him real bad."

I took a deep breath. "He's alive. He's still at South Shore Hospital, and until he regains his strength, he'll probably stay there. Sam and Maloney will be here shortly. They need to ask you some questions. Questions about Arthur Richardson and Peter Mosley." I leaned over and took her hand. "If you're not ready to talk about it, we'll wait."

Tears rolled down Annie's cheeks. "I'm okay. I do want to talk about it," she said. "There's no way Richardson or Peter Mosley can get to Mark or me, is there?"

"Absolutely not. Richardson is behind bars, never to walk the streets again as a free man." I glanced at Annie. "And Peter Mosley is dead." I squeezed her hand tighter.

Annie's eyes moved around, looking for answers. "Richardson killed him, right?"

"Yep," I said just as Marnie came back into the room with both water and juice.

Marnie looked at me and slightly shrugged her shoulders.

"You know what, Casey, I don't care that Peter is dead." Annie started to gasp. "He's the one that beat the shit out of Mark."

I could feel her hand starting to shake.

"After Peter beat Mark until he couldn't move, he injected us with something. I felt a pinch in my arm. Then after that, I don't remember a thing."

"Okay—you're okay now," I whispered.

"I know there's more." Annie started to cry.

"Marnie got you some apple juice.," I said. "She got it from the refrigerator at the nurses' station, so it's nice and cold."

"I want to remember. I want to tell you what happened."

I put a straw into the juice cup and held it for her. "I want you to relax. We'll figure out everything that happened. Marnie and I aren't going anywhere, and Sam and Maloney are on their way here."

Annie had another sip, then Marnie and I helped her get back into bed. "I want to lie down. I need to rest a little."

I could tell she was getting nervous, and I didn't want her to have an anxiety attack. I got a cold facecloth and rubbed her forehead. "Close your eyes," I said.

Chapter 62

Annie was dozing when Sam and Maloney arrived.

I put my finger to my lips then pointed to the door.

Sam, Maloney, Marine, and I walked down to the dayroom so that we could talk freely and not wake Annie.

"Casey, before we get involved in a *Richardson* discussion, I have some other information to share," Sam said. "I got a call from Officer Paul Bishop."

I slid to the edge of my seat.

Sam pulled a piece of paper from his pocket. "We had an interesting conversation. He said he remembers you from the *Tribune*. I briefly told him what was going on and why you wanted to talk to him. He said he still has his notes from the Buster Adams case."

"Where is he living?" I asked.

"North Carolina," Sam said.

"Sam, I'd like you with me when I talk to him. As soon as we can take an hour or so back in my office, we'll set up a teleconference call."

Sam agreed.

I had questions for Officer Bishop regarding Buster Adam's death ten years ago. His answers may help confirm it wasn't accidental. "Any information linking Richardson to Buster's death will help cement the teacher's feet to the floor of a cell the size of a parking space."

"Back to the case at hand," said Sam.

I looked at Maloney and Marnie. "With all that's happened within the last two weeks, I think Richardson panicked and realized we've uncovered valuable information that will put him behind bars for life. Unfortunately, the Commonwealth of Massachusetts banned capital punishment in 1984. I'm sure he knows that too. Otherwise, he'd be a perfect candidate," I said.

We'd just stood and were headed to the door to go back to Annie's room when Nurse Walsh walked in. "My aid said you were down here. I wanted to let you know that we received a call from South Shore Hospital. Mark Mosley has regained consciousness and keeps trying to say, *Annie*."

"Can we go see him?" I asked.

"They're going to monitor him for a couple days, and then the plan is to move him out of ICU. Once he's out of ICU, you should be able to visit. "Not the four of you at once. And, I'd be careful," said Nurse Walsh. He's still in a fragile state, but Casey, I'd suggest that you and Marnie go first. Mark seeing Annie's friends might be more calming than having two police detectives, even without asking any questions, triggering a plethora of emotions."

Nurse Walsh left so that we could discuss the situation surrounding Mark.

"Sam, Mark would probably recover faster if he could transfer to Cape Cod Hospital. Right now, if Mark realizes he's sixty-plus miles away from home in an area he knows nobody and nothing about, he could become depressed and possibly not make it."

"I'll talk to Chief Lowe." Sam nodded and walked out of the dayroom to make the call.

The three of us walked into Annie's room. Sam joined us ten minutes later.

"You were sound asleep, so we took a walk," Marnie said.

"I woke up, and you guys weren't here, but my lunch was." Annie looked at her tray, then at Sam. "I can't wait to have that Raw

Bar lobster roll." she smiled. "Though I'd forget, huh. Nope, I've got a memory like an elephant. At least I didn't lose that."

I couldn't help but chuckle. "You heard the girl," I said.

"How you feeling?" asked Sam.

"I think I might try a mini-powerwalk up and down the corridor tomorrow," said Annie slowly.

I shook my head. "The staff isn't going to know what hit them."

"Casey, can you please move my bed down a little so that I'm not sitting up so straight?"

"Of course."

Sam stood and walked to the side of Annie's bed. "I've got some information to share." He took Annie's hand. "Mark has regained consciousness and keeps trying to say, *Annie*."

Annie's eyes opened wide. "And."

"He's still not ready to do the Irish Jig, but he's heading in the right direction. They plan on moving him out of ICU within a few days." Sam smiled then continued. "I called Chief Lowe, and he's going to try to get Mark transferred to Cape Cod Hospital."

Annie started to cry. "Sorry, I can't help it." Her voice was weak.

I leaned over the rail on the side of Annie's bed. "It's okay. Now, I'll be the wicked witch. I have no doubt you're well on your way to recovery, but you still have some work to do. Mark needs you to be strong, not only for yourself but for him too. Do you understand what I'm telling you?"

"I do." Annie nodded. "And I promise I'll listen to you." She closed her eyes.

"Before you doze off, we're going to go down to the coffee shop and grab a sandwich. Take a snooze, and we'll be back in a little while." I nodded. "Okay?"

Annie managed a smile. "I'll be in la-la land before you get to the elevator."

Chapter 63

I cocked my head and looked at Sam. "I didn't want to ask questions in front of Annie. But, knowing you talked to Chief Lowe and judging from your demeanor, you have information to share with us. It's between lunch and dinner, so there shouldn't be many people in the coffee shop."

"I don't call you Sherlock for nothing." Sam smiled.

"I know you mentioned a sandwich, but why don't we just get a muffin and coffee, then stop on the way home and get some decent food," Marnie said.

Everyone agreed. Marnie and I went to the counter, and the guys found a table in the back corner.

"There were three blueberry muffins, and one cinnamon left." I set them down on the table.

Marnie followed with the coffees.

"I'm all ears. What did the chief say?" I asked.

"He got contact information for Marsha Richardson," Sam said. "He's already touched base with her, and, to no surprise, she wants to meet with him. She did tell him that she left her house in Mashpee because she feared for the safety of herself and her children. The chief assured her that her husband was in custody with no possibility of being released. She said she'd leave the children with her parents and head back to the Cape tomorrow. There was more conversation between Marsha Richardson and Chief Lowe because he said he'd fill me in on the details tomorrow morning."

"So, I'm assuming that you and Maloney will be tied up most of the morning, if not longer," I said. "If you get any information on transferring Mark, will you give me a call?"

"As soon as I hear, you'll hear," said Sam.

"What else is on your mind," I asked.

"Per orders from Chief Lowe, I have to ask Annie some questions. I think she can handle them. Not only did Richardson try to kill her, but she's also an eyewitness to most of the charges. Having worked in the DA's office for so many years, she knows that the information she can provide is key to putting Richardson away for life."

I looked at Marnie and Maloney. "She's strong. She'll be able to handle it."

They agreed.

Annie was sitting up in her chair when we walked back into her room. "Look at me." She smiled. "I've got a magazine, a vending machine package of cookies, and a diet ginger ale. I can't walk without help, but I'm happy to be sitting up and able to take nourishment—even if it isn't white zin and peanuts."

"That's my girl," I said. "Now we've got a little business we have to conduct. Are you up to answering some questions for Sam?"

"Things are coming back to me, and I need to get them out." Annie took a sip of her drink.

Sam slid a chair up and sat beside Annie. "I'm going to ask Marnie to take notes, but I also want to record your answers. I need your okay to do that."

Annie nodded. "You've got my okay to record our conversation."

I went out to the nurses' station to let Nurse Walsh know what was going on and that we needed to shut Annie's door, then I returned to the room.

Sam turned on the recorder. He identified himself then had Annie record her permission to be questioned regarding Arthur Richardson, Peter Mosley, Mark Mosley, and herself. Because of the hundreds of depositions that passed through her hands in the DA's office over the years, she knew how vital this question-and-answer session was to the pending case against Richardson.

There was no doubt of the relationships between Annie, Richardson, and Peter Mosley. One had been her high school art teacher and the other, the older brother of a close friend.

I took a small legal pad and a pen from my purse to jot down any information that might trigger a discussion. I listened as Sam carefully chose his initial questions.

"How did you and Mark meet up with Richardson and Peter?" Sam asked.

Annie thought for a minute. "I was at Mark's house. His brother, Peter, came home. He was kinda living there."

"What do you mean *kinda*?" asked Sam.

"Mark said they argued about a week before and he had told Peter to leave."

"What did Peter want?"

"He wanted to pick up some of his clothes and get a ride to hook up with a friend."

"Did he mention the friend's name?"

"No. Peter said the friend would let him crash at his house until he could find a new place to live. Mark didn't ask for the friend's name, and Peter didn't volunteer it."

"So, since you were the only one with a car, you agreed to take him to wherever it was he was meeting his friend."

Annie took a deep breath. "That's it. I didn't see a problem. Mark was glad to get rid of him. Peter filled a pillowcase with clothes, and we left."

Annie slowly recanted what happened, but now she was starting to struggle.

I looked at Sam and slightly moved my hand sideways to indicate it was time to take a break.

"Annie," I said, "do you want to take a breather?"

"No, just give me a minute." She turned her head to look out the window. "Okay, I'm ready."

"I'm going to let you fill me in on what happened when you left Mark's house. If I need something more specific, I'll stop you." Sam leaned back in his chair.

"Um—Peter said his friend lived in Wellfleet. But, for some reason, the friend didn't want us to drive to his house. He wanted to meet us in a remote area, drop Peter off and leave. We didn't think anything about it. Peter wasn't the best society had to offer, so we figured his friend was also a member of the same low-life community that Peter was a part of. Annie shook her head. "You know I'm very familiar with lower Cape. When we turned off 6A and headed to the Wellfleet flats, I felt a little nervous. But we were supposed to meet the *friend* there so, I kept going."

"Did you see any other vehicles around?" asked Sam.

"Nope," said Annie. "We came to an opening in the middle of nowhere. I wasn't comfortable. I told Peter to take his bag of clothes and get out of the car to wait for his friend. He didn't budge. Mark repeated my instructions. Peter just laughed and pulled a joint and a lighter from his pocket. Before he could flip open the lighter, Mark jumped out of the passenger side, opened the back door, grabbed him, and threw him to the ground." Annie's breathing quickened.

"We're going to take a break," I said. "You're a trooper, but I want you to rest for a bit."

Annie nodded. "I'd like to get back in bed."

Marnie stood on one side, and I stood on the other. Annie held our arms, pivoted around, backed up, and sat on the edge of her bed.

"Hold onto the rail, slide back, and I'll lift your legs. Ready?" I asked.

Annie scooched to the middle of the bed, then gave us a slight smile. "Can you please pull the sheet up?"

I wasn't sure how fragile Annie was, but I could see that reliving whatever happened at the Wellfleet flats triggered unhealthy emotions. I caught Sam's eye and motioned for him to meet me in the corridor.

"I'm going to stretch my legs and get something to drink," I said. "Sam, wanna keep me company?"

"Maloney and I will entertain Annie." Marnie looked at her watch. "Maybe there's a twenty-year-old game show on TV."

"Yeah, maybe Match Game or Let's Make a Deal with Howie Mandel." I laughed. "Won't be gone long."

We got a couple of sodas from the vending machine and walked down to the dayroom.

"I'm no psychiatrist, but I think she's finding it hard to verbally identify the next person who entered the picture. There's no doubt in my mind that person is Arthur Richardson."

"I agree," said Sam. "Let's see how she's doing when we get back to her room. If she indicates she wants to talk, we will. If not, let's not mention it. Tomorrow's another day." He reached over and hugged me, then whispered, "You okay?"

"I am. And Annie is going to be." I tried to smile.

Nurse Walsh was in Annie's room when we returned. She was going over Annie's therapy schedule with her. Sam and I nodded, then walked over to where Marnie and Maloney were sitting. Instead of writing down her workout times, I decided to ask Nurse Walsh for a copy.

"Her therapist was pleased with her progress. He's going to do some more stretching and strengthening exercises later this afternoon," said Nurse Walsh. "After dinner tonight, there's a movie in the lounge. I'll check to see what's playing."

I followed Nurse Walsh to the nurses' station. "Can I please have a copy of her schedule? That way, Marnie and I can figure out the best times to visit."

"Sounds like a plan." She made a copy and handed it to me.

"We'll stick around for another half hour until her dinner comes, then head on back to Hyannisport. I've got to go into my office in the morning, so Marnie and I will plan on being here early afternoon. If you need me for anything before them, give me a call." I started to walk back to Annie's room, then remembered I had another question for Nurse Walsh. "Annie seems to be doing good. Do you think it would be okay if her parents came up tomorrow for a visit? I'll make sure Marnie and I will be here while they are. And I'll suggest that they don't stay all day. I know they need to see her, and she needs to see them."

Nurse Walsh nodded, "I'll okay the visit."

"Thank you," I said and walked back to Annie's room. "Hey, girl, we're going to head home." I laughed. "Enjoy the movie."

Chapter 64

Tuesday

My phone rang. It was Marnie. "Sam left for Barnstable a few minutes ago, and I'm just heading out the door. I'm going to connect with Bishop, but I don't expect it to be very long. I'll have my car. Since the guys are meeting with Chief Lowe later this morning, why don't you and Maloney come to my office. They can head to Barnstable PD, and we'll go to Spaulding. I want to swing by Dunkins' and get us donuts and coffee. That will cheer Annie up," I said.

"Okay with me," Marnie said. "See you in a few."

I brought Watson over to the Martin's house. "I'm not sure what time we'll be back. Probably around dinner time. I'll call if there's a change."

Mrs. Martin smiled. "No problem."

"Thank you. I appreciate you watching the boy."

Traffic was light, so it only took me fifteen minutes to get to Barnstable.

Sam was sitting at my desk flipping through the *Tribune* when I walked through the back door.

"I forgot to tell you I asked Nurse Walsh about letting Mom and Dad McGuire visit Annie, and she okayed it. So, I'm going to give them a call. It would be better if we were there at the same time they are. They wouldn't do it on purpose and may not do it at all, but I don't want them asking any questions that would upset Annie. How long do you think you'll be tied up with the chief?" I asked.

Sam shook his head. "I'm not sure, maybe an hour or two. Why?"

"Marnie and I are heading to Spaulding as soon as she gets here. So, if I call the McGuires, would you and Maloney pick them up around 12:30 and meet us in the lobby at the rehab?"

"We can do that. I was going to say after lunch, so 1:00 is perfect," said Sam.

Sam's phone rang. He mouthed *Bishop*. "Paul, Casey just arrived, so I'm putting you on speakerphone."

I got settled in and nodded that I was ready.

"Good morning, Casey. It's been a while since we've talked," said Officer Bishop. "I understand you're interested in the Buster Adams case. Sam told me that Amanda Adams retained you to look into it."

"Good morning to you, too," I said. "That's correct. Amanda Adams has retained me. I'm not sure what Sam told you, but Buster's mother believes that his death was not accidental, rather that he was murdered. And, that Betsey Harper's death two weeks ago was somehow related to her son's death ten years ago."

"I did read about the Harper girl's murder. Her name came up when I was investigating Buster's death. She wasn't linked to his death, but I always thought she knew more than she let on. I was never happy about how the authorities handled his case, but nobody agreed with me. Solid evidence about it being anything other than accidental was non-existent. It was there, but I just couldn't put my hands on it." Officer Bishop sighed. "I told Sam I kept copies of all my notes. I can overnight FedEx a copy of them to you if you'd like. Once you go through them, we can talk."

"I'd appreciate that," I said. "Do you ever think about coming back to the Cape?"

"No. I did think about moving back when I left the FBI but decided on North Carolina instead."

"Thank you for your help. Sorry to be so abrupt, but I've got an appointment." I said. "Talk soon."

Sam took Paul off speakerphone and walked out to the kitchen to continue their conversation.

I glanced at my watch—9:30. I took my phone from my purse and punched in the number for Annie's parents.

Mom McGuire answered on the first ring. "Casey, have you got any news for us?"

I forgot she could see my name on the caller ID. "I do. Annie is doing much better. Would you and Dad like to see her this afternoon?"

"Dad, we can go see Annie this afternoon." Her voice cracked. "Casey is on the phone."

"Sam and Maloney are going to pick you up around 12:30. Marnie and I will already be at Spaulding, so we'll meet you in the lobby at 1:00," I said. "She's anxious to see you."

"We'll be ready. Thank you," Annie's mother said.

Sam finished talking to Officer Bishop and rejoined me in my office. "It was a brief conversation, but he feels the same way as Amanda Fallon. He did say that he'd come back to the Cape if it involved reopening the Buster Adams' case."

"Then I'd say we're going to be breaking bread with Officer Paul Bishop sometime soon."

"We may be doing just that," Sam said.

I took a deep breath and let it out slowly. "I'll be anxious to see if Richardson's name was cited in Bishop's notes. It was only about two years after Buster's death that Bishop left the Barnstable PD."

I was sitting at my desk, staring out the window, when I saw Maloney pull up. "The other half of this team is here." I laughed.

"Maloney can take his car to the station." Sam walked to the front door. "See you around 1:00." He held the door for Marnie, then joined Maloney.

"Well, we might as well get going," I said. I locked the front door.

"After the meeting with Chief Lowe, Sam is going to pick up Mom and Dad McGuire. I forgot to tell you Nurse Walsh okayed a visit. We're going to meet them in the lobby at 1:00." I picked up my keys and purse. "It's time—"

"You're right." Marnie nodded. "Let's get going."

"When we stop at Dunkins' for coffee, I'll get a dozen donuts for the nurses."

Chapter 65

Annie was still working out with her therapist in the rehab room when we arrived. Nurse Walsh was on the phone, but I caught her attention and pointed to the box of donuts.

Her eyes lit up. Less than two minutes later, she was standing beside me, smiling. "How did you know? It's been one of those days. A cup of coffee and one, maybe two, Dunkin donuts are certainly going to take the edge off. Thank you so much."

"Mental telepathy, or is it *great minds think alike*?" I chuckled.

Nurse Walsh checked her watch. "Annie's almost done. She'll be glad to see you."

"I talked to her parents this morning. They were beside themselves at the news of being able to visit Annie. Sam and Maloney will pick them up, and Marnie and I will meet them in the lobby at 1:00. My question to you is—should I tell Annie?"

"I think you should. It's going to be emotional for both Annie and her parents. A heads-up will give her time to compose herself as best she can."

I glanced up the corridor. "Well, speak of the devil. Look who's trying to sneak up on us." I lifted the box of Dunkins'.

Annie gave us a thumbs up. "They'll never let me out if you spoil them with donuts."

"Not a bad idea." Marnie laughed. "At least we'll know where to find you."

"Can we escort the *little lady* back to her room?" I asked.

Nurse Walsh looked at Annie. "What are you waiting for? As soon as she's settled in, I can have my donut."

The therapist nodded and motioned for Annie to walk herself into her room.

"Watch this," Annie said as she backed up to her chair, braced herself, then lowered her body onto the seat. "I've made some friends here, but I want to come home to you guys." She tapped her fingers on the chair arms and looked at her tray table. "I'm assuming that one of those coffees and maybe two of the donuts in the bag are for me."

"You're just too smart," I said. "You want your donuts or some good news first?"

"How about a bite of donut and good news at the same time?"

Marnie got her set up with a coffee and two donuts while I pulled a couple of chairs for Marnie and me.

I let her take a bite and a sip of coffee, then reached out and took her hands. "You're going to have visitors this afternoon."

She scowled. "What are you talking about?"

"It seems there are two people who can't wait any longer to give you and get from you a big hug and lots of kisses," I said.

She squeezed my hands harder than I thought she could. "My mother and father?" Tears started to run down her cheeks.

"Yep. Sam and Maloney are picking them up. They'll be here around 1:00." I looked at Annie. "I told them how good you were doing. Nurse Walsh gave me the okay for them to come up to see you. Maybe, you'll be able to take a walk with them down the corridor?"

"Not maybe, I will." Annie nodded. "I've always been the strong one. They need to see I'm steps closer to coming home."

"I'll get it okayed by Nurse Walsh. But, right now, I want my coffee and donut."

"While you're eating, I'm going to talk." Annie leaned back in her chair. "I've been doing a lot of thinking. I'm ready to talk to Sam. I've come to terms as best I can with what happened to Mark and me. And, laying here at night with nobody to talk to, I've carried on silent conversations with myself. Working in the DA's office always reminds me that a tiny piece of information regarding a case could be the most crucial evidence to either convict or prove a person innocent."

Marnie shook her head. "I guess you have been doing some thinking."

"Hear me out." Annie continued, "Buster was *murdered* ten years ago. It was reported as accidental, but there are too many questions to accept the finding one hundred percent. Betsy was murdered at her—my— class reunion ten years later. I told you that Betsy and I were not best buds—just friends. Thinking about this shit that's going on now, Betsy was pretty chummy with Arthur Richardson, the art teacher. She was an artist herself. She did beautiful work. There were rumors that Betsy and Richardson had a thing going. He was handsome, and he knew it. He was also married. Most of us didn't pay much attention. Betsy had a reputation of being a flirt."

"Annie, this is a lot of gossip. There have been teacher-student flings throughout the annals of time. Did anyone ever see them together?"

"I did," Annie said. "I never saw them *together together*, but I did see them dancing intimately at the reunions. At our fifth-year reunion, they were seen coming in from outside and were holding hands. I know that's not a biggie, but it is when one's a student, and the other is a teacher."

"Did you notice anything at your ten-year reunion?" Marnie asked.

"Richardson was his flirty self. But not just with Betsy. In fact, he kind of avoided her. She wasn't at all happy. They must have had words because I heard them arguing in the hallway when I left the ballroom to go to the ladies' room. I heard her mention something about a baby. He told her to shut her fuckin' mouth, or he'd shut it for her. I figured they both had too much to drink or one of them was high. And, as I told you before, Betsy didn't do drugs, so it *the high* would have been Richardson."

"Did you see them after that?" I asked.

"I saw him, but not her." Annie gasped. "Holy shit, you don't think he killed her, then came back to the reunion party?"

"It sounds like it," I said. "Sam and Maloney need to hear everything you just told Marnie and me."

"I'll tell them," Annie said. "What time is it. I want to rest a little before my parents get here."

"It's 11:30. Your lunch should be here anytime. I know you've had a couple donuts but try to eat something cause the nurse has to record your food intake. We'll stick around while you eat, then we'll help you get in bed so you can take a cat nap."

Marnie and I stayed with Annie until she dozed off, then told Nurse Walsh we were heading downstairs to be in the lobby when Sam, Maloney, and the McGuires arrived.

I was donut and coffeed-out, but I needed a water. I picked up a couple bottles at the coffee shop then we went outside to get some air.

I looked at Marnie. "Remember the hospital baby picture we found at Betsy's apartment?" I asked. "And remember the picture taken at Boston Harbor of Betsy and some guy? The guy is Richardson."

"Richardson got Betsy pregnant. That's his daughter. A date was written on the back, but I don't remember it. "

"She may have threatened to expose him," I said. "Or she may already have. That would account for Marsha Richardson taking an unplanned trip to New Hampshire."

"Arthur Richardson knew he was screwed when Mark and Annie started playing private eye. His only recourse was to get rid of them. He almost succeeded."

"How does Peter Mosley fit into the picture?" Marnie asked.

"Peter Mosley was a low-life nobody. Richardson knew that. For some reason, Peter thought Richardson was his friend. Peter was Richardson's puppet, just like I told Sam. Richardson cut the strings and killed Peter when the teacher had no more use for him. After all, who would miss Peter Mosley?"

I watched people coming and going from the lobby. It was 12:45. "Sam and company will be here shortly," I said.

Marnie nudged me. "You're being too quiet. What's going on in that scary brain of yours?"

"Just a hunch. But, once I get the reports from Officer Bishop regarding Buster's *accidental* death, merge them with my investigation, and add what we know about Richardson, the cause of death will change from accidental to murder. I hope that Richardson finds himself a cellmate at Souza-Baranowski who will give him a taste of his own medicine."

Chapter 66

It was 1:05 when Sam, Maloney and Mom, and Dad McGuire walked from the parking lot into the lobby. Marnie and I were sitting in the waiting area and immediately got up when we saw them come in.

I could tell Mom had been crying. Dad McGuire was trying to console her. I took her hands in mine. "Annie's waiting for you. Do you want to sit for a few minutes, or are you ready to go on up?"

"I'm okay," she said. "I'll feel better after I see my baby."

Dad McGuire nodded in agreement.

I linked elbows with Mom and guided her in the direction of the elevator. Marnie walked behind us, and Dad, Sam, and Maloney followed.

Fortunately, we were the only ones in the elevator, so we went right to Annie's floor. Mom McGuire was the first one out. She looked down a couple of the corridors, then back to me. "Which way is Annie's room?"

I pointed to the corridor across from where we were standing. "She's waiting, so let's go see what she's up to." I tried to smile.

Halfway down the corridor was Annie's room. I could see Nurse Walsh standing at the counter in the nurses' station. She saw us and walked over to greet us.

I introduced her to Annie's parents.

Nurse Walsh whispered, "Be gentle."

Mom and Dad McGuire walked in first. Annie was sitting in her chair but slowly stood up when they came into the room. "Hi, guys," she said. "Come give me a hug."

They exchanged hugs and kisses, then Annie sat down. Sam slid two chairs over so her parents could sit beside her.

338

I asked Nurse Walsh if we could let them have some alone time.

She saw no problem with that, so Sam, Maloney, Marnie, and I walked down to the dayroom. The news station was boring, but there was nothing else on the TV except soap operas. Sam walked to the other side of the room to make a couple phone calls. Marnie and Maloney went for a walk, and I curled up on a chair and fell asleep. When I woke up, I checked my watch. "Sam, I'm going to walk back down to Annie's room to see how it's going."

"I've got one more call to make. Then I'll meet you there," Sam said.

Mom, Dad, and Annie were sitting around the table. "Well, look at you. They better keep tabs on you, or when they least expect it, you'll bolt." I laughed. "I think you have therapy at 3:00. Maybe we can walk down and watch you. I'll check with Nurse Walsh."

It was 3:15 when Annie's therapist came to get her for her afternoon workout. He suggested that Annie use her walker and bring her parents to the physical therapy room. He said he'd be right behind her if she needed him. He also said they could sit on the sidelines and watch her.

The six of us walked down the corridor, then Sam and I left them and went down to the lobby. I called Marnie to tell her where we were. Ten minutes later, they joined us.

"I'm exhausted," I said. "Do you think therapy has come up with a program for Annie yet?" Or do you think they're still evaluating the situation?"

"I would imagine they've charted a course of action," said Sam. As far as how long she'll be here may be another story. And, then there needs to be a plan in place for after she leaves here. Depending on her progress, they'll probably have her do outpatient for a while. The big question is, where is she going to live? They won't release her to live alone. Mr. and Mrs. McGuire aren't in the best of health and have a small cape. I'm assuming all the bedrooms are on the second floor. There's no way she can negotiate stairs yet."

"Sam, I know we only have one bedroom, but the couch is a queen-sized pull-out." I took a deep breath. "She'd be no problem. If she has a doctor's appointment, I can take her. When she's up to it, she can come to the office with me. If she wants to go to her parents' house, I can take her there too. She's been through a lot. I don't want her to be alone. Besides, the doctor won't let her be alone."

Sam nodded. "When that decision has to be made, she can bunk with us."

I wrapped my arms around his neck and kissed him. "I love you, Sam Summers."

Marnie, Maloney, Sam, and I went back upstairs. Mom and Dad McGuire were standing outside Annie's room.

"They're getting her ready for dinner. I'm proud of my little girl. She's one of a kind, and I wouldn't trade her for the world." Dad McGuire peeked in the door and blew her a kiss. "They want her to rest before dinner. And, I think Mom and me need to go home."

"We'll say our goodbyes and be right back," I said.

Annie smiled when I walked into her room. "Thank you, Casey." They're tired and, to be truthful, so aren't I."

"No problem. We all are. But things went well today," I said.

I looked around the room. "Marnie and I will be up sometime tomorrow. She's going to check in with the DA's office. Mike wants an update on how you're doing."

"He probably wants to send me some work," Annie laughed. "Get going, and I'll see you tomorrow."

I met up with Marnie. "Sam and Maloney are going to take the McGuires home," I said. Then, how about we meet the guys at Seafood Harry's? I don't know about you, but I'm tired and hungry."

"Me too," said Marnie.

340

Chapter 67

Tuesday...two weeks later

Annie was dressed and sitting in her chair when Marnie and I walked into her room.

"You look like you're going somewhere," I said.

"Funny." Annie laughed. "Spaulding's kicking me out. I'm waiting for Nurse Walsh to give me my marching papers."

"It's 11:30. I have a suggestion," Marnie walked over beside me. "How about we leave here, get some lunch, then head to Cape Cod Hospital and pay Mark a visit?"

Annie's mouth opened, but nothing came out.

"Annie McGuire is at a loss for words?" I smiled. "Before you ask—yes, it is okay. Nurse Walsh made the arrangements, and Mark knows you're coming."

Annie wiped a couple tears from her cheeks. "Happy tears," she said.

Ten minutes later, Nurse Walsh came in. After Annie signed the release forms, Nurse Walsh handed her an envelope containing information regarding rehab follow-up, instructions for at-home exercises, a couple of scripts, and a list of emergency telephone numbers should she need them.

Annie stood and started to walk without her walker. "Whoa there, lady." the nurse said. "First of all, I'm going to wheel you to the car. Then, I want you to promise me you'll follow the instructions in the envelope I just gave you."

"Sorry, I was excited." Annie nodded.

I tilted my head in Annie's direction. "She'll behave if she wants a place to recuperate."

"Ah, yes. I forgot she's going to your house," Nurse Walsh said. "I'll be right back with the wheelchair, and we'll get this show on the road."

I went down a few minutes early to get the car. Annie, her therapist, and Nurse Walsh were dealing out hugs and kisses when I pulled up. She got into the passenger side of my car. Marnie put Annie's walker into the truck, then got in behind me. We said our goodbyes, waved, headed out of the parking lot, and turned right onto Service Road.

Not quite a half-hour later, we pulled up to the entrance to Cape Cod Hospital. Marnie went inside and got a wheelchair. Marnie and I helped Annie get out of the car and into the chair. They went into the lobby to wait for me to park. As much as Annie wanted to see Mark, I knew she was nervous. He was teetering on the edge of death when they brought him to South Shore Hospital. Miraculously Mark survived. He still had a long road ahead of him, but knowing Annie was okay and was there for him gave Mark the determination he needed to get back on his feet.

We already knew he was on the third floor in room number 311. We went to the nurses' station, per Nurse Walsh's instructions, to check-in. The attendant behind the desk took our names and directed us to Mark's room. I stuck my head in to see if he was awake. He was. I smiled and waved, but he had no idea who I was. I backed out and pushed Annie in and up beside his bed.

She took her hands and rested them on his. "Well, will you look at us," Annie said. "We're going to be just fine, and ya know why?' She smiled. "Because we've got each other." Her voice started to crack.

Mark turned his hand over to hold hers. "And, nobody can take that away from us."

Annie looked at Marnie and me. "Mark, these are my best friends, Casey and Marnie. If it weren't for them, we wouldn't be here now."

I could see both pain and love in Mark's eyes.

"You're home now. Before you know it, you and Annie will be back out riding those bikes to *Sunday School* for ice cream. I won't be riding a bike, but I'll meet you there." I smiled.

"That's a plan," he said.

Marnie walked up to the bottom of the bed. "Casey and I are going to grab a coffee, sit and gossip, and give you guys some alone time."

Annie smiled. "Thank you."

We nodded and headed out of his room.

"I want to stop at the nurses' station to see if I can get any information about his progress." I shook my head. "I don't know if they'll share anything with us. But, we'll find out."

According to the chalkboard in Mark's room, his attending nurse's last name was Thompson. I asked the attendant behind the desk if Nurse Thompson was available.

"She's with a patient at the moment—no, wait, here she comes."

I turned to look down the corridor. A young girl about four feet ten inches tall, with long blonde hair, pulled back in what appeared to be a ponytail, was walking towards us.

I held my hand out to shake hers. "Nurse Thompson, my name is Casey Quinby. I believe Nurse Walsh from Spaulding Rehab called you regarding our connection to Mark Mosley." I didn't want to say too much. I figured less was better. And, I wanted to see what she knew and if she was going to share.

"Yes, I've been expecting you," Nurse Thompson said. "Since Mark is conscious and alert, we'll have him sign a consent form allowing us to share information regarding his medical records. It's not me making the rules—it's the legal beagles. Actually, I agree with the permission part. So, let me get those forms, and I'll get them in the works."

"We're going to take a walk, so Mark and his friend Annie can be alone for a bit," Marnie said.

"Nurse Walsh told me about Annie." Nurse Thompson shook her head. "They're lucky to be alive."

"They sure are," I said.

Chapter 68

Marnie and I had just got our coffees and sat down when my phone rang. It was Sam.

"We've been in meetings with Chief Lowe all morning. We'll tell you all about it when we see you. I'm assuming you're still at Cape Cod Hospital. We should be there in a few minutes. What room is Mark in?"

"He's in room 311. Annie is with him. Marnie and I are in the coffee shop," I said. "Why don't you guys meet us here."

"We'll do that," Sam said.

I hung up and turned to face Marnie. "I've read Officer Bishop's reports on Buster's case several times over, and each time, I find something to add to my list of questions. I've developed a sequence of events of what, in my opinion, happened. To start with, I don't think Annie knew Betsy was pregnant. Or, if she did, Annie didn't know who the father was." I stopped talking when I saw Sam and Maloney walking in our direction.

Sam stood beside the table with his arms folded. "What are Mrs. and Mrs. Private Investigators of Barnstable Village discussing?"

"Maybe you'd like to join in the conversation. But, I want you both to listen before you give me your opinion or opinions," I said.

I retold my Buster, Betsy, and Richardson relationship regarding Betsy's pregnancy. "Let me finish my story. Buster died just days before their graduation. You remember Betsy and Buster were friends with benefits. That could have been Betsy's assessment of their relationship. Buster may have felt differently. We'll never know the real truth." I shook my head. "We can't prove it because two of the players are dead, but here's my take on what happened."

Sam pulled up closer to the table. "Okay, if I take notes?"

"Perfectly okay," I said. "I think Betsy told Buster she was pregnant. Buster lost it. They had words, then Betsy got pissed off and announced that the father was Artie Richardson. Buster met up with Richardson, but I don't think Richardson was alone. I think Peter Mosley was with him."

"This is starting to sound like an episode from *Law and Order,*" Maloney said.

I took a breath, then continued, "Richardson arranged to meet with Buster in a remote section of Wequaquet Lake to talk, and Buster agreed. He had no idea Peter was lurking in the dense vegetation beside the dirt area where people launched their boats. Between Peter and Richardson, they held Buster underwater until he drowned. That would account for no visual marks on his body. They positioned him in the car to look like he had committed suicide. Peter, from the passenger side, then backed up as far as he could, gunned the engine, and drove as fast as possible into the water." I glanced at Sam and Maloney. "Officer Bishop noted in his report that the driver and passenger side windows were open. That was Peter's way out. In his notes, he mentioned that the *accident* could have been staged. But, from what he wrote, no one else agreed."

"With everything that's happened, your theory makes perfect sense," Maloney said.

"You said you'd tell us about your meeting with Chief Lowe," I said.

"It seems that Marsha Richardson found pictures of Betsy and her husband tucked in a lockbox on a shelf in his workshop. Two of them were copies of the same pictures we found at Betsy's house— the one by the boat in Boston Harbor and the hospital baby shot." Sam shook his head. "There was also a copy of a birth certificate listing Betsy and the mother and Arthur Richardson as the father."

"So that means Betsy gave that information for the record when the baby was born," Marnie said. "We didn't find a copy of that in her box of goodies."

Maloney folded his arms and leaned back in his chair. "My take is that they were still an item—at least up until the class reunion. Marsha Richardson told Chief Lowe that she found the pictures and the certificate a couple of days before the reunion. She was looking for a hammer and screwdriver and came across the locked box. They were having some heavy-duty troubles, and out of curiosity, she wanted to know what was inside."

"Did she tell her husband what she'd found?" I asked.

Sam shrugged. "She did and gave him an ultimatum. He told her his relationship with Betsy was over years ago."

"And," I said.

"Marsha told the chief that she told her husband she'd give him another chance because of their children. He agreed and promised it would never happen again. That he made a mistake, then told her he loved her," said Maloney.

"Let me guess," I said. "Marsha Richardson read the *Tribune* Sunday morning after the ten-year reunion of the class of 2006 and froze when she saw Betsy's name."

"Yep, then she asked her husband if he knew anything about it. He grabbed the paper from her and read the article." Sam sighed. "Marsha said she told him to get out. She said he didn't say another word, snatched his keys from the counter, took the paper, and left."

"Did he ever return to his house?" I asked.

"She said he called and left a message that he was coming by in a couple of days to pick up some clothes and personal stuff. He said he would let her know the day and time and emphatically told her not to be there and not to tell the children he was coming," Sam said. "That's when she decided to pack up the children and go to her parent's house in New Hampshire."

Maloney nodded. "The chief asked Marsha if he could record their meeting, and she agreed in writing. So everything they talked about is considered evidence."

347

"Maloney and I need to talk to Richardson," said Sam. We need him to confess. He was a big man on the campus at the high school, but in the *big house,* the pretty boy will be a *daddy's little girl.* Instilling that thought in his head might get him to cooperate in exchange for where he'll be housed."

"Let's go back upstairs. Annie's probably wondering where we are," I said.

"Good idea. We'll need to talk to Mark about Richardson and his brother at some point. Right now, I want him to know he's safe, and nobody can get to him or harm Annie," Sam said. "She's probably told him that she's staying with us."

Chapter 69

Wednesday

It was 7:00 when I woke up. I tip-toed past the pull-out where Annie was sleeping. Sam was already dressed and having coffee. I motioned toward the deck and whispered, "I'll grab a coffee, then let's go outside and talk."

It was the start of a beautiful day on Cape Cod. The sun was warm, and there wasn't a cloud in the sky.

"I was just about to call Chief Lowe," said Sam. "I want to set up that meeting with Richardson. Maloney and I can interview him at the jail. I don't know if he lawyered up or plans to, but before any meeting can take place, I need to know that."

"Are you heading over to Barnstable PD this morning?" I asked.

"I planned on meeting Maloney there sometime around eightish. I'll wait until he gets there to talk to the chief. I think it would be more productive if both Maloney and I met with him."

We finished our coffee. Sam left to go to the PD, and Annie rolled over and said, "Good morning," as he walked past her and out the front door."

Sam and Maloney met with Chief Lowe and retold Casey's version of Buster Adams' death. And how Richardson and Peter Mosley were involved. Then, Sam continued, "Richardson had an encounter with Betsy at the reunion. They were in the hallway, and Annie was going to the ladies' room. She heard the whole thing. Betsy mentioned something about a baby. Annie said Richardson got real mad and told her to shut her fuckin' mouth or he'd shut it for her. After that, Annie saw him, but not Betsy."

Chief Lowe leaned back in his chair. "This dude is going away forever. We have enough evidence to have him tried for Buster's death, Betsy's death, Peter's death, and the attempted murders of Annie McGuire and Mark Mosley."

"Chief, Maloney and I would like to interview Richardson. Can you arrange that?" I asked.

Chief Lowe nodded. "If he lawyered up, probably with an attorney assigned by the court, you'll have to deal with him too. And, you know those guys, they tell their client to clam up."

"We'll take our chances. I don't care how often an appointed attorney tells his client not to answer our questions. We'll make sure Richardson knows that we know and that one way or another, he's done."

Without another word, the chief called the county jail and requested a meeting between Richardson, Sam, and Maloney. The lieutenant on the duty desk at the Barnstable County House of Correction told Chief Lowe that a court-appointed attorney was representing Richardson. "I expected that," said the chief.

"What time do you want to schedule the meeting for?" asked the lieutenant on the duty desk at the Barnstable County House of Correction.

"Two o'clock," said the chief.

"It's in the books. I'll call the attorney and tell him."

"Thank you," said the chief, then hung up. "You've got a meeting at two o'clock.

Sam nodded. "Well, touch base with you when we finish."

Chapter 70

Sam and Maloney arrived at the House of Correction a half-hour early for their scheduled meeting with Richardson. Sheriff Hardy was in the lobby talking to a couple of his officers when we walked in. He excused himself and walked over to greet us.

"Sam, long time no see," he said.

"I'd like you meet Detective Maloney out of Barnstable PD," said Sam.

We shook hands.

"What brings you to my necks of the woods?" he asked.

Sam folded his arms. "The Arthur Richardson case."

"I've read and heard lots about it." Sheriff Hardy shook his head. "This guy carries many titles. The teacher reference scares me to death. To think that a person would hide behind the title of an educator, then morph into a child predator, con-artist, and murderer. And, most of all, that he got away with it."

"Unfortunately, he did get away with it for a long time." Sam shrugged. "We scheduled a meeting at 2:00 with him and his court-appointed attorney. I don't know who got assigned to him, but I'm anxious to see how Richardson will react to our questions. We've got him dead to rights, but you know how the system works. I'll tell you one thing, though, I'm not letting this guy see the light of day outside of a jail cell."

"Sam, I've known you for a long time. For you to make a statement like that, you've got a good case against him." Sheriff Hardy got serious. "If I can help in any way, please let me know."

Sam looked at his watch. "Let's touch base after the meeting, and I just may take you up on your offer."

Sam and Maloney checked in with the front desk. Five minutes later, an officer came to escort them to one of the interrogation rooms inside the facility.

Attorney Evans stood when Sam and Maloney entered the room. Richardson stayed seated—his hands cuffed and his ankles shackled. The smugness he emitted the day Casey interviewed him at the school was gone. His pretty boy designer clothes were replaced with a wrinkled orange jumpsuit.

Attorney Evans acknowledged that he was Richardson's court-appointed attorney and that Mr. Richardson has agreed to answer questions asked by Detectives Summers and Maloney from the Barnstable Police Department.

Sam wanted to tell the attorney to shut up. This guy must be right out of law school, Sam thought. He better hold on to his seat because he's in for a huge awakening.

Sam started. "Again, let me introduce myself. I'm Detective Summers, the lead detective in Bourne—working on a case with the Barnstable Police Department. Along with Detective Maloney, I have some questions regarding several related cases. I understand you agreed, with your attorney present, to meet with us. Is that correct?"

Richardson looked at his attorney, then nodded.

"You know you are being recorded, so I'd like you to answer our questions verbally."

Again, Richardson looked at his attorney, then said, "Yes, I know this is being recorded, and I'll answer your questions verbally."

Sam thought for a minute, giving Richardson time to stew. "You were an art teacher at Barnstable High School, am I correct?"

"Yes," said Richardson.

"Did you know Buster Adams?"

"Yes."

Sam didn't take his eyes off Richardson.

Did you know Betsy Harper?"

"Yes."

"How did you know these two people?" Sam's face was expressionless.

"I had them as students."

"Did you know them outside of art class?"

Richardson looked at his attorney. "Yes, they were in various clubs I was involved with."

"By involved, you mean as the facilitator of these after-school clubs?"

"Yes."

"Did you have any contact with these individuals in non-related activities?"

Attorney Evans spoke up, "What are you referring to?"

"Nothing, in particular, just general relationships not involving the school or held on school property."

Attorney Evans nodded.

Richardson's face wrinkled. "No."

"How well did you know Buster Adams?"

"He was a jock. Everybody knew Buster. He was outgoing and well-liked," said Richardson.

"So you liked him?" Sam asked.

"You didn't ask me that. Buster was cocky." Richardson's eyes moved from one side to the other. "He was alright, but not one of my favorites."

Sam leaned forward on the table. "What about Betsy Harper? I hear she was very pretty and kind of promiscuous. How well did you know her?"

"She was my student and, I suppose, my friend. She was interested in art—and I was the art teacher."

Sam stayed leaning on the table. His eyes still focused on Richardson. "How about Annie McGuire and Mark Mosley—how well did you know them?"

"They were students and in the same class with Buster and Betsy."

"So you only knew them from school. You had no contact with Annie and Mark other than at school?"

"That's right."

Sam took a deep breath. "So let me ask you—were you and Betsy friends with benefits?"

Richardson's face hardened. "What the hell are you getting at?"

"Mr. Richardson, I'm not trying to upset you. I'm just asking general questions. Do you have a problem with that?" Sam knew he was starting to hit a nerve.

"No. I don't have a problem."

"Then, if you don't have a problem, let's continue," Sam said.

Maloney looked at Sam, then asked, "Mr. Richardson, you're married. Is that correct?"

Richardson snapped his head in the direction of his attorney. "This is bullshit. What does my being married or not married have to do with whatever he's here for?"

"Nothing. Just answer the detective's questions. I'll stop him if I don't think you should answer the question or if we need clarification as to why he's asking a particular question." Attorney Evans nodded.

"Your attorney has directed you to answer my question. Are you married?"

"Yes. I am," Richardson answered.

"And you have two children?" Maloney asked.

"Yes, I do," Richardson answered.

"And they live in Mashpee. Right?" Maloney asked.

Attorney Evans looked at his client. "Let's take a break," he said.

Sam ignored Evans' request. "Right?" Maloney said. "Aren't they currently in New Hampshire?"

"They're visiting their grandparents," said Richardson. "Is there a problem with that?"

"No. No problem at all, sir." Maloney knew he'd wound Richardson up.

"Detective Summers asked you about knowing Mark Mosley, and you said you did. How about his brother, Peter? Did you know Peter Mosley?"

"I knew of him," said Richardson. "He was known as a loser."

"And why's that?" asked Maloney.

"I don't know. That's what I heard," said Richardson.

"Do you own a gun?" asked Maloney.

"I used to have a .38 Special. I haven't seen it for years. I kept it in the nightstand on my side of the bed, but when my kids came along, I put it away in a lockbox somewhere in the house. But, I don't remember where." Richardson fidgeted with the cuffs holding his wrists together.

"Arthur, I want you to think real hard where you last saw your .38 Special," said Maloney.

"I told you I put it in a lockbox when my oldest kid was born."

"Wrong answer." Maloney stood and walked around the table where Sam, Attorney Evans, and Richardson were sitting.

Richardson didn't say anything, just followed Maloney with his eyes.

As quickly as Maloney stood up, he pounded his fist on the table and sat down. "Lying is one thing, but to include your kids in your lie doesn't cut the mustard with me. We obtained a warrant to search your truck. You'll never guess what we found." Maloney stretched across the table. "Councilor, I want to make sure you hear this. We found Arthurs .38 Special. And, when we had it tested against the bullet that killed Peter Mosey—well, can you believe that it was fired from Mr. Richardson's long-lost gun."

Sam, who'd been leaning against the wall near the door, stepped forward. "Arthur, we've got motive, means, and opportunity connecting you to Buster Adams' 10-year-old murder case, Betsy Harper's murder two and a half weeks ago, Peter Mosley's murder on Webb Island in Hanson, and the kidnapping and attempted murders of Annie McGuire and Mark Mosley."

Sam looked from Arthur Richardson to Attorney Evans. I'm not playing games. We have the evidence to put your client away for the rest of his life. As you both are well aware, the State of Massachusetts doesn't have the death penalty. He'll go to the Souza-Baranowski Correctional Center in Lancaster. It's not a nice place to be. I'm sure you can attest to that Councilor. He'll be housed in general population with inmates who committed similar crimes. Arthur will become a *daddy's little girl.*" Sam stopped for a minute to let what he just said sink in. "Attorney Evans, would you like to tell Arthur what that means?"

"No, I'm sure he knows," said Evans. "What are you looking for?"

Sam shrugged. "He pleads guilty to all changes, and as long as he behaves himself, he'll be housed in protective custody." Sam moved to the end of the table and sat beside Maloney.

"Can I have some time to talk to my client?"

"We'll be in Sheriff Hardy's office when you have an answer for us," Sam said.

Maloney knocked on the small window in the door for the deputy to let us out. "You've got one hour, and then the deal's off the table."

Sam and Maloney headed to Sheriff Hardy's office.

"Sam, I think he'll take the deal." Maloney nodded.

"So don't I. I left my briefcase in the sheriff's office. I already had the DA's office draw up the papers for him to sign. There are three copies." Evans can look one over, but remember I told him he has one hour."

Sheriff Hardy was in his office waiting for Sam and Maloney to finish the meeting with Richardson and his attorney. Sam took one set of the papers from his briefcase and asked the front desk deputy to bring them to Attorney Evans. Sam then explained what went on and told the sheriff about Richardson's already approved housing plan.

"I told him he has one hour to make up his mind," said Sam.

Chapter 71

Thursday

I was sitting at the kitchen table with my coffee and the *Tribune* when Annie walked in from the living room. I looked at the time. "What are you doing up so early?" I asked.

"I heard Sam leave a few minutes ago. I feel like I've been given a new lease on life—as the old saying goes. I'm so grateful to my family and my friends. And, oh, by the way—that pull-out couch isn't bad at all. I'm thinking about extending my stay."

I walked over and hugged her. "You're not leaving here until you're ready."

"I know. But, it's over, and I'm ready besides Mark's going to be released from Cape Cod Hospital and admitted to Spaulding within the next few days. At my next outpatient appointment, they're going to do an evaluation and let me know if I can go back to work, move back to my apartment, and start driving again."

"And—I know there's something else you want to tell me," I said.

"Yes, Casey, there is." Annie took a deep breath. "Mark is going to stay with me for a while. He can't be alone, and I'm not sure if I can be alone either. So, we're going to give it a try."

"Speaking of driving—you need a car."

"Yeah, I've been thinking about that." Annie laughed, "Want to take me car hunting?"

"We can do that," I said.

"And, the other thing we have to do is practice walking on the sand," Annie laughed. I don't want to stumble at Marnie and Maloney's wedding."

"Annie, you're back." I made her a coffee and a couple pieces of toast. "Today, we'll take a ride to the beach, then take a walk."

"Casey Quinby, I love you."

357

Epilogue

Three months after Arthur Richardson was arraigned for the kidnapping and attempted murder of Annie McGuire and Mark Mosley, the murder of Betsy Harper, and the murder of Peter Mosley, he went to trial. He listened as the evidence against him was presented by witnesses called to testify. Detective Sam Summers was the last person to present on behalf of the District Attorney's Office. Detective Summers answered questions but never took his eyes off Richardson.

Casey, Marnie, Annie, and Mark sat three rows behind Sam and Maloney.

Richardson was no longer the respected teacher. He was the mere shadow of a man who didn't deserve an ounce of pity. His lawyer leaned over and whispered in Richardson's ear.

They each looked at Detective Summers, then took a deep breath. Attorney Evans nodded and asked to have a sidebar.

Judge Mathews called both sides forward, turned sideways as the attorneys approached, and listened intently to what Attorney Evans had to say. The judge folded his arms and asked if Arthur Richardson was aware of the decision.

Evans nodded, as did the Assistant District Attorney trying the case. They returned to their respective tables and waited for the judge to announce the decision.

Richardson didn't look up. His hands were in his lap, and he was staring at the floor.

Judge Mathews asked Attorney Evans and Arthur Richardson to stand. He reread the charges against Richardson—hesitated, then asked the attorney how his client pled.

"Guilty, your honor," resonated through the courtroom.

The judge gave his speech accepting Richardson's plea, dismissed the jury, and directed the court officer to take Richardson into custody.

Richardson received life without parole and was remanded to Souza-Baranowski Correctional Center in Lancaster.

Annie and Mark became a couple and helped nurture each other back into society. Annie returned to her job at the DA's office. Mark returned to the moving company as a scheduler until he could physically handle the heavy lifting.

Marnie cleaned up her caseload at the District Attorney's office and took Casey's offer to move across the street and become a private investigator.

Since it was February, Marnie and Maloney's beach wedding wasn't going to happen. They changed the date to May—checked out a couple of venues, then decided on the Kelly Chapel behind the Old Yarmouth Inn. But they kept their New York City honeymoon plans, which included Casey and Sam.

Made in the USA
Columbia, SC
04 March 2022